# WHITEWATER

# BY PAUL HORGAN

### NOVELS

The Fault of Angels
No Quarter Given
Main Line West
A Lamp on the Plains
A Distant Trumpet

Far From Cibola
The Habit of Empire
The Common Heart
Give Me Possession
Memories of the Future

Mountain Standard Time (*containing* MAIN LINE WEST, FAR FROM CIBOLA, *and* THE COMMON HEART)

Everything to Live For
Whitewater

### OTHER FICTION

The Return of the Weed
Figures in a Landscape
The Devil in the Desert
One Red Rose For Christmas

The Saintmaker's Christmas Eve
Humble Powers
Toby and the Nighttime (*juvenile*)
Things As They Are

The Peach Stone: *Stories from Four Decades*

### HISTORY AND OTHER NON-FICTION

Men of Arms (*juvenile*)
From the Royal City
New Mexico's Own Chronicle (*with Maurice Garland Fulton*)
Great River: The Rio Grande in North American History
The Centuries of Santa Fe
Rome Eternal
Citizen of New Salem
Conquistadors in North American History
Peter Hurd: *A Portrait Sketch from Life*
Songs After Lincoln
The Heroic Triad: *Essays in the Social Energies
of Three Southwestern Cultures*

# WHITEWATER

by Paul Horgan

FARRAR, STRAUS AND GIROUX ❧ NEW YORK

*for*
EDWARD BISETT

# Contents

All things whisper in the blood.
                    —*Hymn*


Hoy recuerdo a los muertos de mi casa.
                    —Octavio Paz, in *Elegía interrumpida*


And if I die I shall not leave behind me one soul who understood
me. Some think I am better, others that I am worse than
I am. . . .

                    —Mikhail Yuryevich Lermontov, in
                    *A Hero of Our Days* [English by
                    Maurice Baring]

# I. To the Islands

"Is that the best way to reach perception, then?"

"I didn't say that."

"Yes, but, you said—"

"I only mean that you often see more, for example, if you look at an upsidedown reflection in water, than you do if you look at what casts it—any upright sign of life along the shore, you see."

"But which is clearer?"

"That depends on the angle of the light, the stillness of the surface, that sort of thing. But curiously enough, it can add another dimension to what you look at, if you see it in a pure but dislocated way."

"What sort of dimension?"

"Take it another way, then, in terms of time."

"Time?"

"Yes, the reflected sign of life can seem like the past, about which there is so much to learn and remember, while the other, the direct sign, is like the present, which we know and hardly notice by simply living in it."

"Will this be in the exam?"

"No. Any more discussion? —Let's move on, then."

※ ※ ※

It is later. Phillipson Durham (in scholarly jocularity known to a few colleagues as "Beckford" Durham because of his considerable work on the Caliph of Fonthill) is finishing his student papers for the night. Like most of his countrymen, he is a migrant: somewhere along the lines traced on their personal maps of life they have encountered a place, in a certain time, which as they move on means more than any other.

The campus is quiet. His house is secure, with his wife waiting for him in sleep, and his children strenuously dreaming in their own room. The moon rides alone above the lighted three-storey windows of the library's main reading room—a view he enjoys when he looks abstractedly out of his own study window at home.

He is never aware of his condition when he falls into abstraction, but others are, and their startled expression when they look to him for response and find none always puzzles him. Sometimes a girl student of his wonders if she is falling in love with him, for his worn good looks, or the way he would seem to reach into her thought through her eyes, but then she would think, no, he is not looking at me; at someone else.

He angers men students with his occasional abruptness just as they have begun to feel the warmth of some idea taking fire in their minds, and they scold privately, wishing he could be their friend; and then, another time, when he would be a friend, obscurely they feel less comfortable with him than ever.

This much he understands about himself, though: that whatever he does not actually know, he can imagine or suspect in the style of the appropriate truth. But he does not take pleasure from thinking about his temperament, and he looks instead out of the window of his upstairs study into the leafy Appalachian night in the wake of his thoughts.

"My children are their own future, yet the time will come when they too will look back and ask what they have heard, what they have seen, what they know. Each of them must ask this for himself, despite what they all know together. Will each conclude that we are the sum of our acts and dreams, of our doubts no less than our certainties?"

※ ※ ※

In a certain moment of a pale, star-lighted evening long ago, he heard William Breedlove, who was called Billy by everyone, declare at the bow of the canoe while pointing with his paddle,

"There! There! There's our island!"

That voice was excited and constricted, as if held down to keep a secret in the midst of nowhere. They were both then in the last of their high school years, and the time was autumn, when the day's heat was turning into evening cool, and the stars of the low heavens were slowly trembling their unknown messages to earth. The starbeams were so bright in the ash-darkening green of the lower sky that they were reflected, quiver and all, in the still surface of Whitewater Lake, where the canoe spread the only ripple.

"That's our island, and it's the best one," said Billy. He sounded exultant, and by this he made Phillipson Durham feel so. Aware that Billy could sometimes make him feel anything he wanted to, Phil often resisted, and now asked,

"Why is it the best one?" Phil, at the stern, where he knelt, dug his paddle unnecessarily deep so that the canoe turned aside from her long, pure course which the paddlers had held in accord for half the length of Whitewater Lake. "The islands all look alike to me," he added.

"Watch it, watch it, Phil, you're turning us!"

With a twist of his paddle which began in his kneeling thighs and came spiralling up into freedom of effect out of his whole body, Billy brought the canoe back into line. Then with control restored, he explained, over his shoulder,

"I know every one of the seven islands, and the best two are Fourth Island and Fifth Island, and of those two, the Fourth is the one I always take because the trees come right down to the water and the island is like a private little room. —We'll be there in a few minutes, and what we'll do, we'll take the canoe, almost drifting to be quiet, you know, but moving ahead, just enough, and we'll circle the island to be sure nobody's there; and if there isn't, we'll land and make camp."

"To found the colony," murmured Phil. He spoke ironically to counter Billy's exuberance, and hide his own.

Acting without signal, they slowed the movement of the boat and proceeded with a new nerve of stealth. It gave them pleasure to come with caution to even so small a particle of the unknown in life as Fourth Island in Whitewater Lake, which backed up Whitewater Dam, on the Whitewater Draw, forty-nine miles from the town of Belvedere, in Orpha County, in West Central Texas. The lake was declared to be eighteen miles long, and six miles wide at its widest.

"How deep is it?" asked Phil.

Billy answered,

[ 6 ]

"How high is a hill? There are hills under us." Like all leaders, he had the thoughtless power to touch the mystery of common things.

Halfway along rose the seven islands which had been hilltops years ago, then, as now, crowned with groves of salt cedar and willow, cottonwood and mesquite. The town elders of Belvedere remembered from their childhood the old gravelly road that used to follow Whitewater Draw and how it twisted through the hills whose tallest crowns were now all that could be seen of their eroded shapes where the once exposed earth had shown bands of white gypsum and red clay. The road, and all that it had passed through, were now deep under water. Hunters and fishers in their small boats now often followed among the islands the way the road used to go, guided by the same lie of the land, even though it was now concealed under the lake. In a dry vastness, any water was something to see. Belvedere listed Whitewater Lake as among its chief attractions, though it lay nearly fifty miles away. As a lake it was not all that splendid; but the harsh, gritty landscape in which it lay like a jewel made it seem more than it was, even to those who had seen the ocean. People thirsty for change and other forms of pleasure came to the lake on weekends, if only to look. In vacation times they arrived in little throngs. At other times, the place was deserted. No one ever could be sure of what to find there—solitude if that was what he wanted, or fellow creatures, with all their possibilities, or news from elsewhere, or kindness, violence, love, amazement, peacefulness.

"We're coming in between Fourth and Fifth," said Billy on a husky breath.

Darkness was full overhead, but they could see enough by starlight, and by the outline of the islands against the pale band above the horizon. They heard nothing but the reserved drip of their paddles, and the wieldly glide of the canoe in which they knelt feeling their own weight through the balance they held.

"This is the channel," said Billy, of the space between Fourth and Fifth islands. It was an open span of water a fifth of a mile wide. Delicately he spurned the water with his paddle and headed the canoe toward Fourth Island and Phil steered with him. They circled the island until they were on the off-channel side. "It's all right. There's nobody there."

Billy plunged his paddle deep and strong into the water and in a hiss of wake, they beached the canoe on a crusty slope of alkali-white earth against a wall of salt cedar. There among the lower fronds a dark tunnel dimly showed a trail which would give a crouching entry into the island.

The stillness was so great it was like a perfect creation not to be broken. The young men were moved to make as little sound as possible. Water and stars, night time, and rocks aeons older than the slow flood which years ago made the lake behind Whitewater Dam, a drift of night coolness in the air, all wrapped the solitude about them and made them quiet. They hauled the canoe out of the lake into the nocturnal shade of the salt cedars. Brushing the dry trees they stirred out of the whiplike branches a pungent breath smelling of dust held since the last dust storm, and of the pink salt cedar flowers, with their own powdery motes, which together made reminders of drugging hot weather noons. Billy tossed Phil a pack bundle and took up one himself and said, "Let's go."

He led the way through the grove to the low crest of the island and down the other side. The branches whipped at their faces and they sparred at them in the interior darkness of the island, swearing lightly. They were heading to the channel side of Fourth Island.

"I know a place," said Billy, "it has a tiny little beach and three years ago I built a nice little stone wall for a campfire and I bet it's still there. We can make some coffee and then try our luck with some night fishing. There's an old catfish I know. I'm going to get him yet. We're almost there. There. See."

He paused and pointed. The dense woods of the island crown opened out to reveal a small half-moon beach of sand a few feet wide and hardly more than a few inches deep. Phil asked, "Is that what you call your beach?"

"It certainly is, and it will look like a real one, too, if you don't look at it too close. You've seen the Atlantic Coast, but I never have, but I've seen the Gulf Coast, and I know what a beach looks like." He spoke with the calm certainty of the native who addresses the later settler.

A thousand feet away rose Fifth Island, dark and clear against the sky. Suddenly Billy put out his hand and whispered, "Listen!"

What was it? It was something like a clap of air, almost to be felt instead of heard, and when Phil heard it, he had a sudden notion of living in a prehistoric world, before the local flood, even,—he heard the wings of a large bird beating at the stillness over the channel. A bird? What was a bird? asked his pulse, beating its own way. But this was not just any bird, it was the bird of that particular night in that breathheld quiet of the lake and the sky and the dusty rocks; and in another instant as it flew the bird made a swooping and crying call, a sickle-sharp sound that cut apart the silvery night. It made its piercing wonder, and was gone. Phil shivered. In the starry glimmer the far western shore of the lake began to show as darkness made its habit in their eyes. They stirred. Billy said,

"He certainly flew close. He certainly cried out loud. Wait. Listen. There he goes again—" already far down the lake, it seemed, the wings and the cry were searching the farther darkness. To cover the awe which he felt, Phil asked, "What kind of a bird was it?"

"It was a speckled night hawk. I shot one once. I was doing taxidermy then. I didn't do a very good job on it, except for the wings. I found out from them why a glider can soar. The thick leading edge, sustained by forward speed."

How much he knows about how things work, thought Phil. Billy's truths are simple. Mine are always made up of a combination of what I know and what I imagine or suspect.

❦ ❦ ❦

Billy's fire wall of small stones was still there. The two fishermen gathered dry salt cedar branches and made a hot white fire which burned down fast. Soon the smell of coffee joined the weedy air of the lake and the dusty pungency of the island groves. Lying back on the little strip of beach, and touched with edges of light from the settling fire, the two were content in the lordship of solitude. The immense starred heaven was theirs alone, and so were the stilled reflection of the lake, and the faint drift of cooling air off the plains of West Central Texas, and the homely clinging touch of their campfire smoke, and the island which had once been a hill.

"This is the country for me, all right," said Billy. "—How did you and your pappy and mammy ever end up in Belvedere five years ago?"

"Chance. Someone wrote my father about an opening in the print shop, and we just came. We've always 'just come.' My father never owned any place. He never wanted to. He kept saying, 'We'll just try one more place.'"

"What is he looking for, do you suppose?"

"I never knew. My mother never knew. I don't think he ever knew. Sometimes I feel sorry for him about that. Maybe he has always been one of those, you know? who have to find out where they are before they want to lie down and rest."

Billy laughed.

"I know just how that is. Like ' old dog turning around and around following his tail until he knows just where to flop down and make a tight comfortable old shape and go to sleep."

"That's my pappy, as you call him," said Phil, without bitterness, and then chose to change the subject. "I was wondering if there are any snakes on this island."

"No!" Billy sat up in order to deal with a matter of such interest. "Not a one. And you know why?"

Negative silence.

"Because when they built the dam, and the lake filled up—it took ten years, they told me, my grandpa knew, he used to live out here—all of Whitewater Draw was originally absolutely full of rattlers. It was ideal snake country. Still is, roundabout. You've seen other places like the Draw. Chopped walls along the arroyos, you know, where erosion came, and all sorts of little slits there and holes where the gypsum was soft, and in there, you know, all secret and cool where the shade is, and sometimes *far down,* because the earth is not the same toughness everywhere, why, there? you know? the snakes would have their place. That kind of place. So when the lake began to fill, and back up, all the way along the Draw, why what happened? Why, the rattlers had to take to high ground, higher all the time, and at last, what ground was it? Nothing was left but the tops of the hills and these are now the islands. So for a long time the rattlesnakes were thick on the islands. They used to say it was as much as your life was worth to take and land on one of these islands, because you could hardly take a step that you didn't come right on top of some old rattler or other."

"It must be great in the dark."

"So just because it was so great, everybody made it a point, from time to time, to wipe out the snake population, and they must have got every one of them, because for years, they tell me—though snakes can swim, you know—there hasn't been a single rattler on any of these islands. I've never seen one here, and I've been coming to the islands for a long time even before I got to know you."

They were both stirred as though by a memory which reached to them from the first light of Eden. Billy snapped a twig of salt cedar.

"I wish I'd seen it all before!" he exclaimed.

"That's what everybody says who finds out he was born too late," said Phil.

"Nobody is ever born too late. Sometimes I think I was born too soon. There's a lot coming, but it won't all of it get here fast enough for my time."

"Forget the future."

At the idea of forgetting something which had not yet happened, Billy laughed.

"That's wonderful. I must remember that," he said, "I have to learn to say things the way you do. I can only *do* things."

"Oh, no, you can talk, all right."

"Well, talk, yes, maybe; but I for certain can't spell. I never will, try as I do, long as I live. T-a-c, cat," he said.

"The great thing," said Phil, rolling over on his belly, and talking against the breath that was pushed out of him, "is to look back and decide how things used to be because you know how they are right now."

"Yes!" Billy stood up to look as far down the lake as night would let him, "you've got what they call a theory there. Sometimes when I think of everything down under the water there, I see exactly how people were down there, and how they had things fixed, and then I see what everything was like, long before you and I were born." He swept his arms about. "It was once all open air before the dam was built, and the lake backed up. It was like Belvedere is now, or any town."

"Where was the town of Whitewater, exactly?"

"I'll tell you! It was between these two islands, and the next two, above us. My mother's daddy told me. He lived there when it was still a town. They built it there, before the railroad, even, because it seemed like a protected place, with four hills surrounding it, and it had that running creek going right down the middle of it, Whitewater Draw, they called it. But there was trouble about the water. —Well, you see, when the rains would come, cloudbursts, days at a time, after dry times, then the whole town would get flooded. But they would dry out and go right on. But all that water just ran away. Then came the railroad thing."

"Railroad thing?"

"Yes." Billy showed a cross in the air. "The Roscoe, Snyder and Pacific came up this way, and the old Rock Island went across that way, and they both needed water for their locomotives. Where was the water anywhere around here? Right there in Whitewater Draw. So the railroads got lawyers and began buying up water rights and quieting titles. That's how they say it, so they could build the dam and own it, and in time, have the water back up, and make a lake, and supply the pipelines for the railroads."

"Was that the end of the town?"

"Oh, no. People hated to get up and go. They fought, as long as they could, even though the town took more floods before they were through, years apart."

"I don't see why they just didn't move."

"Well," said Billy, "you know? People don't go away from something they know, if it's *all* they know."

"Just the same, you'd think a whole town named Whitewater, Texas, would try to save itself if it happened more than once, before it was too late. And then it *was* too late, when the lake water came and filled. Where did they all go?"

"Some moved to Belvedere, like my grandparents. Some moved to Orpha City, some just moved on. But listen to this. You know something? *The town of Whitewater is still down there,* how deep? Hundred, three hundred, feet? I can't rightly say. But there it is! Down there are streets, crisscrossing, and *making street corners.* If you were down there you could tell where the streets are by the rows of trees that grew along the walks. If you could dive deep enough even now on a clear day you could probably see them. They have backyard fences and old telephone poles. They have a junk yard. When the lake was filling up people used to come before it got so deep and ride over White-water in their new rowboats and look down and see everything. I've seen old photographs of them doing it. The men had on funny hats, derby hats, and shirtsleeves with rubber bands around them, and the women had sunbonnets and umbrellas for the sun, and wore puffy clothes so they all looked shiny and fat. We've got some of the pictures. I'll show you. They're all sort of pale and brown now. Sometimes the lake wavered when the wind blew and then they couldn't see, but other times, it was all there, if they just looked down through the water."

"It's just like looking back," said Phil. "Sometimes you see clearly and sometimes it wavers. But it's all there yet."

"More! Say more!"

"Well, then," said Phil, rising to his knees, "I saw an empty house once, out in the country by a town where we lived for a while." He felt his mind go alive with the surge of his imagination, until he felt transformed from the ordinary likeness people had of him. "The house was dry and cracking open with weather. The paint was all gone. The doors hung open. There was no glass left in all the windows but one, and I smashed that with a rock, and I'll never know why but it made me feel wonderful. I looked in. People used to live there, and I went in and walked around every room. *I felt like them.* It made me feel I wanted to get out of there but I couldn't, right away. Where were they? I wondered, and for a minute, I didn't know where I was. You know? Well, they had iron beds, that were still there, rusty and broken down, and on one wall there was a cracked mirror. I looked in it because I thought I could see one of *their* faces, not mine."

"Come on, Phil! Come on!" cried Billy with amazement. "I get it! I get it!"

"And in one corner of one room, actually there was a pile of old papers."

"Newspapers?"

"No. Letters and papers with writing."

"Wonderful. What did they say?"

"I didn't read them."

*"Didn't read them!"*

"No, I didn't."

"Why not? *To find out.* Why not?"

"I didn't read them because I wanted to think to myself what they said instead of see really what they said."

"I see. I guess I see," commented Billy in a lowered voice. "Yes, maybe you are right. Yes, there is that.—Well: go on":

"Well, nothing, except to make the story complete, there were piles of dried excrement here and there. Hoboes I suppose—"

With scoffing glee, Billy said,

*"Excrement!* Why don't you be *real* nicey-nice, and say *human waste,* like she does in physiology class?"

"Well, there it was, I suppose, to remind us that there is always that in life. All of us. But anyway, when I left there I would have sworn I knew everything and everybody about that house, and I'll bet, down there, in Whitewater, Texas, at the bottom of the lake, I'll bet there are a hundred houses I know just as well because of the one I saw."

Billy got up and jumped around for a second and said,

"So you know the whole town, even though you never saw it!"

"And the people. I know the people."

"You know the people! Look! That means they're not gone. Nothing is gone!"

[ 15 ]

"Time goes, you know."

"Yes, time goes by, but it stays, too, if—"

"—If anybody remembers, no matter who?"

"That's it!"

They had an exalting certainty of having pierced one of the most mysterious of secrets, and one of the most sad. Neither of them could have achieved this alone, at that time of life. They had done it together. The image of the drowned town was all the brighter now in its detail. Billy declared,

"Look. Down there, I bet somewhere near the junk yard there is somebody's old Model T that they didn't think it was worth while to take and haul it away before the water came, and I bet it has a shell of white salt over it now, if we could see it, because this water is so hard and full of alkali. You know who would give his shirt to have that Model T, as a curiosity?"

"No."

"Guy DeLacey, down at the Red Dot Garage. He's already got one, so that means he could use another, the way collectors are."

"He's a collector?"

"Well, he wants to know everything. That means he has to have a lot of things to fool around with and find out. —You know him, don't you?"

"I guess so. Not well."

"You don't like him."

Phil shrugged.

After a brief silence, Billy said,

"Do you know who has the finest mind in Belvedere?"

"No. —In fact," added Phil, intending to respond disagreeably to the challenge in the air, "I don't think there is any such thing in Belvedere as a fine mind. Much less a finest."

"Well, I'm here to tell you you're wrong."

"But of course," continued Phil as if without being interrupted, "we aren't talking about ourselves."

"No. We're not," replied Billy, rejecting the sarcastic joke, "we are not who I mean. I mean Guy."

"DeLacey?"

"Guy DeLacey."

"You'll have to excuse me from taking that."

"I didn't think you would. But it's true, just the same. —Do you know, in the first place, what he's done in his life?"

"All I know is, he has learned something about the internal combustion engine, and gives himself airs about it."

"I agree. He does. All that doctor stuff he puts on. But oh me. What a lot more."

"For example?"

"Well, he ran away from school in Iowa where his uncle was principal and he ran away to be a merchant seaman. Before he was twenty years old he had been around the world twice. That's more than you or I or anyone else in Belvedere ever did."

"What of it? All that matters is what he brought back with him. What's all that got to do with his mind? Or for that matter, the Red Dot Garage?"

Billy was patient because he was filled with thoughts of his friend Guy. He said gently,

"He nearly got killed in Callao. In Hong Kong he thinks *he* may have killed a man. In New Zealand he got married the first time and his wife left him to run away with a half-caste Chinaman and then he says he learned that the marriage was a fake anyway, and he thinks all marriages are. He told me he jumped ship in Rio and thought about becoming a monk but then he heard of some lost mines in the Andes and went to find them with a party of Englishmen, but all he got out of it was malaria. He spent a year in London and all he did was read books in the British Museum. I asked him why, and he said he was trying to find out if he was Karl Marx. I said, Were you? And he answered, No, but he came close once or twice."

[ 17 ]

"Do you really believe all that?" asked Phil.

"Don't you?"

"No."

"Why not? —He told it all to me."

"I don't doubt that he did. But you don't have to believe it. There's just too much. He was just trying to get you interested."

"In what?"

"How do I know? But some people make up things just to get people to listen. I guess it means they're lonely. —You said the first time he got married. Did he get married again?"

"Yes, but she died the second year and he gave up on it, he said. When he wants a woman he gets him one for three dollars."

"Is that all his fine mind leads him to?"

"I figger it's his business. —One funny thing, though." Billy paused, and then went on. "He took me with him once."

"You mean to a whorehouse?"

"Yes. Out on the Orpha road. You know. The Silver Grille and Lounge. Maudie's place."

"I know. I never went in."

"Neither did I."

"But you said you went with him."

"I did. Yes. It was sort of peculiar. He said he absolutely had to have it, but he said I had to go along with him, so I said, Well, and we got in his red pickup truck and went out to the Silver Grille, and when we got there, he pulled up, got out, and slammed the door, and said to me, Now you just sit there and wait for me. Hell no, I said, and I said I was going in too. No, he said, I was not. I said I couldn't stand it. He said I had to, after all we came out there on *his* account. Well, I said, then why am I here at all? Then he just looked at me, a very funny look. Finally he said that I could do him a favor, and I asked What. He said, Well, then, sometime, after you've had it, come on around and tell me all about it. Before I could say yes or no, he went inside. In ten minutes he was back. He didn't say anything, but got in

"Hush! It doesn't matter. But I'll go crazy if I don't hear what they're saying. Let's get in the canoe and drift around our island and over near to them!"

"No," whispered Billy, "we'll swim. The canoe would be too easy to see and we might splash the paddles. Let's get buck naked and slide in and float across to Fifth Island. Be quiet!"

For Billy now took charge of the expedition, in his way.

"The wind is from their way," said Phil, shivering. "They won't hear us if we're careful."

While they pulled off their clothes they could still hear the voices. Secret and safe under darkness, Billy first, then Phil, took the water. It was deeply cold. They held their bellies hollow with their breath and bit their jaws to keep from chattering their teeth until they were fully in the lake. Phil turned his head to listen and heard the island murmurs, and he was sure he was about to discover what he had always known he must know about the planet earth, and the light of God, and the vastness within himself. He would, he was certain. He would because he must. He must because he was ready to hear.

He paced himself in the water by Billy. They floated deep, with heads lifted only to breathe. Underwater, their arms and legs, hardly moving, took them as slowly as drifting wood toward Fifth Island. As they became used to the cold water, it was the cool air which they now felt when they rolled their mouths up for air.

With head down and eyes open in black water, Phil was seeing in mind the sunken town below him. How far? Who could say. Who lived there? Perhaps Billy's old catfish. He had streets, marked out by rotted trees, to swim along, and corners to turn when he came to an intersection. When he felt like it, he could leave town and swim on up the draw, or down the other way to the dam, or follow the sunken hill slopes all the way up to the islands in the air and idle about them, and then go back to his drowned town, if that was where he lived, and find his food,

[ 23 ]

where, maybe, in the underwater, weeds grew and clung to the metal wrecks and discards of human life in the rusting junk yard. But all that was made up in Phil's head, and what he wanted was to know, know, everything real.

Drifting toward Fifth Island Phil could not help it—he had to pause and in all caution turn his head to let the water run out of his ear, so he might listen. The voices were silent, but just as he was about to go under again, he heard them resume, and in his straining chest he felt a thump of relief and longing, and he knew that in another few yards of approach, he would hear what they were saying. The thought made him feel fiery in the cold water. He felt like a man saved, light and formless with gratitude and love, now that life was about to bless him with knowledge.

In silky quiet he went under the water again beside Billy. A few strokes later they were in the deep reflected shadow of Fifth Island. Needing breath at the same rhythm, they came up for air. They could just see each other. Billy lifted a hand carefully and Phil nodded. At last they need go no closer—they were close enough to hear. They heard the heavy voice say words, for the first time clearly:

"Whatever you—"

Before there could be more, a loud clap came on the water between the two islands. Startled, the swimmers dived noisily. It was a catfish—a huge old catfish—who jumped behind them and slapped the water as he came down again into his lake. When they surfaced the voices were silent, but a flashlight on Fifth Island was darting its beam all about to find them.

Discovered, they were denied what they sought. It would have had to come to them in secret, if ever. A shout rose from Fifth Island.

"Who's there! What are you doing out there?" —a cry of rage.

There was a silent instant while they floated upright. It was broken by a shot from a pistol. The bullet skated near them and they dived. While they went fast and hard under water another bullet came chunking in deep near the commotion left by their dive. When they came to the embracing black of the reflection of Fourth Island, they drifted in the open, looking back toward Fifth Island. All was again silent and dark there. No pursuit followed. The night was still. If someone went to break a secret, someone else was just as ready to keep it.

Coming to their beach, they hauled themselves out of the depth of danger and lay panting softly against the crusty, alkaline edge of their island, where they returned to safety and ignorance.

What had they just failed to hear?

The failure did not seem to trouble Billy. After drying by air and pulling on clothes, he was soon asleep.

But it troubled Phil that after all he did not hear what the voices across the water were saying, or who was saying it. It troubled him awake and it troubled him later asleep. He was muted by this failure, which was of a kind to return in dreams.


❧ ❧ ❧


When morning came, it put rosy reflections deep into the water. Nothing was to be seen or heard on Fifth Island. The stillness was so great as the sun appeared, the lake so like a sky without cloud or ripple, the light so ageless and fresh touching the sunwise edges of all things with a purity of the instant, that the whole perfection which surrounded the two youths in its timeless calm seemed to demand of them that they shatter it. It was an Eden to be destroyed. In brusque accord they shed their clothes and dived into the lake. When they broke into the air again Billy gave a yell of exuberance. Small birds fluttered out from the salt cedars. From far away came the longing bellow of a range cow. The light whitened. Eden must be forgotten as the day advanced upon its stirred and simple habits. In due course the islanders fished all morning, caught nothing, and at last it was time to go.

They crossed to Fifth Island and explored the shore line. There was no boat. No one was there. With a fine story of being shot at after midnight on a moonless night on Whitewater Lake, they went home. The first sign of Belvedere which they saw from miles away was the silver-painted municipal water tank which in its distance looked like an immense pearl shining with a soft glow against the horizon haze caused by a long drift of smoke from the lamp-black burners beyond the oilfields of Orpha City.

# II. Belvedere

"Shot at!"

"Yes." Billy told his parents as much as it interested him to tell, and went off to work at the Red Dot.

When he was gone, they watched after him in their wonderings, seeing him still, though he had disappeared in his energetic way.

Every now and then—the town of Belvedere had seen it happen time and again—some one youthful individual came along who seemed to contain and renew all that the elders believed to be the most promising powers of local life. This year, the one whom everybody seemed to expect great things from was William Breedlove. His parents had been told so often enough to believe it, though they made modest disclaimers. But they knew he led the high school by his style, on playing field and cinder track, on the dance floor, in the student assemblies, and even at the Princess Theater, when there was a new film playing which he said everyone ought to see, whether it was so good it had to be seen in bated silence, or so bad that it gave everyone a chance to make up inspired mockeries and shout them out at the great shadows moving across the screen. In creating opinion and directing energy, William Breedlove was the public figure of his senior class.

Recognizing this, his father and mother, even so, complained that they knew less about him, almost, than anybody else in Belvedere. They were proud of him, and glad to see manhood so nearly upon him, even as they felt sad to see his boyhood go, for as it went, it took with it their grasp of his life. When would he cease to need them at all?

"Mother," asked Homer Breedlove late one night, "do you think he might hear a call to the ministry?"

Ellen Breedlove found the idea so striking that she sat up in bed and gazed out at the darkness beyond the bay window which, outside, finally produced a wooden cupola above. But try as she might, she could not see Billy Breedlove, her youngest-born, with his crackling black eyes, his cheeks as hotly ripe as a ready peach, his thick stubble of corn-silk hair, and his thrust of body which seemed to split his garments open even when he was doing nothing—she could not see him making properly mournful cheer in public every Sunday morning at eleven o'clock on the green-carpeted rostrum of the family church, which was shaped like a generous cut of pie, and painted pale brown over its shingled exterior. Weddings, yes—she could imagine him putting man and woman together—with God's blessing, of course. Funerals—never, for Billy could never have anything to do with death.

But perhaps her idea of a minister of God might be at fault, and in her sensible habit of letting go of notions which called for thought beyond her powers, she only sighed and lay back again beside her husband to sleep, if she could, though she always knew when Homer was awake thinking, and this always troubled her; for it led her to thinking also, in a loyal response, and now she knew they were both separately at work wondering why Billy was so unlike his brother and sister. The parents often looked back through their years to find Billy in themselves, but they never could. If in their youth they had smiled at the world, they remembered smiling with modesty and restraint. But William Breedlove. Anything made him laugh out loud, while some things made his ideas, and then his actions, spin like a top. In various matters he seemed to hold dangerous views. Every time he produced a new store of knowledge, or a fresh turn of mind which bewildered his parents, they looked at each other and silently asked a question clear between them—"Where do you suppose he got that?"

※ ※ ※

Homer Breedlove, a man of low energy, but faithful will, brought a quiet, formal air to his work, hoping that he inspired secret vows of loyalty in the men and women who worked under him. He was manager of the wholesale wool warehouse at the end of Van Buren Street, along the tracks of the Roscoe, Snyder and Pacific Railroad at the western edge of Belvedere (population in the last census, 5,453). When he considered a problem, he took a long time to reach a conclusion, examining alternatives. Once he felt he had duly considered all aspects, he sometimes asked himself where his acts of mind came from, humbled by his own intelligence, for which he took no credit. His decision ready, he gave it in a mild voice, glad to consider objections, if any; ready to entertain constructive, not destructive, criticism—a phrase he believed he invented.

One of his abiding desires was to be ready for emergency or death which might render him helpless. Against the contingency, he was careful that his underwear always be clean, and if anyone might have to break into his house to offer help in odd circumstances, he and Ellen made sure that their kitchen and bathroom were always spotless. He gave what he could to good causes, and often responded by saying, "I've never turned anyone down yet," and the statement made his eyes flood briefly at the sound of his own generosity and worthiness.

Was he weak? he sometimes wondered, and then answered anyone who thought so by reflecting that he might be slow and modest, but his conviction as to right action was powerful, and he knew his employers trusted him all the way, as well they might. If he were thanked for being of kind habit, he might smile, and swallow, and tell how, as a young man in agricultural college, many years ago, he had lost his temper, with a result so terrible that he could never bring himself to describe it; but in any case, it had made him vow never to lose his temper again so long as he lived.

"Well, Homer," they said who listened, "that must have been a sight," flatteringly.

"It was. Oh, it was. It scared *me*."

"Liquor?" someone asked.

"I'd just's soon not say any more."

If his dangerous temper was a matter of pride to Mr Breedlove, so was the control he imposed upon it. For years his three children would wonder hopefully what would happen if one day his grip should loosen and the terror he contained—but barely—should escape over them. But this never happened, and of the three, it was Billy, the youngest, who decided suddenly that the whole story was false, and that his father was only what he seemed to be—a tall, heavy-boned, man with a tired look of sweetness in his long, skin-folded face, who would never hurt a fly or break a stick. Billy could tell from his father's very voice that he was a peaceful man. Homer Breedlove spoke and sang in a hooded bass voice that sounded as though he swallowed down one way just as he spoke up or sang the other. How could that voice ever split the ear with rage? Having made nonsense of Homer's pretensions, Billy quite as suddenly knew love for him which was more than a boy's greedy habit of affection for a providing father.

His wife, Ellen Sparkman of this city, met him through music, as they said. While students at different colleges, both were chosen to take part in a choral competition which drew choruses from all over Texas to Fort Worth. Homer merely sang in the bass section of his chorus, but Ellen was given a solo to sing with hers, and sang it so well that Homer sought her out afterwards to introduce himself and congratulate her.

"So think of it. If I hadn't gone there to Forth Worth to sing, I would never have met your mother," he said, awed by the common act of destiny which made every love-match seem unique. "Music is a wonderful maker of friends. Harmony. I hope you children understand me."

Mrs Breedlove was a small woman, with wrenlike darting movements. To see her with Homer, who towered above her, made people smile and speculate. But the smiles and speculations were friendly, since he tried to diminish himself in protective courtesy, so as to make their union appear physically less grotesque. Her spirit was tall, if her figure was short; and between them they managed a declared dignity which was not without its occasional larkish moments, especially at home, in the old white frame house with its shingled cupola. The place lay far across town from the warehouse. It took up a large corner lot with its own unused windmill and earth tank which survived from days gone by, when farm cattle used to water there before the town grew northwestward and pushed the country back. But open country was still to be seen from the Breedloves' porch, and the parents often sat there to receive the glory of the sunset over the plains.

The oldest Breedlove child was a daughter, married and living in Germany where her husband, Captain Calloway, was an army officer on occupation duty in Pfungstadt, in that time of the late 1940s. The next was a son who was on a navy ship at sea, fulfilling his national service before enrolling for pre-dental courses at the University of Oklahoma. Billy was last—and nobody, they said, knew where he was headed; and if he himself knew, he did not say so.

Sometimes the parents would muse upon the quality of the world into which they had brought new lives. It was a great responsibility, they knew; and it turned their hearts to think that the likeness of the world which the child must know could only be that which they made for him at home—and home here meant the family house, and the town of which it was part, and the land chosen by ancestors, and the very nation itself. How differently people regarded the same things! they mused, and hoped their children would love what it had been possible to give them, and not turn away from it and scorn it, but see its beauties, recognize and fulfill its hopes, and sternly improve its failings. Sometimes they thought the young people—those too young to have served in the war, the children who had had to make of the war a form of play—were now heedless and restive. Having missed the great experience of their elders' time, the children later took their own way as if to say they had their world to make, which would be like no other before it. Must hope for a better future mean treason to the past? The parents could never decide.

✻ ✻ ✻

In private Homer and Ellen conscientiously discussed Billy's friends, to determine whether any might be a bad influence. Would anyone lead him to ambitions beyond his natural gifts? Or to aspirations too brilliant for the child of a man who controlled a nonexistent temper and a woman whose wholesome pleasure it was to make a collection, already famous, of thimbles from everywhere, including a thimble of real gold which a close friend, Mrs Tom Bob Gately, the banker's wife, had brought her from Dallas?

Of Billy's best friends, one older, one his own age, they knew nothing alarming.

The first of these was Guy DeLacey, who employed Billy after school and during vacations at the Red Dot Garage. Guy was in his late thirties, and as Ellen and others remarked, too fat for his own good. Though he wore an expression of exaggerated self-respect, he was highly nervous, which was strange, since fat men were expected to be jolly and easygoing. But when Guy was near a person, talking, or working together, or "out having cowffee", some undefined recognition of human responses came to him with troubling intensity, until he seemed to be cocked on a hair-trigger. Like many fat men, he had a certain grandeur of bearing, but this was countered by his extreme nervousness, and the gap left by two missing lower front teeth. He had pale blue eyes which frequently held a gleam. His thinning pale hair was brushed straight back. Because of his work, his grainy face had grimed complexion which would never come clear. Dancing deep inside him was a hungry social spirit. When he spoke, even of idle matters, his voice was uncertain out of excitement, and his grease-veined fingers trembled with his cigarette. Any call to respond was a precious experience for him; possibly complicated

[ 35 ]

by too much physical strain on his heart caused by his weight, it shook his metaphysical heart.

"Well, Mother," Homer remarked, "Guy has seen the world, they say"—though just where, and what of it, few seemed to know.

"I think he must be a fine man, though lonely," said Ellen.

Homer knew the world, and one time asked Billy if Guy—living alone, like that—ever went out to Maudie's.

"I suspect you don't know much about that place," said Homer hopefully, "nor do I, thank God, but you hear things. I just wondered if Guy."

"No, well, I don't know," said Billy.

"What people go there for. It's no place for a good clean-living man, or boy."

"No," said Billy, resolving to go to Maudie's on his own at the first opportunity, which would be difficult to arrange.

When Billy came home from the Red Dot, he was sometimes so soiled by black grease that he would have to hold his arms away to avoid touching anything. Ellen hated to see him so dirty, and exclaimed,

"That Guy DeLacey must give you only the dirtiest jobs to do!"

"I guess he does," was all Billy would say, running upstairs to get clean.

Billy decided that Guy saw himself, and wanted others to see him, as a sort of medical man, a surgeon, and his rusted corrugated iron shack of a garage as a clinic, which in addition to its familiar name had another, to be read on a sign inside Guy's little corner office: "Auto Diagnostic and Repair Center." At work, Guy wore a doctor's smock, soon smudged, and he spent his profits on equipment designed to resemble stethoscopes and other diagnostic apparatus, all of which supported his professional manner which was alarmingly inscrutable while making, as Billy heard him say, a diagnosis of some ailing automobile engine.

Needful of drama, Guy was expert at hinting by attitude and glance, while humming reservedly through the smoke of a cigarette which trembled from his pale lips in his pale wide face, that the patient was in bad shape.

"I'm afraid we have a mighty sick engine here," he would say, as he applied electrodes and took readings on ominous dials and gauges, or, wearing his stethoscope, he leaned to listen to the obscure gasps of failing cylinders. But then, when hope must be all but abandoned, he would brighten and smile through the smoke which closed his small puffed eyes with a watering sting, and say that he believed he could pull her through, though it would not be exactly easy, at which the anxious patron was allowed to breathe again, though not too freely. Homer, who had been through it, said,

"I believe it's just to impress people, but it doesn't do harm to anyone, and he is a good mechanic."

Ellen had a glimmer of a notion, difficult to state, so she remained silent, but her instinct told her that Homer was partly wrong—Guy went through his clinical gestures to impress himself.

But they did agree that there was no harm in Guy, for all his airs and jitters. There must be something fine in somebody—even a grown man—who among other activities spent hours, as Guy did, on building a miniature mountain range upstairs in the house where he boarded. Billy had seen it—it was a marvel of reduced realism, and when it was lighted in a certain way, you wanted to be in the mountain yourself. Guy may have lacked what he respectfully called a formal education, but he never stopped trying to know things. Surely he could only be a good influence on a lively boy, despite their great difference in age?

[ 37 ]

About Phillipson Durham, Billy's other friend, Homer Breedlove knew little, since the Durhams had moved to Belvedere only five or six years ago; but what he knew contained no worries which a reasonable man could not overcome.

Phil's father was the foreman of the Belvedere Printers, and was highly spoken of by the owner, Mayor Dillingham. Mr Durham, a silent, sourly patient man, was a palsied remnant of masculine life. Tall and emaciated, he had to move holding to one piece of office furniture after another, to keep from falling. Still, he was able to do his job. Nobody ever saw Mrs Durham, for she was known and accepted as an invalid, and it was said that her state of health was what had decided the Durham family to remain in Belvedere, instead of moving on after a few years, as had been their lifelong habit, to satisfy the roving urge of the father.

Phil was an only child, which was why, people observed, he seemed so withdrawn in manner. But if he was always in a book, he was generally polite, and at high school, they said if he was given something to do, he did it faithfully, and sometimes with a sort of sardonic flourish. He was slightly built where Billy was thickly made, and his whole effect was dark where Billy's was bright. A color snapshot in Billy's room showed Phil to have black hair and dark eyes under scowling brows, and skin swarthy not with warm color but with subdued ivory and olive. In his body, he looked younger than in his years; in his face, older. With Billy, Ellen reflected, it was just the other way round.

"What they see in each other, so different," she said.

"That's just it," said Homer, and she did not require him to elaborate this, for in their wedded habit, they could complete each other's thought beyond the word.

Homer sometimes heard the two boys talking. Though he

carefully avoided eavesdropping— "After all, though just boys, they're people, and have a right to their privacy," he thought, making his eyes fill at his breadth of spirit—he could not help hearing the difference in their voices, and now and then if he didn't get away fast enough, he would hear what they were saying. One time taking his ease in the front living room, he heard them talking on the porch. Billy asked Phil,

"What are those health problems at your place?"

After a pause, Phil decided to reply; and once decided, he had to speak the truth, difficult as it might be.

"My father," he said, "has a disease called locomotor ataxia."

"Is that why he wobbles?"

"Yes. —You know what it comes from?"

"No."

"Well, all right, it is the long-deferred effect of early syphilis."

"Holy crow."

"He was *quite a man* in his day, he says. His nickname was Sport Durham."

Billy was silent, as if he found it shameful for a son to know such a fact about his father. Phil calmly went on with his report, while Homer, horrified, was unable to retreat from his invisible place for fear of being heard now, when it would matter.

"My mother has been an invalid ever since she had to be told what ailed her husband. He caught it while I was a baby. There were to be no more children in my family. I believe she had doubts and suspicions about his larking around for years, but when they were confirmed by medical evidence, it nearly killed her. She has spent her life ever since waiting for the late symptoms to appear."

"Didn't they cure him?"

"The acute stage of it, yes; but too late to head off this present condition." Phil laughed dryly. "You wouldn't know it to look at him, but evidently he was once a handsome man."

"*Sport,*" repeated Homer silently. What disreputable gaieties were contained within the name.

"No, I wouldn't know it now," remarked Billy gently. "How people change."

A silence fell, as though the youths were looking ahead. Homer could remember trying to find explanations for himself in others when he was that age. He flushed.

"You needn't tell anybody what I've just told you," said Phil.

"No, no, no," said Billy, "of course not—Let's go."

They resolved the unanswerable by violent and meaningless action. They raced from the porch and down the street, whither, Homer could not say. But he knew he also must keep Billy's promise to Phil; and he never even told Ellen about Sport Durham's malady, for he knew she would wonder if it would be safe for Billy to see much of Phil. At her absurd notions, he would smile lovingly, and feel more of a man for them.

Just the same, he could not help wondering what his son and Phil saw as their picture of the world. At this thought, and the illimitable opportunities it brought to mind for youthful errors in ignorance, and for discoveries in joy, passion, or sorrow, Homer felt his long, slow-paced heart turn over with an odd thump in his cavernous breast. "Those two!" he would echo, and think of Phil as almost another son of his own and he would wish that some of Phil's quietude might rub off on Billy, just as Billy seemed able to animate Phil with new energy and purposeful imagination. The differences between them were made plain to him even by their voices. One voice crackled with energy and conviction, and sent its demands of interest straight to anyone who listened. The other sounded forth gravely, with dark timbre which made Homer think Phil could sing, if he would. He once asked him to join the choir, but Phil excused himself on several counts—a Catholic, he had to go to his own church of SS Peter and Paul, instead of the Breedlove United Southern Christian; and more than that, he said he did not have the gift of standing up and facing all those Sunday worshippers in the pale blue church auditorium shaped like the inside of a piece of pie, and opening his mouth in public. This refusal at first sounded both bigoted and snobbish to Homer, but then he made himself change his thought to one more kindly, and he said to himself, "An only child, the son of invalids," explaining much to his own satisfaction. In any case, he could think nothing but good of the sealed alliance, commander and follower, between those two. He could sleep well on it.

※ ※ ※

But sleep eluded him if he thought of Billy's third great attachment—the most absorbing of all. He was thinking of Marilee Underwood, and at the sight in his mind of her quality and image, he would almost grow angry, but he knew he must not let his thoughts dwell on the subject, even though he was aware what she did to him through her artless but binding response to his son Billy. For trying too hard not to, he often let the thought of Marilee cost him hours of rest. If there was any duty involved, he decided, he must let it remain with Marilee's widowed mother, who worked so selflessly to give her child everything a ripening girl demanded. Sometimes in baffled fatherhood, he would say "I don't want to know a single thing more about it," and so he would resign the necessary knowledge to the good sense of anyone—the Underwoods themselves, and Billy, perhaps even Phil—who were closer to the problem than he, if there was a problem, and he was sure there was.

※ ※ ※

Now a junior in the Belvedere public high school, Marilee Underwood a few years ago, at the age of twelve or thirteen, was almost a nun, with eyes downcast and a recognized devotion to the Blessed Mother. When she was finishing the eighth grade in the parochial school of SS Peter and Paul, the nuns all saw themselves in her, and gave thanks in prayer that if for no other work than this they had come to teach in the little plains community of Belvedere. With its dust storms, its summer heat before which all Nature seemed aghast, its bitter winters when northers shrieked across Texas to the Gulf, its time of spring when every disturbance of reawakened creation came as a trial to those who had promised their lives to an unending faithfulness beyond this world, Belvedere was worth suffering if only one soul there offered itself to God in the lovely person of Marilee Underwood.

Marilee's mother was as proud and happy as the sisters at the prospect of her daughter's resolved future—and yet too, she seemed now and then to be rueful at the loss of a posterity on this earth. God knew how hard she worked, she tried not to complain, it was worth it, to keep her child in good health and graced with the simple advantages which all children deserved; but it was only human, Mrs Underwood said in her low moments, to have looked forward to a time when she could rest and take satisfaction like any other mother from the joys of ministering to her grandbabies, as she put it, and have her turn at being taken care of after a long life of busy sacrifice. If the sisters were right about Marilee's vocation, it was a time Mrs Underwood must do without.

She sighed. A woman of ardent passions of loyalty and duty, Mrs Underwood believed also that good sense was first of all rooted in unselfishness. If what had to be had to be, then if it was a good thing to be, she must simply accept it and work with it instead of against it, and in that way bring everybody concerned to contentment. She suffered in general from an anguished propriety. She often said the thing that mattered was for her to be able "to hold her head up," and when Marilee was small and innocently wicked, her mother declared at the end of necessary scoldings that what a child did reflected on their mother, and she was going to see to it that nobody— "Nobody is ever going to be able to point their finger at *me!*"

There were depths in her child from which she was excluded— she knew that. Sometimes when she had to scold, Marilee would listen to her in perfect calm, with her pearly small face empty of expression, her sky-blue eyes steady and far-away. What really lay behind their lovely openness? Mrs Underwood never forgot how one day coming home after playing with neighborhood children, Marilee said to her in gleeful innocence—she was about five years old at the time—"Look here." The child made a circle with her thumb and forefinger.

"Well?" asked her mother, recognizing that this was a game.

"Put your finger in there," said Marilee in her deeply fluted small voice which would never lose its slightly husky tone.

Her mother, in playful wonderment, as Marilee's playmates must have done, put her finger into the little circle of her child's hand. When she did so, Marilee, in derisive glee at having won the game, cried out,

"You put your finger in your father's toilet!"

With a gasp, Mrs Underwood snatched her hand away saying,

"Where did you learn that! What have you and those dirty little children been doing!"

Marilee was astonished at this sudden rage over something which had always made her friends of four and five years of age laugh in delight.

"Nothing!" she said, and burst into tears.

The tears seemed like signs of guilt. Mrs Underwood seized

her and gave her a sharp spanking. How she must fight against the furies of the flesh to subdue them daily for fear they should make irresistible claims in any life! Marilee screamed in outrage and learned to keep secrets from her mother.

A miniature tempest, it was soon over; but it was like others which came up between them as Marilee grew older. They were always followed by periods of loving contrition and calm; but it was a calm which concealed Marilee's growing thirst for escape. It was a solace when at just the right age for it, she decided, before the first hint of woman's nature had reached her exquisitely forming body, to take vows against the carnal in life.

This gave Mrs Underwood peace of heart as she pursued the work which supported her and her child. She was manager and hostess of the Bluebonnet Hotel Coffee Shop in Belvedere. She had worked every day of her life since burying her young husband long ago back in Ohio where she came from. She knew now what dawn looked like in all seasons of the year, for every morning she had to be at the Bluebonnet before anyone else, to open up. She had to close up at night after the tables were all made fresh and ready for next morning, and the kitchen was mopped, and the wooden meatblock was giving off a moist scrubbed fragrance.

Two days a week she was so tired she was fit t'be brushed up in a dustpan and thrown away, she said. These were the two days when the men's luncheon clubs met in the Bluebonnet Coffee Shop and everything had to be managed with no more help than usual. She also had to have a word and a smile, a scornful but attractive ray in her gray eyes, and a hovering raillery on her lips, for members of the clubs as they filed past her cash register to pay their ninety-five cents plus tax. She was still handsome, in an unreachable sort of way, and her male customers liked to stir her up. They rowdily called the cash register her bandit's piano. Her fingers flew making change, and her tongue drilled with what she returned for the compliments of Belvedere's leading citizens.

Among the men was Mayor Dillingham, who always offered her the self-humbling courtesy which had earned him four terms of office. He seemed to say that he knew what she suffered, admired her for it, and was glad she could take the waggeries of his fellow-members in such good spirit. The mayor had an appealing face which he knew how to crinkle with a patient smile. His wife often said of him that a better man never forked a horse—a remark which drove young people into strangled hilarity.

As a small child, Marilee had spent most of her days at the Bluebonnet Coffee Shop, for there was no one at home to care for her. She sat on a low stool behind the cashier's counter, quiet, hardly looking up, for hours. Without knowing it, she showed in her thin little face a longing for escape which made some of the hearty club members wonder what would ever become of her. Too, there was something in her wan features, her wide brow and scrolled lips, that made one or another of the men wish at the hazy edge of his thought that he might know her, say, ten-fifteen years from now, when he might just not have to suppress what might come up.

❦ ❦ ❦

The nuns had no high school at SS Peter and Paul. Presently there was no place for Marilee to go but Belvedere High School, where Phillipson Durham knew her in the first year she attended school there. He was a class ahead of her, but somehow seemed the same age. They saw each other at Mass also. They began to walk home together after church or school. For some while she was quiet and removed in the presence of the heedless, glistening young life all about them. But the better they knew each other—mainly through little blurts of talk and long consequent silences

—the more Phil began to see in her another person whom she protected within the restrained presence she showed to others. Everyone knew she was to become a nun, but one day she said to him,

"If I became a great actress, you could write me a play."

"What about?" he asked, startled.

"Oh, anything—Saint Thérèse of Lisieux, the Little Flower. Do you think I could be her?" she asked hooding her face with her hands to suggest a nun's cowl. She was in a period of looking plain, but a light of pure being poured from her eyes.

"No doubt about it. But I thought you were going to be a nun."

"I still might."

She read his stories—the ones written outside of class—and told him he was already a great author. All he had to do was wait until everybody else knew it too.

"I'll collect things for you to put in your books," she promised.

When she began to give him "things" he was startled by the mocking tone of much that she said. There was a plump, elaborate young man who as assistant principal led the assemblies in the school auditorium.

"Some day," said Marilee, "all his jokes will finally make *him* tired, and he will collapse. You can tell that he would never be able to think of any new ones. He will simply have to kill himself."

Phil saw him anew through her. She was like no other girl in school. He was never certain when she was serious or not. A hazy smile lingered about her lips, and faint shadows came and went across her blue eyes as the expression of her tender brows changed with her thought. He was stirred by all her premonitions of ripening power, none of which he understood. High school athletics drew another comment from her.

"What if they all would put as much into praying together as they do cheering together!"

"I didn't know you went to sports."

"I don't, often, but enough. But maybe they think they're doing the same thing."

"As what?"

"As praying, when they're cheering."

If he was unsettled, though interested, by these views, it was no wonder that other boys were shy of her. Few others ever asked her to dance. One time while Phil was dancing with her she seemed to be at the edge of tears, and when he asked her what was wrong, she said,

"I don't know. Yes, I do. I'm such a lump."

"Oh, no," he said, with a sudden rush of protective feeling.

"Yes. But it wouldn't be so awful to be a lump, but it would be awful to become a nun for that reason!"

"That won't be the reason, Marilee."

"But it may be."

"Maybe I won't let you become a nun," he said.

"How could you stop me? Or stop them?"

"I could make you marry me."

"Don't be a sil. We're not in love."

"You never can tell."

She looked at him sweetly, with something in her eyes that dismissed being a lump for both of them. She pulled herself nearer to him and smiled and they danced, willing to remain in their ages and take each other for granted whenever there were occasions approved by their parents, even though, privately, as nobody else knew, they might be a great actress and a celebrated author. Plain and obscure, Marilee seemed to be making peace with her life.

Summer came, and again the opening of school. When she returned to school Marilee was transformed. Two things caused this. One was the great importance of only a few months' growth in age of a girl leaving childhood. She was suddenly lovely again, but in a new way which made her mother hold her breath with anxiety when she looked at her. The other was the effect of coming to know Billy Breedlove and to be wanted by him.

꙳ ꙳ ꙳

When school opened again, Billy consciously saw Marilee for the first time, though he had been passing her in the halls for several terms. She was now within a shade of being as tall as he. Her hair was dark honey-color and she wore it short and tossed about her clear brow and high-boned cheeks with their warm color. When Billy really looked at her, he saw that her eyes made a kind of blue light of their own. She was not pretty in a regular way, like the other girls he liked, for her nose now had a little bony angle between the eyes, a Roman nose, they said, which gave her a strong instead of pretty profile, but, as the Latin teacher said, one that was aristocratic. Her mouth was classically cut, like the mouth of the Greek plaster statue behind Miss Mallory's desk in the public library, and like that one it was always seen to be slightly open—the lips in the statue parted to suggest the breath of life, and, in Marilee, to give and take the actual breath of life itself, which she now began to do energetically, laughing or talking. Her new voice was like nobody else's in town—strong, low-keyed, and a little husky. Seeing its effect on Billy and other boys, some of the ambitious girls of the time began to imitate it.

"I don't have to ask you, but I want to," she said to Phil. "Billy Breedlove wants me to have a date."

"I know you don't. Go ahead. But don't forget to come back," Phil answered, wondering if she would.

He recognized that he had made no exclusive claim on her,

and with a return of the lumpish feeling they had discussed some time ago, he had to admit that he had no gifts with which to rival those that Billy could offer. He hardly knew Billy then, but was occasionally greeted by him with general—some said political—heartiness.

Phil was left to wonder about love until he should know what it was. Billy knew from the beginning. His body told him first, and he answered it. He captured Marilee, and knew more about her in an hour than Phil in all his years with her. He quickly saw her ruefulness for Phil, a schoolmate of whom he was then only distantly aware, the companion she had left behind. But Billy was not content to leave him behind if he could take him along.

He sought out Phil to make him his friend, and was amazed at what he found. As Marilee was like no other girl he knew, Phil was like no other boy. Billy promised that the three of them together would be something new in Belvedere. In a sudden movement of excitements and recognitions, they made a league among themselves, as Billy's will led them along.

❦ ❦ ❦

In late afternoons, or early evenings, they often went, the three of them, to Whitewater Lake, taking a picnic.

After long deliberation, during which he looked so soberly at Billy until Billy laughed out loud for the speculation far within his father's eyes, Homer Breedlove would let Billy use the family car. Across town, Mrs Underwood would give permission for Marilee to go "so long's there's the three of you going, and not just the one boy". Phil's parents, lonely as they were, feared loneliness for him, and were glad to see him "take some interest," as they said, in other people—even young ones.

Evening fell over the plains like the past and brought a fugitive pang to anyone who watched the horizon slowly vanish. Memory was the light against it.

Billy was always reminded of something by something unexpected. One evening at the lake as they all lay at the water's edge watching the stars appear in the still reflection, he said,

"Ben Grossman."

"Who?" asked Marilee.

"You never knew him, either of you. This all happened before you people moved here."

"Did you know him?"

"He used to give me candy when I went to the store with my mother. They found his car right away, but they didn't find him for weeks. Maybe he was down in that old town below us, because the currents may go down the streets between the rows of trees, and they may even turn the corner now and then. But one day he came up and they found him."

"He was drowned?" asked Phil.

"There was more to it than that."

"What was he like? —do him for us," said Marilee, for Billy had a knack for impersonation. She loved to see him showing off, so she could watch him with her love uppermost, while pretending to be interested in his act.

"Yes," said Billy, throwing a catch of dried tamarisk whips on their ebbing picnic fire. He thought a moment until he had the image of his subject clearly in mind, then squared himself, and then slumped into another figure. In the pale glow from the embers, the other two watched him turn into Ben Grossman.

"He had a funny shape, with his shoulders up high, his head hung forward, like this, and he was skinny everywhere but in his gut, and there he stuck out, this way. His arms hung down loose by his sides and when he walked, his feet flapped out, right and left, and his hands flapped too, at the end of those long loose arms hanging down. He was bald, and I remember the color of his head, and his face, the color of an old cue ball. Gray now but once white. Walk, walk. Flap, flap." Billy showed how. "And when he talked his voice was high and squeezed, this way, like coming from a bad chest cold: 'Good morning, Mrs Breedlove, I see you brought this bad boy in with you today, what are we going to do with him?' And then he always reached in the front counter and got me out some candy, a Tootsie-Roll, or some jelly-beans."

"Where was this? What did he do?" asked Phil.

"Ran a grocery store, the best one in town, full of special things he ordered from New York and Boston, from places he worked as a young man. Funny. My mother said he was a very handsome young man. She knew him then. I couldn't believe it. Oh yes, she said, he was friends with everybody. But he never went any-where. He just got old. He worked every night down at the store, in the little office at the back alley, till all hours, they said. Some nights he just stayed and slept on a cot in the office."

"What did his wife say?" asked Marilee.

"He never had a wife. He was born in Whitewater. His parents were pioneers there. Then he went to school in Belvedere, and then never went to college, but instead went East to learn the grocery business. Nobody ever thought he would, but he came back and lived alone in Belvedere. He had a little house down by the railroad. Nobody we knew was ever inside it. He planted grass but it dried up and blew away and he never tried again, sort of as if he gave up trying to make anything live. Mostly he walked to work and us children yelled at him and waved and he waved back, and sometimes we followed him, because he might have had some candy in his pockets. But not just for that. We liked him. He was funny-looking, but sad, like a clown."

"Show how," demanded Marilee.

Billy drew his mouth down, but managed also to suggest a smile, and put his head on one side and nodded it and shook it. Then coming back to himself, he said,

"He was famous for one thing, though. —He always was the first one to give when they had a drive for anything, like the Red Cross, or the war bonds, or the Milk Fund, and that. He gave so much that anybody else with money had to match him or beat him. Tom Bob Gately, at the bank, always had to give more, just to come out on top."

"He must have had a lot of friends."

"People tried, but he wouldn't let them."

"How do you mean?"

"Well, I heard that he always said not to bother about him, he would be all right, and nobody should take any trouble over him. So after a while everybody gave up, and stopped asking him to supper, or to a party, or go fishing, and that." Billy paused for his next effect. When it was ripe, he said, "And then one day he was missing. —That's right. The store didn't open up, people telephoned each other, went to his house, but he wasn't there. They look for him all day. He wasn't anywhere in town. They checked the bank, but all his money was still there. His car, it was an old jalopy he kept but didn't use much, was also gone and so they began going around the country on all the roads, somebody drove out as far as here, and pretty soon they found it."

"Found what?"

"His car."

"Where?"

"Over there, on that side of the lake, where it's flat, they found tracks turning off the road, and leading to the edge. They followed them, and spang: the tracks went right on over, and the car was under water, but clearly visible, about twenty feet down."

"Oh," said Marilee on an indrawn breath.

"They got Guy DeLacey to bring out his wrecker, and they hauled the old Model A out, but there was no sign of old Ben. They took the car back to town. It was nothing but junk, now, more than ever, and they said Guy could have it and keep it with the rest of his junk out back of the Red Dot."

"I know. I've seen it there," said Phil. "I never knew what it was."

"People came all day long to look at it, and think about their friend."

"Well, but did you ever know what happened to him?" asked Phil.

"So they thought a lot, and thought he might have been kidnapped and robbed, and maybe murdered and his body put in the lake with a heavy old rock tied to it, and all. Maybe somebody thought it, but nobody said it, about what really happened."

"Maybe I know," whispered Marilee.

"What was it?" said Billy solemnly.

"He killed himself," she said. "Stop it, I can't stand it."

"But you don't know why."

"I know we don't. No, don't stop."

He watched Marilee touch away tears that tried to come to her eyes. Phil oddly felt his heart begin to beat rapidly.

"Well," said Billy, "nobody would have been sure ever, but that one day six-eight weeks afterward, some men were out here fishing, my pappy was one of them, and one of them said, *What's that out there, floating?*, and they all thought the same thing, for somebody else said, *I'll tell you what it looks like to me,* and they rowed on over, and it was what they thought."

"Where was this?" asked Phil out of simple nervousness.

"Just what we were saying. Up there, right above old Whitewater. It was Mr Grossman, floating. And you know? This is the thing. Nobody ever understood it. He was stark naked, and nobody ever figured out what became of his clothes, or why he took them off, though they looked everywhere. It was about three o'clock in the afternoon when they brought him back to town. I remember hearing about it, though I didn't really know what to think except by seeing the look on peoples' faces."

Marilee put her face into her hands and shook her head. Billy laid his hand on her gathered shoulder, and went on telling.

"They took him to Mr Doty's, and Mr Doty said when he embalmed him that he saw cancer everywhere in old Ben. Mr Doty told everybody the pain must have been the worst anybody ever had. They felt sad and horrible because they had not been of any help to Ben. Day after day they had just gone shopping and said the usual things, and got out of his store, and forgot him, and all the while he was as kind and nice as ever, and ready to die, and he knew it, and you know? they said he seemed almost apologetic about it when they thought it over later?"

Marilee turned her face against Billy's chest and he put his arm around her and went on speaking to Phil over her head.

"There was a grand funeral and every famous citizen was there—no, all but one, they all thought this was strange, Tom Bob Gately wasn't there, though his wife was, but then she's always everywhere. But not Tom Bob. People all mentioned it. He went to his ranch instead. Everybody said, 'Well, that's Tom Bob, he does just as he pleases.' I think they all wished they could do just as they pleased, like that ornery son of a bitch. But then, they weren't president of the bank."

Billy looked down at Marilee. She was quiet but seemed to be hiding against him. He said,

"Something else. They found old Ben's will in the bank and he left everything he had to found a public library, provided they didn't put his name on it anywhere. That's how that got started. That's when Miss Mallory came to town to be the librarian. That's why you can go and get books every day."

Now the silence was valuable to their thoughts. Phil felt a heavying of his substance, as though a struggle began in his inner flesh, a struggle to know the meaning of all that he could see, hear, smell, touch, and taste, for fear that he might suddenly lose the power of thought; and if that should happen he must die. None of this turmoil was visible. He sat hunched over his drawn-up knees, enclosing his inner storm, as would be his lifelong habit. Billy brought all things to the surface once more by talking again.

"Maybe it's none of my business," he said, "but there's one more thing about Ben. You know how people have to talk, and they have to say this, and say that, and poke around, trying to find out things about anyone. Well, they tried to understand how Ben, even with all that pain, went ahead and did it. And they seemed to think it wasn't just the pain."

Marilee looked up in renewed distress.

"What was it, then?" she said.

"It was his whole life. They said it was because he never fell in love, or got married, or even had an affair, or let himself have any friends, or keep a dog or a kittycat, or anything, and it took a long time, and it took a lot of pain on top of everything else, but finally what happened happened." He waved out toward the now dark lake.

"No, no!" cried Marilee, with her face pressed into Billy's breast again, but her voice was muffled, and they could not understand what she said next.

"What?" said Billy. "What did you say?"

She straightened up, conquering her sympathy with effort, and said in a level tone,

"I said, 'The only worse thing than being in love is not being in love.'"

The fire was almost gone, but Phil could see alarm in Billy's face for depressing her so. Billy jumped up energetically and cried in a comic singsong,

"We're losing our fire. I want some more coffee." He threw on more branches, the flames were born again, and so was his comic sense. "Listen, Marilee," he said, "who's this—see if you can recognize who this is!"

"Don't try to cheer me up," she said, as if he would make a child of her, but she added, "Who?" and he held his hands out to create a new atmosphere of theatre, and then began another impersonation.

He made his shoulders look like a coathanger, and hugged his hands downward before him making his arms seem long and thin. He pulled back his head until he made an Adam's apple where none showed before in his young athlete's neck, and then, in a sandy voice with every grain sounding separately to create accents of fellowship so full of Christian goodwill that he sounded grief-stricken, he declared,

"I'm just so glad, folks, to see so many of us here this marning, fit and ready to give our wirship to the L-a-a-r-d! I get just so thankful fir the blessings that w'receive that sometimes I"—the voice went sore-throated with goodness and gratitude and grief, and under it sounded a scandalous delight in the impersonation, —"I just go down cellar and kick my old dog where he lies snoring on a gunnysack, for the joy of it? Brethern?"

He threw himself down in a comic cramp, and Phil said through his own laughter, while Marilee remained pensive,

"It's the Reverend Lew Priddle, the way he sounds in those manly talks he gives us in those high school assemblies. You even looked like him!"

"I have a theory," said Billy. "—It's all makeup, like actors. When I was in that show last year I saw how all the faces got fixed, and now when I walk down the street, I know how they all get to look the way they do. —Who's this?"

Billy jumped up again and made himself shrink bent over till he was a little old man, with fierce jerky energy in his movements. He created a long mustache by sweeping its shape along each side of his mouth, and he established a temper by switching his head first to one side, then the other, in suspicion of what might be going on around here. Then he shrilled in a thin, sour, forced voice, while brandishing his arms ineffectually,

"C'mon, c'mon, c'mon, get out of here, you there, c'mon, get out. I saw ye, ye can't fool me!"

[ 56 ]

"That's Mr Honeycutt!" cried Marilee, laughing at last.

It was the town marshal, long past the age of retirement, who was retained on the Belvedere city payroll out of sentiment and even a sort of civic pride; for so long as Marshal Honeycutt was in charge of the peace, Belvedere could show that she was the most law-abiding city in West Central Texas, needing only one old man and one state highway patrol car with Highway Patrolman Hardie Jo Stiles to keep order.

"I don't know how you do it," said Phil.

"Oh, well," replied Billy, "it's all part of finding out. That's the thing. Finding out."

"What are you going to become, yourself?"

Marilee said, "I know."

"Yes," said Billy, "we've talked it over. I have decided to become a Personality. You know, how they talk of so-and-so of stage, screen, and radio, being a Personality? I don't mean I'm going to go to Hollywood, or anything, or become a semi-automatic, gas-operated guy, like a fast-talking salesman, or anything, but after all, all you've got in this world to use is yourself. I guess it's a joke, but it won't hurt anybody, as long as they know it's a joke."

"I wish I knew anything that clear about myself," said Phil.

"Oh, you will," said Billy, "if you don't think so much about it."

The truth of this was a blow, accidentally given. To conceal how he felt it, Phil asked,

"Can you do Tom Bob Gately down at the bank?"

Billy gave the effect of lounging back smoking an imaginary cigar, partially closing one eye against the rich, heavy smoke, and slowly looking up, down, over, and into the person of a suppliant for a loan. Through Billy, Tom Bob showed as a menacing bull of a man who eased his belly out of his belt, and lazily raked and comforted his conspicuously weighted groin in a reference to the common virility; he then idly spat as if delivering an opinion, and then suddenly smiled, with handsome and rugged waggery, saying in an unexpectedly high drawl,

"Hi, there, y'old breed bull, what nefarious plot to achieve sudden wealth brings you into the temple of commerce today?"

For Tom Bob was the town's leading banker, master of the fate of many a rancher and businessman through his control of loans.

Once again Phil marvelled at Billy's knack, wondering how much understanding of the feelings which lay under action reached Billy, and vaguely concluding that if Billy should ever discover them, he would either not believe them or else decide that they were crazy. The faculty of judging only by himself was what made it possible for Billy to keep Phil as a friend. He never felt what Phil's friendship was made of—of how much resentment, unwilling love, envy, curiosity, admiration, self-hatred. Unlike Phil, Billy never asked why people did as they did.

"We have to go," said Marilee suddenly. "I am going to drive home."

"My pappy says I am not to let anyone else drive," said Billy with a shake of his head.

"Then I'll walk," she stated calmly.

Billy turned to Phil, and said,

"You know? She would? She really would. —All right, you drive, Marilee. But I'll be right beside you. If he asks, I'll tell my pappy I just let you steer."

The evening was now cool, under a faint wind. The stars turned to ribbons leading down into the deep water. The three friends look leave of the lake with a dreaming stare. At such moments their contentment together was less troublesome than love, for it called forth no stresses, concealed no troubling hopes.

Yet always, as they would return to town, Phil granted in his thoughts to Billy and Marilee their own pairing which made him less than their equal in all unspoken ways.

※ ※ ※

But with all Billy's easy monopoly of Marilee's thoughts and hours, she and Phil still held an interest in common which had nothing to do with Billy.

Belvedere, like most modest towns where everyone seemed pretty well alike, had one tradition of a presence which would have been exceptional anywhere. When people spoke of it, mentioning the memory of the Judge, or the name of his living widow, they always did so with a grudging acceptance of the distance between themselves and those figures who belonged, as if to another world, to the large, silent, impressive house at Crystal Wells, six miles out of town off Highway 31, the road to Orpha City. Visitors would be driven past the estate to see the great grove of cottonwoods which made an oasis in the plains, and the long lane of Lombardy poplars which led for over a mile to the mansion, as it was always called; and then taking a dirt road widely around to the far side of the estate, they could gaze at the upward tumbling of the artesian wells, two of them, widely separated, which threw high into the air thick columns of pale green water crested with domes of breaking crystal fallback which gave its name to the establishment.

It had once known great days. Residents of Whitewater who migrated to Belvedere could remember how it had been when Judge Cochran was alive, and the state he decreed to keep his first wife entertained. They said she was an Easterner of great wealth who felt exiled out here. The Cochrans had a household staff of Negro servants who catered to frequent visitors from far away. The sidings of the Roscoe, Snyder and Pacfic often supported private railroad cars in those days, when the Judge's guests would arrive, to be met by the Judge's varnished carriage, and later, his shining Pierce-Arrow motor car. The Cochrans had only official friends in Belvedere. The first Mrs Cochran was known to view the local society with indifference, and as a result, buried hostility long existed between Crystal Wells and the town. The Judge was rich enough (through marriage) to be treated courteously when business took him to town, but he never felt any need to cultivate the ranchers, the small-town bankers, anyone except the leading physician, a Virginian of his own age who knew a good cigar and was a judge of bourbon.

Yet for all the resentment, Belvedere in an odd way was proud of the rambling brick mansion with its canopy of trees, its vast farm fields irrigated by artesian water, and the rumored splendors within the house. The Judge—who took his law degree at Washington and Lee—had been appointed to his federal bench in Texas after practicing law in Washington. He served until the fancy struck him to resign and write an exhaustive study of the Napoleonic tradition. He acquired a great library of history and biography about Napoleon, and spent days reading and making notes in his long living room which faced out across the fields where he could see the distant artesian wells—the only feature which broke the level landscape. His notes grew and grew, the collection expanded, relics pertaining to his subject multiplied, but he never actually began his book. When his first wife died, he gave up the project, it was said, and, as if he had not already done so, let it be known that he was going into retirement.

The important visitors from the East and from abroad dwindled away. Still active, Judge Cochran would now and then be seen riding his favorite mare, but always alone, until in his sixties he married a second time. To local amazement, he married a young woman of Belvedere who had been born in vanished Whitewater. She outlived him. He died at eighty in 1929, when his wife was forty-one, long after she had earned her living by teaching a class of the dance, which she gave up on becoming Mrs. Sylvester James Cochran.

When his death left her in solitude at Crystal Wells, everyone expected Victoria Cochran to do one of two things—either fill her days by at last becoming the grand lady of the county, entertaining all the local people who had never seen the inside of the famous old house, of which so much was believed by rumour; or to vacate the place and its treasures, and take a small house in town, and again become one with the people from whom she had come long before.

She did neither.

Not wholly a recluse, though she continued to live at Crystal Wells, with only one servant, a comfortable old black cook, she was induced by Major Dillingham to take an interest in the school system, and presently was elected to the school board. Because she was still the grand lady of the plains, with that house which strangers were always taken to gaze at from the distance, the other members tried to elect her president of the school board. But she thanked them and said, "Nonsense"—what they needed was new blood. As a result, the oldest member was elected, and Victoria said almost nothing at meetings, which she faithfully attended. Instead she spent her time knowing the principal, the teachers, and some of the students. Policy interested her less than persons.

Now and then there would be an occasional student, boy or girl, who showed interests and capacities somewhat outside the general style of Belvedere. To these she gave her time, inviting them to Crystal Wells for a chance to tell of what they wanted in the world. In her own day, she had wanted much beyond Whitewater and Belvedere, had gone away to seek it, and had come home again without it. But having seen something of the world, she could imagine what others growing up might desire, and surely, she would say to herself, there would have to be a handful who would realize their desires. She also knew how few people there were in Belvedere to listen, and to understand, what the ambitiously longing boy or girl was trying to say, often by inexplicable action instead of words. She knew how important it was to the young simply to have someone to listen.

"Who is it this year?" she asked the principal during Marilee's junior year.

"The one who has surprised us all is Marilee Underwood."

"Is she good in her studies?"

"Yes, decidedly. But more—she is like someone who has suddenly begun to *see*. We all feel it. —Her mother is the Mrs Underwood who manages the Coffee Shop."

"Oh, yes. I know who she is. Let me meet the child. What does she want to do?"

"We don't know. Perhaps you can help her to find out for herself, Mrs Cochran."

"I'll try. Tell her I'll call for her Wednesday after school. I'll meet her here in your office."

"Thank you. I will."

※ ※ ※

On Wednesday at three-forty-five Marilee in trepidation appeared in answer to the principal's summons and was introduced to Mrs Sylvester James Cochran. She saw Mrs Cochran waiting there and recognized her, but she never thought she'd meet her. Everyone knew who Mrs Cochran was and what she looked like—small and thin, but full of decisive strength. She was in her early sixties a handsome woman, with a severe style. She wore her still dark hair parted in the middle and drawn back above her ears and tied with a narrow black ribbon, like a—like a ballerina, thought Marilee. Her tanned face was gullied with wrinkles, but clear-boned, and carefully serene. Her eyes were lively, darting with interest. She perpetually held a cigarette which showed rouge marks at its tip. She wore no makeup other than lipstick of a deep rose red. She was plainly dressed in a smartly cut gray suit and carried short white gloves.

"Marilee, this is Mrs Cochran. She wants to get to know you."

They exchanged greetings, and Mrs Cochran said,

"Have you time to run out to the house for a glass of iced tea?"

"Yes, thank you. But I don't know why you ask me."

Mrs Cochran laughed.

"That's the remark of somebody who is embarrassed. Don't be. You're better than you think you are. Once upon a time *I* was better than I *thought*. I was mistaken, but it didn't wreck my life after all. But you know? young people sometimes need someone to believe in what they really want to get at. Do you know?"

"No."

"Well, education outside the classroom has something to do with finding out. —Shall we run out to the country for a little while?"

She drove Marilee in her old car, which was kept up in good condition.

"Do you come from here?" asked Marilee.

"I was a child in Whitewater. When we had to move to Belvedere, all I could think of was getting farther away. So here I still am."

She did not sound bitter—only amused at the realities for which most people had to settle.

"Here we are," she said, and turned in at the high stone gate-posts of the lane which led to the rambling house at Crystal Wells Farm. Marilee had never seen it except from the highway and the circling wells road.

Once inside, Mrs Cochran led her through a long dark hallway to a living room which was as large as four classrooms put together, and finally out to a wide shady porch looking upon a lawn where willow trees surrounded a cast-lead fountain where no water now played.

"We'll have our iced tea here," said Mrs Cochran, "I'll go tell Nella."

Alone, Marilee felt an excited beat in her heart. She was in a new world, the one link Belvedere could offer her, or anyone there, to the great world beyond the plains community which, with all its self-satisfied modesties, never seemed to her to represent life. She thought of Phil, and of how he would love to be here.

When she returned, Mrs Cochran settled down with a fresh cigarette and asked a few questions indifferently, but in a warm voice, and Marilee found herself at ease with her. At the end of an hour they were talking like old friends. Marilee could hardly wait to tell others of her visit. To put her at ease, Mrs Cochran said,

"I'll run you home whenever you say. Your mother will be worried."

"She's always worried."

"She wouldn't be a mother otherwise."

"I know. But it's hard."

"Yes. But remember that it's hard for her, too. I have no children, of my own, that is. But some of the students now and then—." She made it clear that she regarded Marilee now as one of her own. "You must come again. —Is there anyone you'd like to bring?"—for Mrs Cochran had heard of Billy Breedlove's possession of Marilee, believed it innocent, but knew it to be strong. She was therefore slightly astonished when Marilee said,

"Oh, yes. Phillipson Durham. My oldest friend. He's a senior. He is going to be an author."

Mrs Cochran was never surprised visibly by anything the young could claim for themselves or say to her. She smiled and said,

"Bring him next time. —Friday?"

"Oh, yes."

"I'll fetch you both, same time, same place."

So, beyond love, began Phil's truest new friendship. In no time, it seemed to him, and to Marilee, they were both intimates of Victoria Cochran. Without self-consciousness she invited them to exchange first names with her. If they felt like it, they were to call her Vicky, and come as often as they liked. Phil was to borrow books that interested him. He was to be free in his visits to roam the house and feast upon its contents. He was lifted into another prospect of life itself by what he saw there. It gave him a critical distance from which to look at Belvedere. Victoria, without malice, but with amusement, could talk about the local life and speak frankly about those aspects of it which she thought foolish or cruel. People in town rarely spoke about themselves or each other in just that way. Through her Marilee and Phil met standards of opinion which answered questions that could not have come clear to them so soon.

They liked looking at her—the way she moved, swiftly, with grace which sometimes mocked itself to make a point; the way she sat, erect and poised at every moment; her seamed face, which showed how beautiful were the bones beneath; the formality of her expression, with arched eyebrows above her long lids, which so often seemed in witty contrast to the simplicity and frankness of her speech.

"You must come often," said Victoria. "But if I have to come and get you each time it will be formal, and we'll have to make arrangements. I dislike arrangements. Do you both have bicycles?"

"Yes," they said.

"Then ride out whenever you feel like it. I'm always here except when the school board meets or when you're in class and can't come anyway."

They felt free in her world. When she spoke to them of her

dead husband, she called him Jim, and so they too thought of him, looking at a long portrait of him at the age of fifty-five. He was handsome in a majestic way, with roughly carved features, light blue eyes, shaggy white hair, and oddly delicate hands. They looked at her to see what she found in him.

"He was a love," she said. "The most sensitive creature I have ever known. I never thought of the difference in our age. Shall I tell you something? He said he was drawn to me because he felt I was disappointed in life but that I refused to admit it. He said he had known so many whining females that after he had seen me a few times he found me a relief. I loved his calm and his lack of curiosity."

"—Were you?" asked Phil, for he had not passed further than one thing she said.

"Was I what?"

"Disappointed."

"Yes. I didn't want to come back, but there was nothing else to do."

"Why? —Or should I not ask. I'm sorry."

"No," said Victoria, "I thought you probably both knew all about me." They shook their heads. She laughed. "Lord! not even to be talked about, any more. Well. It is quite simple. When I was a small child in Whitewater, I made up my mind to become a dancer, I mean someone like Pavlova. I suppose it came from some magazine picture, heaven knows I'd never seen a great dancer. But who knows how we start for anywhere, any of us? Do you know where you are going?"

"No," said Marilee.

"I think so," said Phil.

"Yes, who knows. Yes, well, it lasted, with me, even after I was here in school, and finally my father and mother—they were sweet, really, but of course weak with doubt about all of it—let me go to Dallas to study—or *take ballet,* as they said. They really were sweet. They saved money to send me later to New York. I

[ 66 ]

worked hard. I was very happy." She paused and looked at the two young people. "If I could have one blessing to give to people I would wave my wand and say, 'Let your illusion, whatever it is, never be broken.' Mine lasted a while longer. I was able to go to Europe on a legacy just large enough to let me stay one year in Paris and go on studying. I auditioned actually for the *corps de ballet* at the *Opéra*." She pronounced it in French. Phil thought, "French! in Belvedere!"

"Oh—did they take you?" asked Marilee.

"No. I heard someone refer to me as 'that American' and when they rejected me I was sure it was because I was foreign. But then I remembered they had Russians, and even a few English girls. I began to wonder. Presently I knew."

"Knew what?"

"That I wasn't talented enough. —I had a clue."

"What was it?"

"One day my ballet master grew furious at me over something I did—I honestly don't remember what I did to cause it, but he burst out at me in a fury, and asked whether I was or was not *sérieuse*. I had thought so, but evidently, deep down, I must have lacked something—dedication, no, even solemnity. The other apprentice dancers were so brainless and so, so, self-conscious in another way than I. I decided that was it. I was ambitious—but I suppose not serious enough beyond myself, and so I had to be ready to fail. And fail I did."

"Oh, no."

"Yes. I didn't like it. But I had to know it." Her eyes remained clear and direct, but her mouth trembled a little as she lighted another cigarette.

"What did you do?"

"I came home. Belvedere was ready for a dancing class by then, and I gave them one. —But look there, on the middle table."

She pointed to a small photograph in a slender frame resting on a miniature easel. They went to look at it. Above an illegible dash of writing it showed two women in tight, bell-shaped hats and fur neckpieces and dark coats sitting at a small round sidewalk table in Paris. Their faces were white, heavily made up. They looked famous and professional. One of them reminded the viewers of someone. They turned to look at Victoria. She laughed.

"Yes. That *is* me, with Karsavina, who was dancing in Paris that year. I asked her to be photographed with me after she visited our class one day. There it is, —I even had my stage name picked out. I was going to be Stasia Marinova, and I would have no past, only a glorious future, after I assumed the name. Now I am Mrs Jim Cochran, back where I started from, more or less."

"—But when the Judge died, couldn't you—"

"Start again? It was too late."

She saw that she was hurting them, for it menaced them to hear of defeat and failure.

"But you know?" she said in her cool, amused voice, "I have found out what success is, and I never knew it in those days."

"What is it?"

"Success consists of only one thing: hope, not fulfillment. Now I am absolutely alive with it. —No, no, not for me; but for others, like yourselves. At one time I thought I would die if I ever had to see Whitewater country again—those dry, pink gullies, and smell the dust flying through the air. But the outlandish! How long it takes us to love it—but how inevitably we do, once we confess that we have sprung from it!—Jim taught me that."

Her listeners were subdued, not by the story of an abandoned longing, for they could not imagine any such fate in their lives, but by the abrupt tenderness of the way she spoke. They felt love for her, and concealed it by silence.

Mrs Cochran looked at her watch.

"It may be time now for you to trot home, both of you. —But come again."

Phil said,

"May I look at everything, sometime, I mean bit by bit?"

"Any time. If I'm not home, Nella will let you in." She saw that he would prefer to be alone with the alien splendors of the mansion and make them his with his own imagined explanations of them.

They said goodbye. Riding home, Marilee turned to Phil and called,

"That is where you belong."

They rode for a mile or so and then he answered,

"I know it."

Saying it, he knew, and she accepted, that they were not ruled by the same hopes at that moment.

❧ ❧ ❧

Phil—and before long, everyone—saw how wild Marilee became when she was with Billy. Without saying so, they recognized how she took on aspects of his personality. She now loved everything and everyone as he did when she was with him. She made no more sarcastic and penetrating observations upon school society. Billy watched with pleased approval as she tried to resemble him.

At times she seemed to look back in her life and wish she had always been a boy along with him: think of the years which had been wasted! Then again, she would look ahead, and be proud to be a girl because her being a girl was what kept Billy by her side. She settled for trying to be like a boy in small ways. Billy presented her with a school sweater like his, except that it did not carry the athlete's honor of the varsity capital B on the left breast. They wore the same kind of jeans. They chewed the same kind of gum, though Marilee had been schooled by the nuns at SS

Peter and Paul in gentler years to believe that every time a girl chewed gum the Blessed Mother shed a tear in heaven. Now Billy and Marilee even exchanged mouth to mouth the same piece of chewed gum whenever they felt a pang of closeness which, because it came and went so swiftly, must be instantly given between them, no matter where they were or who saw, or it might be given never.

The Breedloves, too, saw what had overcome their youngest born. They wondered how Mrs Underwood could let it go on so rapidly, but they decided that she had little enough time to give her suddenly grown child proper supervision. But they would muse on Mrs Underwood's fierce self-respect, and Homer only hoped that Billy and Marilee, if they really meant all that was going on, would wait until—he arrested his thought for fear of releasing into enactment the very thing he foresaw. Life seemed to rush at young people so much faster now and at that idea, Homer had a flash of imaginary fury at what he would do if ever—what: if ever Billy did something dishonorable?

"Now Daddy," murmured Ellen.

"Don't *now daddy* me. I know what's right and what's wrong. Even my own flesh and blood will never come between me and that."

Ellen sighed and wondered if she ought to speak to Mrs Underwood, mother to mother, but thought that she should just take care of her own end of things, as she phrased it, not wanting to give precise definition to something which might blow over as fast as it started.

When Mrs Underwood saw what was happening, as the town saw it, she came to her own knowledge too late to have any effect on her child. With a groan, "She's gone on Billy Breedlove," she said. Already in any crowd, when Billy and Marilee arrived together, there was always some quickening, a collective nudge, which went through people, and in spite of themselves, at the sight of the two vital young creatures, observers were lifted further into a feeling of the occasion, festive or otherwise, which had brought them all together: Billy striding with long steps to make up for his lack of towering height, Marilee beside him, with a smile which had the effect of springtime air.

The boy's very name gave Mrs Underwood troubling thoughts. Nobody in town ever thought what the name Breedlove really meant if its two syllables were broken apart and looked at and put together again. Certainly the Breedlove parents in their decorum and patience aroused no popular reminders of the powers which the name abstractly contained. But their youngest! It was like a bolt of fatality when Mrs Underwood, chaperoning a Saturday night dance at the high school, sitting near the dance floor wearing a fixed smile that referred fondly to good times remembered not so long ago as all that in girlhood, happened to see Billy Breedlove cut in on one of the older girls, and hear him say, as they danced away together, "Belly up to me, baby."

Mrs Underwood's heart began to go fast at that. She thought of her child, who was already *gone* on him, and she had a swift, clear vision of the appeal in Billy which had taken her. And yet she must be calm. They were only children. It was unworthy, yes, silly, to think anything else of them. Why, he was only Billy, with a little boy's nickname. Didn't that prove it? Billy Breedlove, belly up to me, baby—everything started with the letter b, like the sounds of infant speech. How could danger be there? Yet how measure the power of joy, however infantile and labial, if to be felt it had to be given from body to body? And so,

"Where is my little girl?" Mrs Underwood mourned to those who would listen. The most merciful answer she could imagine or hear was that the children were just going through a phase.

"Oh, you don't know her," said Mrs Underwood. "She's stronger than I am."

Why did Marilee suppose her mother worked all day every week-day and half a day on Sundays, and slaved to put a little money in the bank every week so nobody would ever have to put

out any charity for *them,* and made her novenas at SS Peter and
Paul? If Marilee didn't know why, she had just better take and
learn, for it was for one thing and one thing only, which was to
do her duty by her child, and see that she grew up well, strong,
good, and a *lady.*

"Oh, mother, for heaven's sake."

"Yes, for heaven's sake—and another thing," and then would
follow bitter words about wearing boy's jeans, and a varsity
sweater, all droopy and saggy because a star athlete and a girl
were not shaped the same across the shoulders and arms and *up
in front,* and then chewing gum, how could anyone forget what
the sisters of SS Peter and Paul always said when a girl chewed
gum?

"And another thing."

"Oh, mother."

"Yes, oh mother. I know I can't give you all the things you
think to want, oh, I know, I was the same as a girl, before we lost
everything, but all that running out to Crystal Wells. *I've* never
been out to Crystal Wells. But *Crystal Wells* is all I hear for days
on end. —What's *that woman* got, to keep all the young folks
running out there day and night?"

*"Mother!* Phil goes, and I'm glad. But I hardly ever, now."

"No, I know I'm probably making more of it than need be. But
oh. It does bitterly shame me that I can't have a grand home for
my baby so she can have her friends here, and entertain them,
and has to rely on the pity of strangers to—"

"Mother, if you keep that sort of talk up, I'll walk right out of
here."

"You won't either, my fine Miss Chickabiddy! I'm your mother
and I'm talking to you and you will hear me—" but Mrs Underwood's vehemence came from deeper complaints than she knew,
and Marilee was the one who recognized that her mother was
sorrowing as much over her own loneliness for the past as over

the present and her daughter's sudden joy in life. Marilee said calmly,

"Mrs Cochran simply takes an interest in young people. She's on the school board."

"To think I voted for her!"

This made Marilee break out into laughter, and through the glimmer of her tears of self-pity Mrs Underwood caught something of her own absurdity from her child's radiant face, and unwillingly gave a short, lip-blown laugh herself, and for a moment the two were close; but the mother recovered her needful distress enough to say, that if anything came along that made a lovely young girl who knew what was right turn into someone who didn't seem to care any longer what was right, then—then: Mrs Underwood did not dare carry her worry further.

"Mother, I *know* what is right. You have no cause to be jealous of Vicky—"

"Vicky! Who is Vicky!"

"Mrs Cochran. We call her that. She said to."

"There. An old woman, a widow, with all that money and so grand, and high school children call her first names. Well. I don't like it. And I am not jealous."

"Vicky Cochran really cares about what young people want to accomplish."

"And I suppose I don't. —All I know is that wearing shorts to go to the supermarket is not right any time any place and nobody can tell me different. What are people saying about *me,* to let you run around that way!"

Marilee's heaven's-*sake* patience and exasperated love for her mother were oddly swept together at moments like these in the gust of her general happiness over Billy. She would stop listening to her mother and simply be there looking at her. The anguished energy of her mother's eyes and mouth, once so pretty, now so spiritless, the drawn marks of sorrow in her scrubbed face, her whitening hair, would be all that the daughter could think of, not what she had to hear; and she would suddenly take her mother in a passionate hug, hugging everything in life so, and tell her to be quiet, and not to worry, and "Mother," she would say huskily, "you are the absolute greatest mother, and I *love* you, you poor dear."

"My honey," her mother would say, and then, "So I am a poor dear?"

"Yes, you are my poor dear."

The daughter made a lullaby out of it, until the mother could almost forget that it was the same daughter who once said, "I like boys the way they are, and myself as I am," and was sure to go her own way. So to Mrs Underwood, a moment of endearment and rest in her child's gratitude, however happy it made her in one way, only seemed another way for Marilee to preserve the secretiveness of her passion; to guard the mystery of how much she might already know; to refute the wonderings that could be read in her mother's longing gaze which asked about *that Billy Breedlove,* with his strong, sweet breathing that a person could hear.

❧ ❧ ❧

There was no harm in it, thought Homer Breedlove, to let his son have the family car now and then, after work, in the early evenings, or at night, to take his friends for a ride; or if the Breedlove car was not available, why, then, it was perfectly all right for Billy to use Guy DeLacey's red pickup truck. The young people had to know their town. What else, in that great space of plains and sky, was there to know?

It was a familiar sight to see one or two carloads of the youth with or without their girls filling their out-of-school hours by riding around town. Up and down Central Avenue, it would seem, over and over again. They would pause for a root beer and drink it as they resumed riding. After the length of Central was observed and judged, passing the Bluebonnet Hotel, and catty-corner from it their favorite meeting place which was the Saddle and Sirloin Café, they would roll on by Tom Bob Gately's bank on the corner of Jackson and Central, to see if they knew anyone going in or coming out. The bank was made in imitation of a Greek temple, with pediment, pillars, and bronze grilles in the front windows, but instead of being constructed of marble, its front was paved with glossy white ceramic tile. Way out north-west on Central was the Gately home, always described as "lovely." It was the most notable residence in town. A little way beyond it, across Cleveland Avenue, was the corner lot of SS Peter and Paul, with its yellow brick church and matching school. A few blocks away from the high school on First Street the Breedlove house stood at the edge of town. The riders would roll along First in the other direction, to the southeast, past the public library at the corner of Polk and on by the bus station with its cement deck and canopy, its walls of yellow brick—the favorite building material of Belvedere—which stood at the corner of Jefferson and First. Two blocks away on First at the corner of Jackson was the Reverend Lew Priddle's church, where they always slowed down to read the current "Message for the Week" which Mr Priddle set out for all to see in front of his tabernacle. He had a glassed bulletin board with a white frame which held a miniature steeple on top of it. Inside the frame a black velvet background was arranged with parallel slits like lines on a page into which white capital letters could be set. The type was large enough to be legible from the street, and passers-by read what was there, often in a hurried glance of discomfort, for if Mr Priddle's messages were clever, as he worked whole hours to make them, they were also intended to be relentless in their suggestions. It was the style for the young people to jeer at them, but they were amazed, as they would never admit, at how many of the white words refused to leave their uneasy memories. On one occasion, they could read that "Flattery Is Like Perfume—Better for Smelling than Swallowing." Again, "Say No More than Half What You Think but Be Sure Your Other Half Is Right Too." Or again, "An Ounce of Prevention Is Better than a Pound of Repentance." They would laugh and jibe, but they were also unwillingly impressed, though some, like Billy, were defiant, and one other—Phil—was embarrassed not at the sentiment but the style. In his thrice-weekly column of local comment, the editor of the *Sentinel* sometimes quoted the messages, which he called "Priddle-isms," and some of the best were quoted in other papers across the state. The preacher's greatest success came when one of the young riders would read and cry "Wow!"

A favorite ride was to switch over from the bus station to Central, which at the southeast edge of town became Highway 31 leading to Orpha City fifty-two miles away. They would ride out as far as Maudie's and turn around, full of talk of what went on inside the roadhouse. Sometimes they took the road to Whitewater Lake, which passed the cemetery at the western side of town. If they didn't drive that way, they drove over eastward on Buchanan to the railroad station to see what was going on by the R. S. & P. tracks, and the warehouses along there. A few fields beyond rose the water tank. In a miniature park by the trackside station stood a monument, with a narrow flower bed carefully tended. There rested, on a granite base, an old railroad handcar set on a few feet of track. It was kept brightly painted and someone had even touched up the hubs, the wheel rims, and the handlebars, with gold paint. It was the most memorable monument to the past of Belvedere, which had been joined to civilization by the coming of the railroad a few generations before. The young people sought the familiar without seeing it, but would have noticed anything missing or new. They loved to bound the town, driving along its outermost roads, where the yellow grass of the open country joined the reaches of the streets and buildings. From that perspective they could note that the whole town was made of one-storey structures, except for the Bluebonnet Hotel (two storeys), the high school (three), and the cotton compress (four), and the steeple of SS Peter and Paul and the water tower which were not measured in storeys. On a few outlying lots they saw rows of farm machinery, all fresh in red or yellow paint, waiting to be sold, and on certain other lots, army surplus quonset huts which were in use as offices and workshops. By the railroad, if they followed the dirt road beside it, they came eventually to a corral, with cattle loading pens and chutes. Coming back into town, they sometimes used the alleys behind the houses, and saw the telephone poles, the trash cans which were emptied twice a week by the public sanitation crews with their automatic reducing trucks of which Mayor Dillingham was proud, and they could smell the smoke of burning rubbish which the trucks need not pause to collect from wire screened oil drums with holes knocked low in their sides to provide proper draft.

Back in the heart of town after a few minutes, the riders would gather at the Saddle and Sirloin, where the booths were the right width to let three boys or girls crowd into a bench made to accommodate two.

This was their social center, out of school hours, and also the place where the downtown people went for coffee during the day. Guy DeLacey was often there, and anyone who had a booth near the window could see what happened on Central Avenue without going outside. A long counter ran opposite the booths. Above the counter was a sign which established the good manners of the place, and for the most part, the young crowd took it to heart. It read, "A Noisy Guy Annoys a Guy." The warning was anonymously observed, for together they all made so much noise that no one separately could be held responsible.

Sometimes in the twilights which lasted so long because the

sky was so vast and there was so little made by man to close it away from sight, the idling car riders would pass some of the older houses of town, and there see old women, who sat and watched the day go, the frail old women, alone, rocking. Whether it was that very day which they watched, or one from the time years ago when with their sun-scabbed husbands they had toiled to make first a ranch home, and then a village, which became a town in Whitewater Draw, and then, when the refugees from Whitewater moved in, a small city in Belvedere, nobody could say, and few cared. They were just the old widows, with nothing left to give, and little enough to keep, except the thoughtless persistence of the wavering past. The energetic young people knew them, but only in the way that they knew the impersonal furniture of the streets, as they rode up and down to see what they could see.

❧ ❧ ❧

The time had come when Mrs Underwood must speak to the proper person about Marilee and Billy. This would be one of the priests—either the irritable old pastor or the generally subdued young curate—at SS Peter and Paul, where she and Marilee went to church.

Monsignor Elmansdorffer received her in his office at the corner of his yellow brick rectory. She quailed when she saw him—it was sure to be one of his bad days. Everyone knew he was in constant pain with rheumatism, but they did not always remember why this should so affect his mind and heart. He was short and twisted in his frame, with a ruddy face and thick grey hair cut short. His glare was piercing, as they knew in church, when between sentences of denunciation he would hold the silence, and the breath of his parishioners, with the scowl of his pale blue eyes. Hell became real for all who heard him promise it to them if they should persist in their ways. In the pulpit his voice was huge, echoing in the plaster vaults above him; in the rectory, or a family dining-room it was mild and purring, but the conviction within remained the same wherever he was. Children were always reluctant to enter his confessional, for the scoldings and the fears they brought away. The line was always longer at Father Judson's box, across the church. The old monsignor had been known to emerge from behind his own green curtained hatchway and on seeing a long line of young people waiting at his curate's confessional, to shout out across the resounding church ordering half of the young sinners to come over to him, who had nobody waiting. "All of you in line after that girl with the red thing on her head, come over here! Quick now!"

In the office, twisting in his chair with irritation, yet trying to give kindliness to his voice, Monsignor Elmensdorffer said, "Yes, yes, and what else?" as Mrs Underwood poured forth her worries.

"And I just simply *know* she is still my dear good, *safe,* darling little Marilee. But, Monsignor, how long can I go on, day after day, and night after night, worrying, and wondering, how she will come home to me this time, what with that fool boy, no, he isn't a fool boy, he's a grand youngster, I can see why she's so gone on him, but what's he know? What's she know? They're babies. And oh. I don't know. Sometimes I ask God why He has sent me this trial. Or why He has sent *her* this trial. Not that *she* thinks of it as such! Monsignor?"

"They are going steady?"

"Steady!" Mrs Underwood scoffed at such an understatement. They were wild over each other.

"And you let her?"

"Let her! You don't know! I talk and I talk and I preach and I preach—"

"That is my job, to preach. Yours is to make her obey."

[ 79 ]

"Oh, I've tried so—"

"Have you tried locking her up?"

"Monsignor!"

"Have you whipped her?"

"Oh, Mon*sign*or!"

"You sound shocked. Well, I will shock you. Not only your child is aimed straight to hell, but so are you!"

She put her hands to her cheeks. He was looking strange— the red of his face was now mottled with white patches. His distorted hands trembled on his desk blotter as he leaned toward her. He glared at her until she thought his eyes would pop out of his head.

"You let them be places alone, do you?"

"Yes, all the young ones have their dates and—"

"And you a married woman, a widow, a mother, don't know what happens in the foul flesh?"

"She isn't foul!"

"I say she is, and he is, and so are the rest of them, when nobody is there to keep them the way they ought to be! Those who fail in that duty are as bad—no, they're worse—than those who let themselves go!"

"Now, you know as well as I do," she said, suddenly angry, "that I have to work for our living, and I can't be with my child all day long and all night long and do that too! I came to ask for advice and all you do to me is—"

Mrs Underwood, appalled at the way she was addressing a priest, as much as by what he had made her listen to, put her face into her hands and sobbed.

He sat watching her. His miserable pains made his body shift and try against his high-backed swivel chair. His mouth and cheeks worked like someone chewing on painful jaws. He thought, This can go on forever. She will go home and think about what I have said, and she will see I am right. I will let her go now.

"Mrs Underwood, you'll have to do more about the matter than sit there and shed tears. Now you must excuse me. I have a morning's work to do. You know your duty. Do it."

She looked up and shrugged helplessly.

"Very well," said the pastor, "send her *to me. I'll* tell her what's what."

"Oh, let me try once more—"

"I will expect her here Saturday morning at ten o'clock."

He stood. She would ordinarily have asked for his blessing. But not today. She did not think he was in any condition to bless anyone.

"I will tell her, Monsignor."

"But you mean she may refuse to come?"

"I will tell her."

Mrs Underwood left the office.

Blinking away her last tears indignantly she went down the steps outside and didn't see Father Judson until he called out to her. He was in the shadow of the rectory, pulling weeds out of a small flower bed. When she answered, he looked at her keenly and asked,

"Did you run into something in there?"

He nodded toward the rectory.

"Oh, if you knew: I can't *talk* to him."

The young priest laughed.

"Neither can I. My job is to listen. —But Monsignor isn't well, you know."

"Oh, I know, and I'm sorry. But."

"Is there anything I can do?"

"It's my Marilee."

"Oh. And young Breedlove?"

Mrs Underwood looked haggard.

"Oh, you knew?"

"I'm afraid everyone in town knows."

"Yes, well, if I could take her off on a trip, or send her to an expensive school far away—. Monsignor wants to talk to her Saturday morning. I dread it, Father! He will be so hard with her! That isn't the way you get anywhere with my girl!"

Father Judson bent down to his weeding. Pulling out some roots, he did it savagely. There was no other way, in obedience, in which to answer. Over his shoulder he said,

"If I can ever help, Mrs Underwood."

She thanked him and left, hurrying back to her work.

❧ ❧ ❧

On Saturday morning Marilee lingered at the corner of Central and Fillmore, rebelliously uncertain whether she would ever go up the rectory steps and ring the bell. Her cheeks were hotly red. She knew what they would try to do to her in the church office. The more she thought of it, the more she began to take pleasure from defying them. In the end, she went smartly up the steps and rang. The old housekeeper, Sister M. Prisca, answered. Until too old to teach, she had had Marilee as a pupil. Her old skin-folded eyes were dimmed by cataracts, and as she peered to see who rang, she saw a young woman radiating every sign of beauty and love, and decided it was some newly married member of the parish come to ask about a connubial matter. But as the heavily glassed front door swung open, it reflected the sky, throwing back light, and she saw who it was.

"Why, Marilee!" cried the old nun, wiping her hands on her apron, "my darling child! How you've grown! Come in, my dear, how often I think of you, and the way you used to recite Browning's 'Guardian Angel.'" The old teacher, now displaced, had a surge of recollection which restored her days of beloved duty, and

striking an attitude, she quaveringly recited a fragment of the
poem she had taught Marilee in grade school:

*I shall feel thee guarding*
*Me, out of all the world; for me discarding*
*Yon heaven thy home, that waits and opens it doors.*

She put out her arms and embraced Marilee, and at once felt her
child to tremble.

"But is there something? You want to see Father?"

"I have to see Monsignor. He sent for me."

"Oh, Monsignor is not well. He hasn't been downstairs for two
days." She looked around in caution and her old face showed an
impish pleasure. "Oh! we've been so peaceful for two days! —
Now don't you tell on me. —How sweet you look, Marilee!"

"I'm so glad to see you, Sister. I was afraid you might be cross
with me."

"Cross!"

"For not going ahead to be a sister."

"Oh, no, you have to find complete happiness in that and not
in something else. If you don't, it is even wrong to think of being
a nun."

"Are you happy, Sister?"

"Oh, I was so happy for so many years. Now I am just con-
tented. It takes strength to be happy. I don't have so much of that
any more."

Marilee impulsively threw her arms around the small old
woman in her voluminous habit and apron. Sister Prisca blushed
and made little toothless noises of fondness; and then said,

"But Father is in the office. He is taking all of Monsignor's
appointments. I'll tell him you're here."

Before Marilee could escape, she was brought to sit opposite
Father Judson. He wore an old buttoned sweater and a shirt with

collar open, and a pair of corduroy trousers, and *huaraches* from Nuevo Laredo. He was thirty-eight years old, but the sight of Marilee made him feel older. He gave her his kindliest, most grey-eyed, tanned, and white-toothed smile. "A handsome priest," said one of his reverend professors of theology in the seminary long ago, "will have many temptations to use his good looks as part of his professional equipment. Let nobody succumb, for on top of divinely derived authority, there is perhaps no advantage more unfair to make use of in the presence of a trembling laity than celibate good looks. It is, in fact, the ultimate vulgarity. The true priest is never vulgar." Father Judson had a passing recollection of this embarrassing law as he smiled at Marilee.

He saw that she was in a mood of defiant seriousness. Sixteen years old, blossom-fresh and natural as light, she was cupped full of the kind of joy that seemed energy itself, which even her air of impassive refusal to cooperate could not conceal. She was properly dressed, something in linen, he supposed, cherry pink, with a white silk neckcloth. Her hair, streaked with gold, hung heavy and shining.

"Hello, Father Judson. My mother said Monsignor Elmensdorffer wanted to see me this morning."

"Yes, he did. But he's a bit under the weather. He asked me to see you instead." She smiled at this, referring silently to dread and relief. "Well, Marilee, do you want me to say anything first, or do you want to say something?"

"I don't want to say anything, Father, except that everybody is excited about me for no reason."

Ah, me, said Father Judson to himself. Aloud, he said,

"I don't think *everybody* is making assumptions that would distress you to hear. But everyone who loves you is concerned for the path you may be following, which may lead you where you would not go of your own free will. Our will is not free when it is subject to ways that mislead."

"My mother is always telling me to listen to reason. I know

what I am doing, and I don't see what reason has to do with it."

"Your mother is right to speak to you, but she also knows that children will not listen to reason in these conditions. They must be ruled by something else at a time like this, a time of real danger. It is always a time of danger for young people before they are old enough to handle the responsibilities which may come with love. Your mother is only trying to use the authority God gave her as a parent."

"Oh, Father, you're so sure. I wish I was so sure."

"It isn't I, Marilee. The Church knows something about human nature."

"It seems so hard."

"It is not concerned with making life easy, but with making it good. Salvation may *have* to be hard."

"Am I to understand that my will is not free now?" she asked, and her heart made a beat she could feel, for she admired Father Judson, and did not want to be rude to him, yet it was not he whom she loved, and who made the image of the world for her.

He saw the fires of rebelliousness deep in her eyes. He was moved by her determination and the fear that now troubled it, and the courage with which she defended the one against the other. He had no doubt that he was gazing at a being consumed with love. It gave him a slightly sick, sweetish feeling. He saw how she was beyond the reach of reason, for what held her had power greater than reason, as well he knew from stumbling self-accusations in the confessional; and he knew how, for the moment, there was only one other power to use in his duty.

"Yes. Your will is not free," he said, "for your feeling prevents you from making a decision in the light of reason. Your will has gone to sleep. You should pray that it awaken. I will pray that Our Lady will protect you. Will you pray to her too?"

"I do already."

"And you still—?"

[ 85 ]

"Oh, Father," said Marilee, and like her mother, put her face into her hands, and shedding angry tears for the choices before her, neither of which she wanted to dishonor, she ran away from the rectory.

The curate followed her out to the yard and with a feeling of tears in his own heart he kept her in sight until now walking rapidly she turned the corner and disappeared beyond the red brick and half-timbered three-storey Tudor mansion which Tom Bob Gately had built on becoming president of the West Central Texas State Bank. It was a hot Saturday morning. "Pitiless," murmured Father Judson, thinking he was referring to the plains sunlight. But his thought went wider, and it made him turn to go across the cement basketball court behind SS Peter and Paul's and enter the church through the sacristy door. The church was empty in the mid-morning. The light within was a hot and relentless yellow, from the strong cast of color through mottled amber panes which were spoken of by the faithful as stained-glass windows ever since their installation years before by the then Father Elmensdorffer. Anthony Judson went to the altar and knelt down and fell into prayer for Marilee who was helpless to help herself.

☙ ☙ ☙

While Marilee and Billy threw themselves into the present, limited as it might be by the dimensions of Belvedere, and which they transcended by their inner flight, Phillipson Durham pursued through the uses of the past a world he was at last allowed to recognize as his own, distant as it might be.

One day when he heard the school board would meet all afternoon in the council room of the city hall, he rode out alone to Crystal Wells wondering if Nella had been told to let him in if he should ever come when the lady was out. He stood so long on the wide porch, which shaded a row of huge plate-glass windows set in the red brick walls of the rambling house, that before he could make up his mind to ring the doorbell, the door opened, and Nella said, "Come right on in, Mrs Cochran is in town. But she said you's always welcome even if she's not in."

He thanked her, for he saw reflected in her face the fondness he had already felt in her employer. Nella was as small-boned and lean as her mistress, with a nimble energy and a shrewd good nature. Her hair was white against her black skin. She made frequent small sounds of general laughter through her shapeless lips which she kept closed even while smiling or laughing. She offered Phil a glass of milk and a sandwich, which he was glad to accept. She said to go on in the living room and see the gold pictures, and she would bring him his tray in a few minutes. As she left she switched on the lights.

By the gold pictures she meant row upon row of heavily framed paintings. The room was so large that it had space for several pools of light from separated tables. Bookcases ran half way up the high walls. They contained books of every variety in English and French. The pictures leaned slightly over the tops of the bookcases so that their heavy glass would not catch reflections from the windows and the bright arid expanse beyond.

Alone there, Phil recognized that he had never before had enough attention to spare, for he was always captured by Victoria Cochran, and to hear her talk he must watch her animated face. Heretofore he had had an impression only of profuse richness in the various rooms of the house, but now he was free to examine the contents in detail. He felt a sort of possessive exultation. He believed that in an obscure way, destiny had put these things here for him to discover—the elements of a world he seemed to have contained in a private vision all his life. Where might he have thought before of such resources as these books, these works of art, this ordered and profuse evidence of civilization itself, however limited it might be to a certain period of the lifetime of any one man—Judge Sylvester James Cochran?

Phil went to see his portrait. Each of the paintings had labels attached to its frame—a small gold plaque lettered in black. Jim Cochran's likeness was painted by Anders Zorn, in sweeping wide gestures of the brush. Judge Cochran was in his judicial robes with the hood of an honorary degree adding velvety color to the heavy throat. His face was a hearty pink, and it carried in its expression a hint of humor—"a majestic scalawag," thought Phil, in a notebook phrase. He could imagine how Victoria must have been kept amused by him, and he fancied that the Judge might have been looking at her over the shoulder of the painter even as the portrait grew. He had an odd shiver at evidences of life which never died. He felt Jim Cochran all about him. In a hollow weight of guilt he thought in the same moment of his own father, grey, wretched, palsied, a burned-out "Sport," and he was ashamed for loving Jim Cochran more, even though he had never seen him in life.

He toured the paintings, engravings, and sculpture. Among other works, he found a portrait of Robert Burns by Nasmith, and imagined he saw there something of Jim Cochran's masculine sweetness in the face. He looked deep into a darkly sparkling painting of a rill with a waterfall by Jakob van Ruisdael. He paused longest before a wide painting by Edouard Manet, showing a small fleet of black fishing boats off Boulogne, with sacking-colored sails on a rolling jade-green sea with whitecaps against a scudding grey sky. Of all the works in the room it took the observer farthest away, into its own existence. Near to it hung a painting by Tissot of an awninged deck of a steam yacht showing men and women in golden shadow, and next a set of oil sketches by Raffet, matching in size, which dramatized episodes of war between hussars in uniforms of the time of Napoleon. There were a water color of a drummer boy by Meissonier, a deep green forest with shafts of dim sunlight by Díaz de la Peña, and a feathery grove alongside a pond with a diffident maiden on the bank talking to a young boatman who wore a little red cap and stood in a skiff, by Corot.

At each side of the living room door was a marble sculpture in a deep niche painted in Pozzuoli red—one a bust of Napoleon, the other a recumbent nude mature woman of flowing beauty with a drapery thrown over her ankles who was identified as Pauline Borghese. Both works were signed Canova. Amidst the dark red walls of the room they showed white with almost white shadows.

He saw that nothing in the house had been changed to resemble what local people would consider up to date. In one corner of the library an alcove was decorated with a suspended tent in silken stripes, against which two tall Chinese vases of a green which looked blue in the shadows held giant sprays of peacock feathers. A low sofa sat against the wall. One end of it was piled with new books and thick newspapers. He went to see them, and found *The New York Times* for the Sunday before. Victoria Cochran was the only resident of Belvedere who regularly received that paper. How could he ask her—but he knew he must—to give him her copies when she was through with them?

Nella came with a tray bearing a tall tumbler of milk and a chicken sandwich.

"Where you want it?" she asked.

"Anywhere, thank you, I'm still wandering around. I'll never see it all."

She set the tray on a desk near a bookcase.

"Here's good. You can sit and eat."

He went to the wide desk where he saw a set of inkwell, paper knife, scissors, carved heraldic seal, and pen-knife, all made of chased silver and each piece set with an aquamarine. He held the seal up to the light and put it down. It caught a flash and he saw that the seal held his initials—"P.D." He marvelled.

"They belonged to the first Miz Judge," said Nella. "When I dust, I call them my pretties."

She left him to eat and drink.

The light was changing outside when he finished travelling along the bookshelves, where he saw dozens of books he wanted to read. Nella returned to take away the tray, but seeing him so taken with the books, she said, as proudly as if they were her own,

"We got lots more up in the attic. All the gold books. You want to see them too?"

She forgot the tray and led him to the stairway, and up two flights, to an attic room which, dimly lighted, ran between windows at opposite ends of the house. It contained another discovery—the Judge's collection of Napoleonic literature, on shelves which reached along all the walls. The volumes were for the most part bound in varying shades of red leather, and were richly stamped in gold. Many of them bore the crowned N and the golden bees of their subject. On a table was a huge folio volume bound in red morocco with a heavy border of golden bees tooled near the edges. It bore the title, *Sacre de Napoléon*. Phil opened it and turned every leaf, discovering the designs of Isabey for the coronation of Napoleon. He moved amidst the thronged courtiers and visitors in their plumes, diadems, furs, velvets, swords, boots, silks, mitres, copes, and croziers, and his eyes grew hot at the sight of glory and splendor, for here was proof again that these had once been achieved and made visible.

When daylight in the attic had faded into gloom, he closed the book and looked around a little wildly, to be sure he was still there, in Crystal Wells, near Belvedere, Texas. He went downstairs, wondering what had so fascinated Judge Cochran about Napoleon that he had resigned from the bench to write about him? And what had he written, if anything? There was one clue—he had evidently served in France as a young attaché, for on a small table stood a framed citation addressed to him, and the badge of a French decoration. Living in France in the 1890s, he must have been seized by the Napoleonic legend. Now it stood as part of the island of Crystal Wells, bearing witness to unproductive glories in a great farm no longer cultivated. Phil, feeling in his youth exempt from decline, and seeing only greatness as man's essential element, felt himself the natural citizen of it, and thought of no difference between past and future.

He was deep in the main hallway gazing at a large engraving when Victoria Cochran came home from her meeting.

❧ ❧ ❧

"Isn't it a wild affair?" she commented, coming to stand beside him to look at the picture. It showed a Gothic abbey with a central tower twice as tall as the building from which it rose. Its fanciful spires and apertures, laces and upward thrusts, like ligaments of stone, against a stormy sky, suggested something imagined and never realized.

"What is it?" he asked.

"Read it." She pointed to the faint engraved lines in the wide margin of the picture. Phil leaned nearer and read, "Fonthill Abbey. Residence of William Beckford."

"He actually lived in such a thing?" asked Phil. "I would love to see it."

"Unfortunately, you cannot."

"Why not? I am going to England some day."

"Of course you are. But Fonthill is gone."

"What happened to it?"

Victoria made an upward sweeping gesture as if to define dimensions of splendid folly, and then dropped her arm grandly, replying,

"It fell—three times—of its own: what: aspiration, I suppose. It was too tall for its weight. But for the owner, who designed it, it couldn't be any the less tall. And it had to fall. —You must read him. I'll let you see his book. —Will you have tea?"

"Oh, yes! Thank you!"—as though starved.

They moved back into the library and when she saw the remnants of Phil's tray she smiled, but rang for Nella.

"I'm so glad you came and that Nella let you in."

"She was lovely. She gave me something to eat."

"How good of her. I'll tell her you think she is lovely. It will enchant her. Have you had a look around?"

But she smiled again, for she saw in his brilliant black and white gaze that he was still entranced by his discoveries. She let her own vision go a trifle hazy the better to see his general effect—his long, tangled hair which framed his clear cheeks, the dark porches of his brows and under them the piercing light of his assaulting thought, the slight rise of his lower lids which gave something wild to his expression, and the swarthy oval of his face with its parted small lips which looked to her like those of a portrait, so vivid their color and animated the spirit behind them. She had not seen him before as strikingly handsome; now she thought he was; and she wondered how he would look tomorrow when his excitement was lowered or lost.

"If you ever build a tower," she said, in a fond bantering tone, "and I expect you to, in one form or another, make sure it doesn't go too high."

"How do you know when it is too high?"

"Lord knows. —No, I think I'd rather have you make it high, high. There's always a chance it might not fall."

She went to a shelf and brought him a copy of *Vathek*. "Take this home. This is the book by Beckford of Fonthill. There's nobody like him. One of his is enough, but I think you'd be interested in this one. I think you are a romantic yourself, though perhaps you won't be one if you stay around here too long."

"What is a romantic?"

"Oh: how impossible to define. —Your friend Breedlove is not a romantic. You are not very much like him. You must make your own definition. No. I *will* say something. Billy will always want and get the possible. I doubt if you would settle for anything but the impossible."

Phil leaned toward her. His eyes were flooded with the light of the future. Years must pass, and a thousand qualifying events, but this was the moment when Phillipson Durham was ordained a scholar, with William Beckford and his period as his acknowledged province. For the moment, he had enough to do to understand what Victoria was lightly and affectionately throwing about in words which certainly laid no emphasis on his troubled sense of his limitations.

"What a board meeting we had," she said lighting her cigarette. "I think they must despair of me. Everything they want in the name of progress, which means things, not people, I have to argue against. The Reverend Lew Priddle looks at me as if I were the village freethinker. I'm afraid he's right."

Phil had a sudden strike of complicity and humor.

"Do they know you take the Sunday *New York Times?*" he asked.

"They must, because of the post office. —Would you like to have my copies every week when I'm done with them?"

How did she know that he had been trying to think of how to ask for them?

"Yes. Thank you. Yes."

She laughed and said,

"Do you know that I love to read even the casts of the performances in the opera announcements? I can tell anybody here who wants to know who is singing and conducting this week. —Not that anybody ever asks." She looked beyond him. "The art shows. The new books. Any ballet performance. I keep up with them all."

"Why do you never go there?"

"I used to, with Jim. Sometimes I think I will again. But alone, and now, I suppose it might be a little painful."

"Painful! To see and hear all those—"

She put her hand to her cheek and made a little circle against her lean jaw with her middle finger. It was a gesture which told what she thought was too private for utterance. Nella came with the tea tray. Busy with cups, Victoria said,

"And if you only think about it, life is bigger than art, and we have a lot of life in our town."

"I don't believe it!" said Phil. "Art is bigger than anything!"

"I hope you always think so. —Melodrama is a kind of art, I suppose, and even a little town can provide that. And comedy."

"I don't see much comedy in Belvedere."

"My dear child, take one look at Mrs Tom Bob Gately. She's a scream, as we used to say."

He had never before heard anyone older make mocking remarks about the style and the eminent persons of Belvedere. His eyes widened. Mrs Gately was the unchallenged leader of Belvedere society.

"I don't know her. But Billy does."

"Yes, I know. She spoils him. I suppose she is a worthy creature. But so ridiculous! So anxiously refined! —I am hopeless. I always seem to be drawn to the unlucky ones, or even in some cases, the disreputable."

"Then you don't like Belvedere, either?"

"Oh, my dear, liking has nothing to do with it. In my time, I have been hungry for something far beyond the plains, and I came home still hungry."

He was silent.

"But how beautiful it can be, here, too, though you probably won't think so—how can anyone tell about it, when so much else is ugly and narrow and foolish—but the moonlight on the cottonwoods leading up to this house, and the early mornings

[ 94 ]

when the wells across the fields just begin to show in the gold light, and yes, even Whitewater Lake, *that* was beautiful, when we used to go for picnics, and want nothing, really, nothing, really want nothing else. . . ." She sighed, not unhappily. "One must always look for the beauty behind the banality. Sometimes it is there."

For a moment she was pretty beyond age. Then she abruptly asked which books interested him the most in the house.

"Yes, I think all those up in the attic—Nella showed me—the ones about Napoleon. What a lot of them!"

"Ah. My husband's hobby. He was going to write the great book about him."

"But he didn't?"

"No. —The more he read about him, the more impossible it became."

"You mean there was too much to say?"

"Oh, no, just the other way. It could all be said in one word, and when Jim found that out, he gave it up. He sent the Napoleonic collection to the attic."

"One word! What was it?"

"The word was 'cheap.' "

"The *Emperor?*"

"Yes, cheap in the sense of vulgar. An impossible cheat and pretender."

"But I always thought he must be one of the most glorious conquerors and rulers in history!"

"It's what he wanted you to think. He wanted to think so himself. But he never really managed to. He knew how hollow all his pretensions were —Didn't someone say that the first madman who thought himself to be Napoleon was Napoleon?"

"But the empire! The pictures in that great book upstairs, the coronation, and all that. And the victories! And his sad end!"

"Well, in the first place, everybody's end is sad, so you can simply take that for granted. In the second place, the victories

[ 95 ]

finally came to nothing, and in the process, destroyed as many millions for his time as Hitler and Stalin did for theirs, in proportion. And why? Because he had to prove something of no interest to anyone but himself. A wretched little swindler. —I hope I have shocked you."

"I think you have, Mrs Cochran."

"Vicky. —But the sooner you know that even heroes have flaws, the more chance you have of being educated. Do you want to be educated?"

Phil looked down and then up again. Shame mingled with desire in his lucent eyes. He was thinking of his parents, and how to escape them, whom he loved, by whose notion of the present and the future he could never be contained, yet by which he was bound.

"I do. I think I know what it has to do for me."

Victoria nodded, reading his thought and keeping it in silence between them. She was thereafter content to observe the enlargement of his response to ideas and people, during his frequent, if brief, visits to Crystal Wells. He recognized that what he found there, in the atmosphere of the cool, dusky, spread of the house, was something which no one else in Belvedere knew of, or if they should know, would be able to grasp. This gave him a feeling of privilege; and that he saw and valued what was left of her life gave Victoria Cochran a pure joy which she had never expected to know again. Her sense of exile from the hopes and places of her earlier life was lessened by his occasional presence—even by the thought of him in the life he led in common with those of his age in Belvedere. She never urged him to come more often—she understood that what was most valuable about his visits to her, and his travels among the Judge's possessions, was his own spontaneous desire for what they could reveal to him. She was convinced that he would one day be a man of consequence, if only he would learn to survive, and in fact use, the suffering she saw in his ardent nature—oh yes, she would think: suffering which his very nature would all unaware call toward himself. Those who accepted disappointment, she knew, were more content than those who could not do so, but must forever strive, if not in act, then in memory.

"The old widows, you know?" she said to him once, "who sit on the porches in Belvedere late every afternoon as long as they are able?"

He nodded.

"I know some of them—they had to move from Whitewater, and they have never liked anything, or really believed anything, ever since."

"It's just because they are old."

"Oh, no. You mustn't think like all the other young people who believe it is just age that makes the difference between what should have been and what is. I know." She laughed and made her little circling gesture of her finger upon her cheek. "Remember that I had my own Whitewater. My ambition didn't end there, but it began there; and when it ended some place else, and I admitted it, and came home, I was free, in an odd way. Within the limits of where I belonged, I was happy again. You know? After a while, not even sorry. I suppose what happened was that I was mainly sure of the truth about myself and"—she laughed like someone much younger—"the rest of the world."

But at this Phillipson Durham rose up and shook his fists at the high ceiling, beyond which arched the universe.

"No!" he cried in almost a singing voice, "no, no, never admit that they are right!"

How she loved him, though she would never say so. She loved him enough to let him strive as ridiculously as he must. She sat as coolly graceful as a ballerina in repose, revealing nothing of what she felt for him, in which ("mercifully," she said in her thought) there was no sign of desire.

He lingered in her speculations every time he left her. She was puzzled that Marilee was so much more taken up with Billy than with Phil. But then she must shrug off the thought, remembering how often she had failed to understand the mysteries of attraction between other lives, and their odd pairings of the physical and the temperamental. As for Marilee, her guess was that Marilee would have liked to claim both Billy and Phil; each had something strong in him which called to her; but if it had to come to a choice, just then, it would have to be Billy, as he was then, in his time of life.

❈ ❈ ❈

Feeling so much more at home in the world of Crystal Wells, Phil, even so, went with Billy and Marilee to the school dances. He would watch the two with pride and longing, wishing he were as free as they to find either joy or love—if these were not the same.

They danced slowly, always, no matter what the music said. Marilee's face, asleep on Billy's hot cheek, was lost in a look of happiness so great that if you caught sight of it, Phil said to himself, and then shut your eyes to keep the image for a second, what remained in your vision seemed really more like an image of suffering than of joy. But then if Phil, or anyone else, cut in, she awoke with a brilliant smile, and Billy gave her away, using one of his special expressions which other students picked up, such as, with a clap on the back of the boy who took her away from him, "All wise, right guy, just this once."

Billy was master of a number of special devices through which to possess everybody and the world. Refusing to be like anyone else, because he had the inner power not to be, he made original gestures; and as soon as they were copied, he invented new expressions of his originality. One of his cheerful, arrogant fancies was to behave as though he were officially in charge of everything. If the school authorities posted a notice on the bulletin board, he would initial it, "Approved, B.B." When he entered a crowded room he would call out reassuringly, "At ease!" Most of all he possessed others by touching them—with a caress, if a girl, or a jab, if a boy—crying out in glee, "I put my sign on you!"

Such was his power that it became an honor to feel his touch and bear his given sign. Everyone understood that Billy both declared and mocked his own authority—for their time of life permitted them to be serious at play, and they loved to play according to Billy's rules.

If a dance was to be remembered as a success, it must end in only one way. Nobody remembered how this way had first happened, but it had come about with natural ease and style.

The jazz band was made up of students under the direction of Dick Ferris, a lean, houndlike young instructor in accounting and other commercial subjects, who could play the saxophone with twisting body and lifted shoulders as he sucked the reed like a greedy baby at the teat. The effect was that of making love to himself through the music, as the couples did to each other out on the floor. When the night was far gone, the band, in a flourish of showmanship, always stood up to play the last piece of their rehearsed program. Moans and protests arose from the couples on the gymnasium floor, but all knew that the night had to end, and their feeling for each other quickened until they felt that they belonged to the best crowd of young people in the world, who would never forget a night like this, or anybody who was there.

At such a moment, Billy danced Marilee to the band platform under a basketball goal at one end of the gymnasium, and helping her up to the stage to stand beside him, he turned to the crowd. Just as the last piece was hanging on to its final chord, someone might call out, "Billy! Do us the *Hitchhiker!*" —a loving clamor which aroused a chorus of cries to add to the demand. They wanted Billy to entertain them, as he had done so many times, but they also wanted any excuse not to see the dance come to its end, and themselves forced to go home. Sometimes he shook his head, cheerfully quelling the tyranny of the crowd, but more often he consented. His consent was a small reflection of his general habit of life.

Turning to the student who played the electric guitar in the band, Billy gave, with rhythmic contortions of his body, and with offbeat snapping of his fingers, a suggestion of a tempo; and the player, dividing an octave at the fifth, set an introduction in 2/4 time, thumb-and-finger, thumb-and-finger, whose very monotony helped to cast a spell, while Billy, pulling his own coat collar up around his ears, and yanking his belt down about his hips, so that he looked in disarray, with his right hand wearily held up to support his tired thumb, poking it in the air along an imaginary road, into a vivid distance in the minds of all who watched, created the atmosphere for his stunt. With practiced skill, he nodded to friends at random below him in the crowd, making silent references to the hardness of life, the exhaustion of the boy who stood half a day by the highway trying with his right thumb to hitch a ride, and managing to suggest that he was both a hopeless vagrant and a fellow like anyone else whom they knew and lived with. He glanced up at the imaginary sky with its beating sun, and he shaded his eyes looking far down the heat-hazed highway for the magic car or truck which would rescue him, pick him up from where he was at, and take him ahead on another stage of his journey, wherever it was leading him for whatever reason, but simply *away,* as most of his listeners longed to be *away.* He made a character for them all. During the plucked introduction, he said, lifting his right hand as if displaying a wound,

"Look at that, ol' thumb is plumb out of joint," and he stared at his thumb comically, as if it were a foreign member.

Finally, holding their established fascination and belief, which he had created by becoming someone else, he began, with an almost imperceptible nod to the guitarist, to talk, not sing, the words, with a smartness of inflection and timing which seemed careless but was instinctively precise. Enacting the characters, and gesturing into life the scenes of the song, he talked:

> *Jerked my thumb at a Model T,*
> *Ol' sombitch wouldn't stop for me.*
>
> *Told him what to go and go.*
> *Here come a pretty gal, woo, woo, woo.*
>
> *Fixed my tie and hiked my pants:*
> *Baby, here's your new romance.*
>
> *But sh' didn slow down and sh' didn stop.*
> *Baby, you can take a hop!*

He mopped his brow:

> *Sun come up like a fryin pan—*
> *Sure is tough for a travelin man.*

He saw something else coming out of the distance and smartened up hopefully:

> *Jerked my thumb at a Coke-Cola truck.*
> *Says "No Riders," you're outta luck.*
>
> *Stand by road inna long hot sun.*
> *Lizard inna ditch, run-run-run.*
>
> *Taperin road inna faraway—*
> *Think I wanna stand right here all day?*
>
> *I'm dead onna plains with bleachin bones*
> *When hot tar shines through the highway stones.*

High, smiling, brief hope:

> *Here come a Cadillac—there it went:*
> *Wouldn't stop for the Pres-eye-dent!*
>
> *Here come a hoopie with a bed-spring tied,*
> *And dogs and chickens all cooped inside,*
>
> *And a Paw and a Maw and a passle of kids,*
> *All of em cryin over don'ts and dids,*
>
> *And a kerosene lamp hung by the tank,*
> *And a sewing machine hid from the bank,*
>
> *And she was a-boilin and a-makin steam,*
> *But her ol' brakes began to scream,*
>
> *Says, Get right in, you're a college boy,*
> *Daughter, meet yer future joy!*
>
> *Sure felt good to ride and sprawl,*
> *And incidentally, that ain't all—*
>
> *Little ol' gal was full of tricks,*
> *Woo, woo, woo! Let daddy fix!*
>
> *Tire blew out, said Lend a hand.*
> *Nuts to that, I'm busy man!*
>
> *Got another ride on a diesel freight,*
> *Says gon to a funeral, gonna be late.*
>
> *Says Can't help that, but here's some likker.*
> *Drink, drink, drink; sick, sick, sicker.*
>
> *Driver says, Get outta my cab.*
> *O.K., tough guy, blab, blab, blab.*

Billy nodded his body in time with the guitar, and with a clown's over-life-sized acceptance of the joke of life, and of death, for both seemed equally comic to all who were there, he finished:

*Walked on home by the bob-war fence,*
*When does the funeral feast commence?*

Whistles and yells broke over his last words, for they all knew them; and Billy returned to himself.

They were ready for what came next—the usual way in which the dances ended that year. With a comic bow to Dick Ferris, Billy began to direct the band and lead the crowd, singing the words, in "Auld Lang Syne." Nobody else could have come up out of the crowd to show them all how they felt about their life on the plains, or their joy and resignation about the end of one of their dances, by feeling it visibly for them. His singing voice was strong, grainy, and unmusical, and with it he lifted theirs, though with an effect of unplanned magnificence they lagged a trifle behind him in the time of the song. The orchestra fell in with him, and something special came out every time. The saxophones were like the voices of newly adolescent boys, dwelling with a mealy flutter and a ducklike reediness on the long notes that made everybody feel noble and serious, and at the same time, ready to laugh or cry, but for what, they would not know until they had children of their own. Closing around the platform, the dancers looked up at Billy and sang with all their hearts. Boys hugged their girls close beside them, and girls fitted themselves into the stances of their boys in acts of immemorial possession.

Billy gave a signal over his shoulder and in response the trumpets put gold derby hats over their golden mouths and played the melody with a faraway pure sadness.

"Should auld acquaintance be forgot, and never brought to mind?" asked the trumpets, wah-wah, and in their hearts the listeners replied, "Never!"

Everyone all through the crowd locked arms until they were one, and because Billy was up there, leading them, knowing just how an orchestra leader acted, and doing it, seriously but with an under-edge of burlesque, and his pale hair shining under the colored lights that went slowly across them all from the rotating gelatins of the projector in the steel girders high under the gymnasium roof, they would always remember the song and Billy together whenever they heard it again anywhere. He held them on the last note and then slowly let his arms down and bowed to them like a great conductor, to make them all laugh again. How blessed, thought Phil coldly, were those who believed the ways of their homeland to be beautiful and sufficient.

On the way home (by the longest possible way) Marilee, Billy, and Phil usually went to have a glass of milk and a hamburger at the Saddle and Sirloin, which stayed open all night, as they could see from blocks away, looking at the yellow neon lariat which played endlessly around the outlines of a red neon steak on the front of the café.

Before they separated going home one night, they saw Marshal Honeycutt testing the locks on the front door of Miss Mallory's public library. Billy said,

"Did you hear the latest?"

"No: what":

"The latest is that Marshal Honeycutt would like to court Miss Mallory."

"You don't think she's in there at *this* time of night!" exclaimed Marilee, "all in the dark, waiting for him?"

"Oh, no, not at all," replied Billy. "But don't you see? One way he can show he loves her is to take extra care of her public library after midnight, isn't it?"

"Well, how would she know?" asked Marilee.

"You'd be surprised how things get around in this town."

"But I know that," said Marilee flatly.

"The old Marshal, himself, you know?" said Billy. "Years ago there was something about him. Nobody will talk about it. But when you mention him, they all look."

"I never heard anything about him," said Phil.

"You haven't been here long enough. There are lots of theories."

"Well," said Phil with a worldly sigh, "we all know the answer about him and Miss Mallory, anyway."

"And what is that?"

"He's too old, and she's all set to die a virgin."

"How old is she?"

"I guess about sixty."

"It must be just a rumor about them," said Phil.

"What if *everything in the world were just a rumor!*" exclaimed Billy with animation.

"Anyway," said Phil, "do you know what virgins really work at?"

"Must we keep using that word?" asked Marilee.

"I'm sorry. —But they always work at keeping everybody else a virgin, too."

"Here's where we say goodnight, Phil," said Marilee, kissing him lightly on the cheek. How easy it would be to love him, she thought, if she weren't helpless over Billy. She had heard that each man wants all women. Was the same, in reverse, true of every woman? She laughed at herself.

"What's so funny?" asked Billy.

"You'll never know," she said. "Goodnight, you sweet solemn Durham."

Phil left them. Hearing their steps recede, he heard also their laughter. The air was chill. He walked faster to keep warm—perhaps to escape the laughter in the growing distance.

# III. Common and Uncommon Knowledge

One afternoon in the public library which Ben Grossman namelessly had left to the city of Belvedere, Monica Mallory sat for a long time on the high swivel chair behind the circulation desk facing the front door.

It was a typical winter afternoon in the Belvedere Public Library. The heat was on in the radiators, which were always too hot or too cold. When warm with steam heat, the particular climate of the library gave drowsy far-away feelings to anyone there. You noticed it when you first came in, and then it took you, and then you yourself helped to create it, that heavy essence in the library air. It was the sum of many elements—the smell of the tarnished gold paint on the hot steam radiators; the weight of much-breathed air, into which people of all ages exhaled the passions which had brought them there along the years, to know their kind and all its selves through communion of the printed page. What lingered in the air was love of learning for its own sake; the odor of longing, of consolation, of sanctity; the transpiration of bodies; the smell of janitor's wax; and the sweetness of dust resting for years on books undisturbed.

Late that afternoon Phil came into the library, hoping that Miss Mallory was too busy to talk to him, for sometimes, when she got started, she would not let him go. Today, especially, he knew the book he wanted, and he did not want to discuss it with her. It was the *Droll Tales* of Balzac, of which he had heard promising reports. It was supposed to have pictures as exciting as its text. He knew where the set of Balzac was kept.

In the shallow, glassed lobby he paused to look at the bulletin board, and to discover with a side glance whether the librarian was at her desk. On the bulletin board was a child's drawing of a landscape with huge flowers springing up in coarse lines on a green crayola hillside. In the sky was lettered "Poems, Second Grade." Below the poster several sheets of handwritten poems were thumbtacked to the cork background. He read the first one as if deeply interested:

> *Spring is a thing*
> *That will bring*
> *A bird to sing.*

He glanced aside. Miss Mallory was not at her desk, though he thought he had seen her from the street. He went quickly into the stack room and found his book. He pulled it a trifle forward on the shelf so he would be able to take it up quickly when he was ready to leave the building. It would be better to wait a little while until more people came in who would occupy Miss Mallory at the desk, so that he could simply sign his card and get his book stamped with its return date and go out the door with his prize under his arm before she could hold him with talk. Meanwhile, he would go to the open reading room space at the front of the building where the new periodicals were kept.

Turning the pages of *The Illustrated London News,* he heard Miss Mallory return to her desk, and he did not look up in greeting. But he felt Miss Mallory's eyes and thoughts upon him.

Her pale eyes had a dreamy look, and the edge of a smile showed past the fingers she held crumpled against her naturally red lips. It was always remarked that her hair had never gone gray, which gave her occasional opportunity to be flustered and modest when people said she was still so young-looking, almost a girl? with her high coloring, her glad nature, and that slim figure? But next time they saw her, Monica might look like an old woman, thin and haggard, with grey skin and a clouded wonderment in her eyes. They never could know what to expect of her. They generally recognized that her mind was as incessantly busy as her fingers, at her various occupations.

All her plans—for she lived dream lives for everyone she knew—all her plans for Phillipson Durham had gone wrong. For a year or so, back there, she had been certain that he and Marilee Underwood would some day have a real romance, solemnized by a wedding at which she would sing. But before she could hardly turn around in her thought, Marilee was seen everywhere with Billy Breedlove. Miss Mallory was uneasy with Billy who always looked at her with a disturbing grin, as though he knew all the strange thoughts she sometimes had, even about him. Her eyes would sting easily at difficult moments, and every time they did so under Billy's smile, she swore she would never look at him again. But how could she help it, if he came to the desk to take out an armload of books about one of his passing obsessions, which ranged from taxidermy to the history of the Olympic Games, to the novels of John Buchan? Billy was not a student, like Phillipson. Miss Mallory said to herself, that Marilee should have gone on to become a nun, instead of the way things were working out, but if she couldn't, then for a lifetime, she would do better with Phillipson Durham than with William Breedlove.

❧ ❧ ❧

As she had no one to live with, Miss Mallory held dialogues with herself, half-aloud, speaking first for one, then the other, of the two persons within her being, both of whom were herself, and yet each of whom, it seemed, thought and gave ideas as if quite independently. She was sometimes fascinated by what one or the other of her persons had to say. Where did ideas come from! she would marvel. As she spoke for each, she would inflect their sentiments, her curled fingers against her lips, her eyes as lively as her mind, in the constant colloquy as "I" and "she" spoke within her lonely life.

"And what, Miss Monica Mallory, do you think you know about the state of holy matrimony, in your single blessedness?" I asked her, and she replied,

"Well, Miss Monica Mallory, if you want to know, I've had my chances . . ."

"Chances," I said, and I said, "you don't count that old fool Honeycutt, I hope. I should hope you'd have better sense than that," I said. So she said,

"Well, you never know. They say a man's never so old but what he—"

"St! Hush that! The idea," I said. "Besides," I said, "you know what they say about Mister Marshal Honeycutt."

"There's never been any proof," she said, just to make me mad, and I said,

"Smoke's fire," and she had to admit that he had a dangerous look about him.

"Dangerous!" I said with my little laugh that I give, but of course all men are dangerous, and oh: here is that feeling again, all warm and squeezed, and I know just how I would look, with my wreath of orange blossoms, and then that long veil, I would have a train from here to there, and one of those ivory white prayerbooks and a set of pearl rosary beads, everybody would wipe their eyes when I went up the aisle. Then she broke in, saying,

"Well, he's twenty years older than you if he's a day."

"Well, all that story about him happened when he was just a young cowboy. Who really knows?"

"Yes, I suppose so, he would be in jail, or hanged, if it were all true, wouldn't he," she said sensibly, for she is nothing if not sensible, and of course so am I. But it really was dreadful, if true.

Honeycutt had a brother, older, and they always said he was the handsome one, when they told about it. Honeycutt was engaged to be married but his brother wanted her, too, and they say he got her, oh, not in marriage, but without it. But Honeycutt didn't let on a thing—at least this is how it was always said when people talked about it, which they didn't do much any more—there were so few left, only some old women who had to leave Whitewater long ago. But the Gately ranch out beyond Whitewater took in a lot of the part that is now under the lake; and old man Gately—Tom Bob's father—always hired extra hands for his roundup every spring after the calves were grown enough. This was long before Tom Bob Gately was born.

"My! the dust!" I said, and she answered,

"The smell was worse, that time we went to that roundup out past Orpha City."

"Yes, and the sweat, you know?" I said and I could hardly

keep from laughing, I love some of my funny ideas, I said, "The men got to look like the cows themselves! They got dust in their eyelashes, and I don't know, they hollered and humped on their horses, and the cows did the same! Remember?"

"Oh, yes. Oh, the things you think of."

"Thank you. —But that time, way back long ago, on the Gately ranch—you know, of course."

"Yes," she said, "I shudder to think."

"If it's true."

"Yes, it may not be."

"No proof."

"But the fact is still there, that much you have to admit."

"Yes. Honeycutt did shoot his brother," she said, "and they say it was because he found out about him and the girl—she was the daughter of the telegraph operator in the Whitewater station, before the water came up the Draw."

I thought she was too positive, and I said to her, I said,

"But just as many people said it was an accident as said the other way."

"Pistols just don't go off."

"They said this one did."

I had to smile, because I said (my Irish wit!), I said,

"The girl went off, too, to New Orleans, some said, and was never seen again."

"Well, so did the Marshal. To LaVaca country, they said he became a deputy sheriff. When he came home years later, the town was gone, the Draw was full, and he settled here. Nobody really remembered much about the old story, except just what some people said did happen."

Monica's two voices fell silent. There was so much to turn over in thought about everybody's separate life. Nobody, for instance, could imagine the life she lived inside. She thought now that there was something infuriating about the contest between animals who would escape if they could, and men who rounded

[ 114 ]

them up to brand, to feed, and to sell. Something even foolish. Men might become just as irrational in various ways as the animals they harried into packs and eddies of bellowing senseless power and subjection.

As for Marshal Honeycutt, of course it was all only gossip, but it was strange how everybody who said as much really believed all of it, even after he became a local peace officer.

"Why else, will you tell me?" said one of the selves, "is the cranky old marshal such a solitary? Far's anyone knows, he hasn't ever taken up with a single soul, man or woman?"

Miss Mallory bridled on her high stool. Regardless, there was something almost like her being a public figure, talked about that way, even if the talk connected her with nobody more likely than Marshal Honeycutt.

"Why do you even let yourself think of it?" asked the relentless other self. "Remember this when you go to Confession!"

❧ ❧ ❧

Phil was becoming drugged in the atmosphere of the library. He had forgotten the staring presence of Miss Mallory across the room when suddenly she called out,

"Phillipson Durham, will you ever be old and peculiar?"

Startled, he turned to look at her. She had her witch's chin in her hand, leaning her elbow on the desk. Her filmy eyes had a dreamy look and the edge of an empty smile showed past the fingers against her almost purple red lips. Today in the library was one of her young days.

"Don't be so startled," she added, standing as if coming up out of a trance. Her best-known public aspect was a comic self with which she, in her Irish character, was most at ease, for she hurried to make the joke about herself before anyone else could do so by any glance or nudge. It was this which won her the general love of the town, in spite of her other times of being flighty and off the track, as a city councilman once said. Shrewd and knowledgeable she was too, and they all admitted it; and before the opposing faces of her nature, her friends on the City Council, to whom she was responsible as a municipal employee at a low salary, said with considered goodwill, "Well, that's Monica."

To his distaste, she walked over to see what Phil was reading.

"Or perhaps you're *young* and peculiar," she remarked. "Anybody who loves to read as much as you do. And then all that writing they say you do. I saw you come in. Did you see me?"

"No."

"Well, I was back in the bookstacks." She looked at him sidewise, and he wondered if she had seen him searching for illicit joys in Balzac. "Oh, yes, I was back in the stacks, and you'll never know what took me there." She laughed against her own absurdity, from which fear could be removed only by sharing it as a joke with someone else, even a youth who gazed warily at her. "I kept wondering if anybody was there. The more I wondered the more I was sure, until I had to go see. Sometimes there seems to be somebody—it's always a man—out of the corner of my eye, but if I make a move, or turn to look, he's always gone. Not an *unpleasant* man, I'm *never* frightened, you know, but somebody *unexpected*. I think the worst of growing old is that so many things are *unexpected*. Don't you?"

"I don't know, Miss Monica." The very essence of his youth in a small plains town was a longing for the unexpected.

"No, how could you," said Miss Mallory, with an indrawn breath. "Well, do you want to know something, Phillipson Durham? I pray for you, but only occasionally. I really think that's all you need, just yet, at any rate."

Saying this, she laughed on a high rippling shriek. He was a little offended, and somewhat frightened. He closed his magazine and stood up.

"I think I have to go now," he said.

"But you haven't gone for any books!"

"No. I'll get one before I go."

"Do you want to be a young gentleman and do something for me?"

"I guess so, Miss Monica."

"Oh, splendid. My handsome young cavalier. That stack of periodicals over there on the floor. Would you take it to the basement for me? They're ready for the bindery and I tied them all tightly with stout twine, but they're so heavy, and my sacroiliac. Just put them in the corner downstairs by the furnace. Fine. My. Oh, thank you, you *are* a beautiful thing, so serious!"

Flushed with embarrassment, for he avoided mirrors believing himself to be far from handsome, he took up two heavy bundles which she showed him and went down to the basement. When he reached the furnace room, he heard Miss Mallory's light rapid steps on the floor above, like the hops of a bird. She was taking her way to the bookstacks, as he knew by the direction of her steps. He set the bundled magazines neatly against the rough cement wall behind the furnace and went upstairs.

Miss Mallory was seated again at the loan desk, now talking to two women who were selling chances on an electric washing machine for a church benefit. She made them laugh at her questions—why should she, an old maid, need a thing like that which was designed for a huge family wash? Both of them were mothers many times over; had reached for and submitted to their place in the natural order of life. Miss Mallory's place outside it gave them memories and thoughts which sent them into near hysterics of suppressed laughter until they hardly dared speak for fear of losing control.

"Only fifty cents a *chance*," said one of the callers, and her last word ended on a blurt of breath which came from her huge bosom involuntarily while tears of guilty amusement at her bawdy thoughts ran down her powdered face. The other felt the contagion of this and, not to be outdone, added,

"A girl should take every chance she can get!" and in her turn exploded in a wheeze of obscene gaiety.

Phil hurried to the stacks to take his book and make his escape with it while the women were preoccupying Miss Mallory so that she would be able to do no more than stamp the return date for him and let him go without her usual insistence on talking about his reading with him. The book was gone. He went around the stack to see if perhaps he was mistaken in the location. But the first place was the correct one, for there stood all of the works of Balzac, dusty and undisturbed, except for a black slit of space where the *Droll Tales* should have been.

It was plain, then, that the librarian had seen him earlier as he lusted after that particular book with its comedies of profane love, from which he had hoped to glean forgetful hours in the only carnal adventures he could know. It was now also plain that Miss Mallory believed it her duty to keep such pleasure from him.

He turned from the stacks and walked behind the loan desk and saw the *Droll Tales* behind the librarian's back through the slats of her high swivel chair. Without a word he walked past the desk to the front door. She called after him, almost using her well-known singing voice,

"No book today, Phil Durham?"

He shook his head and ran down the steps to the street. If life forced chastity upon her, she did her best to force it upon others, he thought bitterly, even to robbing him of reading about love. After walking a few blocks in anger he blew out his breath and shook his head at the general foolishness which seemed to govern his life.

※ ※ ※

Homer Breedlove let him stand for a long moment while considering the matter brought before him, and then said to Billy,

"Yes. You may take it. But mind you be home by ten-thirty, ten-forty-five."

Billy drove the car cautiously out of the family driveway and down as far as the corner. Turning there, he laid on speed and went spurning gravel in a roar along the unpaved road leading to Phil's house, where he pulled up as if riding a bronc'. There was a light in Phil's window on the first floor of the grey, unpainted house whose upstairs rooms contained Mrs Durham, whom nobody ever saw, and her husband, when he was at home. The doctor said climbing the stairs was good for his exercises in coordination. No light showed above. Billy ran to the lighted window which was somewhat screened by bare lilac bushes.

"I've got the car!" he cried softly. "Let's go!"

Phil in silence put his book away, turned off the light and climbed out the window. In a moment they were ripping along the dusty street toward town.

"What'll we do?"

"First, let's ride up and down."

They inspected Central Avenue, and the bus station, and then, without consulting Phil, Billy turned out on Highway 31. When they were past the town limits, he struck Phil's thigh a solid blow with his fist and said,

"We're going to Maudie's again."

"I've never."

"This time I'm going *in*," said Billy.

They rode without speaking for a couple of miles, and then Phil asked,

"Where's Marilee?"

"This is the night she helps her mother with the accounts. —Anyway, Marilee wouldn't care."

"I didn't mean—"

"Well, you know, how you get to feeling."

Phil nodded; he felt an odd reluctance mixed with excitement.

Far down the road they could see the electric sign out in front of the Silver Grille and Lounge. A tall metal stalk made to resemble a yucca plant was outlined in blue neon. The central shaft rose thick and high from the bayonet spikes near the ground. At the top of the shaft the yucca head of blossoms was painted on a flat metal surface and the blue neon outlined its swelling dome. At the top of the dome was a single powerful lamp which went off like a bomb every thirty seconds in a spurt of blinding white light. You could see it from far away before you knew what it was. At night, there was nothing else to see for miles. The sign was widely admired. Few if any customers ever saw in it the tower of desire at whose mindless urging they came there. In the wide far rim of night it simply meant conviviality and entertainment. Against the front of the roadhouse, which was a one-storey building arranged out of two quonset huts joined end to end, with an extension at right angles to the rear built of unpainted stucco, another sign, immobile, read in pink neon, "Maudie's Silver Grille and Lounge." As they drew up to park, Billy and Phil saw half a dozen cars already there and heard the deeply tinned throbbing of the jukebox within.

"Just follow me," said Billy. They were both under age but that was an essential part of the event; and entering as if he were expected, Billy moved his arm generally and nodded Phil to come with him to the bar.

It was a scene which for Phillipson Durham became a standard of the innocently ugly: it could define any sad local hell devoted to the surcease of dreary days. It long later came to him in his habit of fixed irony that those who sought delight in such a place never even thought consciously of their days as dreary, or of their tin shack palaces of pleasure as ugly. All they needed—all perhaps anyone, anywhere, ever needed—was a place, in whatever degree of richness or squalor, a place where appetite could run free without censure.

The amplified recorded music noise was deafening. A few couples were dancing to it in the far quonset hut, where festoons of metallic silver fringe sagged from corner to corner over their heads. Blue and red lights alternately shafted over the dancers. The dance floor was surrounded by linoleum-topped tables. Most of them had beer bottles on them, but one or two had pint bottles of bourbon whiskey which, under the law, had to be brought by the customer and not sold by the house.

Behind the bar was a small, thin, wavy-haired man with the body of an adolescent and the face of a veteran of vice. His expression was one of aggressive innocence. He greeted the high school boys and said,

"Cokes?"

Billy said,

"Two set-ups," and pulled a pint bottle of whiskey from under his jacket.

"Now just look at that," said the bartender, whose name was Happy.

"No, I sure mean it," said Billy, exaggerating the local idiom.

"Where'd you get it?" asked Happy.

"Ain't none of your cordial business, Mister Happy. Just give me and my pardner here a couple of set-ups and tell my friend Maudie we're here."

"You know Maudie?"

"She knows who I am."

Happy laughed.

"You're a sight," he said admiringly. "Just a minute." He disappeared between thick, green curtains at the end of the bar. They could hear his high boot heels tokking sassily along the long corridor that led between the small bedrooms in the cement wing out back.

"Who gave you the liquor?" asked Phil.

"Guy. I get it from Guy any time I want it. —Don't worry. We're not going to get into any trouble. Just a lot of mighty nice feelings."

He hungrily ran his tanned hands along his tightly breeched thighs. Maudie was a time coming, and Billy tapped his fingers on the bar in time to the blighting sound of the jukebox, even as he watched and listened to the television set, a recently installed novelty, which stood above a corner of the bar.

Phil gazed about in a frown, observing every detail of the establishment. His belly contracted with something like sickness as he watched the dancing figures which seemed to swim in and out of blue and red undersea currents. Their faces held every look of contentment. What made him feel sick was that in a place so hideous they should find joy.

The curtain parted and Maudie came forward followed by Happy.

"What's this?" she asked in a sort of manly authority. She was a neat, small woman with close-cropped hair. She looked like a girl enacting her idea of what a prizefighter was like. It was a successful impersonation. When the men of Belvedere spoke of her as a "good scout," their admiration was couched in puzzled wariness. If they understood her nature, which few did, they did not really believe what they knew. They conceded she was shrewd.

"I'm Billy Breedlove, and you know a friend of mine named Guy DeLacey. Me and this other friend here just want a little drink of Guy's liquor, and then we have a mind to see some of your young ladies on a matter of business and pleasure."

Though he sounded like a veteran of places like hers, Maudie hesitated with a cold and empty face, looking first at Phil, then at Billy. In the end, she kept her eyes on Billy's and then with a theatrical effect, she let one corner of her mouth ease into a crooked smile and there was an air of general easement as a result. Happy reached for glasses and soda water, and Maudie said,

"You're quite a little gentleman, aren't you. What're you so mean to Guy for?"

"Mean? To Guy? I'm not mean to Guy."

"Well, if you don't know it, you don't know it."

"He comes out here all the time," declared Billy.

"Yes," said Maudie, "we all know him." She made a sidewise grin and added, "He's never been able to make out here, if you know what I mean. —All right, Happy." She authorized the bartender to serve the two under-age customers, and then turned back to them, speaking and nodding severely. "Now Highway Patrolman Hardic Jo Stiles comes by here about nine-thirty every night and I hear him coming because he always gives a little turn on his siren before he parks. Now I want you two out of here before that. You hear?"

"Of course," said Billy, as though he had understood the arrangement for years.

"All right, show me your money," said Maudie. Billy took out his wallet and opened it.

"That'll do. Bring your drinks back with you."

She waited for them and then led them through the curtains down the corridor to a bleak, square, cement sitting room, with a single floor lamp, whose shade was made to resemble a Mexican *sombrero,* which stood between two worn wicker settees.

There they found two women in their early thirties. Both were highly made up. One had a tiny flat face and wavy blond hair; the other had wavy red hair and a great curved nose, like the bill of a tropical bird. They were both clothed in electric blue satin dresses and pink high-heeled shoes with no stockings. They wore nothing under their dresses. Maudie introduced them—"Myrtle, and Jackie Lou"—and said,

[ 123 ]

"These two cowboys are friends of Guy's. They want to have a drink with you *and.*"

The girls exchanged a look and a laugh at Maudie's style, and then recovered their manners. Maudie ordered, "The back door, afterward, though." They nodded. She left them.

"I like a nice redhead," said Billy.

Jackie Lou smiled, which made her resemble a mackaw. The blonde looked at Phil who said nothing, but gazed, fascinated, with his half-mooned eyes, until his concentration on Myrtle became impolite. The silence grew attenuated, and Billy said,

"Let's all have a drink."

They shared their drinks, and then settled, as couples, into the two settees, with the Mexican *sombrero* between them.

Phil saw Jackie Lou put her arms around Billy, and then he felt Myrtle's hand upon him. Holding his drink in one hand, he put the other hand on the back of her neck, at the cords beneath the skin, which seemed as pitiably exposed as a child's. Under his touch they shifted and strove in echo of the professional charm she worked to summon for him.

His heart fell and his half-risen desire left him. Feeling her life, he saw her working in its practised terms, and a passionless sympathy went through him. Myrtle felt his emotion, and mistook it for the one she worked to arouse. He bent down to her cheek, as if to say goodnight against bad dreams, while his thought said how great was the pity he knew for herself and him, connected as they were by the most ancient of purposes, now meaningless. She looked at him with puzzled eyes, and their unaccustomed expression made them seem mysterious as he looked into them. He set his glass on the floor and took her miniature face in both his hands, and felt all over her cheeks, her flat brow, her baby mouth. She tried to speak—"Say, wat's going—" but he hushed her with his fingertips and then took her hands and held them, simply looking at her.

He felt oddly responsible for her. She was a human being and her claim upon him was that of all human beings who seemed to ask silently for release from their various traps in life. He had never felt farther from desire, or closer to fellow feeling. He saw the scabs of caked powder under her ears, and the difference in color between her creamed face and her unwashed neck. The protrusions of her collarbones seemed to him so vulnerable and childish that he traced them with a finger, as though they were fragile relics rescued from antiquity. He gripped her shoulders, and she said, "That's more like it," but all he sought to know was her substance of flesh simply for the marvel of all flesh. Beyond, he heard Billy laugh like an excited boy with a secret, and he said to himself, "Poor Myrtle, poor Billy, poor Jackie Lou." He put his hand on Myrtle's head, and she said, "Look out, my hair, I just done it," and he said, "Myrtle?" and he pressed her head to his shoulder, and stroked her arm, and said, "Hush, just hush," as if they were to sleep like guiltless children. But she felt his self-protection in this.

She indignantly pushed him away and stood up, and just then they all heard a whirring rise of a police-car siren out front. Jackie Lou broke apart from Billy, and, as the more businesslike of the two inmates, she cawed sharply,

"Out you go, both of you, out the back door, come on. You heard Maudie. That's Hardie Jo out front. He's early tonight. Now come *on*."

In a moment, Billy and Phil were outside in the dark fan of shadow at the rear of the Silver Grille and Lounge. Billy was laughing so hard, but in silence, that he held on to Phil to stand upright. At the same moment, State Trooper Hardie Jo Stiles entered Maudie's by the front door.

With a casual professional air, he looked around, and then asked Happy,

"Is Maudie here?"

In one gesture full of necessary fear and respect for the law, Happy wiped his hands on his apron, twitched his head toward the rear of the Silver Grille to indicate where Maudie was, then hurried to tell her who came. In a moment,

"She'll be right here," said Happy, returning from the long hallway behind the green curtains. Trooper Stiles, standing erect at the bar in such a way as to keep his uniform from wrinkling, and to let his torso show to its best advantage, nodded. In a moment he heard the sound of a car starting out front of the Silver Grille, and then caught an impression of headlights backing, turning, and raying away down the road toward town. He made a habit of knowing most of the cars belonging to leading citizens. From sight and sound he knew which one had just departed, from which parking place. He had habitually noted the license.

Maudie appeared through the curtains and greeted him with her one-sided smile and silently prepared the shot of bourbon which he enjoyed as her guest every evening—no money changed hands. She set the glass in front of him and he left it there, while she leaned on the bar to face him with her hands spread widely along the moist wood. Without feeling anything for him, she admired his looks and his style. Even when washed over by the red and blue changing lights of the dance floor, and the pallid flicker of the television set above the bar, the smooth, healthy, outdoor color of his cleanly modelled face took on none of the sickly look which overcame most of Maudie's customers in her tin rooms.

" 'thing all right?" he asked finally, in a gentle drawl.

"Oh, I suppose so," she replied. "But my sinuses are killing me. I'm going down to Corpus for a while to get over it. This winter dust."

"Unh-hnnh," he said sympathetically. "Alone?"

"No, I'm taking one of the girls."

"Which one?"

"Don't you worry. Not Jackie Lou. I wouldn't do that to you."

"Or to her," he said, with one of his rare, but sincere, efforts at wit.

Maudie sighed.

"You're not kidding," she replied.

"Anyway," he added without opinion, "you like Myrtle."

She nodded.

"Poor kid," she said.

"No, I guess she's lucky, in a way."

Maudie took a deep breath which made her go into a gasping cough, with resulting tears in her eyes. When she could she said,

"Oh, I don't know. I wish I knew."

Hardie Jo had no thought in response to this, and so sat quietly, watching Maudie wipe her eyes. When he thought she could listen again, he said,

"There's quite a Naval Air Station at Corpus Christi."

"Yes, I know. But we're going for a vacation."

"Go on over to Padre Island and look at the sea birds."

Her whole mood brightened at this. The Gulf of Mexico, wild life, the open world—he gave her all these in his mild way. After the Silver Grille, it was a wonderful vision, and he seemed to think she and Myrtle had as much right to it as—as anyone.

"Well," he said, "I'll keep an eye on things for you while you're gone."

"You're real-real sweet," answered Maudie. "I'll send you a postcard."

He stretched, lowered his head, and had a swift glance at himself in the long bar mirror, and gave a neater slant to his wide-brimmed campaign hat, and said,

"I never knew Homer Breedlove to come out here before. No wonder he left by the back door."

While Maudie, after a wide-eyed stare, burst into flat slaps of laughter which he thought he understood, Hardie Jo quickly tossed down his shot of bourbon and departed.

It was the time of night when Hardie Jo often felt good.
Maudie's bourbon always helped, but he knew his state of well-
being arose from more than that. He never put it into words, but
he did not have to—what he meant was that his every physical
sense was pleased with itself. His whole being seemed to be
focussed in the fine awareness of how well his tailored shirt
clung to him, and defined his trim, powerful torso; and how
his trousers with their official stripe hugged him so well that he
was dreamily aroused if he even happened to stroke his thighs.
When that happened he was both the source and the object of
his admiration. Drifting around town in his car, he would let his
thoughts take him into adventures which ended with the imagined praises of amazed women ringing in his head. Who would
ever think that a man who spoke so gently, and was proud of
it, was proud also of the slow, controlled strength of his beauti-
fully kept body which when it demanded enjoyment always
violently completed whatever it started, taking its way to his
full satisfaction, whether subduing a lawbreaker or using a
woman?

That evening touring the town he was curious about an un-
familiar sight revealed by his headlights—a bright pink station
wagon standing beside the little civic park at the darkened railroad depot, where the gilded hand car rested.

Hardie Jo drew alongside the parked car and beamed his
flashlight on its door. There, in large golden script, was painted
the name "Cuddles." He shifted his light. At the wheel of the car
sat a plump young woman with a make-up so vivid and hair so
yolk-yellow that in his finger of light she looked like a whole
stage show all by herself. Her eyes glistened into the miniature

spotlight with liquid sparks set off by her sticky black lashes.

With his trained inscrutability, he left his car and approached hers.

"Ma'am, I believe you're illegally parked?" he said.

"Honey," said Cuddles, "that's my life story. I'm just waiting for a date. But I am early and just sitting here."

"The no-parking signs are plainly visible in this area, ma'am."

"Oh, I suppose so."

He took out his little pad of violation summonses and began to fill in the top sheet. For a moment she stared at him, and then exclaimed,

"You wouldn't! Not at this time of night, with nobody around! It isn't as though I was blocking traffic or—"

"I believe there's no indication of permissible hours on the no-parking signs," he stated.

She slid out from under the wheel to the far side of her car, at the same time unlatching the door near Hardie Jo.

"Oh, come on, Beautiful," she murmured, "get in."

She had spoken the proper word. He entered beside her, willing to risk the small chance of seeing another car come along. The night felt good to him, inside and out. He proceeded upon her with grim confidence.

"That's right," said Cuddles. "I'm just passing through town, I know there's much more for me over at Orpha City, with all the oil field gentlemen. This is just a good will offering for you." Suddenly she cried out on a breath at his effect.

*"Be still, hon,"* he said softly, but with something in his voice that gave her a chill. Oh, yes, he felt good to himself, all right, and he closed his eyes as his power took its way. When Cuddles could not suppress a word or a gasp, he said, keeping his eyes shut the better to see himself, *"Don't talk,"* and she obeyed. All too soon Hardie Jo was done with her. She lay in the car seat

full of wonder. Mildly, he left her, walked around the pink station wagon, got out his flashlight again, copied the number of her car plates, and then came to the driver's door and said,

"Ma'am, I'll just have your driver's license, please."

She sat up.

"You don't mean—not *now!*"

"I'm giving you a ticket."

Bitterly she released a storm of foul profanity and calmly he waited while she dug in her pink patent leather handbag. In a moment the transaction was completed. Her heated threats to expose him to the judge faded when she remembered charges worse than illegal parking—lewd vagrancy, soliciting, and all—and at a brief directive from him, she drove off, leaving him still feeling good, though in a different way.

⚜ ⚜ ⚜

A short while later, cruising along Central, he saw Homer Breedlove's car parked in front of the Saddle and Sirloin. Slowing down, he glanced into the long narrow restaurant and saw Billy Breedlove and that Durham boy of whom he always thought as a "sad-eyed moth-eaten bastard," since he was so unlike the town's other young fellows. "Well, I'll be dogged," said Hardie Jo to himself, and now knew why Maudie laughed. Then he thought that if Phil Durham had gone to Maudie's with Billy, why, there might be something to him after all—something which could explain why Billy was such a good friend to him. Hardie Jo drove on about his work, dimly pleased at how things got found out. As for Homer, and the idea of his going to Maudie's— Hardie Jo had to let himself laugh, too, now.

Seated at the counter with hamburgers and milkshakes, Billy
and Phil were drained of their own hilarity. Presently Billy said,
   "You didn't really think I'd do any more than that, did you, I
mean for Marilee's sake?"
   "I don't know. No, I suppose you wouldn't, after all."
   "You mean you don't know me any better than that?"
   "Well, you're a famous hell-raiser."
   "Yes, I know. But this":
Billy turned from his pungent sandwich and looked earnestly
at Phil.
   "It was just something to do," he said. "How else do you find
about things? —If H.J. hadn't come along when he did, I was
going to get us out of there anyway, before— Hell. We were just
fooling around. Hell. I saw you. You were about as interested in
Myrtle as a jackrabbit. She was getting mad at you."
   "She was?"
   "Yes. —And you know something else? I didn't have enough
money."
   "I saw your wallet."
   "Yes. But I promised my pappy I was going to put that in my
savings account tomorrow." He whacked Phil on the arm. "How
about it?" His contagious glee was reflected in Phil's face.

☙ ☙ ☙

If in his later life Phillipson Durham, as teacher and writer,
was distinguished by a distrust of directness of statement and
flatness of style, this was perhaps traceable to the effect on him

during his Belvedere years of the terms of life there and how they were stated. He encountered an odd combination of eccentric lyricism and raw good will—the first in those aspects of seasonal sweetness and wide grandeur in the landscape which took any newcomer a long time to get used to and to love; the other in the puzzled gracelessness of many people he knew in their use of each other and their stated opinions. He later found that various distant cultures, as he put it with irony, were also concerned with the inescapable failures and shortcomings of humanity, but some had other, more considerate conventions of responding to these, publicly and privately.

For several days Guy DeLacey considered in silence the fact, as he had soon heard, that his boy Billy Breedlove, as he thought of him in the Red Dot Garage, and that friend of his, Phillipson Durham, had gone one night to Maudie's. He imagined what went on, he knew the place, he was invisibly shaken with tremors of rage that he had not been there to know first-hand what Billy had done, and it became his obsession to find out. He knew Billy would never tell him, for all his hints of invitation to learn about Billy and his fleshly life had always been evaded with cheerful finality.

After closing the garage late one evening, Guy went to the Saddle and Sirloin for a cup of coffee, and there saw Phil, sitting at the counter alone. Guy's thought went swiftly through a sequence of actions which promised what he sought. After a casual, but voice-quivered greeting, he said to Phil,

"Have you ever seen my mountain?"

"No."

"I was just going home to do a little more work on it. Come along for a minute and see it?"

Phil wanted to refuse, but his very dislike of Guy, whose mind Billy admired so much, required him to be more polite than he meant to be, and he said,

"Just for a minute, then. I've got a term paper coming up."

"If you're not careful, you'll be valedictorian this year," said Guy. "All right. Let's go."

Guy's red pickup truck was out in front of the place and they drove more or less in silence to the house where Guy rented the rear of the second floor. He had his own entrance up a flight of stairs on the outside of the house.

"Just wait here," said Guy inside the door, "while I go ahead and fix the lights."

In darkness Phil heard Guy, breathing heavily in the far room, moving a chair or two, evidently preparing some sort of effect. Then from an invisible position beyond the door into the next room, Guy called out, "All right, come on, now," and as Phil moved toward the sound, he saw a deep blue light spreading as if in infinity over a plain plaster wall, and in front of it, in silhouette, the jagged crest of a great mountain range. The surrounding darkness made the scale of the scene transcend the miniature. Phil paused at the threshold. The mountain was convincing.

Guy, working electric dials somewhere within, brought a dawn light slowly up on the plaster sky, and then the first strikes of sunlight across the face of the deeply wrinkled flanks of the mountain. The effect was theatrical and realistic both, and it was easy to give imagination to the illusion, so that sized and painted muslin, modelled over fine-mesh chicken wire, seemed to become a distant range of mountains whose face was carved by deep canyons, and lesser declivities which suggested different stages of ancient erosion.

"Wonderful!" exclaimed Phil in spite of himself.

"Isn't it?" said Guy, unable to be modest about his creation. He brought the lights up to full daylight, and the mountain stood in rock browns and greys, with hazy blue shadows in its depths. Phil for the first time was conscious of the dimensions of the model, and saw it to be only about five feet long.

Guy expected him to have more to say about the construction, and so Phil said,

"How long have you been working on it?"

"Oh, several years. I keep thinking of things I want to do to it. The wiring alone took my spare time for a year."

"I should think so."

"How about a beer?" asked Guy, turning the mountain light down to an evening glow.

"I'd better get on to my paper."

"It's already cold—I'll get it."

He was gone before Phil could again refuse; when he returned, Phil asked, idly,

"Why did you build the mountain?"

Guy handed him a pierced can of beer and replied,

"Well, if you can't find one to climb, you can build one, I guess."

This was a comment on the plains where they lived, where no mountain showed; and also, thought Phil, on something to do with Guy's inner life—just what, he could not say. In any case, gazing at the model, he thought it the most ingeniously convincing miniature of any aspect of the world he had ever seen, and he felt almost that he liked Guy. For the moment, Phil was amused to look around the room and see the evidence of Guy's working curiosity and squalid style. The room was heaped with old newspapers, old books, including scatterings of miniature paper editions and piles of clothing—even opened but only partially consumed cans of food. Over the clutter loomed the little mountain, like a transcendent fact in a trivial world. The evening was chilly. In a move meant to seem hospitable, Guy went to an old tin-lined fireplace and lighted the gas under a set of imitation logs which burned with a blue flame and made small red worms of fire seem to crawl on the fabricated bark of the indestructible fuel. Kneeling at his task, and speaking over his shoulder thick with fat, Guy said, with his voice under precarious control,

"Well, how was it out at Maudie's, with you and Billy?"

Phil was astounded. He frowned.

"How did you know?"

"I hear things. —More things than anybody gives me credit for."

"It wasn't much."

"That's what they always say. —Were you together?"

"How do you mean?"

"I mean, did you and Billy—did you see him with one of Maudie's—"

Phil put down his beer and stood up. He asked coldly,

"Are you asking if I watched Billy and Jackie Lou go to bed?"

"Well, you know," said Guy with a pleading smile on his full face which had the texture of corn meal, and in a tone which contained helpless urgency, "if it is a friend of yours, you naturally want to know—"

"Not from me," said Phil.

"Don't be sore," said Guy. "Only he never talks about that end of things with me, and you know, when fellows get together, why, they like to talk about—"

"I *don't* know."

"Listen!" said Guy with animation. "You are his best friend, we all know that. I don't claim anything like that. I just wish he would—I just wish you'd get him to—talk to me sometimes the way other fellows do. You know. Open up a little." Guy was sweating and beseeching without knowing how to say what he lusted to know. "Listen, maybe he doesn't think I know things. If you just told him that I know lots of things, and understand them, and, you know, without thinking anything about them one way or the other, why, then, you know, he might tell me how he does out at Maudie's, and, you know, Marilee, and like that."

Phil stared at him with fascination. There was some spell at work in Guy DeLacey which held him.

"Look, wait!" said Guy. "I'll show you something of what I

mean, about things I know, that nobody else knows, that I don't think one way or the other about! Just wait a minute! Just a minute!"

Guy went into a closet at one end of the heaped room and returned with a rusted metal box of the kind used in small offices in which to keep accounts and petty cash. He fingered a key ring and found a key with which he opened the box and took out a thick packet of letters. He held them toward Phil and said,

"I never showed these to anybody before, not even Billy, but you can tell him that what's in them doesn't make any difference to me at all. I mean, it takes all kinds to make a world. I want Billy to know he could really talk to me about anything." Guy's voice was briefly silenced by heavy saliva which he had to swallow. "Go on, read them. You'll see what I mean. You're his best friend. You'll know how to tell him. Come on, go ahead!"

Phil was mystified. Guy looked to him like a man in full anguish and—could it be?—desire. Phil had the impulse to run away, despising any commerce with Guy DeLacey, but the emotion facing him was too strong to escape from. He sat down again and began to finger the meager evidences of a sorry passion concealed but not quieted throughout a lifetime.

The first letter was typewritten. Its lines were faded by water. Phil looked with reluctance at the dimmed words there. When he recognized to whom the letter was written, he was jabbed by recollections. He remembered the tale of the old Model A long missing and finally dragged up from the lake; and the naked corpse that had been found floating one white afternoon; and the talk about how a certain man had never turned up at the funeral. He was reminded how a man's life had come and gone with no one beside it. The letter, dated years ago at the university at Austin, told Ben Grossman to get over it, whatever it was he thought he had reason to expect, and went on to say that the kind of messing around he remembered so seriously from the days when they were both growing up and taking hunting trips together out on the ranch at Whitewater never meant anything then and meant nothing now, and ought to be just laughed at and forgotten. The writer did not care to be continually reminded of all that by pestering letters. He had better things to think about, such as sorority dates. He hoped he made himself clear for once and all, and signed himself, "Yours with no hard feelings, Tom Bob."

Phil looked up.

"What does it mean?" he asked. "What's the point in my reading it?"

"You mean you don't know?" asked Guy. But a look of wary insinuation in Guy's face made Phil suddenly know what the letter was about. He was disgusted with himself for being party to the discovery of the loyal and despised secret of someone long dead. He had an intimation of consequences, and if he had stopped to think, he would have felt hot and dizzy at the idea that anything, even the idlest event, could lead to lifelong effects never foreseen.

Before Phil could say anything, Guy, in an effort at sounding casual, yet paying respects to eminent precedent, said,

"That was from Tom Bob Gately."

"Where did *you* get it?"

"Oh, there's more there, read them all."

*"Where did you get them?"*

"Now don't sound so uppity, they're rightly mine, I'll tell you where I got them. When they pulled Ben Grossman's jalopy out of Whitewater, they gave it to me as junk, and everything in it. For a long time I didn't fool around with the old heap, but when I did, I found this tin box under the front seat, all sealed with tire tape. I guess old Ben never figgered it would ever be found. I got me a key made to open the box and I've never showed any of it to a soul ever since. Till now. Till you."

"I don't want to read any more of what's here," said Phil. He threw the papers on a cluttered table top.

"Why, you oughtn't to mind like that," observed Guy with an injured air. "I take you into my confidence, and you—this one here, now." He held up a letter in a slitted envelope. "This was addressed to Tom Bob at Austin by Ben, but it was returned to sender unopened. Poor old Ben was trying to be just so nice and make Tom Bob be nice to him again."

"Did *you* open it?"—scornfully.

"Well, there it was, I don't suppose old Ben felt like opening it himself, if Tom Bob sent it back that way. Mighty unkind, it seems to me. —So now this next one is a letter from Ben, sort of a first try that he probably copied and sent later, for it is in pencil with lots of mistakes scratched through. It says he just wants to go to Austin to see Tom Bob and will wait for an answer. I guess he never got one, except the next one sort of is an answer." Guy held up a stiff square thick cardboard, stained yellow. "This one says, '*The Lieutenant-Governor and Mrs Jake LaMar Wildy Have the Honor to Announce the Marriage of Their Daughter Leora to Mr Tom Bob Gately Jr at Austin,* and so on and so on, *June Nineteenth Nineteen-Hundred-and—*' "

"I don't want to hear any more," said Phil.

"So Ben wrote out another one in pencil till he got it right, saying he was leaving Belvedere to go away and learn the grocery business. Then the last one here says he was coming back to open his own store in Belvedere, but Tom Bob need never be worried that he would ever bother him again, or go to see him, or anything like that, but if he saw him it would just be from across the street, and nobody, he says, can object to that. —Of course, this was all years before old Ben went in the lake."

Phil felt himself turning into someone he could hardly recognize. He stood up and was taller than he knew in the rage that went through him. He shook with fury at this betrayal of the helpless dead which could be used for evil against the living. Guy stared at him in amazement.

"What's the matter with you?" he said. "You look all white and funny."

Phil felt his jaws clatter and he bit down on them before he could speak.

"You wanted me to hear all this so I would tell Billy?"

"Oh, I just thought—you know, if he knew I know all about things like that, he wouldn't be so—"

Phil said,

"Burn the letters."

"What!"

"I said, *Burn the letters.* Now. I want to see you do it. Nobody has any right to know what's in them, or use it!"

"You're off your nut!"

"Whether I am or not, you do what I say!"

He took a step toward Guy, who fell back holding the letters away. But in Phil he saw power such as he himself had never felt; and when Phil, unable to speak again because his mouth was dry with fury, pointed to the flame-fluttered gas logs, Guy began to shake with excitement which was not entirely unpleasant—it had been a long time since anybody had shown emotion of any sort about him. After a moment in which his small eyes shifted from side to side, like his thought, he gave in to the sheer moral force which burned in the slight but empowered young man before him, and with much effort, he knelt down and put the letters piece by piece on the top log where in a few seconds they left dead leaves of curled ash which released a musty odor into the room—something like dried river earth. Until the sacrifice was done, Phil stood his ground, while Guy knelt watching his scheme go up the acrid flue of the old house.

"All right. That will do," said Phil, and turned to go.

Guy rose to follow him for a step or two, and said,

"So even when I do what you want me to, you won't tell me anything?" The pathos of impotence was in his voice.

"Your mountain is fine. Goodnight."

As Phil went out the door and down the outer steps, breathing hungrily of the late winter air, he heard Guy call after him from the wooden stoop behind him,

"Well, you'd be surprised to know what people hear about what goes on in this town!"

Phillipson Durham shook his head and ran off down the street, leaving Guy once again hungry to know why nothing he ever tried in his efforts to turn people into friends ever seemed to work.

❦ ❦ ❦

Billy when younger heard in the most natural way something which had ceased to be a secret in Belvedere's levels of power. The general knowledge set going the loose lip of gossip, but the facts were there.

One day the two-tone door chime rang at Homer Breedlove's house, and when the front door slammed, shaking the whole place, Billy looked out of a window upstairs and saw Mrs Tom Bob Gately's Cadillac in the street with its engine running. He could see that the car had a too rich carburetor mixture—the smoke from the exhaust was thick and blue and he wondered why Aunt Leora had not turned the ignition off.

"Ellen! Ellen!" cried Mrs Gately in a high voice, standing thin and stock still in the middle of the front hall.

Mrs Breedlove came running from the kitchen, calling out,

"Why, Leora, whatever is wrong!"

It was a moment before Mrs Gately could speak, but when she could, it was to bring to light something which had long been common knowledge in Belvedere, though in secret, and which now threatened to become public for an unexpected reason.

The town had known for a number of years about Tom Bob Gately and Thyra Doolittle, but nobody had ever spoken of their relationship in circumstances which would cause any trouble. People said to each other that too many owed money to the bank for anyone to go around saying out loud that Tom Bob and Thyra Doolittle were having an affair. Presently all agreed that the affair had been going on for so long that it might as well be taken for granted. A few dared to say that it wasn't for love of Tom Bob Gately that they all kept their mouths shut.

He came of an old Whitewater family, and the statement revealed that the people of Belvedere were arbitrarily measured off into two segments—those who derived from the time before the flood, and those who came after. It was curious that there was power of an obscure sort attached to the former. Newcomers were inclined to hitch their shoulders and resettle the fit of their coats on being made aware of this particular difference—though it was true that some didn't pay it any mind, as they would have said.

When Thyra Doolittle came to Belvedere years ago as a professional performer, she said she was already a widow, with only her music to support her; but she had spirit and self-respect, for she knew the worst about herself and was able to live with it. She was the youngest player in Madame Festini's "All Girl Golden Harmonica Quartette." The company after seasons of diminishing success in chautauqua and other engagements ended its history in Belvedere. It was announced to play two performances in town on the same day—one at a luncheon meeting in the Bluebonnet Coffee Shop, the other in the evening, for the general public, on the Lyceum Concert Series.

The Quartette, in full makeup and costume, though in daylight, played the first performance, and Tom Bob Gately saw Mrs Doolittle for the first time.

When evening came, the ticket sale for the second show was so meagre that it would not cover expenses of the hall, and Madame Festini gave up in anger and discouragement. They played the scheduled performance, of course, with flourishes and musical claims as bright as ever for thirty-four people on folding chairs. But Madame Festini was old, ill, and tired after a disastrous tour across the Middle West and Texas. What was the use of trying to bring novelty cultural entertainment to people starved for music if they wouldn't reach out and support her best efforts? What other musical organization in the United States gave as fine a performance of *The Flight of the Bumblebee* as her girls on their harmonicas—so fast, such a blur of golden buzzing? Her management had told her that this tour was the last chance for the Festini Quartette to prove worthy of future bookings. Belvedere was the last straw. "I can't face it any more," she said, while her assisting *artistes* tried to encourage her, but they too knew they were done for, and she could read their fatal knowledge even through their show business loyalty. She wired for money to return to Chicago which the management refused to send. With two of her members she bought tickets to Kansas City, which was as far as their resources would take them, and that was the last Thyra Doolittle ever heard of them, though she thought of them often, especially of Madame, hoping the best for all of them except one, who was, in her private view, a sl-b and a c-nt—two words which she, being a perfect lady, could never spell out in her thought, but which always made her blurt a laugh of guilty pleasure, while revising her opinion to say that that person simply was not fit companion for *any* lady. Herself, Thyra Doolittle, having no money beyond a week's room and board, stayed in Belvedere, even though, as she told new friends there, it meant giving up her music, for there was no public career to be had in West Central Texas, and having been a star attraction professionally, she did not like the idea of opening a studio in which to take pupils. If there had to be a comedown, she preferred a complete change.

Because of the striking appearance which had always brought a sustaining murmur from her old audiences, Thyra was soon given a position as sales person (as she called herself) in charge of the cosmetics at the Longhorn Drug Store on Central. Within a few days she had her department reorganized, with a gold-lettered sign above the counter reading "Beauty Bar." It was a novel and racy touch which seemed to bring a breath from the great sophisticated world to a county where mixed drinks could not be legally sold.

Thyra was a living poster for the virtues and effects of the products she promoted across her sweet-smelling counter. Her hair was a fiery dark orange. As it slowly grew out it would reveal another color—greying white, and she would vigorously apply a preparation from a fancy bottle at the Beauty Bar to restore its solid color. Her face was white and the skin was tightly drawn over her forehead and cheekbones until it shone. She painted her eyelids with an Egyptian blue and put something over that to make them shine as she turned her glance. Her eyes were pale grey, folded about by a system of tiny wrinkles which you could not see from a little distance. Her natural eyebrows were removed and she pencilled in their substitutes high on the polished bone of her forehead. For her cheeks she chose a thick dusty rouge called *Rose Geranium*. Her nose was large, spatulate at the end, with nostrils flaring open to take an extra abundance of life through the sense of smell. This hint of appetite was emphasized by her mouth, which was small, and painted smaller, as if to represent a kiss which she was keeping for the world at large. Women understood and hated her on sight.

But they had to admit that Thyra was always the first one to aid the ill or the needy. Men said they never saw anyone kinder-hearted. Their wives believed she had better be, to make up for—for the rest of her. But whether or not she helped others in expiation for something in her past—nobody knew—she seemed to have a simple fellow-feeling for the unlucky ones in life, and she would freely confess that she knew something about hard luck herself.

For some time it was her habit on her day off to take the bus to Orpha City fifty-two miles away. She would stay until next morning and come home by the early bus. One time a norther with snow and ice closed the highway until noon. Hurrying back to her beauty counter, she did not wait for the next available bus, but rode back to Belvedere with Tom Bob Gately in his yellow Lincoln Continental. They were seen. All was plain. They had been meeting in Orpha City for all that time. No wonder she wore such expensive clothes to work, which always made her look like a hostess at a drawn-shade tea instead of a working woman. There was no way she could avoid being conspicuous.

She occupied a simple apartment over a garage in back of a doctor's house, which was reached by another of those outdoor wooden staircases seen so often in Belvedere. There she lived an alley life up among telephone insulators, electric light wires, and wooden poles, while along the unpaved alley ranged dogs and cats and children, all natural vagrants, and the garbage truck, and the public service and telephone crews. And there in time she provided a second home—his real one—for Tom Bob Gately.

What she gave him, which he did not find in the Tudor mansion out on the corner of Cleveland and Central—the "lovely-home"—were calm and ease.

He found it wonderful not only to have such a pretty little trick as Thyra to be loved by, and make love to, but also to have a place where he could just go and take off his shoes and his shirt, and leave out his upper dental plate if it was hurting, and sit down, and steadily get drunk whenever he felt like it, without having any little bird-thin woman to clap their hands at him for being the way he was, and walk with high heels all around him on inlaid hardwood floors and talk at him and s'riek at him and clap-clap-clap and clatter-clatter-clatter, saying if she had ever *known* she never would have married him, but now that she *was* married to him, she was not going to stand for disgraceful drunken behavior and if he thought for one minute that she,

Leora Wildy Gately, a lieutenant-governor of Texas's daughter, had to stand there and take any more of (whatever it was this time)—oh, he habitually stopped listening, or tried to, but the only way to succeed was to get out of the house.

Oh, my: he found it good to park his car in the alley and go up the wooden steps to Thyra's place, and just get belly-comfortable. If anybody came down the alley in a highly waxed Cadillac to see where his car was parked, he didn't care. If anybody wanted to divorce him because of it, he didn't care.

This was his strength. In the face of it, his wife Leora was helpless and exasperated. What she would give! to have it come true that if *she* left *him,* it would break his heart and ruin his business, or make him take to drink, but of course he had already done that so that didn't count; or anyway, to have him come to her bedroom some midnight and throw himself on his knees on her pink fur rug and beg her not to ruin him and the bank by making an open scandal but forgive him and take him back on her terms, no matter how hard she chose to make them! Oh, to make a strong man weep! What would she not then do out of the fullness of her heart if he should come to her so?

But he never did, nor did he care, and she knew it. All she could do was deny the whole town with her lifted chin and her hazy look and smile, as though, with all her money and her lovely-home, she were not sipping, sipping away through the hours at the bitter draught she cupped in her fast-knocking heart.

Perhaps she *had* done nothing for years to show Tom Bob that she loved him, but then, shouldn't he *know* it without her telling him? because of all the work she did? and the money she spent of her own for her daddy left her with plenty? to make a lovely-home for them both, where, conscious of her leading position in Belvedere, she gave on a strict calendar a series of parties all year round which were so impressive that they subdued her guests, as she intended?

But did Tom Bob ever give her a word of thanks or praise for her heaps of hot-house flowers from Wichita Falls, and her miles of lace tablecloths, her tons of sterling silver in every form, and her food in every inventive disguise and variety which—creating a phrase adopted by the lady reporter on the society page—she served at her "fingertip" buffets?

Not a word.

He usually went to the kitchen with a couple of men and, interfering comfortably with the pattering labors of the colored help, spent the evening drinking Old Forester bourbon and telling hunting stories from long ago, especially one about an old bobcat, the biggest one ever seen, that lived out at the ranch beyond Whitewater and never had got himself caught yet. The old rascal cat. You had to admire an adversary like that. In a way it'd be too bad ever to get him. Just keep on after him—maybe that was enough. When Tom Bob's friends laughed with plea-sure in his full-blooded geniality, his wife, hearing the laughter as it rumbled as far as the candle-lighted living room, would conceal her resentful shudder. Not to mention how afterward, when everybody had gone home, he came to her bedroom breathing out a whole storm of whiskey and, keeping his eyes squeezed shut as if to preserve an inner dream which would vanish if he looked directly at her, he blindly used her, growling "Take it, take it," in a rude despairing hunger which spoke of how tender he might have been if she had not lain rigid with all entrance to her person closed to him in a helpless spasm of affronted pride. So in the brief, anguished, snorting act, he could only banish all her hard-earned satisfaction at having just a short hour ago shown Bel-vedere what a lovely party was really like.

※ ※ ※

Tom Bob Gately was a careless ruin of a handsome man. Tall
and heavy, he moved with the relaxed strength of an athlete long
away from his playing field. His voice came from deep in his
great cavern of a chest, though Thyra always said it must come
from farther down, where—she pursed her lips demurely at her
wanton thought—he had things like a bull's. He could never
speak quietly, even if he wanted to, which he saw no reason to
do. His hair was almost white and he kept it cut shaggily short,
as if someone took a swipe at it now and then without really
looking at the shears, just the way his "old dead black mammy"
out on the ranch used to cut it when he was a boy—she who lived
far more real within his loving memory than many of his still-liv-
ing intimates. In his dust-brown face he had small blue eyes and
big features. Without making any impression on him, his doctor
warned him regularly about his blood pressure, and drinking too
heavily, and not taking enough exercise. His thumbs looked like
his nose—thick, long, and battered. He read and kept every book
printed about Texas, and when he went back to Austin for a visit
every few years it was his old history professor with whom he
spent most of his time.

Anybody who judged Tom Bob by his huge and sagging
presence, which breathed in its own constant climate of bourbon
fumes, and concluded that he was a dull or stupid man, made a
mistake. In banking hours he was sober enough to work, and
every morning shortly after the bronze doors opened on Central,
he held his daily court at the bank. Ranchers and businessmen
came to pass the time of day, bringing rumors or jokes for him,
and suing for his quizzical gaze, which, in order to keep their
uneasiness alive for the pleasure of it, he often bestowed in long
silences. How could they not be impressed by him? Who could
forget the time years ago during the spring graduation dance at

the high school when the news had been brought specially to him that the United States had gone off the gold standard? The word went through the decorated gymnasium like a current of air. Not one person in fifty, no, a hundred, knew the significance of the information, but how could anyone forget that when he was informed by his cashier, Tom Bob had grimly left the ball at once to go home, everyone said, to place a call to Washington. To Washington! It was tacitly agreed that Tom Bob was the great man of Belvedere, though he had no interest in public office, and was frank to say so. If the occasion arose, and if he cared enough, he could contribute sensibly to a conversation about almost any general topic except science in any form. He had no idea of where life was taking him, now, or in eternity. That he sometimes wondered about this, in a movement of feeling as sensitive as it was private, nobody knew. Thyra Doolittle couldn't tell him anything, but she could refill his glass, and slowly play her fingers along his wide neck, and when he wished, give him ease in her flesh.

The money she got out of him! people said, without really knowing. He gave it, well enough, and he knew what for, though whatever they thought, hardly anybody else really knew what for. With his money Thyra took care of people in need— Negroes, or Mexicans, who lived across the tracks of the Roscoe, Snyder and Pacific Railroad, or anyone stranded ill or hopeless at the Greyhound Bus Station whose agent had her phone number and was urged to call her when she was needed, or an unmarried girl about to bear a child who had gone for help to the nuns at SS Peter and Paul, pleading for secrecy.

For the satisfaction of giving her pain, certain friends wanted to tell Leora Gately what her husband was up to with Thyra Doolittle. But Leora, too, had her strength, which rested in her pride of position. She had worked through the years to make herself into the structure she called Mrs Tom Bob Gately II (it had once been "Jr"), wife of the President of the West Central

Texas State Bank, and well known social leader of the West Central Empire counties.

*While she lived,* Leora would say to herself with urgency, nothing must be allowed to threaten this creation of her style, and *before she died,* if things hadn't changed, she would find some way to change them, in a last assertion of her pride. If she overemphasized everything she said and did, she made her will prevail by doing so, and—though she was small, thin, and ceaselessly in motion—she was strong enough to make others with greater size and simpler inertia do as she wished. She would bet she was more like the Pioneer Woman who settled the West than all those big-armed women who hadn't a fraction of her tenacity. So, her open secret was kept because she wanted it kept. Her falsely sweet loquacity seemed to some a deliberate way to keep others from telling what she refused to hear about herself, her position, Tom Bob, and Thyra.

Of the three, only Leora had passion. If she thought passion had driven Tom Bob to Thyra, she was wrong. All he wanted was comfort, which he didn't find at home, where great energy coupled with an obsession to excel drove him out of the house. Leora could not understand how he could choose as he did. Thyra Doolittle had nothing. She was nobody. Look how she lived. She didn't even try to be somebody. She was common, with all that beauty stuff on her face. How could a man deliberately turn to anything common? She never realized who had driven Tom Bob away.

There were no children to keep him at home. The Gatelys were childless in consequence of a perfunctory indulgence by Tom Bob one night years ago in Villa Acuña after which he had waited too long to see a doctor. Now, Billy Breedlove was just the sort of son Leora wanted. He grew up calling her Aunt Leora. She brought him presents until Homer and Ellen asked her not to. They could not afford to meet their son's appetite for gifts which Leora awakened in order to earn his hugs and kisses, the sparkle of greed in his eyes which she mistook for love, and before he should be entirely spoiled they must put an end to it. She was offended for a while, but felt better when she realized that Billy liked her anyway, not knowing that he also liked everybody. In the end, she sadly belonged to him just as everybody else did, no more, no less.

Sometimes her eyes would fill with tears as she sat talking to his mother and watching him play as a little boy, or later seeing his demonstrations of good manners—a brief phase—when he discovered these on first awareness of girls. In its modest and gloomy propriety, Billy's house was Leora's refuge when she needed one. It was full of what she craved—a family's well-contained love, and never had anyone traced any gossip to its front door. If Homer and Ellen knew what everyone else knew about the leading local scandal, they tried to deny it in their hearts, and thus made Leora at ease with them. During moments of feeling well, instead of being racked by head pains of speculation, she would smile at what local people must think, especially those whose families didn't go back before the rise of the lake above Whitewater: how strange that the prominent Mrs Tom Bob Gately II should be such close friends with those Breedloves, who didn't have anything to speak of, and who lived such a dim little existence, though to be sure, Ellen Breedlove's parents *had* lived in the Draw before the dam was built. But how foolish, Leora would reflect generously, how foolish of anyone to think in that way, when the simple fact was that since nobody in Belvedere could even *begin* to live up to the Gatelys, what could it matter *where* Leora Gately went to find her friends? She gained strength from bestowing her notice.

But when she was unhappy or ill, Leora thought in quite another way, and so she did, when she came running into the house on that day, calling for Ellen Breedlove as though she would lose her mind. Billy could not help hearing it all, which meant that Phil would hear it long later.

***

"I have just left him!"

"Who! Who! Not Tom Bob!"

"No, no. Not Tom Bob. You know that. That's all he wants. I'll never do that! —No, I just left the doctor, and I can't stand it!"

"Hush, Leora, dear, sit down, be quiet, and tell me."

Mrs Gately could not speak again until she had sobbed against Ellen's heart. She went on as though to strangle, with gasping sounds. Presently, drained of shock, if not comforted, she was able to talk.

For some time she had been having this funny feeling, right here, and she didn't want to pay any attention to it, but it kept being there, and sometimes it hurt suddenly, quite horribly, and then all of a sudden it seemed bigger, and she called the doctor and told him over the telephone what it felt like. He told her to come in as soon as possible for an examination. She went today. Hours of it. She came from there just now, but first she stopped at home for something. How could she speak of all her trouble? She began to cry again. Ellen held tightly to her racking little bones, from which such great heavings emerged. The embrace gave Leora strength to continue.

"He has to operate. Immediately. He said I have already waited too long. Too late? Do you know? He said we might be, but we will do everything? Ellen?"

"Hush, Leora, dear, of course it isn't too late. Oh, I am so glad you went to him. Don't be afraid. Don't be."

"Oh, afraid. I'm not afraid if I have to die, we all have to go. I don't want to, nobody does, but that isn't what drives me crazy, Ellen! I can't and I won't!"

Her feeling was filled up again, and the energy of it made her voice split and  go high. As Billy said, she sat there and s'rieked and s'rieked.

"What is it, then, Leora, dear, what is it?"

"I won't die and leave those two together! It's all they want!"

Ellen Breedlove saw how at that point, Leora ceased, for the moment, to be a woman, and became women, with all their worst, instead of best, traits. She also saw that there was no use pretending that she did not know what Leora was talking about, though Leora had never referred to it before.

"Let her have him all to herself?" cried Leora. "Never!" Her voice went cloudy with rage. It sounded heavy, like a boy's voice croaking toward manhood. What she said next made Ellen Breedlove gasp with horror. In her broken, heavier voice, Leora said,

"I'll kill her first!"

"Oh, no, who?"

"Thyra Doolittle! I'll kill her before I let her have my husband when I am gone!"

"Oh, Leora, oh no, for Jesus' sake, amen, Leora, you mustn't sit there and even talk like that!"

Leora opened her large black leather bag and took from it a blue steel revolver and showed it to Ellen.

"I'd like to know why not!" she said. "What have they ever spared me? They have destroyed my life! Now it's my turn!"

"Leora, give me that gun!"

There was an interval of almost silent gasping and weeping while Leora held the gun away from Ellen, and then she said again, but quietly,

"I will, I will kill her before I go—if I have to go."

"No, Leora, you won't do any such thing."

"What *will* I do!" demanded Mrs Gately in a sort of exhausted, desperate amenity.

"You'll forgive her."

*"Forgive her!"*

"Yes, Leora, dear, and him."

"*Him!*"

For a long moment the two women stared at each other in silence to see who was crazy.

But they both knew, and gently, gently Leora crumpled into a whimpering calm before the power of the Ten Commandments as it came to her through Ellen. Ellen took the gun from her hands and said as though comforting a heartbroken child,

"Come, Leora, dear, I'll ride home with you. You'll feel better. You'll be glad to have peace in your heart."

༻ ༻ ༻

That very afternoon Tom Bob Gately took his wife to the hospital, and that same evening, she had a visitor. It was Thyra Doolittle, whom she had sent for. Thyra never forgot a word of what followed, and she told it all later to Tom Bob, who was waiting for her to come home to the alley apartment.

He made himself comfortable by removing his shirt and shoes and upper denture. In the kitchenette he mixed himself a highball—"Old Phorester," he said half-aloud, with the effect that always resulted from removing his teeth, "that'll be just phine, just phine," and with a long sigh of ease which was at the same time an admission of the vague, ever-present malaise of late middle age, he stretched out on the davenport where Thyra kept her toy dogs and cats with fluffed-up silk bows about their necks. When she came home and began to talk, he knew profound shock for the first time in his life.

His temper rose furiously as he listened to Thyra, and then he felt a bolt of sickness about his heart which weakened him and made him sweat feebly. He had a sensation of going sickly pale and when he tried to stand up he could not make his knees hinge open. In his mouth his spittle turned to whiskey-fluff. A hot dryness came to his eyes. Sitting on Thyra's davenport, he stared up at her while she stood in the middle of the alley garage living room under its sloped beaverboard ceiling. In his thick hands his highball glass trembled until it almost spilled. Thyra was standing perfectly steady, even though, as she told him what he had to hear, the tears were streaming down her face and turning her day's beauty into a little mixed mud of blue, black, white, and *Rose Geranium.*

She was telling him goodbye, forever.

"What the phuck are you standin there and talkin about!" roared Tom Bob when she was done.

"Leora is going to die," she repeated. "I saw the doctor and I asked him and he says there isn't much chance. He says he told you too. There's nothing else I can do. Oh my God."

"You cut that out," he said, putting his voice under control. "I know she may have a rough time. I hope not. We're doin everythin we can about her. But whatever happens, that don't have one thing to do with you and me."

"Oh, yes it does," answered Thyra, beginning to cry again into her already sodden, lace-edged handkerchief. "You have to understand. It was like being forgiven by someone on their deathbed. She said she had known all about us for years, and she used to have hate in her heart for me, and this very morning, she went home and got your revolver and said she wanted to kill me, rather than leave me with you after she was gone, but now, facing what she is facing, she has to ask sweet Jesus what to do, and He tells her, There is only one thing to do, and that is, forgive."

Thyra had been undone by the scene. Having had to forgive herself through good works for so long to find herself now forgiven by the creature whom most of all she had wronged in life! Impending death required respect, like impending life, if nothing else did.

"I broke down there, listening to her," said Thyra, "and I just had time before they made me leave, just time to do what would make her happy before it was too late."

"You didn't mean it!" shouted Tom Bob.

"Yes I did, honey, I did, and I do. I told her she could rest easy. I said her forgiveness was what did it. I said I would leave you. I mean it, Tom Bob. God help me, I mean it, honey, and I can't stand it!"

She fell sobbing upon him. He began to recover his strength. His mind felt alive again. He soothed her.

"You understand, honey?" She raised her ruined countenance to his. "No decent person could ever go on again, *after this?*"

A rich power began to surge slowly back into him. He growled against her throbbing temple the words she required of him. He said he would obey, if that was what she wanted. If she couldn't belong to him any more; if out of respect for the dyin or the dead she felt she had to give up what meant the most to her, well, she mustn't worry, he would help her all he could. He would get out and stay out.

All the while he smiled across the room above her head, for tshith! he knew she was just upset, and he had seen a lot of women upset, and when they got over it, they also got over what upset them. Give it a little time, he said to himself, just a little time. After—after Leora goes, it won't make any difference any more. Thyra would let him come back. A little time, out of respect for Leora's memory, and then he would come back. He would bet his stock in the bank that down underneath everythin Thyra was thinkin, she was thinkin exactly what he was thinkin. Right now, she was exhausted. She was ashamed of lookin like she did in front of him, for she always made it a point to be beautiful for him, and now her face was turned away from him.

With a pat on her thin arm which she had flattened against her heavy bosom, he turned from her, heavily gathered up his clothes, and went down the steps to his car, shakin his head at havin been through somethin.

He got into his car and drove along Polk, out of town, past the cemetery at the beginning of the plains, and into the distance on the road to Whitewater, with no thought of where he was driving. He cruised along slowly, his big left wrist loosed and dangling his left hand over the top of the steering wheel, his right hand limply guiding the car at the lower rim of the wheel, his sun-cracked lips open around a soundless little column of tune, and his eyes and thoughts reaching far to the horizon, for he wanted to be alone, and he was, in order to see wisely and spaciously, for he must decide just how long to allow before he could return to Thyra, so she could keep her pride, and yet have a chance to forget her promise, which was a delicate matter to measure, for it involved also just how long he could stand being alone before he did somethin foolish himself, mebbe with somebody else. He drove without noticing the miles or anything else until he had his thoughts in order and his decision reached; then he awoke to where he was, happy at the figure of three weeks which seemed about right to him, and he saw the deep turquoise last blue of the evening on the western rim of the world, and above it, the mystery of the thin crescent of the setting new moon, which cut the infinite dark space about itself with a clarity and sweetness—rather like his own decisiveness cutting the earlier formless dark of his thoughts. He turned around and drove back toward town at eighty-five miles an hour.

"No Marilee?" she asked, on opening the door to find Phillipson Durham alone on the porch. "Come in."

"No—I asked her," he replied. "But she was busy."

"Billy?"

"Yes."

They went far into the house to the living room fireplace where
a wood fire was falling into long-lasting coals.

"Did you bring your story?" she asked.

"Yes."

"I'm ready to listen."

Sitting on the floor before the fireplace, he read aloud to her for
forty minutes. When he was finished, she made no comment. It
was enough that she took him seriously enough to listen. He felt
he could not ask more.

"Are you working on something else?"

"Oh, yes. A novel. In my head."

She did not smile, but said,

"What are you calling it?"

"The title is *A Woman of Our Time.*"

"It sounds important, like Lermontov's *A Hero of Our Days.*"

He smile violently, wrenching his whole body in response.

"I've just finished reading that," he said, "how did you know?"

Did she also know that his book was to be about her?

"I didn't. It just reminded me, somehow."

"That's what I mean," said Phil, looking about the room.

"Mean what."

"I can't explain."

But what he meant was that by definition, a house, a room,
were constrictions of space, and when one entered, one was supposed to feel enclosed. But in the house at Crystal Wells Farm,
when he entered it from the unconstricted world of the plains, he

never felt he was closing himself in but actually was opening his life to a vaster world than that of the horizon and sky outside. Here, through her, all the references he longed to live by seemed to be understood in advance, with scarcely a word needed to define them. If she never thought of him as anything but a youth, he never thought of her as an old woman, or a person of any particular age.

"Tell Marilee I miss her," said Victoria.

"I will. So do I."

"I shouldn't wonder. She is adorable."

"Yes, I found that out just about the time she met Billy."

"Were you in love with her?"

"Not really—but when she fell in love with him, then I wished I had known sooner."

"Still, she won't let you go, will she."

"I don't want her to."

"Or Billy, either."

"No."

"Oh, you darling children. When I think about you all, I marvel at what I was spared."

"Spared?"

"The confusions."

"You mean you were never in love."

"Not at your age. Not with anybody—I was in love with my ambition. It couldn't love me back. I never knew what it was all about until I was back here and married Jim."

"But wasn't that a long time?"

"It would seem late to you, at your age. It didn't to me, at mine. —I don't think I could have known how lucky I was if I'd been any younger."

Phil fell silent, and she knew him well enough to know that it was at just such moments that he longed most to speak.

"What is it?" she asked.

"Well, aren't you lonely?"

"Now?"

"Yes."

"Why, of course," she replied calmly, without any particular inflection, as though the question was foolish, since it held its own self-evident answer.

"Well, then, why do you stay, even if you did come back where you knew there was nothing?"

"Put a log on the fire, please, will you, Phil? —Yes, one sees it all quite differently, coming back with everything one has endured, or hoped for and lost. I thought I would never find anything here. I was lucky when I did. Not everybody does. There is a claim on us."

"A claim?"

"Yes, to look at everything critically, if we have to, but never to despise. Laugh all you like at anything, but see that life embraces what is not yours as well as what is—what you don't want as well as what you do, and let it be. I can die laughing at poor Leora Gately and her fancy parties, and what she calls her drawn-shade teas and 3 p.m. candlelight receptions, and it doesn't take a giant intellect to grasp what they take the place of. When she sends out a gold engraved card asking you to a 'Morning Coke 'n Coffee' she is trying to sing some sort of little song, without a voice. Imagine the million ways—yours, mine, included—people think of to ask for happiness! How many of them can possibly mean much to anyone else?"

He sat half-facing her. The firelight was glimmering in his eyes, which in the intensity of his response to her had taken on their half-moon shapes, with the flat side down. He longed to find happiness in his own circumstance, and yet between his mother and his father, Marilee and Billy, Belvedere and poverty, he could not imagine it.

"Is nobody ever happy, then?" he asked, and she detected a

desperate note of hopefulness that she would agree that nobody ever was so, for if this could be established, then he would at least be accounted for along with everybody in the world. But,

"Oh, yes," she said. "There may be a few common denominators. —The only one I can think of that has worked in my experience may be quite common."

"What. What is that":

"Oh, I think anybody could be happy forever, if they had ever been sure that they were necessary, really necessary, to the life of somebody else."

She said this with the calm which she reserved for her most intimate concerns. It made Phil turn to look into the fire with a heavy heart. Her prescription did not describe him, in his present state of being. She made a small laugh.

"Oh, I thought of all this only today," she went on lightly, "I mean the enduring nature of happiness, by contrast to the fugitive sort, such as I passed on a farm out on the Orpha road. In the yard, a child, a girl of about eight, was swinging with her foot caught in a loop of a single piece of rope, like a stirrup, and she was swinging up, down, around, and back, and on her face was the wildest look of ecstasy I have ever seen on anyone. It made me think of myself at that age, when I dreamed of being a dancer, and actually being off the earth! Levitation! Simple levitation! How ravishing!"

He looked at her so soberly that she laughed at him.

"Oh, yes," she insisted, "the poor heavy body always longs to escape its own gravity! —Don't be so grave, my dear."

He rose suddenly and said,

"Do you mind if I look at something here?"

"Not at all. What is it?"

He went to the desk and took up the silver seal with the aquamarine, which had on its flat undersurface his initials deeply engraved in reverse.

"This," he said. "It seems to me almost magic. My own initials."

"To be sure. I never thought of it," she said. "P.D.—Phillipson Durham. That belonged to my husband's first wife, along with all the rest of the fittings on the desk. Her maiden name was Phyllis Dandridge. I never felt the need to put her things away or disturb anything Jim was used to."

He brought the seal back to his place near the hearth and held it close and saw a little constellation of firelight in all the facets of the stone. He closed one eye and with the other was delivered.

She could look through him, back to his childhood, and also forward to his later life, and see the lyric desires within him as he countered them by the ironic and even the melancholy view which would always show itself first, for fear of seeming foolishly in love with what others might scorn.

He never could resist her humor, when she proclaimed it with a brimming smile as she leaned slightly toward him. She believed it time now for this, and she said,

"Isn't it strange how the oddest things occur to us when we ought to be solemn and sad? Today, also, I thought of a description of Leora Gately."

"What was that":

"I said to myself—you know how she clatters along with no one listening—she always made me think of a clapper looking for a bell."

It was so apt, for what he knew of Mrs Gately, that he lay flat on his back on the floor by the fire and laughed with his arm over his eyes. When he recovered, he sat up and offered her one of their favorite comic subjects of local fame, and said,

"I have a new Lew Priddle for you."

"Tell me—though those Priddle-isms drive me mad."

"Yes. —It says, 'People who never do more than they get paid for, never get paid for more than they do.'"

"You see?" she said, laughing, "doesn't that drive you mad? When you try to disconnect one end of it from the other? It's like a dog with its tail in its mouth. —I saw a Priddle-ism once that made me wince in another way. I suppose actually Lew Priddle is the culture, and the conscience, of Belvedere. This was it: 'Do you deserve to face yourself in the mirror and see there all the good folks you came from?' "

"My God," said Phil, "the man is a master at the art of making everybody squirm. —When we first came here I passed the church and he had this one out front: 'Just Ask Yourself.' I worried about that one for days, when I was young."

"He wanted you to. But I think Priddle is at his greatest when he is not so cute and clever, but when he is short and terrifying. Remember this one? Two words: 'Would You?' "

"It is a ghastly power," said Phil. "I can't deny that he always sets up those inner and widening circles in me. They go out and out, and reach nowhere. —That's what's so wonderful about coming here, Vicky."

"I don't—"

"I mean, I have inner circles here, too, but they always go deeper and closer inside me, inner and inner, not outer and outer. I always go away from here feeling and knowing so much more than when I came. I mean precisely knowing." He sighed. "I probably thought quite stupidly—vulgarly, I suppose—"

"—They're the same thing," she interposed but in such a tone as not to halt him, and he continued.

"—about being rich. But this"—he waved his hand about at the room and its contents, the house, herself, the air of inexhaustible interest there—"is really how to be rich."

"But I'm not rich," she said. "I have barely enough to keep me and Nella, and if she didn't belong to the place, and if I didn't love her, I'd really be a little better off for a lot of things without her. I can do for myself everything she does for me. But." She shrugged. He stared at her and said,

"I'm sorry. I didn't mean to intrude, I just took it for granted that—"

"No, no, please, everyone in town does, too, and I suppose if I would sell this or that thing—a picture, or a sculpture, or even the Napoleon collection, which they tell me is unique in some ways—dealers have been here now and then—I could have a high old time on the proceeds. But if I did, I'd lose something of Jim, you know. I would have to have a powerful reason to lose something of Jim. —In the end, what's left all goes to a nephew of his who already has more land in South Texas than he knows what to do with."

Phil leaned nearer to her and answered,

" 'Necessary,' " he quoted. "I do know what you meant."

"Yes," she said.

"Oh, God," he said, and turned back to look at the fire. She couldn't tell whether he spoke out of love, sorrow, or hopelessness, until he said,

"The worst of it is, I can't do much for my father and mother."

"You're there."

"I know. —But you don't know the awful things I think about when I wonder for how long."

"Don't," she said.

He did not answer, and she allowed the silence which was broken only by the whisper of the fire. At last she added,

"I think they would want you to do what you have to do if the time ever comes."

Without stating it exactly, she had touched upon the hope which he rarely allowed to surface in his thought. He let his head fall to his drawn-up knees, and pronounced a word or two which she could not hear.

"What?" she asked.

"I said, 'Martha Phillipson'—my mother's maiden name. I wish you could have seen her before—*before.*"

"Are you like her?"

"I don't think so. But I don't know."

"Like your father?"

"More, I think. We're both adventurers, except that my adventures are all inside, and his used to be everywhere else. I often wonder what he remembers of them now."

"I will tell you," she said. "It is cruel, but I shall be disappointed in you if you ever refuse to know something because it hurts. He remembers every detail and the older he is and the more infirm, the more vivid and dear it all is to him, and the more he misses it."

"How can he stand it? He was so strong and handsome—and she, she was so pretty. You ought to see the old photographs I found one day in a drawer. They don't want to look at them any more. I hardly can."

"Keep them," she said. "This is not sentimental. They will hurt eventually more than gladden. But there will be moments when you will have to see where you came from. Do you want some advice from an old friend?"

He nodded, loving the "old" friend of a few months.

"Well, nobody ever will have to advise you to look inside yourself. You will always do enough—maybe too much—of that. Look outward, look all about you, *everything* is marvellous. Recognize it!"

"I know it!" he exclaimed, "but every time I talk about it, everybody else just looks at me. They don't know what I'm talking about. Listen!" he knelt up facing her. "You know the most beautiful thing in Belvedere? It's not what they brag about, the lilacs, and the green tile dome on the city hall, and the Greek pillars on the bank. No, it is what happens after the sun has gone down, and the vapor lights on the tall aluminum poles over the highway start to come on! —Do you think I am raving?"

Others might, she thought, but not she. She shook her head, holding her fingers on her cheeks. He went on,

"You know: the sky is still brilliant, but evening is coming, and for the first five minutes or so, the vapor lamps have a color—I think of lime green first, and then aquamarine, like this stone, and the ones on the desk there—and the thing is so magic when it happens it is enough to make you dizzy. Everything on the earth is sort of gray by then, yes, lilac gray, and there are shadows down the streets, but there, while the sky is changing, those lights are the most beautiful things in the United States! And you know? *It's all an accident!* They don't *know* how beautiful the light is!"

She shook her head in agreement, but said nothing, afraid of making him self-conscious, or silent.

"I have an idea," he said, "and I think it tells a lot about this country." He spoke passionately. "The greatest man-made beauties in America are *industrial accidents!* Most everything else they *try* to make beautiful is awful. But now and then something wonderful comes out of factories, or street lamps, or railroads, or grain elevators, and that is some kind of art. I don't know what kind. But it does the same thing as art. And nobody means it to! Do you think I am crazy? But nobody else ever lets me talk this way!"

She shook her head to tell him he was not crazy. She searched his whole head with her eyes—his hair thatch, his intense brows, his innerly lighted eyes, the modelling of his cheeks and the shadows under their clear bones, and finally his mouth, in its animation and hot moist color as he gave expression, without self-consciousness, to the passion for the world that lived only in his mind, unless he could free it to someone else. As it was, she looked modestly away from him, and made her little finger circle, thinking that the one thing she might have been any good at in life was to be a teacher, for she believed that the best teacher was the one who knew how to listen. Her cigarette smoke gave her an excuse for the moisture which came stinging her eyes, as she recognized in him all the formless but furious sweetness of his own ambition—hers had long since gone to sleep—to force the world to assume his vision. He put his magic seal away and went home.

The town did not expect her to, but Leora Gately had become a legend in a way which was still talked about. She did not die. She recovered.

It took her many months, but at last she was again at work presiding more restlessly than before at her feats of social engineering. There was one difference now—her husband did not even nominally live at home, nor did he attend any of her parties. Where was he?

"He's gone to the wanch," she would reply, mispronouncing the word slightly, to lend refinement to a rude subject, with a quick excusing smile, adding, "It's so good for him to relax out there. He says he is just not a social animal, anyway, as he says. You know how killing Tom Bob is. He says all my *fuss,* as he says, is just best left to the ladies!"

As for *fuss,* people who were there remembered the last dinner party the Gatelys ever gave together. Tom Bob was drunk enough to make a point of embarrassing everyone by countering their own best behavior with his exaggerated enactment of the crudeness of the cow-camp. When his wife's favorite dessert—floating island— was served, he did not wait to spoon it up, but drank it at once, and then, "I'll just have some more of that calf-slobber," he bellowed. It was a sort of farewell.

If at first people were inclined to assume that Leora was making up a story to conceal the possibility that Tom Bob then went to live at Thyra Doolittle's apartment in the alley, they soon discovered that this was not true. He never again saw Thyra alone. She remained true to her pledge at Leora's "deathbed." Thyra lived in the same place, and went to work every day as usual, and the years passed, since the crisis, and within only the time of one year, she looked like an old, haggard woman, with her makeup hectic where once it had enhanced natural charms.

Her life was joyless. Moreover, she had no further resources to help the needy. Too often Tom Bob was seen stupefied with Old Forester at the bank, as he never had been seen there before, and more and more he went to his ranch beyond Whitewater for days at a time, accompanied only by an old Negro handyman who could cook for him and get him to bed when he was unable to cross the floor by himself. Virtue, as Lew Priddle was fond of saying, was always sure to triumph in the end.

꽃 꽃 꽃

As the time of the full moon was coming around in April, the bitter, dusty winter began to pull away from the Central Plains. The season was like a signal for quickenings of activity in Belvedere, among young and old.

The candidates for the track team were told to meet out on the field behind the high school after classes. Billy was elected captain, and at his direction, Phil was acclaimed as manager. Billy called practice for every afternoon from now until the great event of May, which was the meet against Orpha City, an occasion of annual rivalry. At the end of the squad meeting, Phil said to Billy,

"How about the movies tonight—you, me and Marilee? We haven't done anything for a while now."

"That's true. We've missed you."

"It hasn't been my fault."

"No. Ours, I guess. But you know how it is."

"Well, then, tonight?"

"Well, you see, she says she has something to talk about, her mother is really having fits over us, and Marilee doesn't know where to turn. We have to talk it over. I'm worried. She says she'd do anything to avoid hurting her mother, but then there's this other thing, too."

Billy sounded splendidly impersonal about the bond between him and Marilee.

"I see. So you don't think so, for tonight."

"I guess not, Phil. But soon, yay?"

"All right. Soon," said Phil.

"We're going to drive out to the lake tonight so we can talk alone," said Billy. "I'll tell you how it comes out."

"Thanks."

"Don't be like that. This is really a problem we've got."

"Yes. I know."

"I hope you do."

"I do."

"Then just have confidence in me."

Phil nodded, and they separated. He went alone that evening to see a film and when he came to Central, where the theatre was, he was as never before aware of the quality of the evening. The main street was almost deserted. Stripped of its daytime human liveliness the town was open to the sky, and he saw that the almost full moon shone in the east even as the sun went down beyond the western rim of the plains. The moon's pale oval against the rising dusty blue shadow of the earth's great curvature struck him to the heart with a pang to invoke sorrow—over what, he could not say. A little chill came and then went as the sun vanished and the moon rode alone and began to shed its steady opulence across the great emptiness of the land. It was an evening and a night which forecast the coming of spring, with all its transforming powers, from which some took general pleasure, others the separate strike at the flesh, made equally of pain and ecstasy.

❧ ❧ ❧

No matter which way you looked, in any daytime, at the end of every street in Belvedere you saw the plains. The long laterals of the land seemed to echo visibly the unseen strands of air moving above the earth. Lakes of light in the sky woven with long twines of silver cloud were enough to melt the heart. In April, dampness rose from even that dry earth along with the breath of wildflowers which were beginning their brief season. Spring seemed to come right into town along every street bringing reminders of what bloomed overnight. People from Belvedere drove out in their cars to see the plains in flower. It was a ritual for young and old alike.

They would drive in a great triangle of many miles, from Belvedere to Orpha City to Euclid, and home, and they would see shasta daisies, white and purple verbena, orange, white, and yellow poppies, and the grape hyacinth, and yellow black-eyed daisies, and Queen Anne's lace. They would see the tender feathery green of new mesquite leafage, and along irrigation canals the wild kaffir corn.

Home again, they were enfolded in the most powerful glory of all, and that was, toward the end of April and in May, the lilacs which stood in bloom against many a house and along many a yard, releasing into the air an invisible dome of fragrance over the whole city which, before the gasoline automobile, old-timers always said they could inhale from far out on the old roads leading in from Orpha, Whitewater, or Euclid. Even the motorists could receive the fragrance once they were back again in the streets of town. If it was wonderful in late afternoon, it would be even more so after dark, when the moon would be up, with the air a little cooler, and everything still, so that you would be able to notice more clearly something by itself, after the confusions of a busy day.

[ 169 ]

Well. It was hard to say just what they felt to be different from other times when spring came, especially as they grew older. Unspoken, perhaps rarely now lighted in the front of the mind, but somewhere deep in the being, came penetrations of the senses by all that seemed to promise new impulse—color, scent, sound—which gave people hopes of being more themselves than ever, and yet better. All life was sharply dearer; and at the same time, all was more sad, for by its very nature, the power brought by spring was transitory, and who felt its fresh loveliness felt also the certainty of its passage. Many a man and woman continued to harbor through all their days the submerged thoughts and desires of youth, while comporting themselves in ways becoming to their actual age. If they ever heard each other say, now and then, with comic rebelliousness, "Yes, but I don't *feel* old," they knew they were not talking about mere aches in their bones. They knew also, preferring not to think about it, that powers beyond their control never ceased the silent work of resolving with finality the contradictions in any life, whether these were ever understood for what they were, or even noticed.

Older people had seen spring go by often enough to believe that it must go. Young people, no. For they were themselves the time of spring, and what others saw once a year, as it came and must go, in the lilacs and the silver wafts of cloud in the sky by day and the pour of the moon by night, the youngsters seemed to keep all year round. For them, a more acute feeling came into the blood, as if spices had entered their veins, and driven them from spirit to flesh, thought to tissue. The young people together, seen at any distance, were like motes of life—perhaps the high school scientists would have said molecules—glistening in constant visible storms of movement, acting and interacting among themselves with what in union would seem like mindless and aimless motive; but taken separately, their storms were all internal, and the turmoil of these mostly suppressed, to be released only in the commonplaces upon which all agreed as signals of opinion at any given moment. The poverty of power to express in which most were confined required everyone to speak in a limited use of the inexhaustible language which was their inheritance. So, too, the need to think freshly was often diverted into the conventions of their hour; and the one or two or three of the young who found ways to escape it became either heroes or outcasts. Parents thought endlessly about their young, but as individuals; and yet the young created a society with its own tyrannies of style which required all to be more or less alike. What remained as the most visible, and the most touching, impression, was the vitality of the students, which incessantly celebrated the process of life of which they were the newest illustrations. Their wilfulness, which they believed to be their own brilliant invention, was but the assertion of forces to which they, like their parents before them in their own season, could only be obedient.

The vital youth in those bodies and eyes and breaths, their intentions and purposes, were all they yet knew; and wouldn't these be all they would ever know, which therefore must last forever?—of that much they were sure.

The wits, the limitations of their certainty, spoke through the young individually, as in a note which Billy wrote to Marilee and passed to her in class. When she read it she felt such a mixed surge of love and suppressed laughter, that she thought she might faint. She managed to control herself, and send him a look across the room which was like a kiss of his eyes by hers.

But there was that about the note which—despite its private passion—she could not help revealing to someone else, who, she decided, must be Phil. She handed it to him when they met in passing after school. It read,

> I am carzy about you angle. Let us keep
> our love scared.

Phil handed it back and said,
   "Yes, but was he making it funny?"

"Oh, no, the crazy darling, he simply can't spell," and she recited the love in the note as he had spelled the words, and its illiteracy seemed to make what it revealed all the more imperative. Laughing with desire, Marilee made Phil see the simple health of Billy in all its abstract power.

"Well, yes," said Phil.

"I thought you'd laugh with me," she said. "Don't be sad."

"All right," he replied, "I won't be sad."

She kissed him lightly and ran away.

※ ※ ※

Throughout the town it was generally known when Billy Breedlove called a meeting of the high school track team and pep squad to be held in the gymnasium on the Friday afternoon before the second Saturday in May. The fathers of the students were as concerned in the games of the school as their sons. Many of them had once sat before the same lockers. Seeing those young bodies hurling themselves through space nowadays, they could see their own in former days. Victory was the idea, as in any war; and war organized by scores, points, rules, fouls, penalties, and waves of spectator excitement or despair meant as much to the parents as to the young. They knew together that the spring sports were in for trouble that year. It was agreed that if anyone could help a poor outlook, Billy was the one to do it.

When, as they remembered, he ran down the field in his football uniform, dodging like a deer, he made everybody feel they were running with him, and if he won a triumph, they were made to feel that they helped him to win. One time after making a touchdown last fall he was pulled off the field so the coach could send in a substitute and give Billy a brief respite. He came to the bench from mid-field trotting slowly and looking nowhere. He hardly seemed to belong there. He seemed to be in another time, when everything that happened was a wonderful deed. He reached the sidelines sweating and streaked with dirt. He carried his helmet under his arm. His shoulder pads were crooked. Under his crimson jersey he breathed like a bellows. His padded thighs moved in short, slow, pistonlike strokes. The air was cracked with cheers for him. Marilee ran forward to meet him. Small as he was, he seemed to loom over her and everyone there. He took her to him. With his loins thrust forward and his shoulders arched over her, he kissed her roughly in front of the whole crowd and then set her away and went to the bench, got his blanket and threw it around himself and sat down. Through that kiss, those watching kissed each other. Marilee turned violently pink and her eyes cast blue lights over those she had to face when she returned to her place in the stand.

"Oh, that dog's-body," she exclaimed in her special slang, a laughing cry of love, disguised as mockery.

They had seen a hero, in his greatness isolated from his fellows, claim the reward of prowess, though they would not have said it so. Supremely he had put his sign on the girl he loved.

The Friday meeting was called to order by Phillipson Durham, the team manager, who then turned it over to the captain.

"I never make speeches, as you know," said Billy, who then went on to speak, putting his sign upon all in another way.

"But I can make a talk when I have to, and somebody has to make one here today. You all know what I'm talking about. I'm talking about the fact that there is too much talk going around to the effect that this track meet tomorrow is already out of our hands. Now nobody denies that we're in a tight spot. Everybody knows why. But this happens to every team sooner or later, and the fact that we lost our three best men last year by graduation puts us in a bad disadvantage against Orpha City. On top of that, we've got another good man out with a knee cartilage. On top of that, Orpha City has got one of the best turnouts this year that they've ever had. And on top of that, certain people I could name who are right here in this room have not been too damn conscientious about not breaking training. And maybe it will snow tomorrow morning in the middle of May, and maybe the pep squad will lose their voices over night, and maybe the Communists have planted a bomb in our locker room.

"All this and more.

"Well, I don't care. All I say is that the meet has not been run off yet, and too many people are sitting around as if we had already lost it. I don't know if we are going to win or lose it, but I do know one thing, I know that anybody who doesn't feel and act as if we are good enough to win it until the very last minute hasn't any right to claim he's a citizen of this city."

He paused and stared at them face by face. He would soon resume.

They all leaned forward to listen, to see him as closely as possible. They were the other half of the ritual drama without which their pledge to earning the right to fight would be empty. They felt abashed and gloried in their abashment; and they felt resentful, and knew that this was part of getting their blood stirred up to a winning pitch. They had all heard much the same message many times before, and knew all the words; yet the pep talk was always new to them, and especially so when Billy made it. If they had to be reviled to become great, then it must be he, their strongest self, who must do it for them. To conjure hope out of a hopeless situation—this they silently challenged him to do.

Billy raised his voice until he sounded hoarse.

"I'm sick and tired of hearing all this talk of letting this one go and laying our plans to win it next year. This isn't next year. This is this year, and we are us, right here and now, and all we've got to work with is us, and I don't care how fast they can run, or how high they can jump, or how far they can throw things over at Orpha City, when they come over here tomorrow morning and line up on our track out there, I want to see every man in this squad act as if he was a better man than any man they've got on theirs. What do you know? Maybe there'll be some surprises. What do you know? Goliath was a pretty big man but a pretty little one knocked him over. Just ask Reverend Priddle about that one. Do I make myself clear? The tougher the spot, the tougher the man. When the going is rough then is the time to show your speed. Do you know what I think?" He threw his rage at them in silence for a long scornful moment, then said, "I think all we need around here is a little show of spirit!"

His voice rang around in the girdered heights of the gymnasium. When its echo died away, he turned abruptly to Phil and said,

"Manager, you can finish up whatever arrangements you need to work out." He lifted his chin at Marilee, who sat with the cheerleaders. "Come on," he ordered, and strode out through the silent ranks of his schoolfellows. Marilee followed him in the dutiful manner of a consort.

He left behind him a sense of outrage which slowly changed to shame and then to memories of him in action. They had all seen him, played alongside him, often enough in his games—football, basketball, track. He was too light for football, too short for basketball, too stocky for track; but now and then he made the most brilliant play of the occasion. Tomorrow he was entered in the broad jump, the low hurdles, the hundred-yard dash, and the mile. They'd bet he would take a first in at least one of these.

What did he have? Why didn't everybody have it?

He had the power to make others want to be like him. They tried, now, as they adjourned the meeting in the gymnasium. It was a power proper to his season of life, and to the time of year in which he drove his spirit into them, in furious bestowal. It was spring, as nobody could escape knowing. It troubled the old and lonely. It inspired the young and heedless.

# IV. A Show of Spirit

And so when night came, drawing its scented darkness from across the plains to the east and bringing after that the rise of the biggest full moon in memory, too bright for stars, and alone in cloudless bounty, what was it young Breedlove thought he couldn't stand?

He couldn't stand the feeling, and do nothing about it, the feeling of night in May when the mockingbirds were all over town, on telephone wires, answering the moonlight with their lifting songs, and when the lilacs were full out of their buds above the sticky bittersweet skin of their branchwood. In his head was the angled skeleton of a grand project in prowess and wizardry—to make a myth for all the future out of what was worth the risk of legal, and perhaps mortal, trouble to achieve. How would it be to rise above the whole city and commit a sign of great daring, his sign, and show contempt for ruin, and make a declaration of triumph for the future, which, left anonymous, would be the marvel of all at daybreak?

This was the night for it, when the moon was sailing full and high, making shadows so black and deep that they had no far end, and showing, where the moonlight fell, such clear, pure, steady things to see that you couldn't blame anybody for seeing more than was there, and believing more than Belvedere, Texas, ever believed about anything.

❦ ❦ ❦

The moonlight was so strong beyond the bay window, and the scent of lilac drifted so steadily on the cool moving air that Homer Breedlove was kept awake. More sharply than he could remember, he had his old feeling about Billy, and he wondered if he should get up, cracking his long bones, and go down to the sleeping porch out back on the ground floor, to see how Billy was, and, if he slept, thrown down in his careless inert body, to wonder how greatly near he might be to manhood. You never really saw your children grow. You only now and then, at a separate moment, were struck by the fact that they had grown.

Every time they did grow, and did take further hold of the world, did the children take away a portion of the life held by their parents, until at last the children had all of it, and the parents had none, and were dead and gone, slowly killed by their own?

Well. What an idea. Hardly awake after all. And yet Homer did have an image in the moon-shattered darkness of how Mrs Underwood, for instance, looked the last time he saw her—thin, and pale, and haunted around the eyes by her wonderings about

Marilee. Homer would be glad to take and shake that pretty little girl, except that he knew he mustn't; but still, it was plain that she had worried her self-sacrificing mother into white hair before her time. Oh, yes, she was a sweet and lively child, and Billy was in charge of her, and why of course: if they were but four years older, and out of college, Homer, and he could speak for Ellen, would be glad and proud to see Billy and Marilee as man and wife. Perhaps then Mrs Underwood could leave off working for a spell, and take a vacation, even a trip, maybe (his breast warmed) she could go with him and Ellen to the Carlsbad Caverns which they had always wanted to see, the twilight flight of the bats, the Rock of Ages underground. They would be glad to take her, for she was good company when not worried, and after the wedding, she would want to let down for a spell. Homer saw the road map and which highways they would follow, driving westward to New Mexico, and on the way back, it would make a real *trip* to go by way of El Paso, a little out of the way, but what of it: visit Juárez, and then coming homeward along the Van Horn, Texas, highway, to see the Hueco Tanks, where outlaws of the old days used to rendezvous before robbing the Butterfield Stage, with black bandannas over their faces.

Well. He sighed. There was no use in all that because they weren't even married yet.

"Oh, Homer," murmured Ellen beside him, "stop fretting and get to sleep. I'm exhausted."

He held his breath briefly and wondered if it was worth disturbing Ellen further by getting up, then, and going down to see how Billy was, just as he used to do when Billy was a little boy. He never knew when she slept or not during his wakeful hours. Ellen needed her sleep. His throat thickened at the thought of her loyal goodness and hard work, her happy nature, so quick, so *ahead* of him. He had never caught her with a humorous riddle which she could not guess. —If she had drifted off now, he should not trouble her by getting up. He was so big that he could not move without stirring all the bed. No. He quieted himself with music, which always had the power to speak to him directly, and govern his feeling.

What if he had gone on with his singing instead of marrying and going into business? Concert tours, recordings, Red Seal, applause, bowing from the stage, signing programs for school children? Instead, this house; this wife, those children; that youngest downstairs who was neat and clean but private and unpredictable. He would not have anything otherwise, if only they were all safe.

Silent to Ellen beside him, Homer summoned up music in his throat with his mouth closed and on his controlled breathing he sounded for his inner ear the orchestral strains with harp chords introducing the piece of music he considered the most beautiful ever written for baritone, which he sang better than anyone else he knew. It was the aria of the evening star from *Tannhäuser,* and when it was time for his entrance with the melody, he embarked in his mind on its long, tasteful, gloomy line, making his eyes water at the loveliness of his performance, which brought him peace and calm, proper, somehow, to this moon-lavished night. He wished along with the refrain that his son Billy could know something as calm and peaceful in himself—Billy whom he wondered about, and whom he desired to visit in the moonlit air to gaze upon him from the doorway of the sleeping porch with a father's baffled, envious concern.

But he did not go, and for his peace of mind, for a few hours of that night, anyhow, it was as well, for Billy was gone.

"A creature of the night"—it was a phrase Billy remembered having read somewhere, and now it described him to himself. Everything he best remembered happened to him at night, he was sure. When he and Phil spent the night months ago out on Fourth Island and got shot at by person or persons unknown, much wondering seemed to have opened up, though he could not say just how. Perhaps before that they had been boys, and were now men, and, speaking for himself, full of new certainties. Since then, other nights. One in particular another full moon ago. In consequence, Billy felt he owned this particular night.

Softly he went away from his sleeping porch along the shadow of a row of tamarisk which led to the shallow earth tank in back of his father's house. There he dipped his hands in the moon-speckled water and splashed his face, which felt hot. Letting his skin dry in the air, he struck out across the open fields that would lead him away from the streets to Phil's house, on one of the other edges of town.

On the way he had to cross the railroad tracks. Where they made a slow curve northward, the rails caught the moonlight and made two ribbons of bright silver leading into nowhere. The shine of points and edges in the moonlight had the power to make his thoughts swell and his flesh feel strenuously active even as he merely walked over the irregular ground of newly plowed fields. But he walked, he was sure, like a great, hitherto unknown, member of the cat species.

He still had the equivalent of four blocks to go to reach the Durhams' house at the corner of Railroad Avenue and Cleveland Street, where the town paving ran out, when he heard a dog begin to bark in the dim distance ahead of him. He paused. He should have been ready for it. Such small matters could destroy the greatest of plans. Standing still, he listened.

It was a large dog, for his voice was deep and his barks were slow-paced. He held his last note in each series of barks, which meant that his muzzle must be turned up toward the moon. He was alone, for no other dog barked with him. He was a sentinel in the night, ready to signal when he heard someone coming. He might be a savage dog, prepared to attack whom he heard. But also, he might simply be sitting on his haunches and addressing the moon, now that he had been stirred up to notice anything. For a great circle all around in the flat land he was the only immediate source of sound. It could be too that his nature was simply responding to the glory of receiving and commanding the whole night.

Billy could not know. But he decided to act as though he did know, and that what he knew was propitious. He decided that this was a lonely dog, making a night song for the need of it, and that the only way to meet him was to go carefully to him and make friends. If he got his hand bitten off instead, why, then, Billy would know that the dog didn't want to make friends, that was all.

He walked on, heading straight for the sound of the dog. Presently he heard the dog break off in the middle of a hornlike howl. The dog was listening for him, so close now. Billy moved slowly toward him, but steadily. Against a dim, dark farmhouse, he could see him, a great collie.

Seeing Billy in turn, he came off his haunches to all fours and began to ruffle a deep growl in his chest, taking in breaths with slavering hauls in his throat. His long heavy body was tense with danger. Billy stopped four feet from him and went down on one knee and put forward his hand.

"Come on, boy," he said in a whispered, chuckling voice. "Come on, boy. Come on." He softly snapped his fingers in the dark. "What that. What that. Come on, boy."

The dog reduced his growling and gazed away across the land as if he were too proper to notice anyone directly.

"That right," breathed Billy. "That right, boy. Come on see your Uncle Billy. Come on, boy."

The collie went silent, and lifted his muzzle toward Billy to sniff of fear, and scenting none, took a step forward, and paused, and then another. His plumy tail made a tentative lift. Billy stayed immovable, softly speaking and reaching for him, and by slow, almost shamed, steps, the dog came to him and let him lay his hand on his head and rough him gently about his dusty long-haired ears and say, "That right, boy. Your old Uncle Billy. Right, boy. Good boy."

He slowly stood up.

"You coming with your old Uncle Billy?"

The collie stood irresolute, and Billy turned and walked on. The dog watched him in silence, and let him go. Billy laughed silently.

"That's the way to fix 'em," he reflected.

It was his night and world. The moon made his skin prickle with electric feelings and he quickened his pace because he could not wait to get Phil and tell him of the enterprise which lay ahead.

The Durhams' old two-storey wooden house stood by itself at the corner of a farm belonging to someone else. The unpainted clapboards were silvered by weathering. No light showed in any of the windows. Phil's window was all but obscured by the grove of lilac bushes, for they now showed dense clusters of bloom fully open at the top.

Billy opened his way through the stiff branches which held the heavily sweet blossoms and their bitter leaves. Stirring the bush as he armed his way into it to the side of the house, he released waves of fragrance. The branches closed behind him and he stood trapped in the lilac grove before Phil's open window which was dark. He ached for the rapt confusion of senses and objects which consumed him as it drove him to action—the moonlight in the lilacs, their breath in his, the valor that seemed never to cease of its stirring in his loins, the gift of his eyes to see in the night, the power in his arms, the spring of his thighs, and the idea of tomorrow and the track meet for which he felt responsible alone.

He heard Phil muttering in sleep and leaned closer as a word or two came clear—"Yes, what else, what else!" groaned Phil.

Billy laughed silently and lifted himself to the windowsill and leaned into the darkness of the little room calling in a strong whisper,

"Phil! Wake up! Phil!"

He turned to hear if he had disturbed anyone upstairs, but there came no creaking sound of parental alertness, and he called Phil again.

༝ ༝ ༝

Phillipson Durham sat up, knowing at once who filled his window against a moonlit sky broken by leaves.

"Billy?"

"Get up and be quiet and get your clothes and come on."

"Where?"

"Don't talk now. Just come on."

Phil took a moment to come fully awake. The dream out of which he had been muttering hung over him still. But in a moment he found his clothes in the dark and handed them to Billy, and let himself out of the window to the ground within the lilac grove. There he pulled on his shirt, trousers, and shoes, and followed Billy out through the bushes and across the road into a field where last year's corn still stood dry and broken. Billy led the way rapidly through the stalks to the far side of the field.

"What were you dreaming of when I woke you?" he asked.

[ 186 ]

Phil said, with a comic sigh,

"It was exactly the wrong minute to call me."

"You were panting about something."

"I often have the same dream."

"What about?"

"It ends before I know for sure. —You remember when we heard the voices over on Fifth Island? I dream that I hear them again, and I am just about to hear what they're saying, when something happens and I wake up."

Billy laughed.

"I've got something better for you to listen to. Listen to this. Look at that."

Free of the field, they saw before them a few scattered houses, and in the distance along the highway east the lights of a car going along clear and fast, and beyond that the whole immense sweep of the plains to the south, where the moonlight lay like snow on the ground, and against all that, rising only a few hundred yards away into the pour of moonlight as though to draw all of it and take it and make it shine for its own, the great pearl of the water tank which seemed to hang in mid-air of itself; for if in the night you half-closed your eyes to look at it, the tower's steel supports vanished away.

"I see it," said Phil, as if seeing the water tower for the first time. There was something awesome in the stroke of moonlight on its roundness, and in the excitement of Billy as he spoke of it.

"I'll tell you what we're going to do," he said, "I'll tell you as we go."

"There's a bucket of green paint over in back of Guy's garage," said Billy, "I know just where, and there's a big brush in a can of kerosene. I know because I used it yesterday, and we'll go by and get them, and then pick up Marilee, she knows, and then we'll come back to the tower and do it. It'll take both you and me. You've got to hold the paint while I handle the brush. How do you like it?"

"The greatest," answered Phil, but with a pang of hopelessness that he was still bounded by Belvedere's view of the worthwhile passions of the world.

"We've got to swear never to tell anybody we did it," said Billy in a hushed voice meant to awe himself as well as Phil. "If they ask us, we've got to tell a lie. Will you?"

"I guess so. —It may be risky."

"To tell a lie? Everybody tells good lies."

"No. To climb up there and do the job."

"Oh, that. Certainly. Certainly it's dangerous. Where would be the spirit in it if it wasn't dangerous? That's what everybody is going to be thinking the minute they see it tomorrow morning. They'll know that the city crew always use safety belts when they go up there. That ol sombitch is ninety feet high. They'll know no city man with their safety belt would go up and do a thing like our thing. They'll think, Now, nobody could have gone up there if he wasn't willing to risk his neck. It's one thing to go up there as a workman with a safety belt, and like that, but it's another to go up there and balance yourself on that catwalk, and lean back out, the way you have to, to reach up and paint big letters on the tank. And then what will they ask? They will ask, What for? And then they'll say, Why, to beat Orpha City, and then they'll know, and then they'll have to beat Orpha to make up for everything. See? See?"

They were heading across upon fields toward the warehouse and into town and Billy paused to turn and gaze at the silver tank abiding so serenely aloft in the moonlight.

"Isn't she a beauty, though," he said softly, for now it was about to belong to him, as if he had the conviction of a citizen who knows that if he is to find beauty in the world, he must first find it at home. "You know, she holds one hundred and one thousand gallons. And that little catwalk up there is only about eighteen inches wide. I checked. Did you know that? We'll have to step carefully, like a couple of actual cats, maybe the very cats they named the catwalk after!"

"What is the best time to go up there?" Phil asked. His belly was hollow over the idea. "Maybe we should wait until just before dawn, so there will be absolutely no one around to catch us."

"Wait a minute," said Billy. "Let me think of a good objection to that." The idea of postponing the great enterprise was painful to him. "Let me see. Yes. I know. The light will be wrong if we wait until then."

"Light? What light?"

"The moonlight. Pretty soon, the moon will be so far along that the near side of the tank will be in shadow, and we won't be able to see what we're doing."

"Well, yes, then. But by the same token, if we are in the bright moonlight before that, anybody could see us."

"Nobody's going to see us! That's where Marilee comes in. She is going to be down there to warn us if anybody is coming. Besides, people only see, mostly, what they expect to see. Have you ever tried anyone on that? I have, and it's true. Nobody's expecting us to be up there! Once up there, I'll be fast. I'll be done in no time. You just hold the old bucket for me."

"You know," said Phil, "I'm not much good in high places."

"Holy crow, neither am I. It always makes me s'rink together down in my balls and feel hollow if I merely look off some place high. That's another reason we have to do it. Everybody feels the same way, and they'll know how we felt! —Take it easy now, the Marshal sometimes checks out around the warehouse about this time, and then he comes back along the tracks, and he might catch us."

Billy pulled Phil down beside him in a miniature forest of winter weeds which, dry and rusty, still stood along the railroad embankment. Before them lay the town, asleep but for the late passengers waiting at the bus station, or the handful of movie-goers walking fast and bemused to their isolated cars at the conclusion of the last show, or a few night workers who came and went for coffee at the Saddle and Sirloin on the corner of Main and Buchanan, catty-corner from the Bluebonnet Hotel and Coffee Shop. The moonlight was so strong that it washed out much of the color in the neon signs of downtown, which gave to darker nights their violent glow in the air. The avenues of town lay northwest-southeast, according to the way the tracks of the Roscoe, Snyder and Pacific crossed the county, and were num-bered instead of named, except for Central Avenue which paral-leled within town the tracks several blocks out on its edge. The cross streets were named for presidents of the United States, omitting Abraham Lincoln, for whose name Jefferson Davis was substituted, and ending with Grover Cleveland, since Belvedere ran out of streets before it did presidents.

This was where throughout their early years the two watchers in the moonlight formed their likeness of the world. The quiet houses on whose roof the moonlight dwelled like peace, the silent streets cupped with shadows under the leafing trees of spring, the invisible but unforgotten courses of people going through their days in Belvedere, each privately remarkable and publicly similar, the weight of the letters spelling home, all had their effect on Billy and Phil as they watched from their weedy brake. Billy seemed content to idle for a moment, which was unlike him. Then with suppressed energy in his voice, he said,

"It's a funny thing. When a man gets married, he is the same man, but he turns into somebody else, too."

"You don't mean, just growing up?"

"No, not just that. I mean the man looks just about the same to everybody else, but he looks different to himself." He paused as though to let the mysteries of the future appear to him; and then he added calmly, "This is the last year I intend to be called Billy."

"Try and stop them," said Phil. An edge of bitterness was in his voice but Billy did not hear it. When had the other two decided to be married? Why had he not been told less casually? He felt newly forlorn. He had never thought of losing Marilee forever, or for that matter, of seeing Billy become for life, as he should have expected, someone else—a married man. To mask his feeling, he repeated, "Try and stop them."

"I'll stop them. —Phil," said Billy in a sort of breathed voice, "I guess you're my best friend, though it's nothing to ever talk about, but I guess I can tell you what I wouldn't want ever to tell anybody else."

"I guess so," said Phil.

Billy was silent for a while, and then said,

"Marilee wanted to go out to Whitewater with me that night you asked us to the movies, you know? It was another night sort of like this one. We have that problem, about her mother and her church—they have been at her again. So we went out that night, and something made her think of Ben Grossman, and she wanted to see where he drove over the bank into the lake. I told her she was morbid and she said yes, she was, but that maybe thinking about people worse off might make her feel better. That's unworthy of you, I said, and she said, Yes it was. We drove around the lake to the place, and I showed it to her. The water was black as tar, right where the old alkali edge dips straight down. I said to her, Now don't you get to thinking about it again, it was a long time ago. And she said, Yes, I know, but I keep thinking how fast it must have been once he went in, I hope it was fast anyway, she said, if there was no way for him to turn around and come out again. I would certainly want to turn around fast and come out again, she said, wouldn't you? I said Yes, sir. Then she hugged my arm and said, Let's get away from here quick. We drove up along the lake road in Guy's pickup that I borrowed."

His voice died away. Thinking of the place, the sort of night, Marilee with Billy driving out alone along the lake, Phil felt a stirring of his blood, a prickling all through him as if cinnamon or fine pepper were there to be felt in him. He said to Billy silently, urgently, Don't, don't! But Billy began to speak in a hush again.

"Marilee, you know, she's the greatest. You know. I don't know. Anyhow. You know how things happen. Oh, remember that old speckled night hawk we heard? He was there again that night. And I heard the old catfish slap himself on the lake when we stopped the car and got out, I know it was him. You couldn't see far, but you felt you could see everything in the moonlight. I never heard a place so still, nobody for miles around. Well. Maybe if just one little thing, anywhere around—what's that!" he suddenly broke off to ask in an alerted whisper.

"Where!" asked Phil, unable so quickly to change the wonder aroused by what Billy meant to tell him.

"There! Someone is moving along the tracks there! Get down!"

From their cover in the weeds they watched a small bent figure go rocking along in a slow limp a little distance away out in the moonlight before them. It was Marshal Honeycutt. He had his flashlight with him, and as he came to the wool warehouse by the tracks, he beamed his light to see the face of each great sliding door on the loading platform above the track. The doors were safely padlocked. All was quiet, just as Marshal Honeycutt intended.

Billy nudged Phil and whispered,

"He thinks he is in charge of everything."

Old age was a joke played by the rest of the world on the progenitors. Poor old dads, what did they know of power, and joy, desire jumping alive, and plans, and purposes? The young could never remember that the grandfathers had known all these before anyone who came after. Crawling along like the kind of beetle which now and then walked upright by unfolding its hind hinges, Marshal Honeycutt seemed to belong to another kingdom than man's. His flashlight rays showed and vanished, showed and vanished, in a regular rhythm.

"Like an old lightning bug that I remember from a visit to East Texas when I was a boy," said Billy.

"You'd think he would have run out of juice by now."

In the urgency to be up and gone which made his thighs ache under restraint, Billy thought the old man would never finish checking the front of the warehouse. If ever the Marshal would finish, and then disappear around the rear side, then they might complete their plans in the weedy embankment—be up and away, or stay and confide. But instead,

"Look at that," whispered Billy. "He's just stopped, there, by the end of the deck."

The old man stood by the edge of the loading deck and swept his light all about him, taking in the whole night. His beam trembled slowly when he fixed upon some shape made obscure and challenging by the strong contrast between bright moonlight and dense shadow; for where these met, they created a sort of negative dazzle, and what was frank and reassuring in daytime could look new and bewildering to an old man in the splendor of the night.

"Go on, get on, get on," urged Billy.

As if he heard, the Marshal suddenly turned his light toward the two watchers. It peered like the eye of a one-eyed cat, and then growing drowsy, it drooped and went out.

"Now!"

But not yet. Marshal Honeycutt, alone in the stillness and comfort of the peace which he had established for himself, stepped to the edge of the deck. There, hunching himself and bending for greater ease in what he must do, he fondled open his loose trousers and in a moment began to urinate into the random grass beyond the boards.

"How do you like that!" breathed Billy savagely.

They could hear the faint whisper of it and they were outraged that the old fool—even if he was a famous killer in the old days—had anything left to make water with. It was an affront to young men, that exhausted reference to man's member of prowess and joy. Made to feel obscene and impatient, they were oddly chastened by such a reminder of prime fellow-manhood coming from a man half simple, who was yet clothed in the power of the municipality.

But as last he was done, and giving in the pour of moonlight an effect somehow rueful, Marshal Honeycutt turned along the loading deck and slowly disappeared around the end of the warehouse to inspect the far side.

"Now!"

They came out of their weedy cover, stirring the dust of early spring that still clung to the brittle stalks, and ran lightly along the tracks until they reached the crossing at Davis Street. There they came down to a walk, and with a strolling gait, such as became anyone going home to bed after a pleasant evening of harmless visiting, they made their illicit way over to First Avenue, where they turned west and followed Buchanan to the alley which divided the block. In the alley they walked a hundred yards, to enter the back yard of the Red Dot Garage. The time for talk was past—action awaited.

❊ ❊ ❊

Cut by the high roof of the hardware store next door, the
moonlight made two triangles, one bright, one dark, out of Guy
DeLacey's alley yard. The garage was locked for the night.
Whatever there wasn't room for inside was in the yard, and
more, too. It was at once junk pile, depot for spare parts canni-
balized from old cars, and outdoor museum.

"Watch it," said Billy, "or you'll break your neck getting
through."

They climbed over Guy's valued collection. In it rested a
likeness of the owner. Many a piece of salvaged or saved junk
bore witness to his imagination and his hunger for the material
discards of the world; for who knew what might not come in
handy one day in making something? And many a rusted relic of
manufacture told of the unsustained energy which had once
seized it to cherish for a job to be done on a good day that never
came.

"Guy is the only one else we're going to tell," said Billy.

"If you think it would be safe." Phil was unable to keep his
contempt for Guy out of his voice, but Billy was too intent on his
purpose to notice it. They were caught up in a plan of coordi-
nated action, and Phil had to admit that this was not the place or
time to tell Billy what he knew of Guy DeLacey's strangled
passions, whose evidence all about Phil now saw with a new eye,
and which, unless he told him, Billy would never see.

"Listen," said Billy, "Guy would know his own green paint,
anyhow, up there on the tank. And if he was here right now, he
would tell us not to break the law by defacing public property,
but he would never tell the police on us. He would just wait for
us and take us to have a cup of coffee afterwards. I have a key to
the back door of the Red Dot. After we're done we will bring the
paint bucket back here and then go inside and scrub ourselves, if

we have to, to get any green paint off us." He laughed. "Anybody caught around town tomorrow with any green paint on them is going to be in trouble."

They emerged from a balanced jumble of old objects and came under the rusted shed of corrugated iron which leaned to the rear of the Red Dot Garage. There they smelled paint. The sliding door of the garage was fresh with it.

"That's what I've been using the paint for," said Billy, "Guy had me painting the door. Here. Take the bucket while I find the brush and my piece of rope."

He handed the two-gallon bucket, half full of paint, to Phil, and then found the brush soaking in turpentine in a shallow coffee can. Coming out from the shadow of the shed, Billy had a length of clothesline looped around his neck, and he held the paint brush, sniffing at it. He said, "That's a smell I like." It was brush three inches wide. He swept it through the air in a grand arc to shake off the excess turpentine. "Get a good hold on that bucket and let's go."

Burdened as they were with the tools of their mission, they now must be doubly cautious as they went.

They kept to the alleys and the shadow side, and they held still if they saw any movement in the streets which crossed the alleys. Once they saw a streak of shadow dart out ahead of them from behind an ashcan, and they admired the silence of it, for it was a cat, who also knew how to use the night. Passing behind a lighted house, they went at a crouch behind the fence, and felt they passed through a perilous strait of spilled light. Sounds of gaiety came across the backyard. Someone was having a party, which had reached the stage of drunken song from men in the kitchen, and, in the front room, high sounds of women who all screamed their commonplaces without listening to each other.

Back in shadow, the marauders reached the next block in the alley, and were only one away from the railroad again. They saw the lights of a car growing along the cross street ahead and they froze near a public service transformer pole until the car should be gone by; but its lights grew and then fanned widely as the car turned and headed straight down the alley toward them. Without a word they both slid to the ground behind the thick wooden pole and ducked their heads. Billy swore in a whisper against his shoulder. The headlights would surely see them as the car bore down upon them. But the car slowed down well short of them and turned in through an open gate as the owner drove it home for the night. It was a close call. Half hoping for another, they went forward again with stealth and approached the end of the last block before the open country.

All was dark again except for amber lights in the upstairs apartment above the doctor's garage. The shades were drawn but light fell dimly on a tangle of telephone and public service wires threaded through the alley treetops. Soft music was playing on a radio within the apartment. Against the south side of the garage rose a great bouquet of the local lilacs in a bush as high as the second storey. Their color was paled by the moonlight and the diffused yellow lamplight from the apartment, but their scent was at full power, and on the breathing of the air, the sweetness of the lilacs entered and pierced everywhere. Billy risked a whisper.

"That's where Thyra Doolittle lives, where Tom Bob Gately used to be with her."

They gazed up at the lighted window which overlooked the alley, and just then, the light went out and they prepared to move on.

But someone within came and opened the window wide. The soft music came louder, and the lilac air went inside, where someone's life, once full, now lonely, made its days and nights. Thyra rested her tired arms on the windowsill and leaned a little way into the disturbing night.

In her floating thoughts, as so often happened in her recent years alone, she invoked an act of passion. Lifting her hands to cover her eyes, she murmured in memory, "Yes, yes," and "How lovely," and "My pretty little dear," while in her imagination love occurred. In a few seconds, her vision faded with her energy, and she returned to the immediate facts of the world. She looked at the moon, and at the high crown of the lilac bush, and at the long lane of the alley, half bright and half as dark as char. Not knowing that anyone was watching, she stretched forth her arms to the unreachable power of the lovely night like a girl in love, and let her voice, ardent, restrained, and loose, sing a few words to go with the gravelly trumpets of the popular love song which filled the world of her one-room kitchenette apartment above the doctor's garage. Years later, when he went to hear *Faust* during his first visit to Paris, Phillipson Durham, amidst the dusty opulence and ceremony of the performance, when Marguerite opened her lattice window to the pour of blue stage light on cloth rose bushes which created the Garden Scene within the proscenium of the Opéra, and addressed herself to the ecstasy waiting in the *"nuit d'amour,"* was carried back to that alley night of dust, ranging cats, and tinny music; for there, also, at the Paris Opéra, was an elderly lady reaching forth her arms, which bent back at the elbows, repeating the rapturous gesture of a virgin girl awaiting her first hour of carnal love, and singing of it in a voice etched by a thousand nights of experience.

Thyra's song ended, and so must she.

The cooling grandeur of the lilac bush made her shiver. She sighed and rubbed her nose with her knuckles and retired out of the moonlight into her box of darkness and unminded survival. Below, the two boys waited in case her music or her light might be resumed, but nothing came, and, with Billy intent on details of the work to come, and with Phil feeling obscurely that he had observed an interlude of respect for the dead, they left Thyra Doolittle's corner of the alley and cut across First Avenue when nothing was coming, and in another minute were on the other side of the tracks approaching open country again.

They gave one look back over town to be sure they were clear of it. An airy continent of white steam was rising and changing above the bank of condensers at the public service plant. They looked the other way, toward the north, and saw their vast pearl, floating in the air on its own crescent of shadow. Now it seemed to wait for them. The idea made their bellies tense with joy and danger. Yes, yes, it was dangerous, and that made what they felt—the "moon-prickling" was the word Phil found for it—even worse, more urgent, and more wonderful. Phil's arm ached remotely from holding the pail of paint carefully away at his leg, and of not spilling any which would make a trail to follow in daylight. He wondered if he were bracingly near to discovery—of what, he could not think. Was it knowledge? Proof of powers? Some act which would grant him a certain freedom for life? He did not know, for such words were far-reaching, and everything he knew, in that time, was local, except in the summoning vistas of his imagination.

᧥ ᧥ ᧥

Marilee's house was at the end of Buchanan Street where the paving once again gave way to a dusty road. It had a picket fence around its little yard. They came toward it from the side, and Billy paused for a moment, as if to complete what he had been saying when the sight of Marshal Honeycutt interrupted him earlier. But if he had something more to add, he thought better of it, and they went on; and in a moment Billy chuckled softly and said,

"Look at that, she left the picket gate open so it wouldn't have to make a creak and a crack when she came out to join us."

They didn't come to the fence but went softly on across the

road. Out of the shadows of her house where her mother lay asleep, Marilee ran lightly into the moonlight to come to them. She touched Billy on the neck with her fingers in a caress but kept silent as they hurried down the road to the entrance of Dillingham Park in which the water tower stood.

The girdered legs of the tower were lost in lilac bushes. Gravelled walks were laid out all around the base of the tower. The tracks, the warehouse, the city, were behind to the south; reaching away to the north was nothing but open country. The silence was edged with the distant tire-song of occasional cars speeding on Highway 31. It was now safe to talk, but excitement kept their voices tense and low. Billy said,

"Here we go up, boys!"

"I'm going up with you," said Marilee.

"Oh, no you're not," said Billy.

"Yes, I am. —Phil, I can go, can't I?"

Phil shrugged.

"I'm not the captain."

She heard something in his voice which made her think of some wound deep within him of which he himself might not know. She put her hands on his cheeks and pressed him there, saying,

"Oh, Phil, you absolute darling, what would we ever do without you!"

"You'd survive," he said.

"No, she's right," said Billy.

"So am I," answered Phil.

"It's all crazy," said Marilee.

Billy sensibly kept to his immediate point.

"No, you see, Marilee, you have a job to do for us down here, which is why we can't all go up."

"Oh, I have?"

"Yes, you have. You have to keep an eye and an ear out in every direction down here to find out the first minute you can if anybody's coming, and if they are, you have to give us a signal, so we can get down fast and away. We're going to deface public property, you know. That's a misdemeanor. Maybe a felony. You didn't come along just for the ride. You're important to the whole thing."

"Oh, dog's-body of the world," breathed Marilee, and Phil could hear the gleeful love in her voice, "I know what you're doing, Billy, you're practicing leadership on me. I don't suppose you can help it. You idiot."

"Thank you," said Billy. "Let's not get to exchanging compliments now. Time is passing. Phil, shuck your clothes off." They began to shed shirts, jeans, shoes. Billy continued, "Now, Marilee, you keep our clothes bunched up so if we have to get down and run off we'll be able to pick them up easy."

"How do I signal you?" she asked.

"Like this: whistle." He made a soft whistle on two notes.

She tried it.

"That's it," he said. "Come on, Phil. Here we go."

Wearing only their shorts and the moonlight on their skins, they moved to the near leg of the tower. There they had to haul themselves like nimble apes up to the first cross-bar of the scaffold ten feet above ground. When they reached it, Billy let down his length of clothesline and Marilee tied it to the handle of the paint bucket. Billy tugged gently at first, felt it hold, then brought up the bucket, in which the wide brush half-floated, then nodding to Phil to reach for it he untied the rope and threw it down to Marilee.

Billy looked up. The first rungs of the steel ladder were within reach now. Phil looked with him, all the way to the end where the rungs looked no greater than small pins. Phil looked quickly down again. Billy turned toward him.

"The matter?" he asked in a harsh whisper.

"I get a gone feeling, looking up there," said Phil.

"Can you make it?"

"I don't know."

"Yes. I see. Too bad. Listen. We can do it one of two ways. You tell me which."

"Billy, it's not like being just scared. I'm scared, yes. But this is something else. I'm just not even *there,* when I look up and think of it."

"I know. Now listen. Nobody is going to turn back now. Now, either I can lead the way up and show you how it's done, just one rung at a time, and you keep your eyes on me, and never look back, or down. That's one way. Or you can go up first and I'll follow you to be there to whack your butt or steady you if you slip. Now how about it. How about it."

The night air stirred across their skins and fondled the heavy lilac clusters below. Marilee looking up called out,

"What's the delay? What's the matter?"

Billy disdained to reply. He made a big breath and said,

"Now, Phil, I felt my gut fall right out of me when I looked up there a minute ago. I know how it is. I'm frank to say I'm scared piss-limber, so don't go to feeling bad all by yourself. Let's just go, how about it?"

"All right," said Phil. "I'll go first, and you come on close after me."

"I'll take the bucket now and give it to you up there. Here you go."

He gave Phil a hoist toward the thin ladder of steel, and looking only at each rung at the level of his eyes, Phil started up. He heard Billy laboring behind him, for the bucket was an awkward burden. But Billy's spirits rose as he saw Phil climbing, climbing, and he made little gasps of happiness and fooling through which Phil heard an occasional word—"sons-a-bitches won't believe it when they—" and "Oh, Lordy, this is—" and once Phil's name, pronounced with scoffing admiration as if to confound anyone who thought Phil might turn out to be a coward. In his anxiety, Phil went too rapidly, and Billy called to him, spacing his words to meet his actions as he climbed,

"Take—it—easy—don't—get—winded—we'll—last—better—."

Phil reduced his pace and began slowly to feel an exhilaration he never expected as they approached the catwalk. The ladder met it through a square hatchway. When he came through it to the narrow deck, he had a sense of triumph.

"Come on, Billy! Come on!" he said, leaning over to take the bucket from him so he could ease himself up to the deck also.

"What did I tell you!" cried Billy.

Their voices must have carried out across the plains as if across water. Phil looked far out over the town. From that height the streets looked like a plan for a town, drawn in scattered Christmas lights.

"Now, don't look down," said Billy. "Face the tank with me."

Only then did either of them see how difficult and full of chance was the job of painting their message on the curved surface of the great sphere. The catwalk was too narrow to allow them to step back from the tank at all. To wield his brush, Billy would have to lean backward as he raised his arm to paint his letters. The protecting rail was little more than knee-high. Half the great sphere was below them, half above.

"Some deal," said Billy, recognizing as Phil did the risk of any movement but one simply upright and perfectly balanced. "We should have brought our safety belts."

Looking up they saw the perfect cheek of the tank curving away in a slow arc toward the sky, and the little lines of rivets which held the metal plates of the tank together, and the welded eyelets where the snap-fasteners of safety belts were usually attached. Phil touched the tank. It was cool to his hand. He knocked it with his knuckles and made a sound which travelled deep within to fade away in rings of watery echo.

"All right. Come on now. Inch along after me," said Billy. "We have to start left of here to get the spacing right and have the words face town."

Moving with sensible caution, he sidestepped along the catwalk and Phil followed him holding the bucket until they were five feet past the hatchway. Billy looked up over his shoulder to see if he was at the center of the moon's pouring light.

"Just right," he said, turning toward Phil and giving him a screwed-up wink.

Phil held the bucket toward him. Billy reached in and grasped the brush and hauled it out dripping. Unconvincingly, he took the stance of how he imagined an artist would behave, his left hand elegantly spread akimbo on the front of his thigh, his right hand aloft with the brush in a mincing flourish, and in his face mockery that made Phil catch his exuberance and laugh. Phil set the bucket on the metal deck.

"How you spell *beat?*" asked Billy, and without waiting for the answer, he began to sweep a capital B as large as he could spread it on the face of the tank. The paint slopped and ran, but the main strokes were so vigorous that the big letter took shape firmly. He dipped for more paint and made the double belly of the B with great sweeps. "E," he said, and they moved along a few steps to make room for it. Phil slid the bucket along between his feet. Billy dipped and slashed away with the style of one inspired. When they reached A he said, "I won a whole page of gold stars in first grade for making good capital A's," and he painted the A with three long, slapped strokes.

Suddenly he thought he heard something and froze still.

"What's that!" he whispered.

They listened but heard nothing.

"What!" asked Phil.

"Hush!"—Billy shook his head sharply to silence him while he cocked his head and strained to hear danger. There was none to threaten from below, but the idea of it belonged to the whole venture, and Billy thought that if perhaps he stopped to listen to it, it might come to be there.

Phil looked down to see if Marilee was trying to reach them with a warning gesture. He saw her just before he shut his eyes; for the look straight down, where she stood with upturned face, so small, a pale blossom against the indeterminate light and shadow of the ground and the bushes, broke his forgetful confidence. A weight of dread made him want to topple away from the tank and enter into a fall which, as it was only in his thought, would never end. His loins turned cold and felt like part of the earth toward which they pulled to be united. His mouth dried. He thought he must never open his eyes again as long as he lived, and therefore must live forever on the catwalk of the water tower. He put his hand to brace against himself upon the tank. His hand could never come away from that single reassuring surface.

"Nothing after all," said Billy, relaxing his alarm. He dipped his brush to make his T. "Move along there now. We have to leave a nice space in here between words."

Sliding the bucket along with his left hand, Phil felt his way with his right along the cheek of the tank. He was unable to speak a sound. Billy noticed nothing of his panic. "Orpha City," he said, "two more words to go, we're doing right nicely."

He swept the great O in one motion, but the paint ran thin and he had to dip and renew the lower curve of the letter. "We got enough paint to last us?" he inquired, but when Phil didn't reply, he said, "You all right?"

Phil's teeth chattered and Billy heard them.

"Well, come *on,*" he said in a husky, fond way, as to a dog, "we only got one word to go after this one, and then we'll go down from here, and get off into the night. Where's that paint?" and he sopped up what he needed to start his huge R. Phil managed to open his eyes and dared to look nowhere but at Billy, who was alive with exuberance. "Beat Orpha City!" Billy exclaimed, "we're getting there!" and reached for more paint. The way Phil looked made Billy respond with his famous leadership. He saw that he must make a joke out of the terror which held Phil all but paralyzed on the height.

With high spirits, as if they were playing around on the ground far below, Billy suddenly said,

"I'm going to put my sign on you!"

At that, he made a swift jab with his dripping brush at Phil's spare naked front to swab his skin with a big X in green paint, laughing with zest in his power.

Too fast for thought, Phil knocked Billy's arm aside to protect himself.

The blow at Billy's arm threw him out of balance. His arm flew out over the rail of the catwalk, and in another second, he tipped backward. The rail caught him behind the knees. Phil reached for him but he was gone. Phil saw one endless glimpse of a slowly turning, fast-falling weight of gleaming body in the moonlight, and saw the white soles of its feet, and he thought he heard a voice spiralling up saying his name on a cry that turned like the air and had no end when he covered his ears. He loosed himself against the cool moon-bathed tank as if to sleep upon it, appalled and safe.

꙳ ꙳ ꙳

Let's see, said Phil to himself. Yes. What needs to be done. Sensible. Of course. Just as soon as I work things out.

He heard a dim wail from below, and said to himself that he must be needed there, Billy must have had the breath knocked out of him. He felt his way against the tank back toward the hatch in the catwalk and when he reached it, he debated, not looking down and with a sense of great intelligence, the question as to which foot he should set first on the ladder for the descent. In the end, he lowered both bare feet to the top rung and felt how cold and thin the metal of it was. There were seventy-seven rungs to find and pass upward before his shaking body until he could be at the lower end of the ladder. In a crucial trial of his will, he started down, moving as slowly as a half-frozen insect.

"Oh, hurry, hurry!" he heard Marilee call.

He gasped in reply, imagining that he was already hurrying. When at last with his eyes shut he smelled the drenching breath of the lilacs he knew he was coming to the girder where the rungs ended ten feet above the ground.

"Oh," Marilee said to Billy in a heavied voice, "I cannot even touch you to help!"

When Phil came to the ground he saw what she meant.

Billy was too broken. They could not touch him for fear of breaking him more. He was lying face upward and pitiably twisted. His eyes were open seeing nothing. He was still fiercely grasping his paintbrush. By the bright moon they could see his heart striking fast like a frightened bird's heart in a little hollow of white skin below his breast bone.

"Oh, Phil, what can we do!"

"I'll run for help." But he was shaking, and Marilee saw that he might fail.

"No! I will! I will find a telephone. Stay with him. Oh, make him hear you and help you to keep him going. Oh, my poor, my poor, poor—"

Her voice trailed away as she ran away to the road.

Phil knelt beside his friend to keep watch.

Billy could not see but he heard. He said in a voice that was all breath, childlike, full of crumbs, slowly, in dreamlike effort, as though to himself only,

"You, Phil. You, Phil."

The swift flicker of his heart under his breast stopped as Phillipson Durham watched. Nothing else changed.

Refusing to know anything, Phil said close to Billy's ear, in one of Billy's own phrases.

"How about it, Billy? How about it?"

There was no reply.

# V. The Dust and the Rain

Shortly after one o'clock that night the air took on a sudden chill when the whole sky to the northeast came forward with a slowly advancing curtain of dust for as wide and high as anyone could see. Those who were sensitive to it awoke because they tasted the dust in the air. It was the sort of dust storm which would come quietly and hang for two or three days over the whole plains land, turning the lilacs to an ashy color, and obscuring the distance, veiling the moon and even the sun. It would take a strong wind from off the Gulf far away to send the laden air westward and out of scent and sight.

Homer Breedlove awoke to the stifling flavor of the dust and lay still for a moment wondering if he dreamed or not, so often had he had that choking sensation when the dust arrived during the still night. But in a few more minutes he knew he was awake, for he heard the sound, dimmed by the hanging dust curtain, of an ambulance siren heading out Van Buren and turning at Central, and then swinging into Buchanan—Clyde Doty's ambulance. Homer said to himself, "Thanks be that all mine are home and safe," and felt sorry for someone, whoever it might be, who needed an ambulance out that way toward the water tower, and on such a night, which had begun in so much clear pale light and now was muted in all ways of sight, sound, and scent.

It seemed to him that even at the risk of disturbing Ellen he must rise and go downstairs and close some windows so that the dust would not come so heavily indoors, though it would find its way through cracks, and she would have to clean house in any case.

He went with heavy gentleness off his side of the bed and out to the hall and downstairs. She felt the mattress heave, but honored his kindly stealth by keeping silent. The front door was open, with only the screen door locked. He closed the main door, and then toured the windows, and then, thinking that since he was downstairs anyway, he might as well see, after all, how Billy was, he started for the sleeping porch. Before he reached there the telephone rang. It made his heart take a heavy jump. Calling so late, so loud? Who had anything to say to him at this time of night? He turned back to the front hall and took the receiver while Ellen turned her head to listen in the dread of after midnight.

꙰ ꙰ ꙰

A sweep of car lights across her window startled Mrs Underwood awake. She sat up and listened. Steps came up on the porch. What time was it? It felt late. She heard a man's slow, gentle, but vibrant words without quite hearing their meaning.

What *man!* Quickly into her dressing gown, she went to the door, turning on the hall and porch lights. She opened the door, for there wasn't anyone on earth she was afraid of, and saw her daughter standing with Highway Patrolman Hardie Jo Stiles.

"My stars above!" she exclaimed.

Hardie Jo looked calmly and politely at Mrs Underwood and said,

"I just brought Miss Marilee home and I turn her over to you, Mrs Underwood. I'll be picking her up in the morning if there's an investigation."

"Investigation!"

"There's been a bad accident, Mrs Underwood. I expect your little lady here will tell you about it. Goodnight, ma'am.—Now, Marilee, I'll be here at ten o'clock to let you know. Young Durham will be there. We're holding him overnight in the jail."

He tipped his hat to them both and went quietly off the porch to his car and drove away. Mrs Underwood was so shocked that she watched him until he was out of sight, as if his departure were the matter of most interest at the moment. Marilee ran past her into the house and into her own room. Finally her mother followed and found her standing in front of her mirror looking at herself as if to see who she was.

"Accident, and I would like to know how you are out of bed and out of the house and coming home with the police, and me not knowing a thing about—"

"Oh, Mother," cried Marilee, turning around and falling into her mother's arms. "Don't, don't, I need you so!"

Mrs Underwood, when appealed to, always changed from what she had been to what someone needed her to be.

"My baby," she said, holding Marilee as tightly in return as she was held. "Tell me. Tell me."

Marilee told her, and afterward, Mrs Underwood took her to bed with her, and held her in her arms all night long, to try, if she could, to halt the shaking that racked her child. A little before dawn she felt Marilee fall asleep out of exhaustion. Mrs Underwood needed her sleep, too, but now she was too happy to sleep, simply glad to have her baby back, by what reason, she refused to think at the moment.

꙳ ꙳ ꙳

By daylight, on the Saturday, as they called it, everyone had the news—how Homer took Ellen straight to the hospital after the phone call. All he told her then was that Billy was badly hurt. They let them see him at once in the emergency receiving room. Clyde Doty was standing by, along with the doctor, and the presence of the funeral director, as he was referred to, told them the worst.

Ellen Breedlove bent close to see her son lying covered with an ambulance blanket. His eyes were shut, the lids closed upward as she had never seen them in his sleep. He looked like a small boy. Or did she only remember that likeness of him? She smiled at his face and went blind with tears. A convulsion of shuddering like that in the climax of love seized her in an extremity of feeling she would never know again in her life, either in love or grief. Homer put his arm about her. Everyone made a group to lead her away. Out of delicacy, Mr Doty did not move to his ambulance with his burden until the Breedloves had driven off homeward. Then he proceeded to his funeral parlor with plans forming in his mind which he felt sure would be approved by the bereaved family and the stunned student body of Belvedere High.

"Now, Mother," murmured Homer when he drove up to the sidewalk of his house.

She had not made a sound. She scarcely heard him. He helped her indoors where she went to sit at the dining room table with her hand under her chin and her eyes streaming as she stared nowhere in silence.

"I almost did go to see if he was all right," said Homer in an anguish of confession, "just before I fell asleep, before midnight, but I was afraid I would disturb you."

She made no comment, and to create change, however trivial in the room, he switched on the prismed hanging lamp over the table which made a small circle of low gold light.

Ellen then looked around at him with vacant sweetness, as if to ask, "Did you say something?", and then she turned her head again to gaze across the room at what she must recognize in the shadows, the death of her youngest child.

A dark cloud of feeling began to gather in Homer Breedlove until he felt sickly in his long hollow belly. He bit his jaws together. He felt the first, slow power of the rage of which he was capable begin to make itself felt, and in his thin heavy arms he knew the desire to destroy whatever they could reach, until he felt fear rise to cover his grief.

"Now, Mother," he said again, to prove to himself that he was in charge of everything. He was actually glad to hear the front door open to distract him from his threat to lose control of himself, and he went to see who came. It was Leora Gately. Her car was out in the street with its door open, its engine running, and all its lights on.

"Oh, my God, where is she?" cried Leora staring at Homer as if he were a stranger. Her eyes were mad. The sight of them reassured him. If he could see that someone else was crazy, then it must be that he was not going crazy himself. He swallowed. The world's shock was in Leora's face. It comforted him.

"She's in there," he said.

Leora went flying past him to the dining room. Her heels made a drilling tattoo on the bare floor and as she caught sight of Ellen sitting at the table in the stillness of disbelief, she began to make a long high wail, and threw herself on the floor, kneeling beside

Ellen, putting her arms about her and weeping with exclamations and choking breaths on little whimpered screams, while Ellen remained silent.

"Oh, my God, my sweet, darling, little Billy, I can't stand it, Ellen, how can I stand it—Clyde Doty called me up, out of respect, he thought I ought to be the first to know, he knew that boy was the world and all to me, and to think that now he—" her voice diminished into a closed shriek that broke into sobs like the sneezing of a cat. Her tiny figure, as energetic as ever since her operation, but thinner and more stringy, was a weed in a strong wind. "He used to kiss me when I brought him toys, until you made me stop spoiling him! Now I wish I had spoiled him," and she started to say "spoiled him to death!" but fear of the word made her halt and she gasped. "Ellen! You haven't said a word to me!" She shook Mrs Breedlove with furious claws and searched her face. Ellen seemed to return to the world.

She put her hand on her friend's bony small face where dabs of makeup had been hastily and inaccurately applied before going out so early in the morning to drive across town in a Cadillac for this event, which was so great an affront to her, Mrs Tom Bob Gately II.

"I know, Leora," said Ellen. "I know, I know."

"Oh, you don't, you don't," shrilled Mrs Gately, yielding up to a fresh spasm of weeping. "If nothing else ever did, this will kill me!"

"I saw him just now," said Ellen. "He looked so young—" and she lost her own voice at the pity for her child which flooded her.

*"You don't understand,"* cried Mrs Gately, "you *had* him. He was *yours*. I never had anything in my life to love, of my own! I loved Billy, but he wasn't really mine, and anyway, now he's gone! I simply can't stand it!"

There was nothing for the sorrowing mother to do but take the barren woman before her into her arms and comfort her for the loss of the son she never had.

Upstairs, Homer knelt by his marriage bed praying with his big face in his long hands that if he had lost a son who was life's image he might not lose himself in anger which might threaten his own very life, if not that of others. The dust that was out of doors seemed now to sift down in a dry rain within Homer's head. As it fell it made a stinging pall over his mind. Through his mind the dust thickened over everything in the world, blurring the clear sense he once had known, like other people, of how it was to love at all in life, and the power about which there was nothing to think, finally, which was as well, for all seemed to be constructed of pairs of opposites in which a man could lose his way—glory and failure; the raptures of goodness and of evil; the ridiculous and the sweet; the hopeless, the mean, the ugly, faced by the beautiful; and all having effect simply because they existed without explanation to a man like himself.

"Please," he prayed in terror and humility.

※ ※ ※

Discussing death, those whom their parents still thought of as children met at Belvedere High to work out plans and make decisions. On their way to school, called together by the disaster which had befallen their captain during the night, they saw the water tower looming dimly in the skyful of dust. Its outlines grew from a blur to a shape as they came along Jeff Davis Avenue and when they reached the corner of Davis and Second, they stopped and pointed. Everything seemed to be made of dust in varying degrees of density, so that nothing was sharp and clear, but still they could read the message from the dead, unfinished, but certain enough in what it told them. The green paint was now simply a darker dust color than the tank and the heavy air: BEAT OR. . . .

They crowded into room 208, the chemistry theatre, taking seats on the rising levels of the semicircular room. They were soon organized into a deliberative body, with a presiding officer, who was thrust forward to take the place of the team manager, Phillipson Durham, who was absent. The discussion in 208 was called to order. It was brief.

The general feeling was they were the victims of an unfair aggression, but what soon emerged was the issue about courage— physical courage and moral courage. They knew they were already defeated by the loss of their best team member and captain; everyone knew those present had the necessary physical courage to do anything; but the real issue was, with defeat certain, and with the message in the air outside there which someone had died to give to them, did not moral courage require that they proceed as planned, no matter what people might say? So put, the issue was carried in a vote, and the chairman went to tell the principal what the students had voted to do.

Walking homeward afterward, some were moody and bitter. Intimate friends said to each other what they really felt.

—Well. They had always suspected that life was like that. They'd better learn it now, for they'd have to learn it later, anyhow. Sacrifice and waste. Death seemed very wasteful.

—Well, yes. But if you got to thinking along those lines, it only made sense if you thought that everything was all just attached to being useful only to things right here, on this earth, only. If that was how you saw things, why, then everything was always going to seem wasteful. So perhaps the best thing was just don't think about it.

—In that case, why?

—Well, for one thing, it was bigger than everything in it.

—That was true. But unless someone like God came along and

told you why something wasteful didn't really turn out to be wasteful after all, what else could you think but that it was?

—Yes, and the dead were dead forever. But people did, you know, people did go on, for if they didn't, what would become of everything? So they went on as long as they had to. And there was a lot to live for.

—Well, you couldn't prove a thing like that.

—Yes you could.

—How.

—You proved it by how everybody proved it just by living.

The dust kept advancing all day, growing heavier in the air, until everyone knew the slow, silent storm was to be one of the three-day drifters, when the sun at noon looked steel blue through the tawny haze. At two o'clock a little throng made its way to Dillingham Field behind Belvedere High, to breathe the gritty air and do what they could to support the team. There they were told that the meet had been cancelled, not by any act of the home team, but at the request of Orpha City, whose team had held a meeting and had voted to call off the track meet out of respect for the grief of Belvedere in the untimely loss of their team captain and schoolmate, William Breedlove. In the face of such goodness of spirit on the part of feared and hated rivals, many teachers, parents, and students of Belvedere felt in their hearts the sentiment of the psalmist, "Oh, grave where is thy victory," and the rest, and some even spoke the words, and felt their eyes smart. If they could not openly admit to the power of the psalm with its ancient feeling, they rubbed their eyes and exclaimed impatiently against the way the dust out of the sky pressed its way everywhere, even into your eyes, dust hauled up from the earth, their substance and their end.

For as long as it took to get the facts on record beyond a reasonable shadow of a doubt, Trooper Stiles told what he knew from direct observation of the events of the previous night. On duty in his cruiser, he had heard the si-reen and had followed the ambulance to the water tower, and the evidence of tragedy. Mayor Dillingham, out of respect for the young folk, preferred to have no official complaint, or other legal proceedings, unless they should be proved absolutely necessary. With pleasure in official speech,

"This is not to say I do not approve of your keeping Mr Durham in custody overnight, Trooper Stiles," said the Mayor. "But he is held without charge. This inquiry is simply to determine if further action may be required."

"Yes, sir," said the trooper, and left further consideration to the Mayor.

The Mayor gazed out the window as though to escape the trouble he was considering. Actually, his thought was clear and full. He had all the information he needed to lead him to a decision, but he felt it his duty to give his mind an opportunity to come to another decision than the one he had already taken in silence. Nothing occurred to him to change his mind. With a quick nod, he turned back to the trooper and said,

"Please bring the boy in here."

In a moment, Hardie Jo returned with Phil, whose aspect shocked Mayor Dillingham.

"You'd better take a chair, son."

Phil sat down.

"Would you like a glass of water?" asked the Mayor.

"No, thank you."

"Well, now then," said the Mayor, and gave it as his judgment that no investigation was further required, and though clearly the law had been broken, he believed the punishment itself was, if he might put it that way, built into the act. He therefore was requesting Trooper Stiles to release young Mr Durham. Was there anything he cared to say?

"No, thank you," said Phil.

"Are your parents informed?" asked the Mayor.

"I don't know."

"They would not inquire as to your absence overnight?"

"Not necessarily. I live on the ground floor and I am often gone before they get up."

"Best go home now, then, son." The Mayor looked at his watch. "I'll inform your father soon's I get to the shop. I expect he's there by now."

The Mayor nodded to the trooper, who indicated with his chin that Phil was to rise and go.

"Trooper, let's just give him a ride home, shall we?"

"Yes, sir."

"Are you all right, Phillipson?" asked the Mayor.

"Yes."

"Now you just hold on to yourself, hear?"

Phil made no answer but the look he gave the Mayor was enough. He left with Hardie Jo. Once in the patrol car, he said,

"Could you take me to her house, instead?"

"I b'lieve so."

They rode in silence until they came to Mrs Underwood's picket fence. As the car rolled to a stop, Hardie Jo said,

"Tell her she will not be interrogated."

"Yes."

"All right. Git on out."

He sounded like one who had taken offense but was powerless to act.

※ ※ ※

At the Belvedere Printers, Mayor Dillingham told Sport Durham of the accident in which his son was involved.

"Oh, shit," replied Mr Durham. As he said it, it was not an indifferent obscenity, but a weary comment on life as he knew it.

※ ※ ※

They walked together in silence for many blocks along Polk, heading toward open country. They could not begin to talk until the populated streets were behind them. Marilee walked proudly erect. A hazy look of knowledge played over her white face. When they were beyond the focus of the town, she weakly reached for his hand and he held hers as they walked. Finally they stopped by an open field. She said,

"Phil, what are we going to do?"

Neither of them could answer, and presently she said,

"Was it awful for you in the jail?"

"I didn't think it was me. I had the strangest idea that I was watching someone else there."

"Were you alone?"

"Yes."

"Did you sleep?"

"Not for hours. I looked out past the bars at the moon. Finally I went down to my cot and I think I went to sleep. I know I did, because I dreamed. I was so happy."

"Happy!"

"In my dream. I don't remember anything but how happy I was, like a god, like Adam, the first day."

"How lucky you were," she said with bitterness.

"Yes. —Just before I drifted off I thought I was going to die. A chill came over the whole plains and I folded my arms over my breast against the cold. That's when I fell asleep. I think if I had not gone to sleep I would have lost my reason. I mean that quite seriously."

"So you were happy instead."

"Yes. —It was mysterious. He was in it somewhere."

"How?"

He could not tell her. The sensation of immense, filling joy remained with him for a moment or two after he was awakened by light growing in the sky. As daylight grew in the jail cell, he seemed to merge with himself again, and all that was real became unbearable.

"I cried into my hands, once I knew I was awake again," he said, "I didn't want anyone to hear me, they had no right to hear me. It was the only time I have cried since it happened."

"Poor darling. I know."

They both felt close to tears together. He said,

"How am I going to live knowing what I did to him?"

"No, you mustn't think that way"—but she saw that she could do nothing to reverse his thought. There was even something in her voice which seemed to confirm his guilt.

"Don't be angry with me."

"I am not," she said. "I have nothing to feel anything with."

In her face he saw the fact of her memory—falling down to her, the turning body white in the full night, and how it struck to earth near to her crouching self, and what she heard, and what she longed to do to no avail. Neither of the two could say whose endurance had been worse.

Marilee's blue eyes now had a steady, liquid purity, like the light from distant stars whose essential life had long ago gone out. She was stronger than her surviving friend. She said,

"Will you go with me to see Billy, later?"

"Good God, no!" he said, stopping in his tracks.

"But I can't go alone! Please come?"

"I'm never going anywhere here again!" he declared in a voice that sounded full of hatred; for what, she knew.

"But with me!" she said.

"I'm sorry, but I can't!"

"I don't want to go any more than you do, but don't you see? I have to? I hate to, and I have to!"

He said nothing. She saw that there was nothing further to be said just then except,

"Well, if you can, and will, I'll be at home waiting for a little while around two o'clock . . ."

They walked back to her house. Marilee broke the silence, saying,

"My poor mother."

"Why."

"I've been so awful to her!"

"That may or may not be so."

"Oh, it's so. When I don't need her, I drive her wild with my ways, but when I do need her, she's still there, as if I weren't such a—"

Phil halted their walk and faced her and kissed her cheek.

"Oh, Phillipson," she cried, and ran up the steps and into the house while he walked home through the hanging gritty air.

🐜 🐜 🐜

Mrs Underwood was in the house awaiting her daughter.

"My poor baby," she cried, hugging Marilee with the gaunt hunger of a deprived woman who had rediscovered how to hold someone in her arms. Marilee's feeling took a swift turn, making her feel worse than faithless.

"Mother, please, don't, please, just don't."

"No, I know, I suppose I mustn't. But how can we help it if—"

Marilee walked past her, went to her room, and shut the door.

That strange child, all different again, thought her mother, looking after her. Mrs Underwood moved to the front room and lay down and covered herself with an afghan she had made years ago for her own mother's last illness. She closed her eyes. A smile came to her face. She was still happy, as she had been all night, without confronting the reason for her joy.

Happy? For the death of Billy Breedlove? But yes, that *was* what she meant, for with Billy gone, every worry about her child and him was also gone. Her heart felt light and its beating went sweetly along in her breast. It reminded her of how fine she felt listening to a simple song she loved.

*Now that you've come, all my griefs are removed,*
*Let me forget that so long you have roved,*
*Let me believe that you love as you loved,*
  *Long, long ago,*
  *Long ago. . . .*

  *Sing me the songs of the long, long ago,*
    *Long, long ago,*
    *Long ago. . . .*

After all these times of troubled wondering, the tearful prayers of her open nights, the glory of Marilee in love, the mindless power of Billy over her, there was now nothing to fear. It was like sudden freedom from captivity. Mrs Underwood clenched her hands to suppress her joy. She told herself she was evil, wicked, to rejoice in the death of a beloved young life, and she insisted that she must set about making it up to Marilee for the dreadful relief of Billys' destruction, but her heart would not stop singing

She wanted now to go to her child to comfort her, but she knew that she would never be able to offer Marilee any comfort that was acceptable, for Marilee knew the truth when she saw it. Was life one long succession of losing her child, by many different ways?

Bothered by joy as much as she had ever been bothered by worry, Mrs. Underwood presently telephoned to the rectory of SS Peter and Paul. When Sister Prisca answered, Mrs Underwood asked,

"Is he still away?"

For the old Monsignor had gone to Mineral Wells to take a course of the Crazy Crystal baths for his aches and pains.

"Yes," replied the housekeeper. "For ten days or so. —Do you want Father Judson?"

"Oh, yes!"

When the curate came on the phone, Mrs Underwood asked him if he could arrange to sing a Requiem High Mass for William Breedlove on Monday morning before the regular funeral which would be held from the Doty Memorial Parlors?

"Yes," he said.

❦ ❦ ❦

When Phil came to his own house, his father was gone to work. Between the screen door and the front door, he found a small packet crumpled together in tissue paper with a note held to it by a rubber band. Before he went upstairs to tell his mother what he must, he read the note and inspected the packet. The note, on paper headed Crystal Wells Farm, Belvedere, Texas, went this way:

*Phil my dear, one time I said to you, "Real tragedy measures humanity at its greatest dimension," and another time you said to me, "Art is bigger than anything." Remember? I am thinking of you and you must let me know when you feel like seeing me. Please keep the enclosed. It has your initials. Think how some fine things last and last.*

Love, Vicky.

In the packet of tissue paper was the silver seal set with the large pale aquamarine into which he had gazed to watch the reflections of firelight in the library at Crystal Wells, and wonder at such a possession, which out of all the initials in the world had his engraved in its mounting.

❧ ❧ ❧

As soon as he walked into her room his mother struggled to rise up in her bed, asking on a heavy breath,

"Phil, what is it!"

He had a childish impulse to go to her side and bury his face in the bedclothes to hide from what came with him. But he walked to the window and looked out into the grainy air. Mrs Durham lunged minutely in his direction but the action seemed large because of her size. On hearing that she was a bedridden invalid, whom no one ever saw, Belvedere had carried about the image of a woman wasting away—frail, emaciated, almost ghostly. Frail she was, nervously; but from years of inaction, and feeding her endless appetite for easily stirred rich foods, she had grown immensely heavy. Her flesh was soft and seemed to roll in waves when she moved. She had no interest in living, aside from seeing her son as he grew, and saying her prayers several times a day, that his life might reflect nothing of what his father and she were responsible for. Her face, once beautiful and animated, with high cheekbones and sweet shadows of mirth and mischief, still in its great enlargement could not engulf her magnificent eyes. Black as polished stones, they returned reflected light. None seemed to come from within her. She looked as old as a woman of her mother's generation.

With hysterical penetration, she saw this morning that overnight her son was almost as mortally cast down as she had been for years. She knew how possible it was to enter upon a slow death.

"Something is terribly wrong! Tell me!" she gasped, holding her bed-gown together over her unshapely flesh.

Without turning, Phil told her what everyone in town now knew about the night's folly, and his part in it. She listened, responding with faintly sounded shudders. Her imagination, having learned to feed on her own betrayals of years ago, followed the events he described; and it leaped ahead to what effect this might have upon him, if his mother was any model to go by. When he fell silent, she lifted her huge, loose-fleshed arms out and called him to her. The strain made her tremble. She was grotesque. She could never be seen by anyone else. She was his mother. He suddenly turned and threw himself into her embrace, grinding his head from side to side upon her wide bosom, and she felt his desire to hide forever.

"No!" she cried hoarsely, "my darling boy, no, no, you must not feel so. How horrible. Oh, how sad it is. But you must not let it mark you. Hush, now, oh, my dear."

Her invalid's odor almost stifled him—it was like a mixture of cream and flannel, something sour and warm, sadly weak; yet he found comfort in it at that moment. He shook his head against her and spoke. It was difficult to hear him, but she understood him. She said,

"Look at me!"

He shook his head again.

"Phil! Look at me—" she raised his head with her shuddering hands, and he saw an old power alive for a moment in her eyes. "I won't have you say things like that. You will destroy yourself if you do what you say. I want you to pray for your friend, and mourn him, and show all respect; but when you say you will never again face any of them in Belvedere, you don't know what you're saying! Look at me! *Look* at me! I will never let you be like me! You must face the world—now. If you don't, you may find it too hard to do it later! Oh, sorrow, yes, but blame, no! Do you hear me?"

Her breathing came in long heaves, and he saw that he had upset her more than she had been for years. But her eyes were full of life, where before for so long there had been only calm disinterest. This wild love and determination were the last responses he could have expected of her. He was amazed at how sharply she recognized his desire to hide, and he knew she was right about it. Because of her great bulk, her efforts exhausted her. She let him go and fell back on her pillows and rolled her head from side to side, murmuring,

"After all I have wanted for you."

The being he had helped to take care of for so long gave way in his thoughts to the young mother he had loved so joyously, whom he had missed so deeply and in silence. The old wisdom and strength which had come to her was now ebbing again; but it was enough to show him the inner life that could still give instead of take. He leaned down and kissed her. She closed her eyes. She said,

"You must promise me."

"Yes, mother. Promise what?"

But she had said all she was capable of at the moment; and besides, she knew he understood what she meant. After a moment, speaking with difficulty, he said,

"Yes. I promise."

She nodded like someone falling asleep in a private world. He left her to it. He was afraid of what he must learn to face; yet sure to keep his pledge.

⚘ ⚘ ⚘

Clyde Doty, having taken personal charge of the "arrangements," was pleased with the extra touches he had given to them. The funeral director was a small, rubicund, plump man with curly silver hair. If he seemed designed to be merry, he made a special effort to be hushed and solemn, as befitted his vocation.

He believed he could properly say that in all their griefs—think only of the number of soldiers he had buried when they came home forever from the recent war—his fellow Belvedereans gave him their fullest confidence, and leaned on him for strength as on a family friend?

Early Sunday afternoon he conducted the family of William Breedlove into the thickly carpeted and draperied room where their son lay in state within a bower of floral pieces whose blooms had been dusted with heightened color, and all of which had been sprayed with a perfume so strong that visitors could taste it in their throats.

Homer and Ellen, muted and thoughtless, remained with their son for ten minutes. Mr Doty believed it courteous to hover nearby, making quiet remarks about the exceptional profusion of the floral tributes, and the number of cards of condolence.

"A mountain of cards, just a mountain of them," he murmured, while his bright red cheeks quivered amiably and his small plump hands squeezed themselves together with simulated emotion. In the musky hush of the softly lighted room even his restrained and practised gestures seemed like bold intrusions.

"We won't be opening up to the general public until after two o'clock," he said, "but we thought you would like to have a Family-Only Prevue."

"Yes," replied Homer, "yes, surely, and everything is very, very lovely, Clyde, and we do surely thank you for all you've done."

"All you've done," echoed Ellen, and took her husband's arm and turned away from her youngest-born. Mr Doty escorted them to the Family Parlor where they could retire to privacy and yet receive whatever friends might ask for them. At the front door Mr Doty saw two figures walking slowly toward his place. Like everyone in town, he knew who Billy's best friends had been. He waited for them at the door, for though it was not quite yet two o'clock, he believed these two should also have the carefully limited privilege of the Family-Only Prevue. Over concealed loudspeakers came the muted throbbing of an electric organ with a consoling message—*"Oh, He walks with me and He talks with me,"* it said to those who knew the words.

※ ※ ※

"Thank you for coming anyway," she said.

"I don't want to go in," said Phil.

"I can't go in alone," answered Marilee.

"I'll wait for you on the porch."

"Please, Phil, darling. Help me."

"I know. But."

She stopped walking and halted him with her hand on his arm. She said,

"I have often wondered. Maybe it was you he really loved the most."

She drew a harsh breath. What made her say a thing like that?

[ 231 ]

She looked amazed, and saw her expression reflected in Phil's face. The thought dismayed him so much that he felt a surge of anger.

"Stop that!" he said in a low, light voice.

"No, what the thing is—we both loved him," she said, explaining everything desperately.

"But I killed him!"

"Stop that, you simply have to stop thinking like that."

"How can I. It's true."

"It was an accident."

'Why didn't I hold still?"

"You had no time to think."

"I don't see how you can go in there," he said.

"I must. I don't know why. Yes, I do. I don't know. Please go with me? I am so afraid."

"All right. But don't make me look at him."

She nodded, they went up the steps, and the plate-glass door was opened silently and thoughtfully before they touched it.

Clyde Doty shook hands with Marilee and tried to with Phil, but Phil put his hands behind him and stood aside, looking anywhere but at the open door of the room where Billy lay. Mr Doty was used to odd forms of grief, some of which often seemed to him like fits of shyness, or embarrassment, and some downright ungrateful and rude. He elaborately left Phil to himself and escorted Marilee in toward the bier. It was evident that he meant to remain with her to provide expert solace, and also to receive hushed compliments on his work, but she turned to him and made a little desperate waft of her hand and said,

"Please, Mr Doty?"

He bowed silently. There were times when the bereaved preferred to be alone, and he prided himself on always knowing when. He left her.

In silence she looked then at silence.

William Breedlove lay in state in a bronze casket lined with puffed white silk. The cover was raised its whole length. He was clothed in his best blue suit, over which Mr Doty, with permission from the school principal, had arranged the gray graduation robe which had been meant to be worn with the whole class two weeks later. Mr Doty could imagine the effect it would have on everyone who came here in the next two days. With white shirt and dark tie—just right. Oh, for such a son!—so they would all think. His head looked like a sculptured head; still, clearly cut, like the one in the Berlin Museum illustration in Marilee's art appreciation book. Its short hair was fletched in tongues of gold overlying each other as though formally carved. His eyes were closed, slightly upward from the lower lid. Below his eyes still showed those small rolls of flesh which always suggested glee. Under his now blameless brows rested a shadow deeper than the one that had given such strong contrast to the light of his eyes in life. A brushing shadow faded away under his cheeks still rounded by the reposeful smile on his carved lips with their curved bevels. His hands were laid one over the other at his groin in a gesture of eternal modesty. But now his hands looked like no part of him. She could not bear to see them and yet she could not turn her eyes from them. They had been artfully manicured. Was that what made the difference? But no—it was their stillness. His hands had never been still, even in sleep. Even in sleep, for she had watched him sleeping as her eyes had grown accustomed to the light of night over Whitewater Lake in an hour when she refused to sleep. His hands had fluttered and played empty in the air above his head where he had flung them like a sleeping child on the short bitter grass near the water's edge. Awake beside him she had watched him breathe, and wondered if his life then breathed within her. When he had awakened from his short deep sleep he had reached his arms to take her to him again, saying, "Mine, now," and again she had said, "Yes," with her life.

Looking at him now she formed his name with her lips, but her voice would not come, and hearing visitors approaching, she left him, to carry in secret her true estate. She returned to Phil in the lobby.

Phil saw in her face how impossible it would have been for him to look upon the dead. Mr Doty came forward to ask if they would sign the visitors' register, but they declined, and were about to go when Homer Breedlove came forth at the sound of their voices.

He put a heavy hand on a shoulder of each of them and said, peering down into their eyes in turn,

"I used to lie awake nights, wondering about that boy, and sometimes I would get up and go downstairs to look in on him and see if he was all right. I almost went down that night. But I didn't. Why didn't I? I wish I had o'. Oh, I wish."

Nodding solemnly at them, he returned to his wife in the private room.

Marilee and Phil went out and walked homeward. The quietly drifting cloud of dust—estimated by the weather reports on KBEL as about five miles high and reaching along a ninety-mile front—settled a chill over the day by interrupting the warmth of the sun, which when seen at all was a wan disc that came and went, like a frequent change between illusion and certainty in the heart of someone who grieved.

They had so much to say to each other that they could say nothing. He walked with her to her house and left her at the weathered porch where ropes of trumpet vine were putting out leaves. She took a step up on the wind-scoured wood, turned, and leaned down to him, and said,

"Kiss me, poor dear?"

He kissed her without being sure to whom she referred. It was a chaste kiss, as between children. His heart felt a little sting of love and he asked far back in his mind what the future might keep for the two of them, when enough time should have passed? Turning away, Marilee covered her face with her hand and ran indoors, not seeing her mother who sat blurred by shadows of lace at the front window where she had seen the exchange at the steps.

"Now what if it was to be *those* two?" wondered Mrs Underwood in a start of a whole new cycle of worry.

※ ※ ※

Phil walking toward his own house followed the unpaved road that led along the edge of town where he must pass the water tank on his right and presently the warehouse on his left. He burrowed his way through the gritty air without looking at either. He knew well enough how they looked. He never wanted to see either place again. Where could he go? Youth itself was a prison from which there could be no escape until a fixed term had been served.

As he reached the corner where Hayes Street faded into open country, a blue Dodge tailgate truck with high cattle bars came to a clanking halt beside him. Tom Bob Gately leaned out of the driver's window and called,

"Hi, there, you, boy, come awn jump in here and take a little ride with me. I want to talk to you."

He sounded thick in the tongue, but he was making signals of affability, ducking his heavy head with its narrow-brim Stetson on the back of his skull. Phil paused uncertainly. He wanted above all things to be alone. But there was a steamy authority in Tom Bob.

"Come *awn*. Take a little *ride*."

Saying this, Tom Bob flung open the passenger's door of the truck with a crash, and Phil, soured by his own lack of independence, went around the battered truck and climbed in beside Tom Bob. The gears crashed immediately and with a lurch and a rankle of tailgate chains, the truck moved off along the dirt road as far as Washington, turned north on Central, then west out on Highway 31.

"Only son of a bitchin place for privacy," declared Tom Bob, "is get in your car and ride."

Until they reached the paved highway the truck made too much jouncing noise for them to speak further. Then, facing out along the straight line of highway which vanished into the earth cloud, Tom Bob found his voice, but not before he took a long pull from a bottle of Old Forester which he hauled out from under the seat with a loving air of exposure as if in anticipation of an almost sexual assuagement. He lofted the bottle to his pulling lips, coughed, pushed at his hat, and made a gust of exploded breath, all with the air of a man unused to revealing the deep thoughts which only a few times in a lifetime might have occasion to want to come free, but then with the power of tyranny beyond control.

"I went by Clyde Doty's Mortuary to take a look at Billy," he said in a heavy voice pebbled by effort and the scars of whiskey. "I came in from the ranch just to pay my respects. For years, now, I watched that boy, but he never knew it. I watched you, too, Ben. You both got somethin."

Phil had a chill of memory and reference, and said,

"My name is not Ben. I am Phillipson Durham."

"Hell yes? Of course your name is Phil. Who the hell ever said otherwise? You damn little phool."

"Well, excuse me, Mr Gately, but you called me Ben."

"I never. Oh, what the hell. It don't signify. The only thing

[ 236 ]

that matters is, you both got somethin, you, Mister Phil Durham, if you please, and that dead ol' Billy back there."

Phil had no notion of how to reply to this. All he could think of was, to say to himself, Why won't everybody just let us alone in this? Why must everybody try to be part of it when it doesn't concern them directly? Don't they know they make it all the worse by intruding? But all he did was to sit forward, his dark face fixed in a strained scowl as he peered ahead into the dust-diminished distance. Now and then an approaching car took form out of the cloud, first showing its headlights like pale blue suns. It was soon clear that he was not expected to say anything, but only to listen to Tom Bob pour out the thoughts and reminders which Billy's death made for him.

"Now you listen, boy. The way *she* always took awn about him"—Phil understood this referred to Leora Gately—"people always figgered he meant more to her than to me. But now you listen. If I had a son. Like him. What I mean. Everythin. Take him huntin. Somebody to work for. Somebody to leave after you. Billy had somethin, and you've got somethin, and let me tell you somethin, it won't go on livin if you stay here in Belvedere. It wouldn't've in Billy if he'd stayed here, and it won't in you if you don't get up and git. You may laugh, but I was like you, in a way, and I was like Billy, in a way, when I was a kid. I know how kids are, thinking about things together, and thinkin things would never change. Well, I had somethin, and I knew it, but I stayed."

He pulled out his bottle again and drank without pausing to offer it to Phil.

"Why did I stay? My daddy had a bank to give me, and a ranch, but I didn't want any son of a bitchin bank, or any old hard-workin ranch, but I took them, and what I do? Evvyone knows what I did. I stayed. And why did I stay? I was too lazy to work for what I wanted. You know what I wanted?"

He turned and forgot the road, the truck, the steering wheel, and hung his heavy mottled face close to Phil until Phil really saw only its eyes, and these were ageless, so that he might have been looking into the nature of a youth through the light of his gaze, and he was startled to see swollen reminders of how bluntly handsome Tom Bob must have been as a young man. The truck lurched toward disaster over the shoulder of the road below which there was a deep borrow pit. Phil quickly seized the wheel and righted the car's direction. Tom Bob took offense.

"And just what was that supposed to mean?"

"Sir?"

"You think I am too drunk to drive m'own truck?"

Just to threaten proof of his claim to control, Tom Bob deliberately headed for the ditch again, smiling at Phil with an impersonation of lost charm, and only in the last moment of chance himself brought the car back to the road again.

"Now how about that?" demanded Tom Bob in triumph. But Phil said nothing, only looked glum and disgusted at such antics, and Tom Bob fell into self-pity and fury.

"Very well, I *could* let you drive, but I won't," he said. "I brought you out here for your own good, not mine, and there's only one way I can tell it to you, and you just sit there and listen to me, you horny little old kid, or you'll do just as bad as I did. —I wanted to stay awn in the university at Austin and take my master's in history, and I even figgered I might as well go awn and get my doctor's, so I could teach. That's all I wanted to do, ever. I mean teach history. Mostly Texas history. I used to think we had to tell our young ones first about their own history right here in Texas, before we could take and have them get to know about the rest of history, and I had an ass full of theories and I knew just what to teach what ought to be taught. My own professor thought I should just go right awn and do it. Do it!

"But you didn't know my daddy. He raised all kinds of hell when he heard what I's up to, and what with one thing and another that are not any of your *Got-damned business"*—he turned to glare at Phil as though to protect private matters from a probing intruder—"I married me a wife they fixed me up with for it didn't make a damn who she was, and I came awn on home and took over my bank."

Tom Bob fell silent while images went past behind his eyes, but he held on to his position as speaker by hanging his shiny, chapped, thick hand in the air toward Phil and shaking it like an orator about to make a point. When his emotion let him continue, Tom Bob said,

"Texas history. Tshee-yit. Too late even to think about it. But you want to know somethin, young feller? I'll tell you the most lonesome thing in the world is, the most lonesome thing in the world is not to have anybody to know what you really are *like*. It don't count when you're growing up. That don't mean anythin. But when I came home to stay, I could give up the master's and the doctor's and take to the bank, and make out fair enough, if ever I'd a-had someone to know that for me. It wouldn't have mattered a-tall what I *did* if someone just knew what I was *like*. They thought they knew when they would see me in the bank, and I just let them think they did. But then long after when it was too late, when I knew I'd never get me any children, and never teach a class, I found me someone who knew what I was really like *by that time* and she made me right happy. I refer to my friend Mrs Doolittle."

Phil pressed his hands together between his knees and asked silently, Oh, no, please don't tell me about any of that. But Tom Bob was alive with memories of his lost happiness. His eloquence was the child of his bottle, and he said,

"I saw Billy and his girl together, the whole town did, and so did you, and I saw you with him, and you's always with the other two, and I tell you, I know what y'all were feelin." He turned to ask with his pouched face whether Phil understood and respected the fact that through the love of young people for each other a man old before his time, sagging, angered, and puzzled by the terms of his life, could apprehend love with references from his own lifetime wants. "Mrs Doolittle and I we made us a right nice little home together, for as long as it lasted."

Like a smiling memory of feeding on the face of a sleeping baby, a wipe of pleasure went across Tom Bob's face and he blinked lazily. His great head lurched loosely on its thick neck and he shaped and then released a commodious blowp of gas through his whiskey-dry mouth. Phil then realized how drunk he was. As if to comment perversely on the discovery, Tom Bob raked his bottle out from under the seat again and again drank immoderately. He emptied the bottle and threw it aside to the highway, not caring where it broke. Phil wished he might ask to be taken home, but knew no way to do this.

"I'd get done at the bank before Mrs Doolittle would get done at the drugstore," said Tom Bob feeling better, "and I'd just go awn home to her place and get my shoes off and my shirt, and sometimes I had me forty winks till she got home. You know somethin? I'll tell you somethin. One time she came awn home, and found me a-lyin there, and she pulled off my socks to make me comfortable, and then you know what? She kissed those socks and smiled at me like a girl. I : tell : you. Lettin me know that way how she felt about *me*. And the way she looked. The nice thing about Mrs Doolittle, she always looked so pretty, she believed in keepin herself fixed up, she was a pretty litto trick, and then she got herself comfortable, and we'd have one, two maybe three drinks, and she liked to play the radio, Amos and Andy, or Major Bowes, and then she would get somethin on the stove, for she was a mighty nice litto cook, she made the best hamburger with fixins that you *ever* tasted, she never would tell me what she did to it, but it was somethin special, and we had hamburgers most evvy night. Then you know what she would do for us sometimes? Why, she would get out her harmonica and settle down with me, just lyin over against me, and she would play awn the harmonica just easy and driftin along, and if I fell asleep she never minded, for she knew the pretty music made me content enough just *to* doze off like that, and it made *her* content to make *me* content. Or next time maybe I'd get wound up and get to talkin and ravin about the pioneers in Live Oak County, history, and she would just sit there and listen, and I never knew what actually did go into that pretty litto head of hers, but I remember she used to say *My-oh-my,* at things I told her, and I don't care what evvyone else thought, *she* thought I was mighty bright, and she used to sigh because she said she wasn't educated up to me." Moisture, not quite tears, began to shine and bead its way down Tom Bob's flushed heavy cheeks. The nourishing sweetness he had once known returned to him. "Well, not evvyone knew it, but Mrs Doolittle was more of a lady than anybody *else* I ever met, no matter what the old bitch cats always said about her and me. Got damn it!" He turned to Phil and his close sac'd blue eyes flared into fiery emphasis. "Now, boy, you take and you marry a girl who knows what you're really like, and you be sure of her, so she won't take and try to make you over into what she *thinks* you're like, which only means what she thinks you ought to turn into to suit *her!* No sir, the woman ought to suit herself to the man! That's what always tickled me to death about that Billy and his girl. You could tell by the way they were together, just the way you could tell about Mrs Doolittle and I. Let me tell you there wasn't anythin, not one litto biddy thing Mrs Doolittle wouldn't do to make me happy, and I been in every Got-damned whorehouse from Matamoros to Juar-*ez.*"

God no, thought Phil, don't let him start talking about that too! But by innocently making clear what he had been talking of all along, Tom Bob was finished with his subject, and without warning he brought the truck to a sliding halt and leaned over and in a grip so tight it gave pain grasped Phil at the thigh and said,

"Learn it from me, learn it from Billy, just you get awn with

your own life as fast as you can, and hell with the rest of them."
He released his grip, but with his knotted fist gave Phil a hard
blow of admonition on the side of his thigh and added, "Just you
be who you are, and nobody else. —That's what built this great
country of ours!" he concluded in a suddenly vague drift of
oratory, and then he swung the truck savagely about facing back
toward town and went clanking along without speaking until
they began to see signs of Belvedere, the first of which was the
water tower suspended as a shape of darker dust in the general
haze.

"Where will you get down?" asked Tom Bob as he drove into
town along Central Avenue.

"Anywhere will do."

With an air of being immediately offended Tom Bob swung to
the curb and stopped the truck, sagging heavily against Phil to
fling open the door for him. Phil got out and shut the door.
Feeling some gesture was called for, he leaned into the truck,
saying,

"Thank you, Mr Gately," attempting to conceal his relief at
being delivered.

Tom Bob was purple red in the face by now, and hardly able to
keep his eyes open. A shapeless mass behind the wheel, he rolled
in little losses and recoveries of control in his seat, and nodding
involuntarily at Phil, he said with a husky weariness that touched
Phil more than all his words,

"Oh, tshee-yit! Nobody kin tell innybody else. Go awn. Get
away." Then a memory from both near and far opened and
closed for Tom Bob, and he added in an attempt at waggish
charm, "There's an old bobcat hangin around out on my ranch.
Why can't we go out and hunt him some weekend?"

Phil knew he should offer to drive Tom Bob Gately all the way
to the other end of Central Avenue where Mrs Tom Bob Gately
II lived in her lovely-home of modified-Tudor-Gothic, but there
was no chance to do this, for as if visibly threatened with rational

caution, Tom Bob suddenly crashed his gears and lunged away from the curb and was lost down the street where the mercury lamps were coming on for evening, showing magic pale in the powdery air.

Then, going home, hoping to meet no one else, Phil began to hear all that Tom Bob had been saying, and he felt a total strike of hopelessness that seemed like despair. It was, he thought, a terrible burden and a responsibility to learn anything at all about the secret life of anyone else. Nobody but God should know everything about anybody. And yet—so Tom Bob had seemed to say—unless someone did, you were bound to be unhappy. Phil wished he could burn Tom Bob's spoken words as he had seen those old water-stained letters go up into ash beyond Guy De-Lacey's miniature mountain range.

Marilee! he cried in his mind, and quite unknowingly broke into a run for a few steps, and then came down to a walk, trudging home once again, toward the edge of town where night was lowering toward him over the plains. "Billy," he said aloud, "you knew. Nobody else does. You did."

Ψ Ψ Ψ

At a few minutes before eight on Monday morning Father Judson waited in the vestibule of SS Peter and Paul for Mrs Underwood and her daughter. The nuns from the parochial school were already in their front pews. The altar was dressed in black and silver for the Requiem Mass about to follow, and in the center aisle, flanked by six tall lighted candles, was an empty catafalque covered with a black pall edged in silver which represented the earthly body of William Breedlove in behalf of whose departed soul the mass would be sung.

[ 243 ]

Oh, said Marilee to herself, walking up the steps of the church beside her mother, if I could be alone for this.

"Good morning," said Anthony Judson.

"Yes, good morning, Father, how can we ever—" said Mrs. Underwood.

"Yes, yes, Mrs Underwood, it is sad."

She looked about cautiously and said,

"I'm so glad *he's* not here, he would never have said mass for a non-Catholic."

"Don't be too hard on Monsignor," replied the curate. "He was strictly raised and he's old and ill."

"I know. But the way he—"

"I waited," said Father Judson, as much to change the difficult subject as anything, "a few moments to see if either of you might want to go to Communion, and if so, whether you'd want to go to Confession."

"Why, I went yesterday, Sunday," said Mrs Underwood. "Perhaps Marilee? I don't know."

There was a sharp pause. Marilee looked straight at the priest with a crackle of blue light in her eyes. Her face was white and shone tightly drawn across her cheekbones and brow. She seemed ageless, thought Father Judson, and he wondered if in all his ministry he had ever seen a face, young or old, more acquainted with grief. Then she said in her marshy cool voice, full of some life which he had never heard in it before,

"Then I think I will, Father Judson."

"Then just fine," said Mrs Underwood, "I'll go in and you can come sit with me when you're ready."

They separated, Mrs Underwood to her place in the right front pew, the confessor and his penitent to the confessional near the main door.

Those established in the pews—the sisters from the school, Mrs Underwood, a few of the anonymous faithful who took frequent reward from the duty of praying for even the unknown dead—

heard the small conspicuous sounds of occupancy in the confessional, and also in the choir loft where Monica Mallory was already at her organ bench waiting to play and sing the responses of the requiem. For as long as she had been in Belvedere, she had been organist and soprano soloist at SS Peter and Paul. In the almost empty church every interior sound was magnified—a missal laid upon a lectern, a purse flicked open and shut, a rosary brushing against polished oak, the creak of a kneeler's bench in the dark of the confessional.

֎ ֎ ֎

She could not soon speak, and he did not press her to, after he murmured blessing and invocation on his side of the lattice of the confessional box.

Her struggle was all at the beginning. How could she bring herself to agree that what she had to confess was a sin? It was all she had thought about for weeks, and especially since Friday night, but always with pride, not repentance. There was, she supposed, nothing new about it to the world whose whole life depended for survival upon it, and perhaps what might seem a passion in miniature, if looked at in the measurements of the history of the world, might not seem so heroic and all-obliterating as it had seemed to the two of them. This somehow did not appear to matter. The fact that it was all a secret, one that he had never told and would never tell, nor would she, made it all the more great and noble. The moon of that night had shone within her ever since. She would never forget the cry of the night hawk, or the unshining yet reflecting lake, or the wry perfume of the desert plants around the shore. How his breathing was alive within her very own breath! She tried to see him in the moon-

[ 245 ]

drenched darkness, but could not really. It did not matter. She
shut her eyes and saw them both so brightly in her own pierced
darkness. They tried to pretend for a little while that they were
children, almost, playing a zestful game, conserving the illusion
that nothing really was going to fulfill its ordained end. But in
the same instants, they knew they were already given with all
their hearts, and she would never forget when she felt how her
pale belly, which was at one and the same moment apprehensive,
soft, and taut, caved in with an overwhelming qualm of desire at
his touch upon it. They tried to say each other's name and the
name of love, but their striving mouths let them give only
swallowed sounds. Her temples were moist under his devouring
touch, and she heard him exclaim with wild sweet pity at this
discovery, and they—

"Yes, child?" said Father Judson in a gentle prompting which
brought her back to where she was. She took a deep breath and
in a single sentence, as flat and as impersonal as she could make
it, she defined her fall from grace, and said, "That is all, Father."

꽃 꽃 꽃

To those waiting, it first seemed rather a long time, and then
an odd delay, and finally an alarming interval before there was a
careful scrape and a sound of rising and walking as Marilee left
the confessional and went up the center aisle to kneel beside her
mother and put her hands into her face and pray her penance.
Even more time passed before Father Judson was heard leaving
his place in the confessional. Out of propriety nobody looked
directly at him as he made his way to the sanctuary and then to
the sacristy to vest for the Mass. He genuflected as he passed the
altar, praying to be given command of his feelings following the

confession he had just heard, and that he might worthily offer up the Holy Sacrifice, for at present all that kept running through his mind was the refrain, "Poor little one. Poor little one." Beyond words, he addressed this compassion for Marilee to heaven, which had already given an answer in return, for he had heard her and had given her absolution.

꙾ ꙾ ꙾

In the organ loft Miss Mallory received from others in the church a heightening of her own ready emotion. Since she was above and behind everyone, she could look freely without being irreverent. Something about the way Marilee walked to her pew, something about how long Father Judson stayed in the box after she had left, something in his bearing as he paused at the altar, gave her chills about the heart which felt both frightening and fascinating. She was suddenly full of the real meaning of the occasion. One of her selves said to the other.

"Why, yes, how could you forget it, it is that darling Billy Breedlove we are burying today," I said, and the other answered,

"Oh, Lordy, all that fame of his, and that charm, and his wildness!"

"Yes," I said, "but look at that poor girl, there!"

"Oh, I don't know," she said, "maybe she got what's coming to her."

"Why, Monica-Mickle, how can you say a thing like—Oh! my God! It can drive you crazy, love, that is, did you know that?"

"Now don't have one of your *things*," she said, and I answered,

"What if I loved that boy myself! Everyone in town loved him. Why shouldn't I have loved him?"

"Yes," she said, "with all you have to give, maybe you loved him more than anybody else! Did you ever think of that?"

"Oh, you're a marvel, you understand everything! What would I do without you!"

"Sauce goose sauce gander," she said, always clever.

"Oh, how I remember," I said—and Miss Mallory's thoughts wavered in her head like the *vox humana,* for she used to watch when Billy came to the library with Phil—she knew how to watch without anybody knowing she watched—and if people thought she knew nothing about life just because she was an old maid and a Catholic and a librarian and peculiar, they could go jump in the lake. Why: she could honestly say she knew more about Billy Breedlove than anybody else, if they just asked her—how he looked, how he did, what he sounded like, that little habit he had of looking with a smile before he answered anything you said to him, and then, when he did talk, how his whole body went into what he said! No wonder that cute Marilee Underwood was so mad about him.

"Probably no one else in Belvedere knows as well as I do," I said, "just what Marilee is suffering right now."

"Yes," she answered, "you are in a heaven-sent position to offer Marilee the proper consolation!"

"You're right," I declared, lifting my head proudly in *my* suffering, "I know a thing or two about being robbed of love, which means being starved for it!"

"Oh, I know," she said, "those whole nights of dreams, almost sort of crazy, and how you have to watch afterward to see if anybody else really thought so, during those days, how strange such days are, of recovering yourself when you drift back to your good sense. You have such good sense!"

"Thank you, if I do say it myself," I said, and I said, "I certainly thank God and my patroness Saint Monica for being there ready to help whenever I remember to ask Their help, They have

[ 248 ]

never failed me, and I will not fail Marilee later, when the time comes for help!"

Miss Mallory was at the same time alert to her duties, and when she saw Father Judson come following the acolytes to the altar, she flipped on the electric switch to start the organ bellows, and as the curate, pale and handsome in his black and silver chasuble, began the prayers at the foot of the altar, she entered upon the *Kyrie*.

"You're a marvel," she said, and I said,

"I know, everyone tells me so."

"I mean, how you keep up! Always so cheerful. And that voice!"

"I know," I had to say, "everyone always shakes their head over what I could have done with it, my high dramatic soprano range, and my firm chest tones."

For at parties, when they heard Miss Mallory sing *One Fine Day* (English or Italian, she gave them their choice) to her own pleased accompaniment in which skipped notes were never missed by listeners, they said she should really have set her cap for the very top years ago, the Metropolitan, Major Bowes, the Firestone Hour, *Blossom Time* on Broadway, anything, no limit. But she would laugh gaily and tell how full her life was, and how glad she was to leave all that to Homer Breedlove, who also sang. Her voice now had a quavering robbed sweetness of which she was unaware, in place of that dramatic attack with which at one time she had made her best effects. If something had been lost with the years, it was a mercy that she did not know it, and in any case she prided herself on the high reliable competence with which she rippled off the responses in the mass, tumbling the heavy-laden Latin syllables of the requiem together, yet always coming out even with the last one which she held and punctuated with the organ.

"I sometimes wonder if it is because I loved everyone so much that I never gave myself up to marriage?" I said. "Was that it? Never called a man to me? *Not that there weren't chances!*"

"Well," she said, "you've been in love with three successive pastors, not excluding Father Judson."

"Oh, but he surely doesn't know it! He mustn't!"

The mass was hardly over when Monica shut off her bellows and scuttled down the spiral stairs of the organ loft to catch Marilee just outside the church. Before Marilee knew what was happening to her, Monica enfolded her blindly in a quivering embrace and in a strident whisper spoke close to her ear with scarcely a pause for breath.

"Oh, I know, I know what you must be feeling. The one you loved and lost will be your ideal all your life, and you'll be faithful to him till you die, I know, I know. That's what it is to love, to really love, you poor little thing."

"Yes, Miss Mallory, thank you. Please," said Marilee, but to no avail, for Monica held her as if to crush her and whispered,

"Plenty of people stay pure all their life, you owe it to the memory of the one you loved, now let me tell you, it isn't so bad, it *isn't so bad,* you get used to it, honey, I always thought you'd be a nun anyway, my, wasn't Father wonderful when he gave the final absolution, I tell you, they don't make them like him any more! Now Marilee, honey, you just count on your poor old Monica, I'll always be there, and you just call me Monica. When I was a tot they called me Monica-Mickle, and I always loved it, it's what I feel more like most of the time, *Monica-Mickle,* honey!", she said in a little-girl voice.

Mrs Underwood came and lifted Monica's arms from their embrace.

"Time we all went now, Monica. You can help Marilee later on."

"Yes. Perfect," said Monica, looking around. "Where is that Phil Durham? I don't see him here, a good friend and a good Catholic, like that?"

"No, I noticed," said Mrs Underwood as they turned away.

Marilee knew why he wasn't there, and wished she too had had the courage to stay away from what was almost impossible to endure. The only thought to help her was the thought of Whitewater where she had gone with Billy on the night of the full moon weeks ago. Why did the moonlight itself seem like the very source of life?

❊ ❊ ❊

Phil heard a car outside and went to the window. It was Victoria Cochran in her old-fashioned, polished sedan. He was with his mother and she heard his excitement when he said,

"Mother, can I bring you anything else?"

"No, dear," whispered his mother. "Go, whoever it is. I want you to be there with them."

He bent and kissed her brow and left her and ran noisily down the stairs and out to the car. Victoria threw open the car door and he leaped in and shut it after him.

"How did you know, how did you know!" he cried, and pounded his fists upon his knees.

"I never go to funerals," replied Victoria, sliding the car's gear forward, and they drew away from the house, "and I thought you couldn't bear to be there today either. I thought we would drift through the country together and see the plains. I never get tired of them.

He turned to stare at her, for she had discovered much to him in that statement.

"No," he said, "nor do I, though I didn't know it until now!"

She smiled.

"I thought it would take you longer. I thought you wouldn't really see them until you went away, and came back."

"I wouldn't have," he said, "without you."

"Yes, in time. Perhaps not so soon. But in time. Where we bury our dead you know. That is where we always are, no matter where we go."

"Ah, Vicky."

She let him give way to feeling as she meant him to. It would have been strained and false for them to avoid the matter of the occasion. She was resolved to let him be purged, but not by organized mortuary horrors arranged by Clyde Doty and presided over by Lew Priddle. It was years before he realized that she came that morning to answer his most exhausting need. In time he must speak; rage, if he must, and even laugh, knowing she would understand how he meant laughter that day.

"Do you know the most disgusting thing about all of it?" he said angrily.

"Perhaps not."

"It is that everything is public. Why does it all have to be so public?"

"But how pitiful—they do it all," said Victoria, "to help themselves."

"What has any of that to do with me?" he demanded in furious arrogance. "I only want to be let alone. How can his parents stand to be pulled this way and that, and almost congratulated, like people at the center of some grand event!"

"It *is* a grand event. What else have they, most of them? except the biggest facts—birth, marriage, death?"

"That should all be nobody else's affair! I don't want anybody doing anything about me in any of that, and I despise it if anybody tries to make me go through public things!"

His face was flushed and his eyes rayed forth liquid bolts of feeling. Driving him in the vast empty land to spare him nearness to what he so hated, Victoria saw that it was useless to try to lead him just then to see universal beauties of life in whose midst the ceremonial vulgarities that so enraged him were but small incidents. She could only help him now, when he so bitterly needed help, by abetting his sense of outrage at the local conventions of death which seemed to him obscene and indulgent mockeries of his own suffering. As he raged along, her eyes were screwed up in sympathetic pain for what he was enduring in memory and imagination. She said,

"I think—horrid as the details surely are—people are trying to help themselves through troubling moments by making ceremonies out of what you think ought to be so private. I agree with you, of course, that it is all miserably inadequate. I wouldn't be caught dead at a funeral, if you'll excuse a feeble joke. But I think I can understand why others need them."

"Need them!"

"Yes, people have always tried to do honor to the largest acts of life."

"Then it is just *this* damn place, and the way *they* do things that is so horrible?"

"Partly. Not entirely. Did you see the pictures of Napoleon's funeral when he was brought back to Paris?"

"Yes."

"Really, my dear, it was the same—oh, more plumes and horses and trumpets and troops and muffled drums, but whether emperor or high school boy—"

She broke off for he was leaning intently forward, trying to transcend the meaning of the day. Finally he said,

"I suppose people have always done something of the sort?"

"Oh, yes. Always. From the most primitive to the *Invalides.*"

"But why do I feel like a double criminal—first for what I did to him, and now for refusing to go near the funeral?"

"Oh, I think I know." She gently put her gloved hand on his arm and said sweetly, "You feel so deeply that you have no way to express the only part—the proper part—of what you feel. Only people who love life so greatly can be so enraged at its short-comings."

She knew how to change the subject when necessary. With a smile at herself, she said, "I just love a car," leaning forward for a moment. He was struck by the simplicity of this wonder at a thing so common as a motor car, which, to her, in a long earlier day, he thought, must have seemed amazing. That she could still so remember it turned his thought, however trivially, away from himself. "Don't you?" she asked lightly.

He did not answer and she drove several miles in silence. The distance was a hazy dust-violet. They might have been at sea in a small boat for all they could discern of land features. She saw that his removal from the familiar was doing him good. Slowly, slowly, by her words, her company, and the complicity she shared in this idle drive about the back roads of the county, she brought him to a belief beyond fury. He did not at the time know this but in after-years he recognized what Victoria Cochran accomplished for him on the day of Billy's burial—to scorn the shoddy observances of Belvedere without dishonoring the humble dignities within every gesture of celebration of life's stages, however unworthy its terms.

For in the physical bitterness of that dusty open empire, she longed (anyone else but "the village freethinker" would have said "prayed") that he would love the land, if only in memory, with all its gritty hardness, which had given him his first wounds. Such wounds—how well she knew—would in retrospect come to seem like early caresses.

He suddenly rubbed his eyes and shook his head violently.

"But I keep coming back to the fact that I did it!" he exclaimed.

"Tell me exactly what happened," said Victoria calmly.

He could do so, rapidly, accurately, and in cleansing anguish.

She took a deep breath and stretched straight back from her driving wheel and said, in all the accents of a summing up of fate, which did honor to suffering and at the same time gave opening to the light of an endurable future,

"Phillipson, promise me something?"

"Anything."

"It won't be easy."

"Anything."

"Promise me never to try *not* to think about what happened."

"Never fear! I'll never be able to forget it."

"Yes, you will. But not if you try to forget it."

"I will?"

"Yes. And promise that if you think of it, you will grieve because he's gone. But not because of how he went."

To her amazement, and his own, he leaned toward her and kissed her lean cheek.

They drove on, and presently he said,

"I wonder if they're there yet?"

"Where?"

"At the cemetery, after the thing at Mr Doty's."

"I don't know. We can take a back road and drive over that way and see, from a distance, if you like."

"I just wonder. From a distance it wouldn't be so ghastly."

She saw that he couldn't bear to stay entirely away.

"No, it wouldn't. From a distance."

They were far from the cemetery, which was three miles out from town southwest of the hospital, at the point where the paved surface ended and a hard-packed dirt road ran on to the southwest and Whitewater. A thought struck Phil and he laughed strangely.

"What is it?" asked Victoria.

"Nothing. It just occurred to me that if I ever felt like going to the lake again, I would have to pass the cemetery where he will be buried."

"True enough," she said mildly.

"Therefore I will never go by that way again."

He knew how today the salt cedar groves on the seven islands must be powdery with sky-sift, and how they would stay that way until a heavy rain came or a strong clean wind off the Gulf three hundred miles away.

The essential life of the town went along, that morning, with people at their jobs; but more than might have been expected to do so were aware of the long procession of cars slowly advancing toward the cemetery shortly before noon.

From far across the open country, Victoria and Phil saw in the distance a flowing stream of cars all with headlights ritually turned on.

"Yes," said Phil, "now let's drive away again."

¤ ¤ ¤

Because the sun was hidden they could cast no shadows. The field of the cemetery with its little city of upright stones faded into the empty plains all about in which there was nothing to impede the eye. There was a chill in the dusty air which drew those present into themselves, as grief and decorum brought them to bow their heads by the graveside. Lew Priddle stood at one end, and at the other, Homer and Ellen. On either side, the sizable throng huddled trying to see what lay between them. From afar they would all be meaningless dots in the moted landscape; yet in their common presence, they each felt like a center of life, so intense was their emotion.

Lew Priddle gave a sharp sidelong glance at Mrs Tom Bob Gately, for he saw the signs of strain in her. He hoped she wasn't going to break down, for her face was working and she kept biting her lips and pinching the thin runnels of skin beside her mouth as if to remind herself of her own flesh and feeling beyond the moment. Facing her were the Breedloves, with Marilee and her mother. They too saw Leora. Ellen caught her eye and by the heroic quietude of her own face brought Leora out of her self-concern.

Mrs Thyra Doolittle was at a little distance from the center of things, but by an accidental shifting of the mourners she caught clear sight of Marilee, who saw nobody. Thyra made a silent inward gasp and held her breath at what she read in Marilee's face. She said to herself that she would bet anything she was right in what she was thinking of. How could people ever really talk to each other: but Thyra told herself she must try, she must try to find a way to reach Marilee if it was a matter of helping.

Everything tasted of the falling sky and all proceeded in order for many minutes. Actions were slow and mournfully reverent. Father Judson, who stood with the farthest of the mourners, recited his own prayers in silence for Billy as the minister read psalms in an eloquent countryman's voice which was proper to their universal realism. Humble beauties came to abide in the hearts and minds of the listeners, who even as they listened, felt that their lives could not be clouded throughout all days by mortality, grief, or hard circumstance in land and weather.

Closing his Bible, Lew Priddle shut his eyes and lifted his face to the sky in silent prayer for a long moment. Then slowly opening his long arms widely to take all the people with him, he began to sing a hymn he knew they loved, and gradually they joined him. Their modest voices reinforced each other. Even from a small distance, their sound would be lost in the illimitable open country; but they heard each other, and were heartened:

> *Now evening puts amen to day,*
> *Calm is the cloud upon the hill.*
> *We are comforted in our way.*
> *Wondrous is God's sovereign will.*

*Tree is down but seed is deep.*
*The child a sire will soon fulfill.*
*Branch will rise while root's asleep.*
*Wondrous is God's sovereign will.*

*After the rain the rivers flood.*
*Thanks from the humble heart do spill.*
*All things whisper in the blood.*
*Wondrous is God's sovereign will.*

*Amen.*

Secretly, everyone there knew it would all be over in a few moments, and they were glad. Mr Priddle and Mr Doty exchanged a swift glance of relief and satisfaction at how well matters had gone. In a moment the sign would be given for the coffin to begin slowly sinking into its deep, nicely cut, box-shaped pit.

§ § §

"So I surely," said Monica Mallory to herself, feeling the words race through her mind. "Oh, of course, I said. Why who else, as I say."

"But don't feel that way," came the internal answer. "Oh, Monica! Oh, oh, no, *they'll see you—*"

But the second inner voice was too late. There was a smothered cry, and then a small but possessed figure ran forward through the ordered throng near the grave, and fell upon one end of the polished coffin, caressing it with claw-tensed hands. It was Monica Mallory, wild in light freedom beyond the time and place. Swept with bereavement in her own emptiness, the threw herself on the coffin shrieking,

[ 258 ]

"I loved him, oh, my God, how I loved him! Nobody ever knew how much I loved him, but, I loved him, my dear darling, and he never knew! And oh! My God!" Her voice rose even higher and she gazed distantly about at all the shocked observers who were not yet able to overcome and recover her, and she screamed, "And now he will never, ever, know!"

She began to pound on the bronze-finished casket which Clyde Doty had assured the Breedloves was a good investment. Monica's act at last moved those whom it outraged to come forward and lift her away. They led her to one of the waiting cars and she went, suddenly docile under restored propriety—even with relief that she was free at last to be frankly crazy, saying to her rescuers,

"Thank you, thank you, you are very kind. Where are we going?"

As they drove her away, she wiped her eyes and ordered her garments with an air of comic self-reproof. Wondering how she could ever do a thing like that and if she might ever do such a thing again, she asked,

"Do you think anyone noticed?"

❧ ❧ ❧

By evening the air was again perceptibly in motion across the great space of the high west central plains. The dust was being vastly swept away to the west toward New Mexico and the Rocky Mountains by a wind coming off the shoulder of South America across the Gulf of Mexico and over Texas. Rain was probable, and then certain, and then suddenly it came in a crashing cloudburst, as if spring were making a violent advance in the lands where it had been halted by the invasion of the dust.

In Belvedere the streets were flooded within half an hour.

"You can't go back to the wanch in this," declared Leora Gately to her husband who had come to town for the funeral but had decided to drink instead of attending. He had spent the whole day at her house, as she called it, for though he owned it, he never lived there any more, to her fury, because the proper way was for her to leave him, not the other way round. But he still belonged publicly to her, and as such, was the possession of her pride, which demanded his presence in her marriage. By the time she returned from the funeral he was grandly drunk, lost in a haze of comfort and well-being which infuriated her because within it he was removed from her effect upon him.

"Very well," he mimicked, his speech thickened by whiskey and the absence of his upper denture which he habitually left out nowadays. "I can't go back to the rants in this. If it is not asking too muts, I'll just phind me a bed here in this house somewhere."

"St!" she exclaimed with her tongue and teeth. "Don't talk like that. Your bedroom is ready and has always been kept ready for you at all times! I don't know why you act like that. I spend my life making and keeping a lovely-home"—she was by now wearing a damp dish towel about her head, attacking the thick layers of dust which had fallen during the past three days over her precious objects and spaces—"and then this dust storm, and there isn't a crack anywhere that isn't full of it, and I let Mattie go for the day and I will have to do it myself, I can't stand dirt, thank God for the rain, though it needn't rain this hard, all we need is a nice long shower to settle the dust and wash it away. But's I say, you don't seem too grateful for all I do to make a home for you, never staying here, and staying out there alone with that smelly old nigra on the wanch, God knows what you eat, and where you sleep, or how often anything gets washed or cleaned!"

Tom Bob heard hardly any of her whirring clatter, but something she said did reach him, and he said not to her, but aloud to himself, that he guessed what he needed after a day of nothing but drink was a little solid food.

She heard him and said,

"Well, you can go and scramble yourself some eggs, then, I have enough to do to get this place clean again."

For since he never looked as drunk as he might be, she thought him capable of fending for himself, though she didn't like the color of his face, which showed a darker flush than she could ever remember. But with all warning about his blood pressure, he had always refused to take precautions, and she thought she owed it to herself not to open herself to profane and filthy language by making one more warning that he should drink no more.

Tom Bob came heavily out of his deep leather armchair, moving like a power that was thoughtless of its own lost splendor. His blooded flush was set off by his thick white thatch of hair. His small blue eyes still held the contentment Leora had worked to dislodge by her complaints. Starting for the pantry he felt happily that he was escaping into freedom, but she suddenly thought of what a mess he would make in her perfectly kept kitchen, and she came tattering after him on her high heels to get him some supper after all. As Tom Bob switched on the fluorescent tubes of light in the kitchen ceiling, the primrose yellow telephone extension rang on the kitchen wall, just as in the advertisement, and he answered it.

"Hi, honey," he said genially into the receiver. "Why hell yes, you can talk to her." He handed the receiver to Leora and said, "It' Ellen."

Mrs Gately took the phone while Tom Bob wandered off into the rank of deep freezes and electric ice boxes where his wife kept enough food to withstand siege. She watched him not seeing him, but seeing instead, as her pale eyes shifted from side to side across Tom Bob's receding figure, an instant vision of what Ellen Breedlove was telling her.

"No!" shrieked Leora, and again, "Oh, no!," and then, "Ellen! You must run right out of the house! It isn't safe! He might do anything!" She listened to the anguished quacking of the voice at the other end, and said, "Yes, of course I know it's a cloudburst outside, but I'd rather you got wet than killed by your own husband!—Well if you won't, you won't. But I'll send Tom Bob right over, he's right here, he's been here all day. You stay upstairs and lock your door till he gets there! Oh!"

She put the phone away and ran to the food room.

"Tom Bob, pull yourself together and get right on over to the Breedloves'—Ellen says Homer has gone out of his head, after all these years, he's lost control, and he's breaking whatever he can get his hands on! He shouted at her to just keep out of his way if she knew what was good for her! She says it is grieving over Billy, she saw it coming, she says. Now go *on!* Take my car, it's better for you in this weather than that beat-up old truck!"

He was staring at her wondering thickly if this was just something else she made up out of her own empty notion of what people did. Mebbe Homer just went and kicked over a floor lamp or a buckhorn ash tray stand, and mebbe he would just settle down when he felt like it. Women. Tshee-yit. Nine-tenths of the time they got theirselves all 'tirred up over nothin.

"Tom Bob Gately, do you hear me? She's in danger! I can't go out in this, this downpour would be the end of me, frail and small, ever since my operation, now you get on over there and take care of Homer! She says you're the only one he would listen to. Oh, *will* you!"

Her passion reached him. He sighed and rubbed his head, mumbling agreement, went out to the garage, and drove off in grand lurches, with a pleased sense that he wouldn't be responsible even if sober, for you couldn't see anything much in the sheeting downpour, but just drive by guess and by God, and mebbe only somebody high's a kite could have driven it anyhow.

He turned right on Central and into Cleveland, feeling his way happily along the wrong side of the deserted street. He did not expect to meet any other car, and it was therefore amazing when his rear view mirror caught the dancing wet light of a car coming up behind him, just before he was due to turn left into First Avenue and head out that way to Homer's house on the northwest side of town.

The light was suddenly a lot prettier, he thought, for now part of it was red, it must be another light that was turned on which now began to spin in steady flashes. Above the pounding of the storm he began to hear a siren. He'd be a son of a bits if it didn't sound just like the police was after him. He pulled a little further to the wrong side and halted. The car behind drew up beside him and then Highway Patrolman Stiles, soaked with rain, was on the seat next to him shining a flashlight into his face.

"Tom Bob?" said Hardie Jo, "do you think you ought to be out driving?"

"Now, H.J., don't *you* go to devillin me. I get plenty of *it* from my wife. What ' matter ' you, boy?"

"Tom Bob, you're under the influence."

"Tshee-yit! I had me a phnort or two, but not's you could say more'n I could handle. Just let me go on now, Hardie Jo. Homer Breedlove is feeling mighty bad about that boy of his and I'm just on my way to comphort him?"

"Well," said Hardie Jo with professional humor suitable to dealing with the city's leading banker, "just's so you didn't say you's sober as a judge, Tom Bob. But you take care, hear? Get on over to the right hand side of the street, hear? and take it easy."

Tom Bob nodded kindly and the trooper dashed back to his own car. Driving with care and perfect control, Tom Bob went on through the storm to draw up at last in front of Homer's house. The lights were all on, upstairs and down, and the front door was open in the deep wooden porch.

"Gret God ammighty!" said Tom Bob at what he heard as he came splashing up on the porch and into the elliptical front hall, and then, at what he saw in the living room, "Gret God ammighty!"

All the furniture was overturned and some of it was broken. In the dark dining room beyond, Tom Bob could just discern the huge narrow figure of Homer Breedlove reaching to the wall to overturn Ellen Breedlove's most cherished article of furniture—a glass cabinet with mahogany supports which contained her thimble collection and her treasures of glass and china, which she polished regularly once a month whether they were used or not.

"Homer!" bellowed Tom Bob, but his voice was loud only in his own ears. Homer did not heed him, but extending his long arms with hands like hooks at the ends, he slowly, and with a long, velvety sound of whimpering through tears that ran down the hollows of his root-vegetable face, pulled the cabinet away from upright and let it slowly crash with every melody of broken glass.

Tom Bob switched on the dining room light and said,

"Homer, you Got-damned phool, cut this out!"

Homer looked around at him, blinded by the chandelier, and shook his head as if reasonably refusing an absurd proposition. He picked up a china soup tureen off the sideboard and hurled it against the pantry door, sobbing the words,

"I spend my life trying to do right for the rest of them, and hold on to myself, and this is what I get! Don't anyone talk to me about the goodness of God! *I'll God them,* all right!"

"Now, Homer, he's gone, everyone has to go, you and I both, and Billy, and everyone. Now you just get a-holt of yourself!"

Finishing the statement, Tom Bob was next aware of himself on the floor, staring up at Homer Breedlove, who gazed down at him with resentment against any excitement except that which he himself was providing. A white pain cleaved Tom Bob's head, and his skin was a mottled purple. His right arm was suddenly absent—it had no feeling, nor had his right leg, which was why suddenly he had gone to the floor. His face seemed half its usual size, and his right eye was almost an inch lower than his left one. A hot tingling suffused all that part of him which could still know sensation.

"Homer?" he thought he said, but it was not a word of pleading that resulted, but only a moist sound on constricted breath.

Homer viewed him with suddenly rational horror. Tom Bob Gately was at last having the stroke everyone had predicted for him years ago.

"Why, no," said Homer, shocked out of himself by the look of his old friend. "Tom Bob, you all right?"

Tom Bob made a baby's gesture whose meaning was obscure. He was unable to move his body. Homer, restored to himself with a sick feeling, felt a slow mournfulness rise in his breast when he saw how guilty he was for causing Tom Bob just the extra excitement he could not bear. He leaned down to lift Tom Bob, but Tom Bob was too heavy and helpless to be lifted alone. He ran to the stair in the hall and called upward, "Ellen?" but she was still locked in their bedroom, now terrified as much by the sudden silence below, followed by her husband's cry of her name, as by all the commotion of the past half hour.

"Oh, Lord," murmured Homer, "forgive what I said. Thou knowest I did not mean it in the depths of my grief. Help me now to help Tom Bob," and without thought, he ran out of the front porch where the rain fell in a curtain of light off the eaves. He saw a lighted car at the curb behind Leora Gately's Cadillac. It was a highway patrolman's car with its red signal light revolving. It must contain Hardie Jo Stiles. Homer ran out to fetch him and Hardie Jo met him halfway.

"I figgered I'd just better tag along and see if he's goin be able to drive home," said Hardie Jo. "But I never—"

He never expected to find what he found on the dining room floor. Ellen came to join them now, for from upstairs she had seen the trooper come into the house. In a moment Hardie Jo called for Clyde Doty's ambulance and in another Ellen telephoned Leora.

Though he could not speak understandably, Tom Bob could hear all they said in his presence. When he heard Hardie Jo say

[ 265 ]

they would get him right to the hospital he summoned every power left in him, which focussed in his left eye and his left hand. He could not make words with any clarity, but he was a strong man and he made his meaning plain to them by signs of fury which seemed to threaten further disasters in his forlorn body, telling them that he refused under any circumstances to be taken to any hospital. His habit of command was firm, and their habit of compliance so simple through all the years, that when the ambulance came, and Clyde himself with it, they took him home to Leora instead of out to St Mary's at Van Buren and Fifth.

※ ※ ※

Leora received him with astonishing calm and good sense. Her doctor was on the way. They would decide later if Tom Bob should be moved to the hospital. For the moment, here, his room was already prepared, the bed turned back, pillows propped, a glass of water with a bent drinking tube on the night table, Tom Bob's pajamas and bathrobe laid out waiting for him, two electric warming pads already turned on "low" inside the bed, milk warming on the "low-medium" on the electric range downstairs, and a portable radio already moved from the knotty-pine den and plugged in the bedroom waiting for him. Receiving her all-but-destroyed husband Leora was wistfully heroic, to everyone's admiration, as she saw. At last, he was home. Helpless, he was hers completely.

After the first things had been done for him by the doctor, a council was held, and it was decided that there was little else to do for him but give him bed rest and care, which he could have at home just as well as at St Mary's. "Better," declared Leora, her heart beating with the joy of usefulness and possession. Tom Bob was her prisoner on her own terms. All of Belvedere would soon hear from her that he was home to stay.

❦ ❦ ❦

In the past week, since the funeral, Phil had not gone to town, but this afternoon, urged by his mother, and fearful of his inability to concentrate, he had made himself walk down to Buchanan and Central, to see the world, and to discover whether he still belonged to it. Out of habit, he entered the Saddle and Sirloin and sat at the counter to drink a cup of coffee. Facing him was the mirrored wall behind the counter and there was his other self. He could not look at it. He turned sharply to gaze out to the street through the front window, and in a second, he saw Marilee going past. She walked with her head held high, not so much in pride, as to seem detached, even invisible, in the presence of the sidewalk life of Belvedere.

Phil in an instant was out of the café and after her. He called her. She paused, turned, and saw him.

"I was just drinking coffee. Will you join me?"

In silence she came to him and they returned to the café where he took his cup to a booth and they sat down side by side. She refused anything to drink.

"How are you?" he asked.

"You know? I haven't the slightest idea."

"What do you mean?"

"I don't even know that."

He tried to hold her eyes with his, but she glanced beyond him with a faint smile. He heard someone enter behind him and saw her wave a greeting.

"Who is it?"

"Guy."

"Oh, no, not now," said Phil in a groan.

Guy DeLacey came to the booth and asked,

"Mind if I just sit down a minute?"

"Not at all," said Marilee.

Guy sat down facing the other two and filled his corner of the booth, cushioned by his own full flesh. His mealy face showed the beard of a day and a half. He waved toward the counter for coffee, and when it came, he stirred it in silence, looking down. Presently he was the first to speak again.

"Well," he said, while his smoking cigarette trembled in his plump fingers on the table top, "I guess there won't be much to ever say about him except that we miss him."

"Don't talk about him," said Phil.

"Let him," said Marilee.

"I have the right," stated Guy. "He was my friend, too," staring indignantly at Marilee, who smiled at him, which made Phil stare at her in his turn.

"Don't you stare at me, too," she said to Phil.

"I wasn't," he said.

"Excuse me," said Guy.

But they had both been searching her with their eyes, for different purposes, but equal longing—Phil, to know what she thought of him now; Guy, to know all that she knew, in all ways, about Billy. Guy abruptly turned to Phil, hoping to appease the dislike he felt in him.

"Any time you want to use my old red pickup," he said ingratiatingly, "just take it. You don't even have to ask me. I leave it out behind the Red Dot for my particular friends, just like Billy always used it."

"Thank you, Guy," replied Phil, with a turn of distaste in his entrails. "I don't—" but he let it go.

Marilee looked above them at her own thoughts. Their odd

feeling about each other was of no interest to her. She turned her head sharply and ran her hand through her heavy honey-colored hair.

"I am not going to attend graduation," she said. "I've had enough."

"Enough what?" asked Guy.

"Enough public emotion."

"But Monday evening? You're not graduating," said Guy.

"No, I don't blame you," said Phil. "I must go. I have to get my diploma. My parents are waiting for it."

"Have the school mail it to you," she said with comic contempt.

"They wouldn't do that. You have to be present to get it."

"Anyway," she declared, "I won't have to go because I am not going to graduate this year. If I had to graduate, I'd have to go too, or my mother would never forgive me."

"Parents get more out of it than their young ones," stated Guy, the childless.

"That mother," said Marilee. "You people will never know."

"What people?" demanded Phil. "I'm not *you people*. You needn't put me off like that."

"I know." She leaned and touched his cheek with hers. "I only mean that *nobody* else will ever know what she has done for me all her life. How could they? when I am only discovering it myself? Until something happens to you, you don't ever, really, ever, think about anybody else, do you, and the way they feel? And the way they give up things for you that they wouldn't ever have done otherwise?"

There was a weight of love in all she was saying, her words common and inarticulate, but her emotion was neither, and the two who listened to her were stirred by the wonder in her face. Guy tingled with a feeling he could not recognize. It made him feel robbed of lifelong exchange with any other human being. Phil scowled at her with worry. She sounded like someone gone far away and remembering the long ago.

Marilee clasped her hands on the table top and lowered her head to them and her hair fell forward concealing the pale sweet cheek they would otherwise have seen, and she said, low, but they heard her,

"I would hate, hate, ever to do anything ever again to make my mother ashamed, after all she has done for me." A little blurt of inadvertent laughter escaped Marilee but it sounded equally like a choked sigh, "She always says the great thing is to be able to hold your head up and look everybody straight in the eye."

She sat up and faced Phil so that he saw her eyes were full of extra light.

"Have you ever made a point of looking everybody straight in the eye?" she said, with an effort at her old system of comedy. He shook his head. The sight of her in this mood made his heart fall and then jump up again, with love.

She caught his feeling, but shook her head and stood up as if to evade private emotion, too, and said,

"I must go."

"May I go along?" asked Phil.

"No, please. I have to be dull, some shopping, and I promised to stop and see Mrs Doolittle who has some perfume samples to give me, and you know."

"Goodbye," he said.

He watched her go, while Guy watched his face, and saw there the kind of longing he always wanted to know about.

"I'll get this," said Guy, going to the counter to pay the cashier, hungry for opportunities to be well thought of.

"Then this one," said Thyra Doolittle, touching a drop of perfume to the back of her hand with a glass applicator and extending it to Marilee to inhale across the counter of the Beauty Bar in the Longhorn Drug Store, "is *Paris After Dark*. It's not as spicy as *Who Cares,* but it's a little heavier and it lasts longer. I think I like it best. M'm?"

"Yes, lovely," said Marilee, wondering why everyone in the world was looking at her so today. Thyra kept her head down, but her eyes looked steadily up at Marilee and they were filled with a subject far more interesting and serious than perfume samples. Marilee added, "Did you say you could let me have some of this? I suppose it is expensive."

"The most. But I have a nice free tiny sample I got you here to give to you, honey. Just a minute."

Thyra disappeared below the counter to find her treasure. Marilee gazed about. The Longhorn was almost empty. Over the Beauty Bar hovered an invisible cloud of combined scents, rising from the many toiletries and other preparations which Thyra displayed and sold. The air seemed to express Thyra's natural climate—mustily sweet, faintly stale, as of dried and disguised sweat, suggestive of ardent devices to capture a little while of love in a fading lifetime. Thyra reappeared with a small box of golden cardboard which she pressed into Marilee's grasp. As she did so, she kept Marilee's hand and said,

"Honey?"

"What?" exclaimed Marilee softly, startled.

"Now, honey, don't be scared, or offended, but I've been through quite a lot, and *nothing* shocks me, or makes me hide something out of shame, when there's something to take care of that's terribly important? All I mean is, if there's anything you just simply have to talk to somebody about and you don't have anybody else to talk to that won't say a word to anyone, why, here I am? I mean, some things begin to be seen by everybody after a while, but sometimes someone can see them before anybody else can, and then is the time to find out for sure, and to get help, if someone needs it. Honey, you don't mind, do you?"

Thyra gave her hand a squeeze and released it. Marilee was paper-white and felt that she must be visibly trembling, but her trembling was all within her. She looked around. Nobody was paying any attention to anyone at the Beauty Bar.

"Mrs Doolittle—" she began, and at the sound of her own voice, tears started toward her eyes, which made her angry.

"Now just say Thyra. When it comes to this thing, we're all the same age, because we're all women, honey. Go on, tell me. Come on. You need someone. Let me help. Nobody is going to hear you now. Bend over and we'll look at these new lipsticks together. Poor little darling. I saw it all coming and I wanted to but I couldn't say anything, and what good would it have done, anyway, who could blame you, he was such a darling, and he had that way with him of having everything be the way he wanted it."

"How did you know?" asked Marilee, looking down into the golden-lighted glass counter full of beauty aids, none of which she had needed.

"Why, there's a definite change about a person's look when it happens, but most people don't see it right off. Doctors can tell sometimes even without an examination, long before anything grows. Just some look. I don't know. I always know when I see it."

"When did you know?"

"At the funeral. That day. I saw something and then I wondered and then I was sure. Honey, are you sure?"

"I don't know. I suppose so."

"Yes. Well, I know someone over at Orpha. You just let me call him and make an appointment, and nobody will know, and we'll run over there in my little Liza Jane"—which was what Thyra called her old Chevrolet—"and we can get back the same day, and then when we know, we can plan what to do. He's a first-rate doctor and he will be just as kind and private as we want him to be."

"You mean—he'll do something?"

"Oh, no, honey, no, never, and I wouldn't want him to, and neither would you, that's a crime, and besides, you'd never forgive yourself. *I know*. No, I mean, he'll make some tests, so we can be sure. That's all, and nobody need ever know we went to Orpha for that. I have some things to shop for anyway. We'll go Monday. —Now you'd better not let yourself cry, or anything, here. Some of those old hens might come in and get to thinking. Women are awful, the way they think they can get right to the truth by making it up, when nine times out of ten they just make up what they wish was true, and then tell it, and most of the time it's bad news about someone."

"Do you think anybody else knows, Thyra?"

"Oh, my God, no, I don't think so. Not yet."

"My mother. What it would do to her. It would kill her, I think."

"Now just wait. We'll see about that if and when. Now look up and let's talk about this letter, someone is coming, so give me a big smile, honey, and remember, I just thought you might need someone, I wasn't prying?"

"Oh, no, thank you, Mrs Doolittle, Thyra, I have been out of my mind. —What's this letter?" she asked brightly as two women came to the Beauty Bar and looked over its wares nearby.

"A letter from Monica Mallory, over at Orpha City, that place, you know," said Thyra. "I've had three of them this one week! Listen."

"I had one too," said Marilee.

"Yes. Listen:"

*Dear Thyra Doolittle, you dear, I know you are keeping me
in your prayers, and I just have to write to my dear friends and
say how happy I am, and how good everyone is to me here.
The food is fine, some lovely people, and I have to play and
sing for them every day. I often think of your wonderful
work and I remember you in my prayers. I wonder if I ever
told you about the recital I gave in Evanston the year I was
taking my degree in library science. I sang Panis Angelicus,
by Cesar Franck. He was organist at the old church of Saint
Clothilde in Paris, France. Also sang Un bel di (Puccini).
How long ago it seems. All so plain. Write to your old Monica-
Mickle.*

> *In Xst*
> *(Miss) Monica Mallory*

"All three letters were the same, just about the same things in
each," said Thyra.

"Yes, my letter was just like it," said Marilee.

"If we get a chance, over there shopping, some day, at Orpha
City," stated Thyra, with a lifted voice to reach the other customers, and to justify anything they might hear later of a certain
trip to Orpha City by Mrs Doolittle and that little Underwood
thing, "we just ought to drop by the Home and see Monica!"

"Yes. Let's."

For Monica was a patient in the Good Shepherd Home at
Orpha City, a private sanitarium, where she could plan to spend
the rest of her life, peering expectantly out the window, when she
was not at the piano, or engaged in writing her letter, which
went forth in many almost identical copies every week.

"Monday?" said Thyra.

"Yes," said Marilee. "Let me know."

[ 274 ]

Thyra watched her go and then turned her attention to the other women. It was odd. They made her heart heavy, while the girl filled it with life, however troubled.

"Yes?" she said, "may I help you?"

One of the customers turned. It was Leora Gately.

"Just looking," she said.

"Fine."

"I thought:" said Leora, and then paused in awkward satisfaction. She had forgotten how rapidly Thyra Doolittle had aged. Innocently, Thyra nodded with encouragement. "Well," resumed Leora, "I thought, then, that you know, there is so little he can enjoy, would you care to stop by the house late some afternoon and see Tom Bob? He can't really talk, only make a word now and then, but perhaps he'd be glad to see you for a minute?"

Thyra pressed her hands together below the counter. Was this noble charity or was it disguised triumph on the part of Mrs Gately? She didn't know. Perhaps Mrs Gately herself didn't know. In any case, it was not a time to be thinking of herself. Thyra said,

"I'll come. Thank you, Mrs Gately."

Mrs Gately nodded and with a flickering regret at her impulsive invitation, she wondered how Tom Bob would really feel about seeing Thyra. She left the store, moving in little dartings like a bird. The friend with her said, and this was all Thyra could hear,

"Well, Leora, in your place, I hardly think I—"

*❈ ❈ ❈*

It was a measure of what she carried in memory that Thyra
Doolittle went that same afternoon after work to call at the
Gatelys'.

"Oh?" said Leora. "I didn't think quite so soon. But come in.
I'll see about him. Just sit down a minute, Mrs Doolittle."

She left Thyra in the Hollywood-Spanish living room, with its
mottled caramel plaster and amber light bulbs, and hurried to
Tom Bob's room where she flew about making neat things
neater. He did not watch her, though he could hear and know
what she was doing. As she worked, she said,

"I saw an old friend of yours, friend? well anyway, I must say I
don't know what came over me, but anyway, I thought you
might be glad to see her for a minute, after all, she did keep her
promise to me, but's I say, I don't mean she has to come again
and keep coming, but just this once, so I said why don't you run
in sometime, not meaning today, but today she came, and she's
downstairs right now. Let me see if you are all right."

She came to the bed and turned the light full on him which
hurt his good eye. She smoothed the bedclothes and made neat
the collar of his pajamas for him—for *him,* who never used to
sleep in anything but his skin here in town or in his sweated
undershirt out at the ranch. Once a day she bathed him with
warm water and wood alcohol, content that his naked virility did
not offend her, now that it had no power to threaten her. She felt
tender toward his body and the baby care it needed.

"There!" she said, playful yet exasperated because Thyra was
waiting below. A formless sound came from Tom Bob and she
supposed he was asking who the visitor was.

"Thyra Doolittle," she said, smoothing his heavy white locks
off his brow, but failing to recognize the quick storm of refusal
and the soundless call for pity that showed in his eye. To be seen

[ 276 ]

by his sweetheart as he now was—this was humiliation he must not be asked to endure. He tried to speak but could not. His breath made tubelike sounds of protest in his bull chest, and Leora said,

"Now don't get so excited, she won't stay long, I'll see to *that,* I thought you'd be pleased, but not as pleased as all that!"

Giving the effect of being offended, she tapped rapidly out of the room and went downstairs to bring Thyra.

Thyra came into his room and stood at the foot of the bed and looked upon him. One side of him looked like the heavy, warm, profane, rebellious, and generous lover she knew so well; the other side like no one at all. But there was enough of him to summon up their past together. A ragged pain seemed to cleave her breast. She smiled her pink, powdery, blue-shadowed smile, and said brightly, in a dry sound,

"Well? Tom Bob? I certainly am glad to see you again. My, you don't look so sick to me, two or three weeks, and."

Leora stood at the head of the bed beside him as if to receive and filter all her words to him. Thyra stopped speaking. Tom Bob glared at her with his left eye clear as the useless right one wept slowly. She knew that he hated to have her look at him now, and she never would have come if she could have known how changed he was. But still—his rough white hair was brushed aside from his brow and he resembled an elderly boy spruced up for a party. There was white beard stubble glistening on his jaws in the pitiless light of the side-lamp. His skin was a hearty pink. She thought she had memorized his appearance for life, but now she knew again little aspects she had forgotten. She treasured these. Not daring to touch any part of him, she patted the bedclothes, and said,

"I had only a minute. I have to be running along. Just think of it! Seeing you again!"

She nodded to Leora, and went alone out of the room, downstairs, and out to her car, and drove off along Central working against her sobs. Half a block later she was passing SS Peter and Paul. Jamming the car to a halt, she ran across the street and into the darkened church. It seemed immense because almost the only light was the crimson altar lamp which seemed infinitely far away. She knew Catholics believed that when the red lamp was burning it meant God was there in the tabernacle. She knelt in the last pew and prayed through her shaking bones, in an act of love,

"Oh, God, You know I don't belong here, and I know I have no right to be heard, but oh, God in heaven, please, please, let him die."

❅ ❅ ❅

The Durhams had no telephone. When Marilee wanted to reach Phil on Sunday evening she had to walk to his house along the country-edge of town. The early June evening was long and light. The scent of the plains was aloft—an air compounded of spicelike aroma of wild grass, of turned earth, of watery freshness coming from how far who could say, perhaps from Whitewater Lake, perhaps from as far away as the Gulf. The upper heaven was brushed dark as though by charcoal and the lower showed a band of yellow light, and between the two somewhere hung the evening star, which looked huge in that clarity and which pulsated unevenly like the irresolution of one whose mind is not made up but whose choices are plain.

"Phil," she called, knocking on the faded wood of the screen door. Mrs Durham could not answer, but her husband came, in his lurching step, and said,

"Come in, Marilee? Come in? Phil's in his room back there with all the doors closed, his *study* he calls it, I'll get him."

[ 278 ]

"Oh, no, just let me wait out here. I have a message for him, that's all," she replied.

It was strange how she could see Phillipson Durham in even his father's wreckage. Mr Durham was thin and palsied, bent from his work at the composing stone; but he was swarthy like his son, and his black eyes held some spirit in them yet which reached out. Quiet and well-spoken, he was a man who had been forced to accept boundaries and diminishings, unlike his son who fought against them in his mind. Oh, my God, said Marilee silently in desperation waiting for Phil to come out to the porch, help him! Help me! Help everybody!

Sport Durham stood forgetful of his small duty as he watched the play of thought over her face. In the clear twilight she was so beautiful in her odd way that for a moment he felt no age at all. Love known and lost spoke through them both, and seemed to make almost a third presence between them, though it meant something so different to each.

"Please, then?" asked Marilee, "Mr Durham?"

"Oh, yes. I'll get him."

Sport helped himself, hand after hand, to retreat within the door and down the hall, and when he opened an intermediate door before going along the distant corridor to the "study," she caught a glimpse of his figure in silhouette which seemed to be dancing to some random merriment, instead of to the ill-transmitted messages of his ruined nerves.

In a moment Phil came running to her, closing the main door to the house to let them be alone. His eagerness made her heart sink.

"Hi!" he cried, hugging her. If—if she had come to him this evening, perhaps it meant he was free to think of what he wanted to say sooner or later.

She greeted him in her cool, breathy voice, and said,

"I brought you a message. —Mrs Gately called Mother and said she knew we saw you all the time, and so would we please tell you to come to see her right away."

"Mrs Gately?"

"Yes, she says she has something for you."

"One million seven hundred thousand dollars and two cents."

"Well, anyway, you're supposed to go to their house."

"When?"

"Now, I suppose."

"Will you go with me?"

"No. I can't stand her."

"Can I come back after I see her? Where will you be?"

"Home. But don't, till after Monday."

"Monday? You mean after Commencement?" He sighed inwardly, but he supposed she could not bear to think of anything else but Commencement without Billy, even if she were not going to attend. Reasonably, he said, "I understand."

"Just Monday. Will you wait till after then, Phil?"

"Marilee, I want to be with you—"

"I know, Phil. I want you to. But after Monday, then?"

"All right. I guess so. But then, really, everything has to be over then, Commencement, everything, and we can't go on forever and ever, thinking and just remembering—can we?"

"It still isn't yesterday, even, for me. It's still today, all of it."

"Yes, oh yes. Forgive me."

"No. It's not you. —Come on, I'll walk to the corner of Central with you."

She took his hand as sweetly as ever before, and they went off together.

"Look at that star," he said.

"I did."

Its purity and glory exalted him. It could tell him nothing, but gave him the ease of heart which must come with the granting of any great wish. They walked in silence as the darkness sifted lower over the plains all about, and the darling lights of town came clear.

At the corner of Cleveland and Central they halted to say goodbye.

"Good night. Till *after Monday?*"

"Yes." She squeezed his hand. "Phillipson, do you think you could say a prayer?"

Before he could ask why she spoke so formally, she left him.

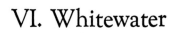

VI. Whitewater

"We'll just go right up to Tom Bob's room," said Leora. "Just come along. Be careful. My floors have just been waxed, they're slippery, but they look so nice?"

Phil followed her up the Spanish-tiled stairs. Her voice fretted back over her shoulder with an extra edge of refinement as she said, with pleasure in medical jargon,

"Tom Bob's been a little upset, I never know what over, but we've been having a few symptoms—loss of functions, elimination, and that, Doctor says bladder?"

They went along the upstairs hall to Tom Bob's room where Leora steered Phil to the foot of the bed and stood beside him. Phil after a quick horrified glance at Tom Bob looked slightly aside and kept his gaze on a rack of hunting rifles on the wall. Leora neatly slipped a small package out from under the folded catnap blanket which lay across the end of the bed. She put on her haziest smile and raised her voice a little as if to address a women's club audience, and showing the little package, she said,

"Now, Phil Durham, we all know you were his best friend, Billy's, I mean, and he meant the world and all to Tom Bob and I, so we always tried to give him something nice, birthdays, Christmas, first long pants, everything. So for his graduation we got him this graduation present, but now we can't—there's nobody—" her voice choked and still smiling her committee smile she let tears tremble on her powdered eyelashes and continued—"I don't mean there's nobody, but he's gone, and I thought and thought, and I said, I can't return it, it's already engraved, and it's no earthly use to Tom Bob or I, and so we thought we wanted for *you* to have it, for *your* graduation present, now that Billy can't, and we hope you don't mind, we don't know you so well, but please, here it is, and will you think of Billy when you wear it?"

She handed over the little box in its tissue paper sealed with a gold sticker. Phil saw from her face that he must open it right then. Not looking at Tom Bob he felt the fierce glare of that one good eye upon him. He could hear the slow tubelike breathing of Tom Bob. He pulled at the tissue paper and revealed a purple velvet case. He opened it. Within it was a gold wrist watch with a gold link band. Everything was golden about the watch—its face, hands, numerals. He turned it over to read the chiselled letters on its back: *Billy from Aunt Leora and Tom Bob Graduation 1949.*

"It's all wound up, and it's a self-winding," said Leora, rubbing her eyes, and then touching the watch delicately to admire it for Phil, who was still silent. "It has this sweep second hand," she insisted, "and there it tells the day of the month and the year, and if you press it here, you will get a little chime to tell you what time it is in the dark?"

Her rising inflection begged for appreciation.

"It's a beauty," finally said Phil, with a maimed smile. His father would have to work three months to pay for such a watch. How could he accept it?

"Try it on, see if it fits," urged Leora, feeling that the scene was somehow a failure. A latent sweetness in her longing gave him an odd pang as he looked at her busy, thin face. He slipped the watch on his left wrist. "You see?" she carolled. "Perfect. Just perfect." Raising her voice, though her husband could hear well, she said, "Tom Bob, isn't it absolutely perfect? I'm so glad we thought of this! It is, isn't it!"

They both looked at Tom Bob as though he could reply. To their astonishment, then, he made an effort that made him sweat in the light of the bed lamp that shined on him day and night, and he produced sounds that could be words. Leora repeated what she thought he said:

"*Drop that?*" she shrilled, "Is that what you said, Tom Bob? Why should he *drop* it? We really and truly gave it to him!"

No, no, no, urged Tom Bob with his breath and his glare and his good hand, that was not what he meant. He tried again and made the same sounds, staring at Phil with such force gathered deep out of memory that it was in its way more eloquent than speech.

"Yes!" said Phil suddenly, glad that he could understand Tom Bob who tried so hard to communicate. "*Bobcat!* You said *bobcat!*"

Tom Bob's deep breath eased out in a sigh of thanks that he had been understood.

"Oh, you men," said Leora playfully, "nothing but hunting," and just then the telephone rang. "Excuse me, I'll have to run along and answer that. I'll be right back, Phil Durham. Don't go."

She went to the phone at the end of the hall, and Phil stood smiling at Tom Bob, who gave the effect of smiling back, while through their minds went similar successions of pictures, different in detail, but telling the same general story of hunters out on the ranch beyond Whitewater trailing the wary old bobcat who had played hide and seek for so many years with Tom Bob and his friends.

☙ ☙ ☙

The ranch was so big and the rocky highland where the bobcat lived was so far away from the headquarters that they would have to go out in the truck, with all the camping gear they needed, and pitch camp and stay out all night. In fact, they might do well to think of hunting him by night, for he was an inquisitive old rascal, and the campfire light, and the smoke, and the smell of bacon cooking in an ashy skillet, and the odd movements of men around the fire sending shafts of shadow like spokes out on the ground and even upon the smoky air, would attract his notice, and you couldn't tell, but he just might come haunching along one of the ledges and take his way up into the high branches of one of the two tall pine trees that grew up out of the rock and there spend an hour or two watching them.

If the question arose as to whether animals could or could not think, why, they would probably in the end after many stories based on personal observation come to the same conclusion, which would be: of course they could think. It would be evidence of thought that he would stay up in the tree planning what to do and watching for the exact moment when to do it. He would be too smart to make any noise until just before he leapt, and then what a great sound he would make, was it cry, or snarl, or scream, or all three strung together like strands in a rope? Anybody who had seen him—and several had, though nobody had ever got a good shot at him—knew how big and powerful he was, and how he could bound away using cover like an Indian.

If they didn't attract him by night, never mind, for they would drink all the bourbon they felt like drinking, enough so that the tar-black coffee would never keep them awake, and they would yawn, and scratch their bellies, and go off a little way to piss together not giving a damn, and then come back to haul out their bedrolls from the truck and unroll them upwind of the fire and climb in and gradually notice the ache made by the sizable pebbles under them which they wouldn't bother to get rid of. They would feel their very flesh sag heavily down from their bones toward the ground, which was the nearest piece of the top part of the whole earth itself, and join it with unrecognized kinship in its dry smells of dust and herb, grass and rock, falling asleep leaving the dream of the bobcat behind until daylight.

Sometime between two and three o'clock, stone cold and hard as rock with stiff aching muscles from which the bourbon had faded, they might awaken to see two black pines towering above the rocks against the night sky filled with general starlight; and in the very branches of the pines, held as if by claws, and shining through the black traceries of the boughs, would be the lower stars, bright beyond telling, just for that moment caught to earth by the guardian trees, somehow free of the mystery of stars farther away in the upper heavens.

The fire would be long dead. Perhaps a wind before morning would come low along the ground. Where would he be, the old rascal, at an hour like that? The daylight would soon come and it would be time to use it again, probably to go along the ledges until they were led into that long ravine which closed at its end under a swell of hill. That would be a great place to trap him—no way out, and twin boulders to block the way, and a heavy old fallen dead tree. Everybody thought many times they'd catch him there, and he was still out there free and clever. Would it be best to all to keep him that way, and hunt him again and again, and never catch him, but have him to go after as long as they could get away from everyone and everything and be as free as he?

❧ ❧ ❧

"Yes, I know," said Phil, as if he and Tom Bob had shared thoughts and pictures in every detail. They had enough of the time and place in common to know much together, and for the first time since his stroke, Tom Bob again felt within reach of life, if only for a moment.

Down the hall Leora's voice went on at the telephone. It seemed to create as it spoke the very wire which would carry its words across town to Ellen Breedlove who was listening to her.

Phil smiled warmly at Tom Bob, and said, without the voice usually aimed at invalids and children,

"Yes, that old bobcat. We'll go get him yet—"

Even so, Tom Bob would now have none of that. He refused indulgence which must now be meaningless. With a strong yet fallible man's pugnacious realism he faced the true facts of his helpless condition, and to demonstrate it, he made an extreme gesture, sparing nothing to the healthy, darkly reserved young man who stood facing him. Tom Bob swept his good arm across the bedclothes and pulled them off his helpless recumbent form. He wore only a pajama coat. His burly figure was like a piece of his own country—the rough, crusty, but finally livable landscape of the bare high counties, with a shrubbed ravine which closed at its end under a swell of old hill, at whose groin the tumbled rubble of lost powers, like boulders rolled together under a dead stump of a heavy fallen tree, lay forgotten and useless. Staring at that angry nakedness, Phil had no recognition or thought of human flesh in the sympathetic sense. Tom Bob was a man filled with mortal disgust at what life had brought him to, after joys and glories of the flesh. A pale yellow flexible tube connected him to a white enamelled vessel which lay along the ledge of his heavy inert flank. The catheter was to Tom Bob his final indignity. Phil shook his head. He refused to look any further at the mockery of manhood. He could think of nothing to say. He felt a shrinking of his own loins at the sight before him. Even as he coldly wondered how that flesh which sagged heavily on its bones, pulled by unresisted gravity toward the mattress, toward the floor, the foundations of the house, and finally to the very earth itself, could ever have been fired and driven by love, Phil despised his own detachment with which he now viewed a fellow man in the loss of his powers. Stop it, stop it, he cried to himself silently, not knowing why, or what he would have stopped. Was it that the prophecy of the vision exposed on the bed was too terrifying to endure? As though he heard this thought, Tom Bob having shown in silence what he meant to show whipped the bedclothes across his body and turned his head aside on his pillow as far as he could. It was an act of departure, mourning, and dismissal. In a moment,

"Thank you for the watch," said Phil, seeking refuge in proper convention. "I'll keep it. I think Billy would say yes."

Mrs Gately came in as he spoke.

"Then that's fine," she said. "Poor Ellen had some happy news for a change. I'm so glad for her. Nancy wrote from Germany, they are stationed there, you know, the Calloways, they're going to have another child, so Homer and Ellen will have another grandbaby, and Captain Calloway got word that they'll be shipped home for the baby to be born here, Nancy will come right home here to her Mama. Ellen is so happy. Or would be if she could. You know, and all. And then young Homer will be here all summer, out of the navy, and before he goes up to

Norman to college in the fall. Oh, things. Maybe they do. I don't mean exactly work out for the best, but they go on. Ellen will have something to live for. Imagine. Only two weeks ago. Poor Billy. I don't know."

Tom Bob had removed his attention, as if forever. Phil said, "Thank you, Mrs Gately. I must go now."

As they went downstairs to the door, Leora said,

"Will you wear it to Commencement tomorrow night? For Billy. I'll be there."

He saw her nervous bullying for what it was, and accepted it with resignation.

"All right. I will."

He did wear it the next night, but never again. Years later he could never recall what finally became of it.

꙳ ꙳ ꙳

At Commencement exercises, Victoria Cochran, with the other members of the school board, sat on the stage of the high school auditorium. When Phil came up to the stage in line to receive his diploma she caught his eye. She neither smiled nor nodded, but a gleam which she gave him fortified him against emotion at that moment, and he was glad that as a result he could remain merely a sardonic observer, without impressions or feelings. He had dreaded the event, and now the fact that it had no sentimental or grieving power to reach his nerves or his heart, as it reached those of everyone else present, gave him a sudden sense of new strength as though he had just come into a stage of growth, and could realize it at the very instant.

When the graduated class marched out up the center aisle of the Belvedere High School auditorium, and broke its ranks to receive embraces and congratulations at the front door, Phil found his father wavering on the support of his rubber-tipped cane. They shook hands silently, and Phil took off his rented grey graduation gown and cap and made a neat bundle, depositing it on the trestle table set up for the purpose in the long hallway which rang with excited voices. He looked about for Marilee, but with pride he knew she would not be there, for he knew why. With a nod to his father, indicating that they might as well get started on their invalid's walk homeward, Phil turned to the outer door. Mayor Richard Dillingham was waiting for him.

"Congratulations, son," said the Mayor, "I think I know more than most folk here tonight what it meant to you to be up there and take your sheepskin without your friend. Now I have talked to my good friend here"—the Mayor put his hand on Sport Durham's shoulder in the role of the benevolent employer suing for equality with his employee—"and I am prepared, with his approval, to offer you a job with the Belvedere Printers. Now you can take more time to consider how you would like to work with us in the years ahead? We're glad to have your daddy with us, and I just know he'd be glad to see you join up and carry on a family tradition?"

All of his cool and comforting detachment fell away from Phil. He saw with ingratitude and anger the pleased hopeful look in his father's face, which meant that a plot had been worked out to keep him in Belvedere forever. The Mayor's ponderous gentleness seemed menacing, his waiting smile a superior assumption that the boy would jump at the chance which was held out to him. Phil felt a chilled sensation along his face bones. He believed he turned white under his swarthy skin. He began to think of things to say in the name of freedom, but was restrained, not by respect, but by inexperience. The Mayor had nothing if not experience of people. Allowing his smile to sound in his voice, he said confidently,

"Well, now, Phil, I see we've caught you by surprise and you don't know how to thank us. Mebbe you just better go on out to Whitewater and go fishing, and think it over for a few days, perhaps you need a little vacation, and then you come back and tell me when you want to start to work."

Phil nodded and ran down the wide flight of steps and away from Belvedere High. But in a few minutes he recovered himself and waited. Sport Durham followed in his difficult pace, and, within a block, caught up with him, irritated by the fact that you never, just almost never, could tell what would or would not please your own boy. What did he want, another gold watch?

❈ ❈ ❈

When Phil awoke his first thought, full of joy, was that it was now "after Monday." He was free to find Marilee. A barrier had been passed.

It was going to be a day of wan sky and still heat, but now when he walked rapidly along the edge of town to her house, the early sun was still golden, not white, and long shadows retained a hint of the night's faint moisture, making cool patches against the shadow sides of everything.

Her house was empty.

Mrs Underwood would be long since at work down at the Bluebonnet, he expected that. But when he knocked and called for Marilee there was no answer. So early. Where could she have gone? Perhaps she went with her mother, to have breakfast at the Coffee Shop, seven blocks straight along Buchanan. He went to seek her there.

"No," said Mrs Underwood, as soon as she was free of customers at the cash register, "she was gone when I got up and came to work. That girl. Sometimes I."

[ 294 ]

"But was she gone all night?"

"No, no, she came home, late, she went over to Orpha yesterday to go shopping with Mrs Doolittle, so Mrs Doolittle dropped her off home at around eleven o'clock, and she tiptoed in so's not to wake me, but of course I never go to sleep till she's home, but I learned long ago that it made her cross if she knew I's lying awake for her, so I never said anything, and she just went on to her room, and her light went out pretty soon. No, she was home, safe and all right, last night. But I just simply didn't wake up to hear her when she must have got up and gone out so early this morning. She usually leaves me a note. But this time she didn't. Excuse me."

She left Phil at the counter and went about her business for a few minutes.

What are you trying to do to me? he asked Marilee angrily in his thoughts and then he ducked his head at his selfish preoccupation, and said to himself that she was probably just off taking a walk somewhere, or going to see Mrs Doolittle, whom he could ask later when the Longhorn opened up, or—this was it—maybe she had gone to see some of her old friends the sisters of SS Peter and Paul. They were always asking him to come by and see them, and he never did, but now he might, to ask if they had seen her today. He saw her clear questing eyes and the lift of her fresh cheeks, and the way she stood so fine in her bones and proud, as though she were taller than she actually was. He wanted to hear her voice, now, right now, more than anything, that cool, faintly husky sound that nobody else made. It was ten minutes to eight. If he took his time about it, by the time he got to the Longhorn Drug, Mrs Doolittle might just be opening up, and he could ask her.

"No, not this morning," said Thyra, looking at him for a moment too long for his easiness. "I drove her home last night about eleven, but no, I haven't seen her since?"

"I just thought," he said.

[ 295 ]

"Surely. Well, if I see her—she said she might drop by today—I'll tell her you're looking for her. Where will you be?"

"Looking for her," he replied, smiling, and she saw him as she might have years ago, his beautiful, unmarked, male youth which called her and she wondered once again if any woman ever got over it, "thanks Mrs Doolittle."

"Surely. —Phil?"

"Yes, ma'am?"

"Nothing. I just."

"Well, then," he said, leaving her. She watched after him, wondering if she could run out in the street and call him back and tell him what she wished he would do. But she had an idea that it was what he wanted to do anyway, and, herself a lifelong victim of busybodies who told her what she ought to do with her life, she sighed and let him go and returned her attention to the Beauty Bar. There she had a whole carton of Vacation Vanities to open up that had come in yesterday while she was off at Orpha City with Marilee. She thought the best thing just now was to keep busy. She couldn't wait to see what they had sent her from the wholesalers, and she set to work with a nail file to strip the gummed tape along the seams of the carton. She hoped they had filled her order for *Aloha Tan,* which had the cleverest container she had ever seen advertised—a gold-colored pineapple with a spray dispenser concealed in the green enamelled spikes at the top.

The parochial school of SS Peter and Paul let out a week later for summer vacation than the Belvedere public schools. The school windows were open. Phil could see and hear the children at their lessons, and in each classroom a nun facing them. They were all too busy to have visitors. Marilee would not call on them at this time of day. He wandered along the walk and turned the corner by the rectory. Father Judson, in a striped sport shirt and golf slacks and loafers, was watering his few sprigs of grass that aspired amidst the strewn gravel of the front lawn.

"Good morning, Durham."

"Good morning, Father."

"You're out bright and early."

"Well, not early enough to find Marilee. Have you seen her, Father?"

"Not since that Monday."

"I see."

"You weren't there."

"No."

"Are you pulling out all right?"

"I don't know. Sometimes it's—"

"Yes. Well, hold on."

"Yes, Father."

"Will you be around all summer?"

"I guess so. My father wants me to stay here and work."

"Maybe he needs you. And your mother."

"They need me, all right."

There was a pause beaded by the starry drops of the hose spray hitting the dust and rolling it into little pungent pills. The curate's silence seemed to tell Phil that any man must be where he is needed, which was no comfort to him, since he already knew this as a son and as a Christian, and disliked what he knew. To preserve a social air, Phil asked,

"Will you be here this summer, too, Father?"

"I hope Monsignor will give me a couple of weeks off somewhere. I haven't asked him yet. He'll be home next week." Father Judson grinned like a schoolboy. "I'll have to time the question pretty neatly."

If he thought to make Phil smile, he was mistaken. Phil nodded soberly, lost in his own concern, and said,

"Well, thanks, Father, excuse me, I've got to look for someone, I guess I told you."

"Yes. You did."

More than you think, said Father Judson to himself. He wanted to watch Phil walk away and around the corner, but something told him that the young man, whether he knew it or not, would hate to be watched; so he turned his hose and his gaze in the other direction where a little colony of moss roses clung to some rocks in the hot shadow of the bare rectory.

※ ※ ※

Phil felt lost in his own streets, now open to the torrid morning. The familiar town looked as alien to him as—as old Whitewater, which he had once tried to see but could not bcause of the depths under the wind ripples on the lake's surface. Yet in a strange way, everything in Belvedere looked painfully clear this morning, so that the sharp angle of a business building on a corner cut his eye with pain as he saw it. The steak and lariat neon sign of the Saddle and Sirloin, though paled by the beating sunlight, continued its electric life even with nobody to notice it, which irritated him because of its idiocy. His growing worry and pain made him feel that he was merely imagining his own town of Belvedere and all the people and places he knew so well, and this made him the more uneasy, not to recognize thoughtlessly what was real, but to see everything as if for the first time, and find it menacing. At Polk and Second he turned the corner of the post office and saw the national flag hanging limp and motionless in the still air. He longed for a breeze to make it stir, as a flag should. He went to the library but since Miss Monica Mallory's removal to the Good Shepherd Home there was no one as yet to keep the library doors open. Still, he walked up the steps to peer in at the doors with his face to the glass. He knew where all the books were, but saw no one—except in thought, for there he saw Miss Mallory, and the letter she had written to him four days ago from the Home:

*Dear Phillipson Durham, you dear, I know you are keeping me in your thought and prayers, and I have just got to write to my dear good friends and say how happy I am, and how good everyone is to me here, quite the celebrity they make me. The food is fine, some lovely people, and I have to play and sing for them every day. Please say a prayer for me. Did I ever tell you about my recital in Evanston the year I was taking my degree in library science. I sang Panis Angelicus by Cesar Franck, he was organist of the church of Saint Clothilde in Paris, France. Also sang Un bel di, Mme Butterfly, (Puccini). How long ago it seems, now, just so plain. Write your old "library hostess" Miss Monica, my how you used to devour books, quite a satisfaction, you have a great career ahead of you.*

*In Xst,*
*(Miss) Monica Mallory.*

Her grateful happiness set his teeth on edge as he recalled the letter. He walked down the library steps. On a concrete bench under a tree at the library corner a long yellow cat was crouched with wide-eyed alertness staring straight ahead, while behind it a small boy about five years old was creeping toward it with his hands extended to seize the animal. Phil heard the boy say urgently to himself, "Oh, if I could only—." Suddenly aware, the cat flew itself sideways off the bench and ran with high rump around the building and out of sight. The boy halted and shrugged at Phil as if to say, "You can't catch them all." Phil nodded severely at the boy and walked on. He would have liked to pet the cat. Why did everything seem farcically to illustrate the sense of futility in his hope and his desire?

It was a measure of his distraction that it occurred to him to go around to the Red Dot to see if Guy DeLacey might by chance know anything of whom he sought; but he found a card stuck in the unlocked front door of the Auto Diagnostic and Repair Center which read in uneven handwriting, "Gone for coffee back in 5 min.," and he knew Guy would be at the Saddle and Sirloin; but when he thought of following him there, he was put off by what he thought of Guy. He must continue his wandering quest alone until he should find her.

Phil had not felt particularly young at any age; but now in his forlorn want, he felt not only young but ineffectual, not yet a man, too old to be a boy. The sight of her, and he knew she might be just around the next corner, or over in the Bluebonnet after all chatting with her mother in impatient fondness, or leaning on Mrs Doolittle's counter over its display of female witcheries and spells, would make him return to his world where he would no longer have to wander under the daylight where all that he knew so well looked so strange.

But she was not around the next corner, nor over in the Bluebonnet, nor at the Longhorn. He went to her house again, but nothing had changed there. A lovely easing certainty came to him and he knew where she must be. He hurried to his own house, took his bicycle, and rode fast out to Crystal Wells.

　　　※　※　※

Victoria Cochran was reading in the hot mid-morning shade of her side porch. Before she saw him, she heard Phil on his bicycle tires coming up the gravelled lane of the cottonwoods. She went around to meet him at the steps. When without his usual little ceremonies of politeness he asked his question, she replied,

"No, she isn't here, I haven't seen her. —Come in." Then seeing his exaggerated concern, she laughed, and added, "But she must be within easy reach. You can't mislay a beautiful girl all that easily in our little town."

He joined her and she led the way into the cool dim interior. He found it difficult to settle down. He paced and she let him.

"You see," he said, "I'm worried about her. She promised to talk to me today, but not before. —I suppose it has all been more terrible for her, even, than for me. I can help her, if she will let me."

"Oh, yes, surely, well, she will. But you must not think it can happen overnight."

"Oh, no. No, that's true, isn't it."

"Speaking of your helping anyone, has anyone been able to help you? Has she tried?"

He stared at her moon-faced. It had never occurred to him that someone should search him out to put away his dreams of falling.

"Well, no."

"Phil, I love you for that."

"For what!"

"For thinking of her instead of yourself."

"Oh, I don't know."

"Well, I do. —Don't run away for a minute or so. She'll be there when you find her. I want to talk to you."

He consented to sit down. She said,

"Have you written anything?"

"Not since then."

"But before?"

"Yes. Several little pieces. And my *Observations.*"

"What are they?"

"A sort of notebook. All about Belvedere—and my thoughts, too. Not to be read by anybody."

"I see. —What's next?"

"My job." He told her about it.

"And then?"

He exhaled and kept silent.

She respected his silence with one of her own, but her eyes worked back and forth between him and the far prospect out the distant window of the artesian wells rising and tumbling beyond the weedy fields of the unworked farm. In expert knowledge, she thought of the tyranny of Phil's longing which never ceased of its work behind the concealment forced on him by the crippled family, the self-respecting, arid, little town, the boundless emptiness of the high plains. She could not say what might lie ahead for him, but she knew with an inner force which almost made itself visible in her bony frame that he must have his chance—like *every* human creature, she insisted belligerently—to become himself according to his desire.

"And after a while?" she asked.

"They say my job is permanent."

"Do you want it?"

"No. But what I want is not to be had."

"I see. What is that?"

"Perhaps if I could go to college somewhere."

"Is it money?"

"Oh, yes. And besides. What about them, at home?"

"Yes. I see."

Victoria lighted a cigarette. Her eyes wandered along the long wall of the room. She half-closed them gazing at the Manet fishing boats which for years had been so real to her that she sometimes had felt she could sail in one of them. She returned from her journey and said,

"How brave she has been."

"Yes. I think so. More than I. I couldn't go near any of it afterward."

"How dear you are to her in her thoughts."

"Do you think so?"

'Oh, yes, I saw it when she first brought you here."

"Oh, but Billy."

"Yes, I know, Billy. But he was one part of life, and you are another. In time she would have known that. I think she still will. Don't expect too much of any woman, or of yourself, either," and then fell silent for fear of casting a bad spell over what Marilee and Phil might desire of each other in time.

He jumped up, reminded sharply of his search. She let him go. Her eyes contained every possibility, and as he said goodbye, looking into her gaze, he was shaken with both love and hope.

When he was gone, Victoria went to make herself a cup of tea into which she poured rum. Her hands were unsteady enough to make the china clatter. Aloud she told herself to be quiet. Nobody, she assured herself, can do much to help anybody. But the worst of it was to decide which, of a set of human lives in widely different circumstances, deserved most to be helped, the young, or the old? Not for the first time in her life, she longed for God, Whom she might interrogate, but for the fact that officially she disavowed Him. Even in the dilemma she pondered on behalf of others, she had the power to laugh at herself for her double-mindedness, and now did so.

⚘ ⚘ ⚘

In early afternoon he went to talk to Mrs Underwood again. He was now reduced to just the state in which to become infected by her habitual condition of panic.

"I'm just nigh out of my mind," she said, letting the business smile leave her face for him, and revealing the hollow marks of trouble down her cheeks. "Phil. You don't suppose she's run away?"

"Away? Why in the world? Where'd she go?" His heart made a single pound at her words.

"Dear Lord only knows. But I've asked everyone, and at eleven I called a taxi and ran out to the house, and she wasn't there, no note or anything, and she's not been in here, and I just don't. Phil, if you don't think me just plain silly, would you go on over to the bus station and see if they? I don't want to telephone, it'll sound crazy, me not knowing if my own child went and took a bus for somewhere. But if you just happened in? You know? They wouldn't think?"

"Yes. I know. Yes. I will."

"I'll be right here."

"I'll tell you right away."

The bus station was at First and Jefferson. It took him eight minutes to reach there.

⚘ ⚘ ⚘

The 2:28 bus from Wichita Falls for Del Rio was due in for a ten-minute stop at Belvedere. The station was filling up. Passengers were buying tickets and the agent was too busy at the moment to be asked whether a young lady, high school age,

[ 304 ]

broad clear brow, hair as gold as dark honey but floating lightly about her head, eyes casting forth blue light so that you felt you were being gazed at by two blue flowers, lips scrolled like a statue's parted a little with undefined appetite for only the sweetness of life, had taken a bus for anywhere today? Phil would have to wait until the Del Rio bus had come and gone.

In a corner of the waiting room clustered a dark-skinned family, holding their meagre possessions like hopes made visible. They were old-Mexico Mexicans, going back to their own Rio Grande border, and Thyra Doolittle was with them to help them get on their bus and start for home. With gifts of wrapped sandwiches, and a six-pack of Coke, and her own fellow-feeling, she had tried to make them understand what her words could not tell, for she spoke no Spanish and they hardly any English. Their eyes were like dark moons as they looked at her with silent acceptance and dignity—a mother, a father, and four children in descending age from five years.

"Now at Del Rio?" she said in a loud, questioning tone to invite their understanding which they placidly withheld, "you be sure and go straight to the bridge and across the border? So when you get there, then you have a little something to eat? Here."

She handed the father a five-dollar bill which he folded in his fist.

From a distance Marshal Honeycutt watched the transaction and sternly nodded with approval. On hand to make his usual "spot-check," as he called it, of passengers coming and going, he had no doubt that his presence kept those Mexicans in line. Phil walked by him to speak to Thyra.

"Oh, hello, there," she said.

"Hello, Mrs Doolittle."

"Did you ever find her?"

"Not yet. I came here. I just thought—"

"She took a bus, you think? Oh, I doubt it. Still—no, I doubt it."

"Her mother is worried crazy."

"Yes."

Is it really any of my business? Thyra asked herself. But if it isn't, why did everybody need her, first the girl, then the boy, even those Mexicans, and who else knew everything about this other thing but herself? It certainly would be meddling, and God knew she had reason to despise busybodies; but she could not hold off any longer. Thank God she wasn't pretending to act out of higher moral duty, it was just that she hated to think of that girl going through hell on earth, when this boy, who was eating his heart out because he couldn't find her, might be the very one to redeem everything.

"Phil," she said, "let me talk to you for a minute?"

She led him to a more quiet corner of the waiting room, near the pay phone booth, where to the crowd that came and went they looked no more involved than anybody else in the hardest troubles in life, and she said,

"Phil. How well do you know her?"

"Why, I guess, better than—you know, we grew up together, sort of. I guess I know her better than anybody else—now."

"Yes, well, I thought so, now that Billy's gone. Well, could you do something for her—I mean something very big, you know, that you don't do maybe more than once in a lifetime?"

"Anything."

"Phil. She's in trouble."

"In trouble?"

"Let me tell you," and as much of the truth shone forth from Thyra's heavy eyes as through her words. For a few seconds Phil did not hear her for looking at her, and when he began to hear, he did not immediately know what she was talking about. But presently he was listening with his whole self, and she went on,

"So we went to Orpha, and we went to see this friend of mine, this doctor, and of course I knew it before she even told me, or before he went over her, but he went over her, and so of course it was just what—"

Words left her when she had to tell this staring boy what he should hear. In a fleeting gesture of primitive grace and modesty, Thyra made with her brown-spotted hands a girl's exquisite gesture over her own old tight-girdled belly, outlining a shell of life for an unborn child. As she did so she looked down with a half-smile of reference to the child she had long ago conceived out of wedlock, as she had then said, and whom she had never allowed to come to birth. Thereafter in all her days she had done her best to expiate in the troubled lives of others that unborn death.

When Phil understood her gesture, he felt his heart stop, and before it beat again, he claimed his love in it, swearing to find and shelter her and her child, forever.

The Del Rio bus came in. People streamed toward it. With a little lift of pride, Thyra watched her Mexicans straggle through the gate successfully.

"Oh, yes," said Phil. "I see. Oh God."

"If someone *loved* her, you know? Or could, in time?" said Thyra, urging him with her eyes, though he could not look into them. He said aside, so that she hardly heard him,

"But I will, if she will. I want nothing else."

"You darling! I knew it! Oh, this will make the difference—oh, you will both be so happy!"

She reached up to him and wetly kissed his cheek.

It seemed to awaken him to action.

"Yes. —Now let's see!" he exclaimed.

Thyra pointed to the Marshal who stood by the gate glaring at everyone who passed him. She said,

"Ask him. He thinks he has to see every bus that comes in or goes out. He may have seen her."

Phil went to the old man who viewed him as an enemy since the scandal of the water tank.

[ 307 ]

"Marshal, do you know Marilee Underwood?"

"I do?"

"Do you know if she happened to get on a bus here, today?"

"She did not? She went elsewhere?"

"Oh! Did you see her, sir?"

"I did not see her, sir!"

"Then how do you know she went elsewhere?"

"People think certain people don't know anything!"

"I am trying to find her, Marshal, it's important, sir."

"Why didn't you ask me in the first place?"

"God, I didn't know you knew!"

"Well, it is my business to know. All right. Hardie Jo Stiles saw her and he told me."

"Where? When?"

"Some time in the morning. He was out on routine patrol, that's what we call it, routine patrol, and he saw her going the other way."

"Yes, but which way was that?"

"She was driving out the Whitewater Road in Guy DeLacey's red pickup."

"Alone?"

"He never mentioned anybody else."

"Thank you, Marshal."

Phil went back to Thyra, wishing he had persisted earlier in following Guy to the coffee counter. His head felt light with relief. He told Thyra what he had learned.

"I'll call up Guy," he said, "and ask when he expects her back in his pickup."

"Here," said Thyra, digging energetically in her box-shaped, black-leather, gold-snapped handbag. "Here's a dime—" for she must be of service.

Phil called the Red Dot Garage and had to wait until Guy, coming from the sidewalk out front, answered.

"Guy?"

"H'hi, Phil."

"Hi. Well, listen, Guy, what did Marilee say when she borrowed your pickup today?"

"She didn't say anything."

"What do you mean?"

"I just mean she never borrowed it. Didn't anyone borrow it. Last time I saw it, it was out back with the key in it."

"Are you sure? Because."

Since the burning of the letters under the command of Phil's moral fury, Guy felt a humbling, secretly thrilling, eagerness to propitiate him. He now said, sandily,

"I'll go out back and look if it'd make you feel any better."

"Yes. Please."

"Hold on."

Phil heard Guy retreat out of earshot, and as he waited for him to return, he frowned and said to himself that he disliked mysteries.

"Hello?" said Guy, now breathless.

"Yes?"

"It's gone, sure enough. How did you know?"

"Hardie Jo Stiles saw her driving out the Whitewater Road in it earlier today. He told the Marshal and the Marshal told me. I'm at the bus station."

"Well I'll be."

"I thought probably she told you when she'd bring it back."

"Well, we'll just have to expect it when we see it."

"Well, I guess so. Thanks. When she gets back, tell her I've been looking for her all day, will you, please?"

"Sure thing."

Phil left the phone and moved to the window where Thyra was leaning to watch the heavy bus turn widely out of the deckway and head for Del Rio. She waved to her Mexicans who did not see her.

"What did he say?" asked Thyra turning to Phil, for whom

she felt a marvelling sort of love, that he should resolve to save that girl from her mother, and the whole town.

"He didn't see her, but the pickup is gone."

"Oh? She just took it?"

"Must have."

"Oh, *why:* what do you suppose she—"

"Mrs Doolittle, when she found out how things were, what did she say? Didn't she say what she ought to do next, or anything? I have to find her, but if I only knew what she was thinking, I could—"

"I know. It is awful not to know just where to turn. No, she didn't say anything, but she couldn't help feeling a lot, when we found things out over at Orpha, but then, you know, it was all so much, she had to talk about other things. —Oh, yes, one thing she kept talking about, things she couldn't answer yet, she kept asking me about someone I didn't know. I could not tell her a thing about him but she seemed to think everybody knew about him, but he used to live here before my time, and when I asked who he was, she said he didn't do any harm to anyone, and then she laughed a little, but not really laughing, you know? and kept still after that."

"Who was he?"

"A man named Ben Grossman."

"Oh, no! Oh, God no, Mrs Doolittle!"

"Why, yes. Why not, Phil? Is there something funny about him?"

"Oh, God, Mrs Doolittle, where's your car? Have you got your car here?"

"Why, yes, Liza Jane is parked right outside. Surely. But why?"

"Are the keys in it?"

"Why, yes!"

"I've got to take it. May I take it? Oh, God, if I'm not too late! I know where she went and why!"

He ran out to the street and got into the car and drove away on

Jefferson, turned the corner three blocks later on Fourth, going faster all the time, and turned left on Polk which led out of town, to Whitewater Lake forty-nine miles away.

❦ ❦ ❦

Left behind at the bus station, Thyra Doolittle wondered for a moment, then shrugging her shoulders at the mysteries of the young, went up to Marshal Honeycutt who was about to leave the loading ramp for the storeroom behind the bus station, where he took his frequent naps when on duty, as he thought of it.

"Marshal," she asked, "who was Ben Grossman?"

"Oh. Ben Grossman. Yes, I knew him, everybody knew him. I was one of them that got his car out of the lake and I identified him officially when they brought him back to town."

"What?"

"He drownded himself out to Whitewater Lake years ago. Drove right over the edge car and all. Had an incurable disease. Now you'll just have to excuse me," he added irritably, "I have work to do."

He made his way in his old beetle's walk to the storeroom where he found his corner padded with sacking and let himself down to catch his breath just for a moment. Soon he nodded and dozed, thinking he was home in bed, warm in his soiled and mellow blankets which stank of his own comfort, habit, and peace, safe against both past and present.

Phil drove so fast that he made the far horizon wheel perceptibly, and yet even then in its flatness it seemed slow to change. In
the white light of summer, the dark band of smoke far away
above the oil fields of Orpha City made the only contrast his eye
could distinguish on the earth.

His heart and mind were full of wordless prayer. He felt dread
so great that it was like starvation in his belly. As he neared the
lake he could begin to see the crowns of the seven islands rising
with their crusts of gyp, shadowed by the feathery groves. The
lake and its islands and its far shores of faded pink, and its white
sky with faint stretches of monotonous blue looked like a postcard scene of itself, such as tourists mailed away after a day's
fishing or a late-afternoon picnic. White alkali edges along the
water line showed where even in the brief history since the in-
undation the minerals of the water had risen to make their
crusty, almost coral-like desposits. There was no moving life to be
seen.

Phil took the rim road along the lakeside, throwing high after
him a rising plume of white dust. Here and there old ruts led
aside from the road down to the crusty edge of the water, tracing
the habits of fishermen, swimmers, lovers, picnickers, where,
leaning precariously over, they could look suddenly straight
down as the edge fell deeply away. He knew just where to go,
for, the flattest and most accessible, it was a famous place, as the
litter of brief happinesses there proclaimed—the rubbish of plea-
sured appetites, from the most convulsive to the most absent-
minded: latex, first wilted, then sun-brittled; empty bottles;
chewing gum, candy bar wrappers, empty food cans. An open
bare stretch framed by ranks of salt cedar went levelly to the edge
of the water.

He drove upon it and came to a sliding halt. He ran from the car to the dusty shore, where fresh tire tracks led him unmistakably. Before he even knelt down to look into the water, which was so clear, so clear, before it went black to the deep, he knew he was too late, for what was there twenty feet down, on a crusted shelf of alkaline coral. Without telling himself to do so, he threw off his shoes and coat and dived into the lake and wooed his way down to the clear darkness at the ledge where the red pickup was caught precariously. The bitter water made his eyes sting, for he must keep them open, for he must see. In the last power of the light filtered from the white sky before it darkened with the deep of the lake, he saw her water-veiled face within the cabin of the car. Slow wafts of current moved her hair like strands of any plant proper to under-lake life. Was she smiling faintly? The current moved. Or were her brows gathered in suffering?

Unless he would stay, also, and forever, he must struggle to the air. But he would bring her with him from the past, from the water, from the primal element.

He began to tug at the handle of the truck door. It resisted him, taking almost the last of his breath and strength. With his blood howling in his ears he broke toward the daylight for air, lost in his return to the present.

As he did so, a car raced to a halt at the lake's edge. Acting on a message given by Thyra Doolittle, State Trooper Hardie Jo Stiles came to investigate. With him in charge, there was little for Phil to do. Given his state, this was just as well, for he was hardly capable of the simplest response, which did not mean he was incapable of thought: "They are wedded. He called her to him through his child."

※ ※ ※

In small towns, news travelled fast, and those who could contribute to it did so with dutiful satisfaction. A man who kept the cemetery far out the road by which Polk Street entered the plains said he remembered seeing her that morning, for she came into the grounds and spent quite a while by the grave of Billy Breedlove. Then she got back into that red pickup, which he thought did look familiar, and as she drove on out the gate, she turned toward Whitewater.

When Phil was able to go later to see Mrs Underwood she was already home and she already knew. Father Judson was with her. When Mrs Underwood embraced Phil what he felt was not her flesh but the striving hunger of her bones.

"Oh, I know, I know," she said, woefully maintaining control of herself by saying for Phil what he would have said, "You don't know what to say. You don't know what to say." She put his hand against her cheek and he felt her tears creep across his knuckles. "My baby," she said, turning to the curate, "you know what I just can't bear to think of, Father?"

"I believe I do, Mrs Underwood. I think I can tell you not to be troubled about that."

"You do?"

"Yes."

"But Monsignor Elmendorffer—"

"He is still away."

"Oh," she said, "if I had to live my life out and know she was not in heaven—"

"No, Mrs Underwood. She was not herself."

"She wasn't?"—like a child.

"No. Her will was not free. No one could have done what she did in all the circumstances who was not drawn out of her mind."

[ 314 ]

"Then you will bless her and bury her?"

"Yes."

Mrs Underwood nodded energetically at something properly settled, while looking at Phil as if she were trying to remember who he was.

Phil felt like part of a silent conspiracy to keep the whole truth from Mrs Underwood. Only himself and Mrs Doolittle—and possibly Father Judson?—knew of the life Marilee had carried within her. They would not have to warn each other to say nothing.

※ ※ ※

All the summer long he refused to receive comment, whether in sympathy or curiosity, from anyone, about either Marilee or Billy. The tragedy of the one always called up that of the other. When he saw that anyone was about to enter into inquiries he stopped them by some darkening of his countenance; a withdrawal which had the power of a warning. Even in the print shop, where soon enough he went to work, he kept the friendly employees at their distance when they hungered to come too close to his feeling.

He recognized nothing of it at the time, but many things about the print shop all that summer added healing effects to thoughtless time itself. His work demanded little mind, but often much muscle; and he felt satisfaction in tiredness at the end of a day of lifting great blocks and slabs of beautiful fresh paper of all weights and colors; cutting them into precise forms with the electric guillotine of the trimming machine; and wrapping them into fine reams or cubes bearing the repeated name on the packaging tape, Belvedere Printers, Belvedere Prin . . . He associated each new day with the pungent fragrance of printer's ink and often went to watch the pressmen with their spatulas dab a black, a white, a blue, a red, a sienna, on the press to achieve a proper mix as the rubber rollers went over the counter-rotating distributing plates until the mixture was ready for a series of test pulls, and when the required hue was achieved, he was given peace at such a simple yet skilled achievement.

Above all, it was the mixture of rhythms in the shop which delivered him from his recent self: the slow, steady clanking of the hand press as it was fed sheet by sheet, and the faster, marked, electric drone of the power press, which, sounding together, made speech difficult to hear, and he learned that printers—at least in Belvedere—tended to be silent men, which he felt to be a grace in his state of spirit.

Even the sight of his father at the compositor's stone, or moving his shaking fingers with implausible certainty over the font cases, was, in its slow, measured way, a consolation as a part of the continuity of life, for from those palsied motions evolved a completed thing, in sequence—from mind, to idea, to word, to type, to stick, to composition, to galley, to proof, and finally to job.

When at odd moments the presses fell silent, Mayor Dillingham enjoyed filling the gap by touring the stations of his employees, to whom in his own mind he bore a fatherly, yet ageless, relation, and he could then be counted on for a new joke, at whose end his fellow-craftsmen, as he preferred to style them, always responded with exaggerated laughter, and even, in the extremity of a particularly flat joke, a slapped knee, such as surely followed when the Mayor tried out in successive corners of the shop the one about the elderly flea: "What did the elderly flea," the Mayor would begin, hardly able to wheeze through his own premature laughter, "what did the elderly flea do when he got rich?" And when the listener made his expected "?", the Mayor, growing red in the face with goodwill and gaiety, gave the answer: "He bought a dog!" Oh, innocence, said Phillipson to himself, some people have it all their lives!

His only released life that summer was made possible by Victoria Cochran. On the summer evenings he ranged the shelves at Crystal Wells and took away as many books at a time as he could carry; brought them back and exchanged them for others; and Victoria said to herself that he wasn't merely extending a taste for reading—it was more like the opening of a sluice through which the pouring stream of the past swept him. She never spoke to him about any book unless he spoke of it first. At home, he would read almost the whole night through.

On most evenings of the week, Phil brought to Victoria at Crystal Wells the news of town, for she never went out of her cool rambling house when the heat was on the plains. They would have the local news together, and then talk of other matters, some near, some far.

᪥ ᪥ ᪥

When the pastor SS Peter and Paul returned from his course of easing baths at Mineral Wells and learned that his assistant had given sanctified burial to a suicide, he lost all the benefit of his cure. He went into a rage, sent the curate away to the Bishop for discipline, and nobody in Belvedere ever saw Father Judson again.

All the Breedloves were reunited during the summer. The grandchild was safely born. When the young parents had to move on again, Homer said to Ellen,

"Well, Mother, we have each other."

But as they smiled at this, the eyes of each told of the day which must come when one of them would be alone.

Mrs Underwood went back to work at the Bluebonnet in due

course, and when commended for her strong spirit, she said that unless she took and laid down and died *right that minute,* herself, she had to say to herself, that other people had their troubles too, and why should she go on putting her troubles on everybody else? Instead, she entered upon a grim cheerfulness which made many people uneasy, until with the passing of time they forgot why she had to be cheerful.

In July, when Belvedere was host to the West Central Plains Rodeo, Guy DeLacey's mountain, with its lighting effects rigged to repeat its changes slowly and constantly, was exhibited in the window of the Chamber of Commerce. He had added a miniature windmill in the foreground whose wheel turned steadily. The display drew crowds.

Later in the summer the City Council considered repainting the water tower. Mayor Dillingham, saying he had given the matter his best thought, had been of two minds—first, the unfinished painted message on the great silver sphere should be left as a sort of memorial, for a while, anyway, to the git-up-and-git which had put it there; then again, he had concluded that it was time to erase abiding evidence of the double tragedy that had fallen on the city earlier in the year, and he therefore now proposed granting authorization to the city engineer to have his crews, protected with all safety devices, repaint the water tank as expeditiously as conditions might allow. The Council so voted.

※ ※ ※

"Here's that book," said Phil one evening to Victoria. He put the copy of *Vathek* on the library table in whose region of light she was sitting.

"Oh. Thank you. I'd forgotten."

"I read it several times. It is very odd."

"Oh, yes. To me, the man behind it is more interesting than the book itself. I imagine you'll think just the opposite. But of course, it is not supposed to show life."

"No, I thought so, finally. —Do you remember where he says the tower in the story was built—wait a minute:" he picked up the book and found a page, and read aloud, "—built *through the insolent desire to penetrate the secrets of heaven?*"

"Oh, yes, now I do. And of course, his own tower—" she waved toward the hallway where the engraving of Fonthill hung against the claret-red wall "—fell down three times, and the third time it was not rebuilt. Except for the fact that I'm not really a pessimist I'd launch into a little aria on vanity and its ends."

"Yes," said Phil abstractedly. "But he was really writing about —you know—the sensual part of things."

"Oh, yes," she replied in a teasing fond tone, to shock him, "the sort of thing people explore out at Maudie's, if nowhere else."

"Well, all that. I don't know why not. But I know, though, that I'll never be a voluptuary."

"That's a splendid word. Where on earth did you pick it up?"

"Oh," he said, "it's just one of my old words."

They both laughed. She rejoiced to see him in even a brief moment of humor, but made no comment upon it.

She searched his expression. She saw the prediction, whose exact terms she could not know, of the possibly lyric but authoritative scholar, social historian, and teacher he was to become, whose doctoral thesis on William Beckford would lead to a row of well-regarded books on the precursors of neo-Gothic Romanticism, in literature, painting, and architecture. It would always be marvellous: what could come from what.

Increasingly during the hot evening visits of the summer she considered how, after having lost both Billy and Marilee, he seemed to have a crystal of character formed in him. Through those two, if something had forever gone out of his life, much else had come. The moment arrived when, in her loving judgment, she could say to him,

"You must no longer let yourself carry the blame for all that happened. I've said this before, but I never got to the real reason. You *must* get on with what you want to do and are able to do."

"Do you believe I can?"

"Of course."

"Nobody else does."

"Do you know what you want?"

"Yes. We have talked about it. I see no way."

"There has to be much else to take the place of what you've lost. Something through which you will live."

"Except for you, there is nothing here."

"Then you must leave."

"There is no way," he replied, and then in a sarcastic imitation of a plains preacher, he quoted: "'Hearken unto thy father that begat thee, and despise not thy mother when she is old.' Proverbs 23:22."

Feeling so much bitterness in him, she felt she must respond lightly, and said,

"I didn't know you Catholics studied the Bible."

"We don't. I do."

She was sorry, but not entirely unprepared, to feel a sort of distant hostility come up in him through his dilemma. But she believed that he had to confront his need and its obstacles or nothing would lie ahead for him. He left her abruptly. She sorrowed for his anger, but thought it better for it to be directed toward her than toward himself. He came to see her less often during the rest of the summer.

But on one brief later visit he noticed a change in the room where they usually sat and talked.

"Where are the fishing boats?" he asked. The wall where they had hung ever since Jim Cochran had brought his paintings from Paris now showed a vacant spot, darker than the wallpaper around it.

"Oh? It's been gone for weeks. I thought you must have noticed." But she smiled at his habit of seeing nothing but what immediately engaged him, and then of pouring his whole self into whatever vision he sought to give, or receive.

"No," he said. "How can you live without it? It is the one you love best."

"Yes, well, it has gone to Chicago for cleaning and restoring. It was getting cracks from this dry climate. And the little flecks of white in the sea were turning rather yellow under the old varnish."

"How long will it take them to fix it?"

"The man didn't know. He said they would have to go over it quite carefully."

"The man? What man."

"The man from Chicago who came out to look it over. And of course he went at all other paintings. He'd seen them before, while Jim was alive."

"When was he here?"

"A while ago. I found his name somewhere and sent for him. Of them all, he loved the Manet particularly."

"Oh, so do I," said Phil. "I always think how you always sit and look *into* it, not just *at* it. You probably don't even know you do it."

"Oh, yes I do," said Victoria. "Like the Chinese philosopher."

"What Chinese philosopher?"

"There's a sweet tale about a great Chinese artist whose paintings were so transporting that one day a Chinese philosopher, studying one of the master's pictures, walked right into it, up the mountain path, through a lovely little grove of tiny pine trees, and higher, where the mountain path took him, into a strand of clouds, and never came back. —Sometimes I feel I could, if I really wanted to, sail away in one of those fishing boats of Manet's."

He jumped to his feet.

"Oh, how great—that must be everything about art!"

"Well," she said, "*almost* everything."

※ ※ ※

One afternoon he arrived unexpectedly at Crystal Wells in a state of elation. When Victoria opened the door she had a thin white towel classically folded like a wimple about her head, for she and Nella were cleaning house against the summer's dust. Phil exclaimed at her appearance in delight.

"You look like a Van Eyck!"

She rejoiced to see him in such high spirits. To sustain his mood, she turned and shrieked over her shoulder into the house,

"Nella! Phil just called me a Dutch frump!"

He protested, and she turned back to him.

"Good Lord," she said, "look at *you*. You are ready to jump out of your skin. What on earth?"

"You won't believe it!" he cried. "I hardly do! It is wonderful, and it is ghastly."

"Come in and sit down and make sense."

Presently he was able to do so and she listened with every satisfactory display of amazement.

During the afternoon, at the Belvedere Printers, Richad Dillingham took him aside in the front office and told him that a committee of citizens led by a source who preferred to remain anonymous had after due consideration of the tragic events of the preceding spring, undertaken to provide the means through which the student, Phillipson Durham, who had been graduated with honors from Belvedere High School, could now go forward with higher education, all the way through graduate school, in the college or university "of his choice"; and accordingly that an account in his name for the requisite funds had been opened in the West Central Texas State Bank. No single donor desired to be thanked for what was really a privilege, to provide opportunity for an outstanding student. The decision and the choice were now entirely up to the young man in question.

"But my family!" was Phil's first response.

"Your father is fully aware of our action," said the Mayor, "and we have his full approval."

"I may go with his permission?"

"That is the impression I have desired to convey."

"Yes," said Victoria, laughing in excitement, "that is the sort of talk he uses."

Phil sought out his father in the composing room and asked him directly about what he had heard. Sport Durham without ceasing his play of trembling fingers over the cases from which he was assembling a piece of copy for galley proof confirmed what his employer had said. He and Phil's mother were willing for him to seize his chance.

"To go away?"

"Yes, you damn little fool," said Sport, "what do you keep standing there for?"

Phil could not say, "For you, for my mother," but with freedom in hand, he felt chained more than ever since the decision was now his alone.

"Well?" said Victoria.

"How can I?"

"You will because you must," she said.

Their eyes clashed, but they both knew whose vision would prevail.

"One thing, though." She nodded, and he continued, "I don't much like. —Well, I think the Gatelys must have put up the money, and I don't much like them. They probably kept it anonymous for fear they'd be asked for other things. Rich people are like that."

"They are?"

"So I am told."

"Well, you must simply take comfort from not knowing, and put it out of your mind. I don't wildly admire Leora myself, but there may be some longing sweetness somewhere in her—"

"Then you think it was she?"

"Oh, Lord, how do I know?"

Feeling impatient with him, she smiled, even so, for she saw that the very greatness of his desire was making him seek for obstacles to put in its way, for fear of being finally disappointed.

When he left her that evening, she said to herself that there went the last, for her, of any enlivened future interest in her plains homeland. In the early autumn before he departed for the university across the nation, she gave him a farewell present. It was a portable typewriter. She said,

"Think of the books already hidden in this small contraption!"

He threw his arms around her and kissed her. Having mastered the art of letting go, she suffered him like the weather, and just as vagrantly he was gone. Presently a new resolution was clear in her mind—never again, at her time of life, to let her feeling become caught up in the life of another.

Of possessions at home he wanted few, and took with him, aside from simple necessities, the photographs of his parents in their youth, and the seal from Crystal Wells which in all chance bore his initials and in whose faceted light he could always recall the hours of his deliverance. Of Marilee and Billy he needed nothing tangible.

At the end, with immense effort, Martha Phillipson Durham reached her upstairs window to see him go. It was her last look at her son, and she knew it. He was, so it almost seemed, taking her life with him. She supposed it must be a law that this be so. The idea did not keep her heart from breaking.

# VII. The Homecomings

It is understood by all but a few students who are governed by other matters than learning that Professor Durham knows more than those whom he teaches, and he is willing to let the impression stand. Another war has come and gone. He served in it and brought "experience" away with him, only to see still another growing in useless carnage by the day. He has attained identification as an authority in a certain vein of knowledge. He has recognized that not where one was most happy, but most troubled, there is home, forever.

When his mother died he asked if there was time for him to come home, and he was told not to do so. "I can take care of everything," said his father. "You'll do more for me now by going on where you are." The fact was that Sport Durham had become so much more palsied and unwell himself that he did not want his son to see him.

Phil went to a parish church remote from the university where he was studying and requested a requiem mass for the repose of the soul of Martha Phillipson Durham. He attended it on a weekday in a church otherwise empty. The human yet impersonal love of the tremendous words which he followed in his missal seemed to him to image eternity; and he was exalted in the thought of his mother received into unending light. Only such a reward could justify her life. He bent his head and felt that he understood the act of prayer.

When at the end of the mass he went to the sacristy to thank the celebrant—the rector, an old man—Phil's oddly joyful peace still shone in his face. The rector looked keenly at him and finally said,

"Are you married?"

"No, Father."

"Have you ever considered becoming a priest?"

Phil was shocked.

"Oh, no!"

"Why not?"

"I couldn't imagine having the courage to touch the Host."

"You feel unworthy? All the more reason."

"I'm sorry. Please excuse me."

He hastened away as though not God but Satan were pursuing him.

It was not until his father was dying a few years later that Phillipson Durham returned to Belvedere.

Sport said to him one evening, then,

"Everything is about love."

Startled by such a farewell from such a father, the son thought, "Really? Even in that ruined life? Even, still, in this town?" How little he had bothered to listen in earlier years to hear if his father might have something to say worth hearing. He then said to himself, "History begins when we bury our fathers."

All whom he knew—the living who were still in Belvedere—spoke to him kindly but as to a stranger, which of course he had become; but they did not speak so eloquently as the dead of his youth. Still, on that journey, he wondered if he could now bear to see the graves he had shunned years ago. Before searching them out, he knew fear of old stirrings, but needlessly; for he found not Billy, but Homer and Ellen—and, surely, Lew Priddle?—in the inscription on stone:

> *A beloved son,*
> *He soon was taken,*
> *We'll see him yet,*
> *When all awaken—*

and instead of Marilee, Mrs Underwood, who had chosen for her child's monument a lamb with its forelegs folded about a slender staff headed with a banner and a cross.

No one had told him before, but Victoria Cochran was also long gone. When he married in graduate school, she had written to say that she believed he must not need her any further. He should give himself, and even his memories, to his wife. He protested this decision in vain, and persuaded his wife to write to Victoria; but there was never any answer. He knew then that the love Victoria had borne him was far more than he ever suspected; otherwise, why should it have to be closed off now, as a matter of duty? He was hurt for knowing so little then, and so much now, about still another life that was gone. He wished his wife had come back to Belvedere with him, but she was unable to, for she was carrying their first child, and was obliged to be cautious in her exertions.

He went alone to see Crystal Wells once more.

A caretaker let him look around. The house was vacant, still furnished, but all its splendors which had once lived in his desire and vision seemed diminished and moldy; and now he too thought how footless was all the agitation released and commanded by the Emperor, within the gold-crowned, bee-bordered red morocco volumes which remained, drying and cracking through indifference, in their dark attic shelves. The red walls downstairs were bare—darker patches, now fading, showed where the Judge's pictures had once hung, all of which were now gone. Shadowed with cobwebs, the earth-red niches were vacant of their sculptures. Perhaps some plains college, hungry for "culture," now had "a collection," or some south Texas ranch house had been professionally redecorated to accommodate what even a furniture store, confronted with gold frames and marble carving, would declare as Art.

He went into the yard, and across the dried fields toward the artesian wells. They were now silent, for the water table had been falling alarmingly, and one of Mayor Dillingham's successors had hired a geologist to make a recommendation, which said that all artesian wells yielding over so many gallons per day must be capped, and the flow conserved, or in another generation Belvedere would become a ghost town.

The words made Phillipson Durham smile with pressed lips. It was already that, for him. He had a sudden sense of the dearness of life anywhere—even here, where he had sought escape.

ﷺ ﷺ ﷺ

On his way home to the university after the burial of his father, he changed trains at Chicago. There were several hours to fill. The wintry stretches of the lake lay under a strange yellow light like thin smoke, and so did the streets along the front. He walked along the outer drive. After the events of his last return to Belvedere, he was now reached by emotions which had not invaded him at the time. He was in a condition of thought and feeling which made him love every life but his own; and now he begged to be free of the sense of how he had failed his father and his mother. Should he have insisted on staying with them through his young life for as long as they needed him? He remembered a searching look on young Father Judson's face at some moment or other—he could not exactly remember when—but it had seemed to tell him that sacrifice of oneself should come before anything else. He knew Martha and Sport Durham must have longed for him to stay. But they thought more of him than of themselves, and he tightened his fists in his overcoat pockets and burrowed his way with downcast head through the cold wind off the lake. He prayed that in his own time he would have the strength—as much, and the same kind as that possessed by those two failed parents—if any child of his should have to make a longing choice between what was owed to himself and what to his begetters. Now that his parents were both gone, he had a vision of their empty hours after he had left them. In vain he told himself that in his fulfillment lay their own. He shook his head against the past.

"Lord," he said silently, "let me have as much life as I have had death." With hunger he thought how it would be when he came home at last, to find his wife, and the signs in her face of the need that had given their coming child between them. There, he thought, he would be saved.

But the day was not yet through with him.

Looking for distraction from the memories which seemed to make him one with the long grey stillness of the icy lake, and the heavy clouds, and the darkness of the city where in mid-day the windows showed pinpoints of electric light, he turned his walk from the lakeside and went to the Art Institute. The galleries there would lift him away from himself.

In the checkroom of the museum he left his hat, overcoat, scarf and galoshes, then lingered a few minutes in the lobby to warm his hands and face. Presently, feeling anonymous and at peace, he went up the wide stone stairway and idled his way into the galleries. Almost at once he was unexpectedly thrown back into the midst of what he thought he had bidden goodbye to forever.

There, on the wall, he saw it—the jade green sea off Boulogne-sur-Mer, with the black fishing boats moving toward the darker horizon of the painted sweep of grey sky. With hot thought, he came close to read the frame, and saw that the painting was a purchase of the Rumson Fund in 1949, and for the first time he knew where the means had come from to give him his life. His bitterness at the impossibility of acknowledgment made him fear for making a public spectacle of himself. He was stricken with a gratitude made equally of wonder and shame.

Putting on his dark outdoor glasses to hide behind, he returned to the lobby and at the book counter bought a catalog, to trace the provenance of the painting, and saw, "Formerly Collection of Judge James Sylvester Cochran." He found a postcard reproduction in color.

He now keeps the postcard on his study desk, under a silver lamp with a green glass shade. Every time he thinkingly regards it, it tells him of the time when life turned outward for him, and of Victoria, through whose lightly given experience his imagination at last left town forever.

When there is a peaceful moment in which to think about it, Professor Durham reflects that even the great lives of long ago were once colloquial; and then the sense of their agitation makes him feel the tug of the familiar, the unevaluated time of his own youth—names, places, all—as though it too must be historically precious: the commonplace become legendary.

But enough of night thoughts, he says, when it is late enough to put aside the last student papers for tomorrow. He turns out the lamp above the postcard. He goes softly to the nursery. His eyes take the silvery darkness of their room where the night light shines low near the floor. He stands to watch the children draw their dreaming breath. Carefully leaning down to their small faces, he kisses in them his image and their mother's, the combination of which has brought something entirely new into the world. Under his caress, the children stir faintly, luxuriously, like kits warm in sleep, and he leaves them, to go safely beside his wife where, though asleep, she will know when he is there.

All is well. Why must he keep watch for anything more?

It is odd, it is even amusing, and any teacher knows this, he muses drowsily, how in the classes which pass by, term after term, certain types of young persons recur, so that a new face, a new energy, this year, will remind him of others from last year, or the year before, or even longer ago.

He has often thought that each of us from childhood on contains an ideal likeness of love which is unique; and that our lives, most often in secret, are spent in looking to fulfill this ideal in someone else. If once we find it, we must possess it, if only in dream.

So it is that he keeps expecting to see two particular images among the heedless and ardent faces of the students who pass by him year after year.

[ 335 ]

Surely, he thinks, it is necessary for the peace of his soul, and his house, that he should never find the faces which he dreads to find, though he must keep looking; just as he keeps asking in all his unspoken nature what it was that he could never quite hear—what the voices were saying to each other on that night long ago on Fifth Island in Whitewater Lake, above the drowned town, with its likenesses to all towns and all history. What could they have told him? Whatever it might have been, would it have made a difference in his life? One voice was heavy, the other light. When they come back to him, as they still occasionally do, he wonders if he listens to them in memory as if to hear the dialogue of body and soul? Heart and mind? The dialogue of life between its completive polarities?

Who were they who spoke just beyond hearing? Lovers? Plotters? Runaways? The very listeners themselves—each other? Sometimes listening at night, falling asleep long after his wife, like any Homer Breedlove in his bed, and without putting any name to whom he addresses, he takes comfort both from asking and answering.

—Do you hear them?

—What:

—What they are saying? They don't know their sound can be heard so clearly. It is like thought without words. Their voices carry across the calm lake. They must be on the near side of the island. Their sound seems to come from just below that red star—it is Mars, setting.

—Should we listen?

—So long as we do not know who they are.

—How many of them are there?

—Oh, just the two of them. They sound young. One voice is like a heavy tendril of air, warm, caressing. The other is like the sound of leaves that are stirred.

—Do you suppose they can hear us?

—No. We are quiet in the dark water. The faint wind, the salt cedars on the islands, absorb our sounds. Let us drift closer.

—Those two are like memories of everyone else, somewhere, some time, aren't they?

—Yes. Of us, whoever we are. Be quiet. We are coming closer now. Let us listen to hear if the voices